THE BRIDGE TO ALWAYS

THE BRIDGE TO ALWAYS

LYNDA MARRON

First published by Eriu in 2025
An imprint of Bonnier Books UK
5th Floor, HYLO, 103–105 Bunhill Row,
London, EC1Y 8LZ

Owned by Bonnier Books
Sveavägen 56, Stockholm, Sweden

𝕏 – @eriu_books
◉ – @eriubooks

Trade Paperback – 9781804186152
Ebook – 9781804441947
Audio – 9781804442173

All rights reserved. No part of the publication may be reproduced, stored in a retrieval system, transmitted or circulated in any form or by any means, electronic, mechanical, photocopying, recording or otherwise, without prior permission in writing of the publisher.

A CIP catalogue of this book is available from the British Library.

Designed by Bonnier Books Art Dept
Printed and bound in Great Britain by Clays Ltd, Elcograf S.p.A

1 3 5 7 9 10 8 6 4 2

Copyright © Lynda Marron, 2025

Lynda Marron has asserted their moral right to be identified as the author of this Work in accordance with the Copyright, Designs and Patents Act 1988.

Every reasonable effort has been made to trace copyright holders of material reproduced in this book, but if any have been inadvertently overlooked the publishers would be glad to hear from them.

www.bonnierbooks.co.uk

To the hippie, maxi-skirted, hoop-earringed, student teacher who told me to write what I feel. I wish I remembered your name. You may have saved my life.

'From the first moment of life, she sought connection: heartbeat sounds, the taste of warm skin, a hand to hold. The most natural thing in the world was to lay my pinkie against her newborn palm and watch as she wrapped her fingers around my own, two humans forming a pact, a bridge to always. We are not made to be alone.'

Daniel P. Wheatley
Paris Diaries

1.

May Day in Dublin, Ten Years Ago

* * *

'Would you like a sausage?'

Not the best opening line, maybe, but the words were out of her mouth before she realised how attractive he was. He had floppy, boyband-blond hair and the sort of hard, compact body that made even a rented tuxedo look sexy as hell. She straightened her shoulders, held the tray a little higher, and smiled a little wider.

It worked.

'You're gorgeous,' he said. This guy had the whole opening-line thing nailed.

She laughed.

He lifted one of the sticky glazed sausages on a cocktail stick and raised it to his mouth.

Involuntarily, her tongue crossed her top lip, anticipating the taste.

Now *he* laughed.

He ate the sausage whole and took another.

'*That* good?' she asked, giving him her best twinkle.

'Hmmm,' he smirked. He had blue eyes beneath pale lashes, and he looked at her as if there wasn't another soul in the world. No one had ever looked at her with such flattering attention. 'I'm Tim,' he said, and waited for her response.

'Maeve Gaffney,' she said, but a wave of sound crossed the room and swallowed her voice. Tim made a quizzical expression and leaned towards her.

'MAEVE,' she said again.

'*Dance?*' With the tiniest tip of his head, he motioned towards the crowd in evening dress bouncing to 'Uptown Funk' on the dance floor.

She looked down at her work clothes – cheap black jeans from Penneys, cheap black t-shirt from Tesco, and a pair of Doc Martens on the cusp between worn-in and worn-through.

'I think not,' she said, but with a smile.

He ran his hand from her shoulder, down the outside of her arm, to her elbow. She felt her muscles flex under his touch. Almost involuntarily, her body edged closer to his.

He noticed and held his ground.

'You look like a Greek goddess,' he said into her ear.

She laughed. 'I do love to be flattered.'

'What time do you finish work?'

'Two.'

'*Two?*' He grimaced.

'Yeah.' She shrugged an apology.

His hand rounded the point of her elbow. The tips of his fingers found the tender, bare skin of her forearm. She tightened her grip on the silver-plated tray of sausages.

He leaned in close, so that she felt the heat of his breath on her earlobe.

'I'll wait,' he said.

'Will you?' She leaned in.

His lips brushed against her neck.

'I will.'

2.

Summer in Dublin, Now

* * *

In ones and twos, the mourners made their way through the rain to the red-brick building on the North Circular Road. It was modern and purpose-built, aiming for dignified but hitting closer to depressingly utilitarian. In the small porch, a laminated sign exhorted visitors to please leave umbrellas in the bucket provided. A pair of heavy doors led to the main reception room, which was wide and bright. Long pews in light beech were arranged either side of a short aisle, so those who wanted could consider this a church, of sorts. There were no banks of votive candles, though, and no incense, only a plug-in diffuser of essential oils – rosemary, for memories, and lavender to soothe unquiet minds. No saints or martyrs were depicted in the stained-glass windows, only flowers and birds and gaudy sunsets. There was no altar, only a podium with a shiny brass reading light, and an empty dais standing ready.

To the right-hand side of this non-altar another pair of heavy doors led to the Private Reflection Room. This was a lower-ceilinged space, much smaller and darker, designed to accommodate immediate family members only. Three pale walls were lined with chairs upholstered in dove-grey tweed. Here Maeve sat, almost alone, her long legs stretched out in front of her so they reached beneath her mother's coffin.

They didn't have much longer together. The lid of Greta Gaffney's oak casket was standing upright, propped against the wall behind her head. Her name and dates were engraved on a shiny brass plaque, putting an incontrovertible end to any further discussion on the tiresome subject of her prognosis. Fifty-six was young to die, but not tragically so. It was just very, very sad. *A happy release*, her mother's only cousin had said when Maeve phoned her from the hospital.

They'd be coming soon, the nice men in tidy suits, Thomas and – she'd forgotten the other one's name. They'd come to secure that lid in place, with shiny brass screws, no doubt, and that would be it, the worst over.

Maeve felt obliged to remind herself that she would never again look at her mother's face. The finality of it was simultaneously obvious and incomprehensible. She made an effort to imprint this image of a dead woman in her memory bank, as if it was precious, just because it was the last.

'You look terrible, Mam,' she whispered, and watched for even the faintest hint of a reaction. 'It's only me here. You can relax.'

It was the last thing Greta had insisted on, that no one be let gawp at her corpse.

'Not Emer either,' she'd said, with her fingers clinging to Maeve's wrist. 'Nine is too young. Let her remember her gran fat and alive, not skinny and . . .'

Neither of them had finished the sentence.

After all the failed diets and resolutions, there was a special cruelty to the way the flesh had melted off Greta's bones those last few weeks, the words *losing weight* suddenly becoming fearful. There was an awful morning, near the end, when Maeve had walked into the ward, up to the usual bed, and was not certain that the skeletal figure propped up on the pillows was really her mother. Breath held, she had searched the woman's eyes for a signal of recognition.

'Maeve,' the creature had said, gently, and was again, appallingly, her mother.

Now, with the powdery makeup and the stiff hair, skin taut against a bony skull, with the eyes and mouth stitched closed, the shut face might have belonged to a stranger. Her hands, though—

Maeve wiped away tears with a balled-up tissue. They came and came, like some biological excretory function that was entirely beyond her control. Like snot with a cold, or sweat on a hot day, they flowed.

'Ah, shit,' she said, and sniffed hard. She'd have to get up from this chair soon. Thomas or his colleague would push the closed casket out to the waiting dais, where a line of mourners would file past, would touch their fingertips to their lips and press them against that implacable lid. They would turn and shake Maeve's hand, tell her how sorry they were for her loss, and go home for their dinners, satisfied that they needn't drive all the way out to the crematorium the next morning. The traffic in Dublin was desperate; only the genuinely bereaved would brave the Red Cow roundabout.

Tomorrow's funeral service would likely be a quiet affair. Regardless, Maeve would be expected to deliver some kind of eulogy, to *say a few brief words* that would capture the essence of Greta Gaffney in a manner that was moving and genuine, preferably not maudlin or self-pitying, and definitely not angry or bitter.

My mother was a cantankerous wagon, said Maeve, honestly, but only inside her head. *She was a pig-headed woman who never listened to a word of advice. She held everyone around her to impossibly high standards. She held herself to impossibly high standards. She was her own worst enemy, and mine. She disagreed with every word I ever said. She crossed me at every turn. She drove me mad. I'll be glad to see the back of her.*

Maeve imagined the dark-coated mourners scattered around half-filled pews, heads bent in respect and one ear cocked, listening, like crows.

But *who* would be there? That was the question.

Greta, like her daughter, was an only child and a single mother. Her own parents weren't that long gone, but dead is dead. There were no siblings. There was no husband or partner. The one cousin would surely turn up, maybe a few old friends and a handful of loyal work colleagues. A few people would come just for Maeve, a couple of the girls from schooldays, maybe her boss.

Maybe her father.

She pulled a scrunchie off her wrist and scraped her hair into a ponytail. It was hard to sit still.

'Will he come, Mam, do you think?' She addressed the words, not to the empty body, but to the chair in the corner where some instinct told her that her mother's ghost was sitting up straight, watching her. She didn't know her father's name, or what he looked like, and now she probably never would. She would never know whether or not he turned up, but she would have quite a few different words to say if she thought the man who abandoned her pregnant mother was sitting in the congregation.

My mother kept me. She kept me and loved me. Every single thing she did, she did for me. She devoted her entire adult life to me. And after me, to Emer. I don't know what we'll do without her.

Maeve pulled a fresh tissue from the packet on her lap and blew her nose.

'Why didn't you tell me his name?'

There was no answer from the woman in the wooden box.

'Was he all that bad? Was he, *really*?'

No answer.

'I could kill you, Mam, for doing this to me.'

Hah. A silent laugh broke in her throat.

She could almost hear her mother's voice saying that stupid thing about what doesn't kill you making you stronger. It made no sense. All the battling only made you harder, harder but more brittle, so that something else down the line – something a bendier person might have managed well enough – is the thing that snaps you in two.

'Could you not have given me that much, at least, Mam? Just a name, would that have killed you?'

A soft knock sounded on the door then and Maeve sucked in a breath. She cleared her throat and swallowed against the soreness. The other tidy-suited man, not Thomas, stepped into the room with a horrible softness about him that made Maeve want to slap him.

'It's time, Maeve,' he said, dipping his head towards the coffin lid.

'Oh right. Yes, of course. Thanks.' She stuffed soggy tissues into her pocket. 'I'll leave you to it.'

She stood at the side of the coffin and put her hand over her mother's, repelled in that instant by the cold stillness of it, and gripped in the next by guilt at that repulsion, torn, again, between her own feelings and her mother's expectations.

'Bye, Mam,' she said, and turned to leave.

She was at the door when she heard it, a faint voice.

'What did you say?' she asked, turning back, but not-Thomas already had the coffin lid lifted in his arms.

'Sorry?' he said, pausing mid-lift, the weight of the lid showing in the way the muscles of his upper arms strained against the sleeves of his suit.

'No, no,' said Maeve. 'It's nothing.'

Embarrassed, she left quickly and took her place in the front left-hand pew, that least coveted of seats. With all her will, she blocked out the sounds that followed her from the other room, wood against wood, determined tapping, final fixing. And then she heard the voice again. She was momentarily distracted from the words by the curiosity that the voice was a blend of her own and her mother's, as if Greta's ghost had taken up residence between her ears, but then the words came clear.

Let it go, Maeve, said Greta. *Let it go.*

3.

Am agus Foighne a Thógann Seilide go Corcaigh
It's Time and Patience That Gets a Snail to Cork

* * *

It was the last stretch of the journey, that final sixteen miles from Cork city out to Drohid, that got her. Her head began to ache as she took the exit onto the N71, heading for the Wild Atlantic Way. Something about the viaduct, that huge derelict railway bridge that spanned the road, made a balloon of anxiety expand in her chest.

'Nearly there,' she said, with no expectation of a response. Emer had fallen asleep somewhere around Fermoy. In the rear-view mirror, Maeve could see her daughter's head tipped sideways against the car window. Not once had she asked if they were nearly there. Emer was dead against this move, Maeve knew that, but Emer didn't know all the facts. A nine-year-old couldn't see the bigger picture. With one hand on the wheel, she took her cardigan from the passenger seat and threw it over Emer's bare legs. She indulged a yawn, then took a lime Tic Tac from the packet on the dash – Emer's choice.

This is madness, said the voice in her head.

Go away, Mam. Maeve let her window halfway down, enough to let a blast of cool air hit her face.

Her mother was annoyed with her, Maeve thought. Nothing new there. Ever since Maeve had moved home with newborn Emer, Greta's life's mission had been to keep her daughter on the straight and narrow. It was Greta who'd pulled strings to get Maeve a job in an upmarket fabric shop. It was Greta who'd bought Maeve a sewing machine, second-hand but a good one, and it was Greta who'd paid for the evening course that gave Maeve the confidence to call herself an interior designer.

Will you never learn, Maeve?

I'm following my heart.

Oho! Isn't that lovely now? There it was, her mother's trademark sarcasm.

Something you never did, Mam.

Follow your head, Maeve. Hearts have feck all sense of direction.

The thing was, it was also Greta who had given Maeve the most detrimental piece of advice of her life. As far as Greta was concerned, men were overrated. They had their uses, the obvious ones, but women could easily learn how to unblock a U-bend, and brute force, when required, was available for hire. No, in Greta's experience, women were more content and more productive when they weren't expending their energy on the happiness of men. Greta and Maeve and Emer were a perfect family, in Greta's opinion. They accommodated each other and backed each other up. There was nobody, no man, pulling against them. They were all on the same side. But Greta wasn't here anymore, not in any substantial way, and Maeve and Emer weren't enough, not on their own. They weren't enough to stand against the whole world. They needed someone else on their team.

Let it go, I said.

I don't want to.

Maeve had stood at the top of the crematorium and scanned the crowd for likely paternal suspects, but no man had caught her eye and smiled. No man's face had shown an uncanny resemblance to her own. No man had lowered his head in shame.

Her father had not shown up.

Surprise, surprise.

Greta wouldn't have expected him to, but Maeve, this one time, had allowed herself to hope.

Maeve.

No, Mam.

The road swung sharply to the right, onto a bridge that spanned a wide, stony riverbed, then left again to run parallel to the bank. On the right, a sheer rock face loomed over the road, but on the far side of the river, a forested ridge caught the day's last light and shimmered green and gold.

It was at the crematorium that Maeve had decided. She wasn't going to let Emer live like this, only half-knowing who she was. Greta couldn't counsel caution any longer. There had been too much caution, far too much. It was that thing again, her mantra, about what didn't kill you making you stronger. Greta *had* become stronger. Her soul had become denser, more compacted. She'd become wary of everything and everyone outside their triumvirate. She'd become a rock, impervious and unmoving. That wasn't how Maeve wanted to live her life.

The day her mother died was the worst day of Maeve's life, but she woke the next morning with a feeling of liberation. She was free of her mother's disapproval and perpetual bloody caution.

Maeve drummed the steering wheel. She wasn't blind to the contradiction. It was Greta's careful house-keeping and tidy savings that amounted to a modest inheritance, enough to make a start with. It was Greta, by dying, who gave Maeve the opportunity to live her life the way *she* wanted. It was Greta – cautious, steady Greta – who gave Maeve the chance to take a chance. If she thought about it that way, she *owed* it to her mother to make this work.

The wall of rock receded and the road opened out. Maeve checked the clock and tutted to herself. It was almost ten. She hadn't intended to be this late. She wouldn't be able to collect the key to the house from the estate agent at this hour. God, he'd been such a culchie; he didn't have a clue what a little gem he had on his hands. Much as she'd enjoyed flirting with the man, and cajoling him into a fast sale, she couldn't imagine he'd welcome a phone call at this hour.

They'd go straight to the hotel tonight, and in the morning, they'd breakfast early, get the key and open up the house. Then, they would get the things Emer needed for school. That would be interesting. The removals truck with their furniture, what little there was, would arrive at lunchtime. She'd have one day to make the place feel like home before they moved in. It wasn't ideal, she knew, but children were adaptable. Everyone said so.

A sign at the side of the road broadcast a welcome to West Cork. A hundred yards further along another sign welcomed her, more specifically, to Drohid. Beyond that was a huge spot-lit billboard with a pair of yellow glasses hovering over crinkled blue eyes that were not entirely unlike her mother's.

Should have gone to Specsavers, Maeve read, and at the same time heard the words in her head.

'Oh, shut up,' she said, and swung the wheel to follow the sign for The Drohid Arms, West Cork's Premier Accommodation.

4.

An Bó Riach
The Brindled Cow

* * *

Agnes Beecher wouldn't usually have wandered onto the Barry farmyard in a light cotton sundress and a pair of open sandals, but Cork was in the grip of a late heatwave; she couldn't bear the thought of pulling on socks and wellies. Anyway, she wouldn't be there long. She was only dropping off a cherry madeira to pay Malachi back for the help he'd given her with a recent plumbing emergency. It was all a bit embarrassing, and she didn't want the debt, or the thought of it, hanging over her.

Agnes held the door to the back porch half open and called out. The farmhouse was small. If he was inside, he'd hear her.

'Are you in, Malachi?' Even to herself, her voice sounded thin and reedy. *When did that happen?* She hated getting old. She was every inch the aged spinster now, from her helmet of white curls to her bunioned toes.

There was no answer from the house, but Bran came trotting and licked her hand in a friendly *come-hither* sort of way. Malachi's Land Rover was parked in its usual spot. If the collie and the car were in situ, Malachi wasn't too far off. She walked to the middle of the yard and called again.

'Hel*looo?*'

'Agnes!' It was a half-shout, the sound of a big man trying to throw his voice a long distance, but quietly. Malachi's head emerged from the door of the cowshed. He beckoned to her, holding his finger to his lips. 'Calf coming,' he whispered, drawing her into the dim interior.

'Oh,' she said, and followed him through the shed, which was mostly empty and conspicuously clean. They came to a hip-high block wall that divided the biggest stall from the rest. On the other side, a lone cow stood looking anxious in a scatter of fresh straw. Malachi filled a bucket of water from a tap on the wall and stretched to put it down on the far side. The cow made a long, miserable droning sound. The dark reddish-brown hide of her belly was tight as a drum, stretched, so that her black stripes stood out even more than usual.

'It's her first calf,' he whispered. 'I want to keep an eye on her.'

'That's your precious brindled heifer?' Agnes had heard all about this particular cow, an impulse buy at a mart last spring. If you were stuck for a conversation starter with Malachi Barry, you only had to ask him about his plans for rearing a herd of rare breeds.

'That's her, my first Bó Riach.' He crossed his arms against the top of the wall and leaned over it. 'Along with my second, fingers crossed.' The angle of his body belied his pretence of calm.

'Will it be long?' Even as she asked, the cow strained and raised her tail. The tip of a hoof appeared, then disappeared. 'Oh, goodness.'

'No time at all,' said Malachi, with a broad smile. 'That looks good.'

'You can tell?'

'Ah, yeah. The hoof pointing down like that, that's what you want.'

'I see.'

They stood side by side, watching as the cow rested and then strained again, over and over, shifting her weight and lowing.

'Is it not very late in the year to be calving?'

Malachi tipped his head closer to hers so that he could keep his voice low.

'Maybe. There's pros and cons. The calf should be smaller, that's easier on her.' He nodded to the cow. 'If the winter's as mild as last year, we should be fine. And I've planted the top field for winter feed, in case we need it.'

Agnes smiled at the way Malachi used *we*, meaning himself and his herd. At least *he* had his herd. And Bran, of course.

'You have it all thought out,' she said, with a teasing nudge.

'I hope so,' he said, and then, 'look. Here we go.'

Agnes saw a small nose appearing this time behind two neatly folded hooves.

'Like a little swimmer,' she said.

'Good girl,' said Malachi, addressing, Agnes realised, his cow. He kept up a rhythmic chant of encouragement as the animal bellowed in earnest. 'Go on now. Tha-*aat*'s a good girl.'

'Should you not help her?' said Agnes, concerned to see the little black nose retreating for a third time.

'She's grand.'

And she was. The nose pressed forward again, determined this time, and was followed, all in a slippery rush, by a head, a body, and two hind legs. The new calf, bound in the bluish gauze of its caul, tumbled to the floor and lay still. Perfectly still.

'Is it alright?' asked Agnes.

'Probably,' said Malachi. He stood up straight, on alert, waiting.

The cow turned and bent her head over her calf. With long strokes of her tongue, she broke and licked away the caul, but still the calf didn't move.

Malachi swung his leg over the wall and crossed the stall in two big strides. Kneeling beside the calf, he cleared its nostrils with his fingers. He grabbed a handful of straw and began to rub the calf's damp skin, drying it off and rubbing hard.

'Come on,' he said, in a hoarse whisper. 'Come *on* now.'

Agnes held her breath.

'That's it now,' said Malachi, louder, the relief audible.

At first Agnes couldn't tell what had happened, but then she saw it, the rise and fall of the calf's breathing.

'Lazy fecker.'

The calf twitched its ears and snorted. Malachi laughed, and Agnes saw how much the animal meant to him.

'Can I help?' she said. She wanted to touch it, the calf. She wanted to feel this brand-new life under her hands.

Malachi looked up. 'You'd only ruin your lovely new dress.'

Agnes looked down at her wholly unsuitable attire. She laughed.

'This dress hasn't been new since you were in nappies.' She sat her bum on the low wall and swung her two legs over. Malachi tipped up his chin and grinned at her.

'Here,' he said, handing her a fistful of straw. 'You keep rubbing her down and I'll get a bucket of mush for her poor mother. Be careful, though. Don't turn your back on her.'

Malachi climbed out and Agnes did as she was told. She rubbed and rubbed, belly and back and skinny little haunches, while the cow carried on her licking. In only a couple of minutes, the soft new coat was standing up in auburn tufts. In jerks, the calf lifted her body upright. She looked straight into Agnes' face with her big, wet, brown eyes. Then, her mother, crossly, nosed her belly, pushing her to stand. Agnes, still on her knees in the straw, shifted backwards until the soles of her sandals were pressed against the wall.

Trembling all over with the effort of it, the calf rose up, then, knock-kneed, the legs folded. She wobbled and fell. Her mother moaned and pushed her up all over again, and this time she stood. She shook and she tottered, but she stood up on her own.

'Come on out now,' said Malachi, reappearing with a steaming bucket hanging from one hand and the handles of two mugs of tea gripped in the other. Bran trotted in at Malachi's heel and settled himself in a rectangle of sunlight that followed them through the open shed door.

Agnes tried to be discreet in wiping tears from her cheeks. Malachi, as she might have known, paid no heed.

'I brought a cake,' she said, climbing out of the stall and pointing out the madeira sponge she'd abandoned on the corner of the wall.

'Half-price, was it, from the out-of-date section?' said Malachi, even though the cake, in its greaseproof wrapping, was obviously home-made.

'What will you call her?' Agnes, ignoring the jab, took a squirt of soap from a bottle on the ground and washed her hands under the tap.

'*Call* her? I suppose I'll call her How-up-now-musha like I call all the rest of them.'

Agnes took the mug of tea he held out to her.

'How about Daisy?'

'Don't be ridiculous. Does it bother you if I cut the cake with my penknife here?'

'Go ahead. Flora?'

'Like the margarine? That seems harsh, even from a Protestant.'

Agnes couldn't help laughing.

'Feckless?'

'Feckless?!'

'Aimless? Pointless? Graceless?'

'What are you on about, woman?'

'Like in *Cold Comfort Farm* . . .'

'Is that some mad English carry-on?'

'Bella, then?'

'You want me to walk down my front field shouting *Bella*? Is it a laughing stock you want to make of me? Why Bella?'

'Well, you keep calling her mother Beau, which makes no sense. Beau is for a boy.'

'Not *Beau*, Bó, B-O-fada, the Irish for cow.'

'*Oh*, I see.' These were the trials Agnes had faced all her life, the perilous side-effects of having been sent to boarding school in England. Nobody ever believed she was as Irish as they were.

'They're a very rare breed, this pair. There's a legend that the Bó Riach got a bit big-headed about how hardy she was, how she could survive all weathers. She made it through the whole winter and then what did she do but taunt the month of March, saying there was nothing March could throw at her that she couldn't handle.'

Malachi paused. Agnes knew he was only spinning out the story to throw a cover over her embarrassment.

'Go on.'

'Well, March says, we'll see about that, and goes and borrows three days from April, so that poor Bó Riach is pounded with storms and gales and floods for three days longer than she should have been.'

'And what happened?'

'She died.'

'The end?'
'The. End.'
'Well, that's cheerful.'
They leaned against the top of the wall, sipping their tea as the calf suckled.
'I'm not calling her anything.'
'Ah, Mal.'
He didn't take his eye off the calf.
'You can call her whatever you want.'

5.

Corcoran's Drapery

* * *

The main street in Drohid ran parallel to the southern bank of the river, with businesses stretching from the town's only hotel at one end to the last brave pub situated across the street from the Garda station at the upstream, western end. Between these hospitable establishments was a double row of tall, mostly mid-Victorian buildings housing eleven more pubs, three cafés, a bank, a post-office, a library, and a dozen or so family-operated shops striving to keep the denizens of Drohid in coats and belt buckles, mops and lightbulbs, iced buns, black puddings, sliotars, fishing poles, and an admirably wide variety of fuchsia-themed souvenirs. To the credit of the town council, chain stores, vape shops, and fast-food outlets had been confined to a small shopping centre at the edge of town. Main Street, with the exception of one mobile phone outlet that had snuck in early, was a postcard-pretty picture of a traditional Irish town, with traditional wooden shopfronts in bold colours and a fine display of traditional painted signage. In the warm light of a late August afternoon, the town looked handsome, if a little on the quiet side, what with the tourists mostly gone and the locals grabbing their last opportunity for a day at the beach.

Corcoran's Drapery sat at the exact centre of the street, facing the bank. The double-fronted, three-storey building stood out from its multi-coloured neighbours because it was painted top to bottom in pearly white. Only the family name on the sign above the door was in vivid green. The letters were high-lighted in gold leaf, which had cost extra, but Nóinín Corcoran understood the importance of branding, and anyway, it looked *fabulous*.

Nóinín strolled around the shop, turning hangers on rails so they all faced the same way, and price tags inwards so that a casual browser had a moment to fall into lust with that cashmere sweater or Italian shirt before facing the reality of how much it would cost. Hers was the sort of shop that promised quality garments, outfits worth paying for, clothes that marked the wearer as worthy of respect. The family business, always steady, had boomed during the heady days of the Celtic Tiger as the newly minted business class fell over themselves to purchase commodious homes at inflated prices in pristine new estates like Chestnut Rise and Oakfield. They'd come to Corcoran's, where their own mothers might have stretched to buying a new suit for a First Communion, and took obvious pleasure in stocking their wardrobes with quality garments without ever once asking the price or checking the bill.

Those were the days. Nóinín allowed herself a nostalgic sigh. After the economic bubble burst, they still came, as if to save face, to prove that, no, they weren't one of those poor fools who'd fallen foul of negative equity or foreclosure. Even if they did slink off to the city on Saturdays to buy cheap tops in Penneys – for hacking about, you know – they still came to Nóinín for the First Communion outfits. Yes, Nóinín and Corcoran's Drapery had ridden out the banking crisis, the pandemic, and the energy crisis. She was right to be proud.

She turned off the display lights in the men's department – the last electricity bill wasn't paid yet – and walked down the thickly carpeted staircase to take her place behind the counter. The *Classics in the Background* playlist she'd chosen on Spotify had moved on to something depressing, some adagio or other. Nóinín pulled her phone out of a drawer and selected something she recognised. Vivaldi – *Autumn* – that would do. She took a cloth and a tin of polish from a low shelf. Just as she sprayed the wooden counter-top, the door swung open, and the shop bell chimed. Nóinín took her time rubbing her polishing cloth in grand big circles over the counter – better to be caught busy – and gave a welcoming nod to the woman and child who stepped inside. She let customers get their bearings before moving in on them. It gave her a chance to suss out their taste, and their spending power.

The woman was tall, exceptionally so, with enviable hair cascading over her shoulders in dark, old-fashioned waves that brought Wonder Woman to mind. She was a few years younger than herself, Nóinín guessed, not what you would call spectacularly beautiful, but she had a very good figure – a clothes-horse figure. She was dressed in dark skinny jeans – not a slave to fashion, then – with a white shirt and a bouclé tweed jacket that was certainly not Chanel, but stylish enough all the same, probably Zara. The black leather bag hanging from her shoulder was from Polène. Interesting. Nóinín stretched her neck slightly to get a look at the shoes. The shoes were always the giveaway. The woman wore black ballet flats with a scalloped edge that looked suspiciously like Chloé. Nóinín couldn't quite contain a grin. Things were looking up. She tossed her polishing cloth onto the low shelf and busied herself rearranging a display of bracelets as the woman approached the counter.

'He-llo,' she said, almost singing it. She smiled broadly and held out her hand in a practised manner that reminded Nóinín of royalty approaching celebrity commoners at a charity gala.

'Hello.'

'Maeve Gaffney,' said the woman, shaking Nóinín's hand with a grip much firmer than she was expecting.

'Nóinín Corcoran.' Nóinín readjusted her own grasp to match Maeve Gaffney's, and ended up holding on an uncomfortable second too long. 'Are you on holidays?'

'We've just moved here,' said Maeve Gaffney. 'It's a lovely town.'

'Well, we think so, but then I suppose we have to.' She gave a bright, tinkling laugh. 'What part of town—?'

The woman didn't let her finish the question.

'You have beautiful things.'

'Thank you. Where—?'

A second time, the woman cut her off.

'It's my daughter we're shopping for today.' Maeve Gaffney put her hand to the child's back and pushed her forward. The daughter was pale-faced and blue-eyed, a skinny little mouse without any of her mother's sparkle. Warily, she held out her hand towards Nóinín.

'Emer,' she said, and after a quick glance for approval from her mother. 'Emer G-Gaffney.'

'Lovely to meet you, Emer,' said Nóinín.

'Emer needs the school uniform for the convent primary school,' said Maeve Gaffney.

'No problem. You'll be starting tomorrow, so.' Nóinín invited them to follow her. She was careful to stay just one step ahead and to keep looking back as they climbed the wide steps together, all the way to the top floor, where school uniforms were kept. 'Do you know which teacher you have, Emer?'

'I-I-I don't,' said Emer. An awkward gap opened up.

'Do you stock the P.E. uniform here as well?' asked her mother, filling it.

'Oh yes,' said Nóinín happily. 'They wear a tracksuit, shorts for fine weather, and they've just brought in a school scarf. It's smashing.' She was pushing her luck now, but *someone* had to be the first to buy the new school scarf.

'We'd better take two, I suppose.'

'Of the scarf?' said Nóinín, taking the last few steps at a run so that she could flip the light switches.

'Of everything,' said Maeve Gaffney.

6.

The Drohid Arms

* * *

Paddy O'Driscoll ran a tight ship. He walked the hotel every morning, every floor, top to bottom. He checked that room service trays weren't left lying outside bedroom doors, that vacated rooms were turned over quickly, that bedspreads were tightly tucked, taps descaled, and toilet paper hung the right way round. Paddy checked *everything*.

On the top landing, he leaned out of a window to make sure the kitchen staff weren't smoking outside the back door. The car park was chock-a-block as usual, he saw. He needed more space. He noticed some grass growing unchecked in the gutters. *Clear drains*, he added to his mental list of tasks for MacSweeney, the hotel manager who, in Paddy's opinion, kept his own hands too clean by far. Turning a large vase to centre it, he checked that the orange-staining anthers had been removed from the lilies. All these tasks made Paddy feel good. They let him believe, for twenty minutes or so every morning, that operating the Drohid Arms was his primary concern.

At the top of the lobby staircase, Paddy paused to check his reflection in a gilded girandole mirror. His tie was straight, but he squeezed the fat knot of it between his thumb and forefinger to confirm its correctness. He pushed back his shoulders, consciously adding breadth to his bantam stature, gave one firm tug to the hem of his suit jacket, and ran a slim, freckled hand from left to right over the crown of his head.

Turning away from the mirror, he saw the same tall, good-looking woman he'd noticed earlier in the breakfast room. She was leaning over the reception desk with one leg bent at the knee – a fine grabbable arse on her, and MacSweeney practically dribbling. The pasty daughter, dressed in what looked like the convent uniform, was standing waiting by the grand piano. She was clearly on the verge of running her greasy fingers over his keys. Paddy trotted down the shallow steps and brushed past the girl, letting the tip of his elbow catch her shoulder.

'Oh, sorry, pet,' he said as she leapt away from the piano. Job done. It was *that* easy.

'Everything okay for you, Ms. Gaffney?' asked MacSweeney.

Smarmy gobshite, thought Paddy slipping in next to him.

'Lovely. Thank you. Everything was very nice.' Ms. Gaffney didn't look up. She appeared to be engrossed in the complimentary copy of the *Drohid Echo* on the reception desk.

He couldn't place her accent. There was a hint of Dublin – the roundy-vowelled variety that Paddy liked to hear in his hotel, the sort that was acquired in expensive schools and on the sidelines of rugby matches – but it was only a hint. The baseline was well-bred country, somewhere in the midlands, maybe, where the land was good and the farms were massive. He switched pages on the computer screen to see what address she'd given. He scrolled down the list of residents – there she was: Maeve Gaffney, two guests only, one adult and one child, with an address given as 3 Weavers' Row, Drohid, Co. Cork.

Interesting.

'Well sure, I hope you enjoyed your stay with us anyway,' he said, upping the ante on his West Cork bit.

'Very much.'

'Is it a long way you've to go to get home?'

Maeve Gaffney looked up at him with a distracted smile.

'Some distance,' she said, 'but I'm looking forward to the journey.'

7.

The Convent School

* * *

It didn't go well, the meeting with the principal of the convent primary school. From the moment she stepped out of her car outside the school gates Maeve felt herself the target of hard stares. Granted, her vintage Saab regularly turned heads, but these women, in their high-chassis Mammy wagons, seemed to take it as a personal affront. Maeve caught every eye she could and smiled widely.

'Come on, Chicken,' she said. Emer was taking her own sweet time gathering her things.

'*C-coming*.' There it was, the stammer that had reappeared since Greta's death. Emer was white as a sheet, obviously a ball of nerves. Maeve stopped her at the front of the car, adjusted her scarf and popped the collar of her blazer.

'That's more like it,' she said, with one hand on each of Emer's shoulders. 'They're going to love you – you know that.'

'I-I-I don't know that.'

'*I* know that. Trust your mother.'

At the school door, a tiny old nun, bent almost double, was cheerfully welcoming every girl.

'Could you direct us to the principal's office, please?' Maeve asked, crouching to her haunches to bring herself level with the woman's face.

'A new girl, is it?' asked the nun in return.

'It is, indeed.' Maeve switched her smile to high beam.

'I'm Sr. Francis.' she said, gently, to Emer. 'Come with me, then.'

At snail's pace, she led them down a parquet-floored corridor. Doorways at regular intervals along the left-hand side were labelled with class names and the names of their teachers. The right-hand wall was broken only by high windows, each with its top pane propped open on a metal arm, all extending into the yard outside by the exact same degree. Every shoulder-height windowsill was graced by a plaster-cast figurine, women in flowing robes of blue or brown, a bald man with a baby in his arms, a different bald man with a bird perched on his hand, and each statue flanked by an honour guard of fresh flowers in cut-glass vases. Halfway down the corridor, Sr. Francis tut-tutted and came to a hard stop. Maeve put her hand out to prevent Emer from colliding with her. She watched her daughter's eyes widen as the ancient nun took a neatly pressed white handkerchief from the pocket of her navy cardigan and, without comment, wiped a cluster of water droplets from the grey gloss paint of the sill. Maeve let her elbow brush Emer's and gave her a tiny wink. *Odd but harmless*, she endeavoured to say. Sr. Francis stowed her handkerchief and walked on. Emer skipped once, so that she was back in step with Maeve.

At last, they faced a brass sign engraved with the words *Sr. Mary Joseph, Principal*. The little nun put a hand on Maeve's sleeve and squeezed.

'God bless you, child,' she said, and departed without another word.

Maeve turned to Emer and stretched her face into a deliberately comical expression.

'Not one bit weird,' she whispered, to defuse the terror.

Emer said nothing, just swallowed hard. She looked as if she might vomit.

'Breathe, love.'

Obediently, Emer took a shaky breath.

Maeve administered two sharp raps of her knuckle to the office door, eliciting, from the other side, a proportionately sharp response.

'Come,' cried a voice, presumably that of Sr. Mary Joseph.

Maeve shepherded Emer through the door, then strode across the office and offered her hand to the nun seated behind a heavy desk.

'Maeve Gaffney,' she said, working hard to maintain her usual easy manner. 'Good morning, Sister.'

The nun leaned forward in her oak throne and allowed the tips of her fingers to twine briefly with Maeve's own, then withdrew her hand to the security of her lap. Maeve had the unsettling sensation of having shaken hands with an empty glove.

'Please sit down, Mrs Gaffney.' She nodded towards a wooden chair with a high back and unusually low seat. 'I've been expecting you.'

Managing not to smirk, Maeve sat and found that she was forced to turn her legs chastely to one side.

'It's Ms., but please, call me Maeve.' She raised what she hoped was an open, friendly smile, which Sr. Mary Joseph neither acknowledged nor reciprocated. Instead, the principal held her finger over an empty space on the enrolment form that would usually be filled with a student's father's name.

'Deceased?' she said, very quietly, to Maeve.

This was the sort of shit, Maeve knew, that her mother had put up with.

She breathed in slowly.

Don't rise to her.

'Not to my knowledge, no.'

'I see,' said Sr. Mary Joseph, and she scribbled one illegible word into the space.

Maeve steadied her nerve and held out her arm to guide Emer forward. 'And this is my lovely daughter, Emer. Emer, say good morning—'

A pause ensued. Maeve gave Emer a long, reassuring nod.

'Hello.' Emer stepped close and held her hand out in front of her. A count of two passed before she added, 'S-Sister.'

Maeve held her breath.

Sr. Mary Joseph, seeming unaccustomed to shaking the hands of her pupils, held Emer's fingers briefly, then shifted to sit further back in her seat.

'You're coming to us from a national school in Dublin.' Sr. Mary Joseph dipped her head and raised one eyebrow.

'Yes,' said Emer. A beat. 'Yes, Sister.'

Sr. Mary Joseph granted Emer a nod of satisfaction, then placed her hand on a yellow cardboard file on the desk.

'I have a report here from your headmaster.' She tapped the file repeatedly, in a vaguely threatening manner, but otherwise gave no indication as to its content.

'Yes, Sister.'

'Well, Emer, the thing to do now is put your head down and work hard, and with any luck' – here Sr. Mary Joseph paused to include both mother and daughter – 'with any luck, we three will have no cause at all to meet again.'

So saying, Sr. Mary Joseph rose to her feet.

'Good morning, Mrs Gaffney,' she said, inclining her head graciously in Maeve's direction. 'You may go.'

Maeve opened her mouth to correct the nun, then thought better of it. She rested her hand on Emer's shoulder.

'See you later, Chicken?' she said.

Emer nodded and Maeve gave her a small squeeze. This was all for her benefit, she'd see that in the end.

8.

Weavers' Row

* * *

With unnecessary vehemence, Maeve executed a tight three-point turn and positioned her car neatly against the shrubs that separated the laneway from the riverside walk.

'Who died and put her in charge?' She thumped the steering wheel with the heel of her hand. 'Holier than thou bullshit.' She swung her legs out to the uneven pavement and slammed the car door.

She'd long ago learned how to deal with those men who assumed she was an easy pull, but a pinch-faced bitch in a habit could still make her feel like a six-year-old who'd wet her pants.

'Sorry,' she said, patting the car's bonnet. 'I shouldn't take it out on you.'

The key to the front door of Number Three Weavers' Row was a four-inch-long cast iron affair that looked like something a wicked witch might use to lock a Disney princess in a cage.

Maeve liked the satisfying clunking sound it made as the mechanism turned, but found she had to give the door a hard nudge with her shoulder before it budged. The timber had swollen, and the door had sunk in its frame, settling into a position of recalcitrance. That explained why, when she had viewed the house, the estate agent had been standing waiting for her with the door propped wide open.

Derelict was the word the man had used, bluntly, sensing that rarest of boons, the buyer who is actively searching for the house nobody else wants.

'Fixer-upper,' Maeve had replied, describing at once the house and her intended relationship to it.

Insanity, said Greta, getting her spoke in.

Maeve had ignored her.

* * *

Maybe the agent wasn't a total dope after all, she thought now. She could forgive him, though. He'd helped get the sale through in time for Emer to start the school year in her new home. It had been tight, but it was done. That was the main thing. And that tyrannical despot of a nun wasn't going to ruin her day.

She'd have to take the door off its hinges, sand it back, maybe take a plane to it, then undercoat it. She felt a surge of excitement at the prospect of combing through paint catalogues.

This was her *métier*: finding the gems, the dilapidated shacks whose disrepair concealed their bones, then turning them into something special, with the sort of style money couldn't buy. Or rather, she corrected herself, the sort of style only a *lot* of money could buy. She'd done it for other people, managed refurbishment projects and then written them up as features for *Belle Maison*, an eco-conscious homes magazine. This was the first time she was getting to do the work for herself, to create a home of her own. Getting paid to write up her progress as an ongoing feature was the cherry on the cake.

She closed the door and hung her bag on a big black hook at the back of it. There were only two tiny rooms on the ground floor, both currently stacked high with cardboard boxes – all her worldly goods succinctly labelled with red marker in her daughter's careful hand. A narrow staircase led to two sloped-ceiling bedrooms and a mouldy bathroom in the attic. The wallpaper was peeling in strips off the walls, the floors were covered with rust-stained linoleum, and the upstairs floors inclined undeniably westwards, but Number Three Weavers' Row had lit up a bulb inside Maeve's brain. It ticked every box. It was bursting with potential. The location was marvellous: Drohid was sixteen miles from Cork city, and only six from the Atlantic Ocean. And as for the situation – only a few feet away from the riverbank – well, it was perfect.

She would bring the original woodwork back to life, restore the sash windows, rescue the cast iron fireplaces, and revive that poor neglected garden. She would put her heart and her back into it. She would make something remarkable out of this house, something that would make people stop and stare and wonder at her creativity. She would prove her worth.

Two nights at the Drohid Arms was one too many for Maeve. It was convenient, being right opposite the entrance to Weavers' Row, but wildly expensive. Maeve had only booked it as a treat for Emer, a softener before she realised quite how basic their new accommodation was going to be.

'Is this really it, Mam?' Emer had said when she and Maeve stood on the doorstep of Number Three. 'You're not joking me?'

Poor Emer. Maeve had taken the key out of her pocket and waved it in the air like a magic wand.

'This is our great adventure, Chicken.' She'd brought out her warmest, most convincing smile. 'We are going to make this place the talk of the town.'

Maeve had checked out of the hotel before delivering Emer into the suspect care of Sr. Mary Joseph. It was up to her, now, as fast as humanly possible, to make a home of this place.

She looked around and took in the scale of her task.

A good start is half the work, said Greta.

'Yeah, yeah,' said Maeve, rolling her eyes, her hip poised to evade the quick whip of a tea towel that should have punished her insolence. Tears welled at the realisation of one more thing that would never again happen. She shook them off.

Her eye fell on the *Drohid Echo* sticking out of her handbag. She'd make a cup of tea, she thought, have a look through the small ads, see if there was a local handyman she might hire.

In a box labelled *Important: Mammy's Tea*, Maeve found her kettle, two mugs, and a box of teabags. She stood the kettle on the bare kitchen floor and made the tea. Casually, as if it mattered not at all, she spread the local paper out on a box labelled *Mammy's Shoes*. She skimmed the headlines – *Planning Granted for Expanded Shopping Centre* and *New Showers for Drohid GAA* – then licked the pad of her middle finger and coolly turned over the first page. It was all a sham, though: she knew exactly what she was looking for. The paper had been lying open on the hotel reception desk. After one glance, she had stuffed it into her bag and resisted looking at it again, until now. Surrendering at last to the hollow ache in her chest, she flipped the pages to the centre spread.

Aha, came Greta's voice in her head, *now I know why you insisted on buying the* Cork Examiner *every Saturday.*

Not now, Mam, please.

You were looking for him, weren't you? Always, always on the look-out for that eejit.

I was not.

New beginnings, my eye. It's him you came for, isn't that it?

Maeve bent her attention to the photograph at dead centre.

There was no doubt about it. It was him.

Still finding balls to go to, is he?

'Leave me alone,' Maeve said aloud, throwing daggers to all four corners of the room.

Have it your own way, said Greta, and she was gone.

The article was a feature on the Lughnasa Ball, a charity gala that had, evidently, taken place the previous Friday night. The page was filled with the flashy smiles of fashionable people, the sort her mother had warned her against, saying they were all only carbon copies of each other with no minds of their own.

And there he was, in a custom-fitted suit and a neat bow tie: Tim Corcoran.

Christ, she thought, biting her knuckle, still sexy as hell.

Tim's arm was wrapped around a shiny, well-groomed woman, a woman she recognised, but Maeve folded the paper so that the figure was reduced to a sliver of gold sequins against his hip. He had hardly changed in the decade since she'd last seen him. His blond hair still fell over his forehead – almost indecently. His mouth was open, fixed in a broad smile that showed his straight, white teeth. It was the same smile that had charmed her, but it didn't, Maeve thought, reach all the way to his eyes anymore.

9.

Back Then, in Dublin

* * *

She was aware of him. All night, while she cleared glasses and wiped tabletops, he was at the fringes of her vision. He didn't approach the bar, didn't look at her, didn't once make eye contact. He stood at the nearside of a gang of lads, in profile, shoulders straight, one hand in his pocket and a casual pint in the other. Some fella slapped him on the top of his head and ruffled his hair. He laughed and smoothed it into place. On the dance floor, he turned his back to her, but she knew that he knew she could see him, that his moves were a peacock's display.

'What's so funny, missus?' Bernie, her manager, asked, catching her smile.

'Ah, you know, culchies. They'd make you laugh.'

'Fuckin' gobshites,' said Bernie. 'I wouldn't touch one of that lot with a forty-foot pole.'

At five past two Maeve was pouring Dettol into a mop bucket.

'Get outta here,' Bernie said, taking the handle of the bucket.

'Are you sure?'

Bernie pressed her crankiest face into action. 'Go on, would ya, before I change me mind.'

Maeve pulled her jacket and her handbag from a press at the end of the bar. She looked around the room. There was no one left except the staff, crashing empties into bins, lifting chairs onto tables, hoovering.

He's gone, she thought. She shouldered her bag and fiddled with the zip of her jacket.

'You're some wan,' said Bernie, without looking up from her mopping.

'What?'

'He's sittin' on the wall outside, waitin' for ya, like a bleedin' gom. Would ya *go on*?'

* * *

He stood up from the wall as she approached.

'You waited,' she said. She didn't slow her pace and kept moving towards the college gates.

'Ah yeah,' he said, falling into step alongside her. 'Do you fancy a kebab or something?'

'A *kebab*?' She gave him the eyebrow.

He faltered. 'Or something.'

Maeve stretched her neck from side to side. 'I'm dying for a slice of toast, to be honest.'

He went quiet, probably trying to figure her out. Maeve wondered if she was too tired for this lark. She should go home, get some sleep. She should tell him she'd ring him in a few days.

'I should really—' She looked at the way his hair, freshly cut, was lying at the nape of his neck.

'Lyons or Barry's?' he asked, nudging his arm against hers.

Tea? Was he serious? She looked at the way his shoulders filled out his suit jacket, broad compared to the slimness of his body.

'Have you bread?'

'Lyons or Barry's?' he insisted.

She laughed.

'Barry's.' The Cork brand of tea.

'I have bread,' he said.

'Alright,' she said. 'Yeah, go on.'

* * *

They walked side by side down Nassau Street. Tim told her about the small town in Cork where he'd grown up, the Gaelic football team he'd been on, about his cousin, Billy, who'd been selected for the Cork hurling team but got the top of his right baby finger sliced off in a training session.

'Could he not still play?'

'Well, the fella that took the finger off him . . . Billy was after taking his girlfriend. It was an untenable situation.'

'Right. I can see that.'

He told her he had one younger sister.

'A desperate swot. She's doing law in UCC. Fucking insufferable. What about you?'

'Me? I've no siblings.'

'None? Have you cousins?'

She shook her head.

'Aunts? Uncles? Grandparents?'

'Nope. It's just me and my mam.'

He gave her a long look, then changed the subject. He told her that he was about to finish a degree in journalism. The plan was to head stateside straightaway, he said, find an internship, get some real experience.

'Do you want to be famous?'

'I do, yeah.' He grinned, mocking himself. 'Pulitzer or bust, right?'

'Right,' she said. 'And why not?'

He nodded, a bit shyly, she thought, as if he was embarrassed to have displayed such naked ambition.

He didn't try to put his arm around her, or hold her hand, or touch her, or anything.

Once, when a couple of stocious old drunks blocked the path, asking had they any spare change, he stepped around her back to put his body between her and them, holding his arms out wide to distract them.

'Alright there, lads.'

They walked on, past Merrion Square and over the canal, then turned into a warren of quiet streets lined with red-brick terraces, the stands of the Aviva stadium reaching into the sky behind the rooftops.

'You live out here?' She took in the tidy gardens, tiled footpaths and classy front doors flanked by bay trees in pots.

'It's only rented.'

'Are you rich, Tim?'

'Hah!' He scoffed. 'Don't I wish. No, we Corcorans have what you'd call a veneer of wealth.'

'All fur coat and no knickers?'

He didn't laugh. He considered the phrase and gave a quick nod.

'Can we go with all hat and no cattle?'

'Sorry. I didn't mean—'

'No, no. You're spot on.' He held the gate open for her, ushering her along the short, narrow path. 'The landlord's an old buddy of Dad's. Gives us a good deal.' He turned the key in the front door, and stood aside to let her in.

'Thanks,' she said. She liked it – the old-fashioned courtliness of him. He was gallant.

'Looks like someone's still up,' he said, as he led her into the kitchen. A guy in a Cork jersey with long hair hanging over his eyes was shaking coffee granules directly from the jar into a NASA mug.

'How's it going?' he said, with a jerk of his head that included Tim and lingered on Maeve.

'Good, thanks,' said Maeve.

'Grand, yeah,' said Tim. 'Pulling another all-nighter, are you, Buddy?'

The housemate rolled his eyes in mock despair.

'For my sins. I'll leave ye to it, so.' Stirring his coffee with the handle of a fork, he left the room.

'Sit yourself down, there,' said Tim, pulling a chair out from the kitchen table. He offered her a choice of white sliced pan, toasted, or custard creams. She stuck with toast. He scalded the teapot, she noticed, before he put the teabags in, and gave her the choice of a Creme Egg mug or a Jedward mug.

'Jedward, definitely,' she said.

'I'm not trying to be smart now,' he said, while she was scraping a knife along the top of the fridge-hard butter, 'but will we take it upstairs?'

'The tea?' She couldn't make out whether he was a pure innocent or a total player.

'Yeah. It's just, you know, the other lads – they'll only be taking the piss . . .'

'Alright,' she said. She pulled her phone out of her bag and started typing a text. He looked a question at her.

'My mam,' she said. 'So she won't be frantic.'

He smiled. 'I'll bring the biscuits, too, will I?'

10.

Nothing but a Light Breeze Forecast

* * *

Agnes pulled the gates closed across her driveway before crossing the road to lean over Malachi's fence and say hello to Bella. The calf and her mother spent most of their time in the front field. He might as well have called them Pride and Joy, she thought, as Bella sucked on her finger.

'I'll bring you back something nice,' she said, and turned to walk into town.

The morning had dawned bright and sunny, with nothing but a light breeze forecast, so Agnes had opted to leave her car at home. It was all downhill from *Ard na Mara*, which made the prospect more inviting, though she'd probably regret her moment of enthusiasm when it came to trudging home.

The woven basket hung over her arm held only her purse, an empty plastic bag, and one book, *The Gadfly* by E.L. Voynich, which she planned to return to the library. She had put her name down for the latest Banville, and had her fingers crossed that it would be in. As she walked, she ran through a mental shopping list: *The Irish Times*, of course; some new season honey would be a nice treat; a crusty loaf from the farmers' market; and she had her heart set on a breast of duck for her Sunday lunch. The empty plastic bag, she hoped to fill with blackberries from the hedgerow on her way home. She would make a nice sauce for the duck, she thought, and have the rest mashed into cream for dessert.

It had been a while – months really – since Agnes had felt such a spring in her step. She was grateful for it. She hadn't allowed herself to consider what a relief it would be to have her finances re-invigorated. Inflation levels having made a mockery of her dwindling income, there had been nothing for it but to sell off what little was left of her father's property. It wasn't what she'd wanted, but it was done. Her last resort had been liquidated, but for the first time in a long time, her account was in the black. She would have to live carefully if she wanted to keep it that way.

All that remained now of the great Beecher fortune was the stone hunting lodge she had chosen as her own retreat – *Ard na Mara* – with its wind-racked trees and elevated view of the estuary where the sweet water of the river mingled with the salty Atlantic. It wasn't the ideal place, perhaps, for a woman in her seventies to live alone, but Agnes had welcomed the isolation. She couldn't have borne it, after she was forced to sell Cavendish House, to have had the eyes of the town upon her, pitying her. She was simultaneously too posh and too poor to fit in. People in Drohid treated her like some antique piece of furniture – a grandmother clock – that had come with the town, handed down through generations, thoroughly out of date, useless, but impossible to discard. They recognised her uncomfortable position, treated her kindly, and waited for her to wind down and die.

* * *

Agnes was successful in her hunt for duck, but disappointed in the quest for Banville.

'You're number eight on the list, Miss Beecher,' said Cáit, the nice young woman behind the desk. 'You'll be waiting a few weeks yet.'

'That's perfectly alright.' Agnes chose instead an old Elizabeth Bowen novel that she'd read before but thought she would probably enjoy again, the one about the Big House.

Deflated but determined to retain the buoyant mood of the morning, Agnes joined the queue inside the new French bakery. She was lost in admiration of a large and very pretty pear frangipane tart when the boy behind the counter addressed her.

''Morning Miss Beecher. What can I get you?'

Agnes studied the boy's face but didn't recognise him. How did he know her name? It irked her that even now, as she edged into old age, people still talked about her, pointed her out to their children. There goes Miss Beecher, of Beecher Mills and Beecher Brewery, Beecher Park and the grand house in Cavendish Place. There goes sad old Miss Beecher with her nose in the air. Precious little she has to be stuck-up about now.

'A chocolate eclair, please,' she said.

The boy unfolded a pastry box, big enough to hold a half dozen cakes, and looked up with an eyebrow cocked to inquire what else she wanted.

'That's all,' she said. 'There's no need for a box.'

'No bother at all, Miss Beecher,' he said and, with mortifying care, placed the eclair into a small paper bag and folded it closed.

Agnes felt tired all of a sudden. Maybe it was the heat, or maybe she'd had enough of being looked at. Either way, she set off for home. At the bank, she crossed to the shady side of Main Street, watching her own reflection coming to meet her in the window of Corcoran's Drapery. This was what people saw – a small, wan-looking woman in sensible shoes and a costume that was decades out of date. She looked ghostly, she thought, as if she'd escaped from a period drama. She was a walking anachronism.

She moved away and increased her speed. She passed the turn-off for the bridge – the way home in her old life – and carried on instead, past the Drohid Arms. At the top of Weavers' Row, she slowed. She would allow herself just one glance at the house whose sale had replenished her coffers.

The *For Sale* sign had been taken down and a bright yellow car was parked at the end of the row, its doors all wide open. The front door of the house too, and all the windows, were gaping. The *thump, thump, thump* of modern music came blaring from inside. Agnes was about to move on when a figure emerged – a woman carrying a rolled-up piece of pinkish carpet. She flung it into the boot of the car and, turning, slapped dust off her hands. Looking up the row, she saw Agnes standing there, frozen. The woman smiled and raised one hand in a friendly way.

Automatically, Agnes smiled in return and nodded politely, but her heartbeat quickened, and she lost her nerve. Briskly, she walked away.

She should have introduced herself, she thought, as the town gave way to countryside. Of course, she should. But then, introducing herself was not really something Agnes Beecher had ever had to do.

11.

The Lair

* * *

'You can't be bringing that dog in here.' Paddy O'Driscoll lifted his chin in the direction of an empty chair to indicate that the border collie's presence would be overlooked on this occasion and that Malachi Barry should take a seat. He bent his head again over the papers on his desk, the picture of a busy businessman.

They were in a windowless room at the back of the hotel, set up to look like something O'Driscoll must have seen in some gangster film. The staging was ruined, however, by the fact that the bare bulb hanging from the ceiling was an energy-saving LED, and that its harsh blue light bounced cruelly off its owner's scalp.

Malachi opted not to sit. He stood in front of the cluttered desk and occupied himself in studying the feat of engineering that was O'Driscoll's comb-over.

Remarkable, he thought, but succeeded in keeping the compliment to himself. He dropped his right hand and let his fingers rest on Bran's head. Bran, good soldier that he was, stood to attention at his master's side. Together they waited.

O'Driscoll gathered up a sheaf of papers from his desk and held them in one hand. He opened a drawer, rooted around in the depths of it, and extracted a blue paper clip. He opened a second drawer and took his time selecting a blue cardboard folder. He tapped the stack of papers against the desk to straighten the edges, carefully attached the paper clip, and slid the documents inside the folder. Finally, he placed the folder on the desk in front of him and rested his praying hands on top of it. *You'd love to know what's inside this*, his actions said, *and I'm not telling*. He looked towards Malachi, but the slight squint in his eye gave the impression that half his mind was on something else.

'Right so,' he said. Theoretically, Paddy was smiling. The corners of his mouth turned up and the tips of his small, keen teeth showed, but the vertical crease between his narrowed eyes left no room for doubt about the depth of his irritation. 'What can I do for you?'

'It was you who summoned me, I believe,' said Malachi. He'd found Sean Leahy, one of O'Driscoll's bouncers, parked in his farmyard, too afraid of a barking dog to risk getting out of his car and too afraid of his boss to risk leaving without conveying the message.

'Well, yes, I thought you and I should have a little chat.'

'I'll talk all you want *after* you drop your objection to my new barn.'

'Your new barn, as I've told you before, would be a blight on the landscape.'

'Bullshit.'

'*Ah now*. Look, Malachi.' O'Driscoll pressed his palms together and leaned forward in the manner of a headmaster remonstrating with a brazen child. 'I shelled out a packet to old man Beecher for my site. I've jumped through hoops for the planners, and I danced a flippin' slip jig to land this celebrity architect that my wife wants. And *just* when I'm making headway, *just* when I've the foundations dug, *you* decide to plonk a great big fucking *shed* right in the middle of my fucking *sea view*. I mean, seriously now, anyone would think you were deliberately trying to ruin my entire *fucking* retirement. It's not very neighbourly, Malachi. Now, is it?'

The speech struck Malachi as a tad over-rehearsed. He stuck to his own line.

'You know as well as I do that the location of the barn is all down to regulations. And what's wrong with having a barn in your view anyway? Would a few agricultural buildings not suit Mrs. O'Driscoll's pastoral aesthetic?'

'She doesn't want it.'

'She'll have to learn to live with it. I'm following all the guidelines. The planners can't refuse the barn. They *won't* refuse it, and you know it, otherwise we wouldn't be having this little chat, now, would we, *Paddy*?'

O'Driscoll flinched at the familiarity.

'I'll hold it up for years,' he growled.

At Malachi's side, Bran bared his teeth but made no sound.

'I'll appeal,' Malachi said, with his hand over the scruff of Bran's neck, 'over and over, for as long as it takes.'

'You'll lose. You know the influence I've got.'

'It'll cost you a fortune.'

'I've got a fortune.'

'Grand, so. We know where we stand.' Malachi turned to leave.

'Wait,' said O'Driscoll.

Malachi stood, unmoving.

'I have a proposal,' said O'Driscoll, in an entirely friendlier tone of voice. 'Sit down a minute, why don't you?'

Malachi pulled the chair back from O'Driscoll's desk, making more distance between them, and sat on it.

'Go on.'

'I'll tell you what. Give me the deeds of your grandmother's house down on Weavers' Row and I'll drop the planning objection.'

'How much are you offering?'

'Offering? Ah here, Malachi. That house has been lying empty this last fifteen years, and we both know the reason why. Nobody in their right mind would buy it. I'm offering to take it off your hands, and I'll make the planning headache go away at the same time.'

'What do you want with it?'

'The hotel could do with a bit of extra what-do-you-call-it, *parking* space.'

He'd knock it, so.

'Don't you already have Number One?'

'That's right.' O'Driscoll sat well back in his chair and didn't elaborate. Malachi knew he'd taken the deeds in return for a bad debt run up in the hotel bar. The man's hunger for acquisition knew no limit.

'I see.'

'You don't strike me as the sentimental type, Malachi.' Malachi hated the way O'Driscoll kept repeating his name.

'I'm not, but I'm not an idiot either. I'd be looking two hundred grand for that house.'

'Hah! Now, who's bullshitting?' O'Driscoll sat back in his chair and let it swing a bit. Clearly, he was having fun. 'I'll give you fifty, out of goodwill.'

It struck Malachi that O'Driscoll didn't give a shit about the barn. What he wanted was his car park.

'Come back to me with a real offer, Paddy, and we can talk.'

Paddy O'Driscoll tapped his fingertips off each other, counting money in his head, no doubt.

'Fifty-five and a half. That's my best and final offer. Take it or leave it.'

'I'll think about it, Paddy,' said Malachi. He straightened his shoulders and walked out, Bran marching by his side.

'You do that, Malachi Barry,' he heard O'Driscoll say as the fire-safety hinge swung the door shut behind them.

12.

Home

* * *

Emer was *so lucky*, she was often told, in having inherited her mother's long legs. Given a choice, she'd have taken her mammy's brown eyes and bouncy hair, her pretty face, *her ability to talk*, but more useful, she thought, on this occasion, would have been her mother's infallible internal compass. She had learned the route from school to the new house off by heart: straight down Convent Hill, past the rows of tall, pale houses, all the way to the river, then over the bridge, up Bridge Street, a left turn onto Main Street, and then left again at the sign that said *Cul de Sac*. It was pronounced culldy-sack, Mammy said, and made their new address all the more desirable. *Fierce posh altogether.* The old stone wall bordering the right-hand side of the lane was curtained with yellow lichen and pennywort, the plant Granny insisted was good for your liver.

'It grows in the damp,' she'd said, picking a leaf for Emer to taste. 'That's the clue, you see, that it will keep you from overheating.'

A terrace of three workers' cottages ran down the left, each with a narrow front door and a six-paned sash window to either side. A skinny footpath ran the length of the row, but at each entranceway a limestone doorstep jutted out, forcing Emer to choose between putting her left foot up on the step, or her right foot out on the road. There wasn't much worry of a car coming down the lane as it was too tight for parking, and anyway, as declared by the *Cul de Sac* sign, it was a dead end. Regardless,

Emer preferred to play it safe and took the option to step up rather than out.

There was nobody to see her, either way. The first two houses were empty, abandoned, with rough boards covering broken windowpanes and clumps of dandelions growing around the doorsteps. Number Three was in no better condition, but there were signs of life. Mammy's car was pulled right up to the doorstep of the house, its four doors and hatchback all open. She could hear music, Ed Sheeran singing 'Bad Habits', and Mammy doing a harmony.

Emer squeezed between the back of the car and the house. As she placed her left foot on the doorstep, a black plastic bag, stuffed full of something rotten, flew across her path, close enough that drops of rancid liquid sprayed her face.

'Aagh,' Emer let out a yelp. 'Mam!'

'Oh hi, Chicken.' There was Mammy, with a second, threatening rubbish sack swinging in her hand. 'You're home.'

Emer went to step inside.

'Go back!'

'What?'

'Don't say what.'

'*Why?*'

'Cross the threshold with your right foot first.'

'What?'

'Emer!'

'S-sorry. *Why?*'

'It's good luck.'

Emer threw her right foot forward and goose-stepped down the hall and into the room that, only yesterday, had resembled a museum piece on 1950s Ireland, with roses chasing each other up the wallpaper and a Belfast sink full of crusty dishes.

'I'm keeping the sink,' said Mammy. 'Everything else had to go.'

The sink, true enough, still stood under the back window, propped up on wooden posts. Otherwise, the entire previous contents of the room had been removed, presumably to the back of the car.

'I've already made three trips to the dump.'

Mammy was in her element, up to her eyeballs in chaos. Emer watched her throw the last black sack into the boot and pull off her extra thick rubber gloves. She was in her working clothes now, her check shirt, blue jeans and hiking boots, her hair pinned in a messy bun at the top of her head.

'How was school?'

'Fine,' said Emer. There was no point in telling her mother she'd had to stand at the top of the class, so that everyone could stare at *the new girl*, or that nobody else wore the stupid school scarf, or that she was put sitting next to a girl who smelled like Brussels sprouts, or that everyone talked too fast and Emer couldn't understand what they said.

She stood at the centre of the bare floor and surveyed the empty room. There wasn't anything to comment on, other than its emptiness, and the corresponding hollow feeling in her belly.

'What did the t-teacher say to the p-pencils on the first day of school?' she asked, instead.

'Go on, tell me.' Mammy was scrubbing her nails with a brush under the running tap.

Emer pointed her index fingers in the shape of two little guns.

'*Look sharp*, they're c-coming to get you!'

'Good one,' Mammy said, drying her hands on one of Granny's embroidered towels. She gave Emer a small, sad sort of smile. 'Are you hungry?'

'A bit.'

'C'mon so – we'll run up to the chipper.' She unhooked her bag and walked out the door.

Emer dropped her school bag on the floor and piled her blazer and scarf on top of it, then ran outside.

'I'll just have to empty the boot at the dump on the way,' Mammy said. She was already perched in the driver's seat, with the window rolled down and her elbow leaning out. 'Pull the door shut.'

The door was warped. When the bottom half met the frame, the top half stayed ajar by half an inch. Try as she might, Emer wasn't strong enough to make the lock meet its latch. She looked to her mother for help, but she could tell that Mammy's mind was already moving up the road.

'Leave it,' she called, through the car window. Mammy was losing patience. 'There's nothing in there anybody would want to steal.'

More's the pity. Emer thought of her brand-new blazer and scarf. She dashed to jump into the moving car. Mammy drove with one hand on the wheel, the other scrolling a playlist on her phone until Harry Styles was singing 'Keep Driving' at full blast. She sang along in her strong mezzo voice, tapping out the rhythm on Emer's knee.

'Do you want a batter burger?' she asked, between choruses.

'Yes, p-please,' said Emer.

'Only if you sing with me.'

Emer waited through a couple of lines before she took a breath and found the words.

'Louder!'

They sang together. Then Mammy laughed, and Emer laughed too.

Emer rolled down her window and leaned out, the rushing air cool against her face. There was no better feeling than this, being in the car, the two of them, moving fast and singing, when Mammy was happy.

13.

Cavendish Place

* * *

Originally a British barracks town, Drohid could boast any number of interesting buildings, but was short of desirable dwellings. There was the Old Mill, built of handsome granite, that threw a long shadow over the weir. Paddy O'Driscoll, amongst others, had more than once tried to prise it away from the absentee descendant who owned it, but all had failed, and the great stone blocks carried on shedding their layers into the riverbed. There was the Old Rectory too, a mid-Victorian neo-gothic horror house, with a row of tidy two-storey Victorian semi-Ds that ran away from it, all respectable but not what you'd call impressive. The local Big House, formerly occupied by His Majesty's magistrate, had been razed to the ground in the fiery 1920s and even a century later was considered too cursed for restoration. Four and a half miles out of town at a point where the river was deep but narrow, there stood the more ancient ruin of a McCarthy castle, but you couldn't count that either, not with the witchy ring of hawthorn surrounding it and the buddleias sprouting from the chimneys.

No, the truth was that in the whole town and surrounding areas of Drohid there was only one truly desirable address, and that was Cavendish Place.

Cavendish Place was formed by two tall terraces of three houses each, all three-storey over basement, facing each other, and one grand house taking up the centre. Never mind that all were damp and draughty. Any bodily discomfort was compensated for by the graceful Georgian proportions, the limestone and brick double-fronted façades, by the garden square at their centre with its private playground where precious offspring were safely enclosed, and of course by the status of their position on the north side of the river, well removed from the grubby, money-handling business end of town. The fourth side of Cavendish Place was protected by tall, wrought iron railings, granting passers-by on the Cork Road a fleeting peek, a moment to admire and dream of a Lotto win.

These seven were the most desirable homes in Drohid, with the one detached home in the centre, Cavendish House, easily pipping the others to the post in the Best Home stakes.

The rear garden of Cavendish House stretched out along the river, catching sunshine all day from the south and all evening from the west. A small wooden dock had been built to extend over the riverbank, not that anyone would be launching a boat in this day and age, but it was a pleasant place to serve drinks before dinner. A stepped pathway was artfully designed to lead visitors through tall grasses and perennial blooms, past an old wishing well and on towards the French doors of the drawing room, where their willowy, well-coiffed hostess and her charming husband would invite them to make themselves at home, if only for an hour or two.

On this particular September evening, however, the French doors of the drawing room stood firmly closed as willowy, well-coiffed Nóinín Corcoran relaxed into her customary chair at the head of the kitchen table with the menacingly satisfied demeanour of a cheetah returned from the hunt.

Tim Corcoran, her charming husband, watched as she kicked off her tan court shoes and curled her toes to stretch her arches.

He placed a soup plate in front of her and dipped a ladle into the china tureen.

'Thought I'd try something new,' he said. 'It's boeuf bourguignon.'

Nóinín, looking lost in her own thoughts, didn't seem to hear him. She blew on her spoon and took a careful sip. Tim served Pamela and Tadgh before taking his own seat at the opposite end.

'It's yummy,' said Pamela, with a smile for her daddy.

'Yes. Delicious,' said Nóinín, too politely. 'Pass the salt, please, Pammy, would you?'

Tim lowered his eyes to his plate but kept his voice light. 'Good day at the shop?'

'Not great. The sooner this weather turns the better.'

* * *

Both Nóinín's family and Tim's were *Old Drohid*, well-heeled Catholic families that had come into their own in a garrison town as soon as the British left. Nóinín's family had owned then, and still owned, a swathe of the town's commercial property, including the all-important hotel. Nobody stayed in the Drohid Arms, as far as anyone could tell, except for the odd salesman or visiting politicians on expenses, but the Riverview Dining Room was the setting for every special occasion in the personal history of any citizen of Drohid. It was, effectively, the Good Front Room of the whole town.

Tim's great-grandfather, back in August 1922, had hopped into the truck directly behind Michael Collins' car as the general left the Drohid Arms. The convoy, of course, was attacked out by Béal na Bláth and Collins shot. It was Tadgh Corcoran who had cradled the Big Fella's head in his lap while Collins' brains, and the pride of a nation, spilled onto the road. The glory of this close association with a local hero was of such significance it had ensured not only that Tadgh Corcoran dined out and did well in business all his life, but even that it rubbed off down the generations. The eventual nuptials of Nóinín O'Driscoll and Tim Corcoran was deemed a fitting match, further bolstering the unimpeachable standing of both families. They were Drohid's golden couple – prosperous, polished, a credit to the place. Even their matching fair hair and blue eyes served to mark them out, these two, as successful beings, the jewels of the town, hard and shiny.

People wanted to associate with the Corcorans. They wanted to latch on to them, even for a short time, that they might become inoculated with whatever sparkle dust it was that made the Corcorans special. It was no stretch to say that something so frivolous as a Corcoran's Drapery bag in hand was enough to make the plebeian citizen of Drohid walk a little taller.

* * *

'I might invest in a line of classy leisurewear,' Nóinín said now, thinking out loud in lieu of making conversation.

Tim could think of no meaningful reply.

'You mean fancy tracksuits, Mammy?' said Pamela.

Nóinín laughed at that. She sat up straight.

'How was the first day back at school, guys?'

'Fine,' Tadgh was non-committal.

'There's a new girl in my class,' said Pamela.

'Is she nice?'

'I can't tell. She was quiet as a mouse.'

'She might be a bit shy.'

'No, I mean, she doesn't speak at all, like.'

'Don't say like, precious. You should try to be nice to her.'

'I would, but I can't get near her. She's stuck beside smelly Veronica Waugh.'

'Pamela!'

'Sorry.'

Soup spoons clicked against the sides of faded Wedgewood bowls.

'What's this new girl's name?' It was Tim himself who asked. There was nobody else to blame, he thought, afterwards. He walked himself into it.

'Emer Gaffney,' said Pamela. 'She's from Dublin.'

Tim reached out for the bread knife and began cutting a slice from the loaf on the table.

'Oh!' said Nóinín, with a burst of enthusiasm. She pointed her spoon at Tim. '*Emer*. That's right. That's the girl who was with the woman I was telling you about, Tim.'

Tim concentrated on cutting a dead straight slice of bread.

'You know – your woman who bought the school uniform, the whole kit and caboodle, in duplicate, and paid in cash.'

'That's a good thing, surely?'

'Well, yes. Nothing wrong with that, but my father's in a fury over this same woman because she outbid him on Agnes Beecher's house.'

'What would your father be doing with Agnes Beecher's place? It's in the back of beyond.'

Nóinín threw her eyes up to the ceiling.

'Ah Tim, for God's sake. Keep up, would you? Agnes Beecher still owned that cottage at the end of Weavers' Row.'

'Your poor father – still trying to catch up with Old Beecher, is he?'

'That's a bit rich out of you, Tim, when you're sitting pretty in the very house where Miss Beecher grew up.'

Tim's mouth twitched at the reminder that it was O'Driscoll money that had set them up in life.

'Those houses in Weavers' Row are only fit for knocking.' He spat the words.

'Exactly. That's what Daddy said. Then this woman came and bid crazy money. Now Daddy has the one at the top, and she has the one at the end.'

'Who owns the one in the middle?'

'That ugly farmer Alison fancies. From out Knockliscrena way?'

Tim laughed at that. The man-hunting exploits of their next-door neighbour was a rich source of entertainment for the Corcorans.

'I know him. Malachi Barry.'

'Uh huh.' She sipped her wine.

'Slice of bread?'

Nóinín batted away his proffered piece of sourdough. Her face was clenched in concentration as she fished in her memory for the correct piece of information, and then lit up when she grasped it.

'Maeve – that was her name – Maeve Gaffney.'

'Ah, *fuck*!' The breadknife clattered to the floor.

'*Tim!*' said Nóinín, pointing with her eyes to their two young children gathered around the family dinner table. He grabbed a tea towel and wrapped it around the injured digit. Nóinín leapt from her seat and pulled open a cupboard door, searching for the first aid kit. After some rummaging, she held up a small Peppa Pig plaster. It was pink and had bananas and strawberries on it.

'Will this do?' she said.

'*Sorry*, sorry,' said Tim, holding his hand above his head to stem the bleeding. 'I think I've done some serious damage.'

14.

It Gets Deep in the Middle

* * *

'Come on, Bran,' said Malachi Barry, holding the car door open. 'We'll walk first.'

Malachi was procrastinating, and he knew it, but Bran wasn't about to complain. He hopped across the driver's seat and onto the road at Malachi's heel.

A vintage Saab was parked at the end of the lane – 1991 900SE in Monte Carlo yellow. *Very* nice, and converted to electric, Malachi noted. He wondered, for the umpteenth time, what it would cost to get a similar job done on his Defender.

'Go on, boy,' he said. Bran, needing no second invitation, took off down the riverbank heading east, away from the town centre and into the rising sun. Malachi picked up his pace, but let his mind wander.

He felt guilty about letting the homeplace go, but there was no merit in leaving it there to rot. Selling his grandmother's house meant he'd avoid a battle with the County Planning Office for his new barn. *If* O'Driscoll could be trusted, that was, which was no sure thing.

He *could* put the house on the open market, but it looked like Agnes Beecher had just nabbed the only person on the planet foolish enough to buy a house on Weavers' Row. Agnes, whose ancestors had once owned the whole terrace, had called up to the farm to let Malachi know that Paddy O'Driscoll had failed in his effort to buy Number Three from her.

'I was quite pleased he was outbid,' she had said, 'if I'm honest.' Her fine-boned face turned pink. Malachi had seen and recognised the look of guilt, but he'd said nothing.

They were at the edge of town now, coming up on the big construction site, where the latest new housing estate was being built. It annoyed Malachi to look at it. With all the fuss the planners made about a barn, he couldn't understand how they'd ever granted permission for sixty houses on the bank of the river. Of course, Paddy O'Driscoll had a finger in that pie too. Nobody wanted to say no to the biggest employer in town. It was all a fix.

Malachi bent and picked up a stone from the edge of the path and skimmed it across the water. Seven, eight, nine bounces, he counted out of habit. Satisfied, he turned to his companion for a bit of praise, but Bran had spotted a rabbit and was poking his nose into the hedgerow in the hope of provoking a chase.

'Bran!' He had to shout to gain the dog's attention. Bran pricked an ear and looked up but then went straight back to his poking.

'Daft fecker.' Malachi turned on his heel and started back towards town. He might as well bite the bullet. It galled him to give Paddy O'Driscoll what he wanted, but it was the cleanest option, all things considered. Better get it over with.

Bran came bounding from behind and assumed his customary position at Malachi's heel.

'Decided to join me, did you?'

Bran looked up with soulful eyes.

'You're a chancer, that's what you are,' Malachi said, but he pulled a dog treat from the pocket of his waxed jacket.

The morning sun was at their backs now and Malachi didn't have to squint against it anymore. The river was low and spinach green after all the weeks of mad heat. Wide stony beaches were exposed below the banks on both sides and the water seemed hardly to flow at all. It snaked around the town with only the merest shiver of life to it.

* * *

He was coming up on the turn for Weavers' Row when he saw her, the woman, a hundred yards further upstream, walking out from the south bank towards the middle of the river. Malachi sped up and jogged to the spot where her shoes were lying. The legs of her khaki cargo pants were rolled up high, but the fabric was already stained dark with water. Her attention was fixed on the opposite bank where Corcoran's jetty jutted out into the river. She edged further into the flowing water, finding her footing on the riverbed with tentative steps.

'Hello!' Malachi raised his chin and projected his voice across the distance between them. She showed no reaction. He wondered whether he should jump down from the riverbank to the stony beach, but stalled, thinking that might look a bit dramatic.

'Hey! Hello!' He shouted this time and Bran, following the direction of Malachi's attention, splashed into the water and barked sharply. At last, the woman turned around.

'Be careful there. It gets deep in the middle.'

'Does it?' said the woman. She waded towards him with one hand raised to shield her eyes. 'I wanted to see if I could walk across to the other side.'

Sunlight flashed off the water droplets on her bare legs. She was taller even than he'd guessed, but not in the least willowy. Her shoulders were broad, and her arms weren't slim. They looked as if they'd been made strong from work, rather than toned in a gym. Her face too was impressive, with high cheekbones, a wide brow and a strong jawline. Not beautiful, exactly. *A handsome woman*, that was the phrase, he thought. There was something familiar about her, a scratch of a memory at the back of his head, or maybe it was just the way she looked a bit like Wonder Woman.

'No. You could swim it, maybe, on a day like this,' he said as she came closer. 'Mind you, the crowd over the way wouldn't thank you for landing in their garden.'

'It's a beautiful house,' she said, looking back over her shoulder.

'Yerra . . .' He was hardly going to launch into a tirade against the Drohid mafia with this woman. He got a grip on himself. 'If you say so,' he said.

She was standing just below him now.

'Maeve Gaffney,' she said, holding her right hand up towards him. He leaned down and took it. Without really thinking about it, he pulled her up onto the bank beside him. Suddenly, they were very close, as close as dance partners, close enough that he could smell toothpaste on her breath.

'Oh,' she said. 'Thanks.' Her laugh came from somewhere low in her throat, a warm, contagious sort of sound.

'Malachi Barry.' He stepped away and let go of her hand.

'I should get moving,' she said. She twisted her long hair into a knot at the back of her head and secured it with a band that she slipped off her wrist with her teeth. 'I'm supposed to be working right now.'

'Me too.' He turned to leave.

'Are you going that way?' She inclined her head towards the gap in the hedgerow.

'I am.'

'Me too,' she said, and they walked together back to Weavers' Row.

15.

A Giant Appears

* * *

Emer's first full week at the convent had been a trial. Everything was a test. The other girls asked questions. Where did she come from? What did she think of Cork? Did she have any brothers? Emer was too slow to grasp the words and took too long to find the answers. Snobby cow, she heard one girl say, when she apologised for misunderstanding.

By Thursday, she had deduced that, in Cork, a schoolbag was called a sack; trousers were called pants; one washed the ware, not the dishes; a sconce was a look; and savage was a compliment. Yes was *yahh* and no was *nyahh,* with precious little difference between the two. *I do yahh* meant I don't, two positives apparently making a negative. Out meant very, as in *happy out*; pure also meant very, as in *pure mank;* it was essential to add *like* or *girl*, or both, to the end of every sentence, and Tanora was the name of a drink, not a singer.

'Nyahh, girl.' The Brussels sprouts girl, whose name was Veronica, had laughed when Emer tried to talk to her. 'I dunno what you're saying, like.'

And then at hometime on Friday, as if by some miracle, a pretty girl with shiny blonde hair had sidled up beside her at the coat rack.

'Very retro,' she said, picking up the end of Emer's school scarf and waggling it.

'Thanks?' Emer couldn't tell whether she was being made fun of, or not.

'I love it.'

'Really?'

'I do.' The girl smiled but Emer was still doubtful. '*Really*. I'm going to ask Mammy to get me one.'

Emer's shoulders dropped in relief.

'We might, we might start a t-trend,' she said.

'Exactly,' said the girl. 'Do you want to walk home with me? I live near your house.'

Emer felt a blush rise in her cheeks at the thought of this glossy girl knowing where she lived, but the girl didn't seem bothered one way or the other.

'O-okay,' she said, warily, untwisting the straps of her bag.

'Great. Let's go.' The girl cleared a path through the crowd at the doorway, then turned to Emer. 'I'm Pamela, by the way. Pamela Corcoran.'

* * *

Emer and Pamela Corcoran parted ways at the bottom of Convent Hill, after Pamela had introduced Emer to Mimi in the sweet shop and bought them each a bar of chocolate. Pamela headed out the Cork Road and Emer crossed the bridge and made her way to Weavers' Row. *Not so bad*, she thought. It was Friday, and she had a Chomp in her pocket, like.

Her mother's car was in its usual position with the doors gaping. *Un*usually, a second car, a big, mucky, navy blue Land Rover, was parked in the laneway. Emer had to turn sideways to get past it. She shoved open the front door of Number Three and went inside.

The house was emptier than usual, in that her mother wasn't there, though her sledgehammer leaned against the wheelbarrow that was parked in the centre of the so-called sitting room.

'I'm home,' she sang out.

There was no reply.

'Hello,' she tried again. '*Hello?*'

A muffled call came from behind her back. Emer spun on her heel.

'Coming!' Her mother's voice, Emer would have sworn, came from inside the wall.

'Mam?' said Emer, but not loudly enough, it seemed, to penetrate to whatever dimension her mother now inhabited.

Emer moved closer to the wall, studying the climbing rose wallpaper for clues. A loud crash on the other side made her hop back. Then her ear tuned to the beat of footsteps approaching the front door.

The familiar silhouette of her mother appeared against the light.

'Hiya, Chicken. Good day at school?'

Emer nodded, but her attention was taken by the taller, bulkier body coming through the doorway. Bizarrely, the man had an antique wall clock tucked under his left arm, as if he was playing the role of Father Time.

'This is Malachi,' said her mother. 'Malachi Barry.'

The tall man bowed slightly, confirming his identity. He held a giant-sized hand out to Emer, which, dutifully, she shook. It was rough, but warm and dry, and he didn't squeeze really hard like her mam had when she was teaching Emer how to shake hands. He had a big head, like a giant in a story, and a kind of bumpy face.

'You can call me Mal,' he said.

'Emer G-Gaffney,' Emer said, and stepped back.

Mal smiled and gave her a double nod of his head, one nod in acknowledgement of her name, and another, she thought, to say he liked her. Something inside Emer went out to him, like a tendril of young ivy.

'Mal—' Maeve paused, and Mal shrugged. '*Malachi* has agreed to sell me his granny's house. He's been very kind.'

'Divil the bit,' he said, under his breath.

Emer hadn't a clue what he meant. She looked again at the wall with the climbing roses.

'That's it, next door,' said Mammy. 'I have a plan.'

16.

The Pear Frangipane Tart

* * *

The front door to Number Three Weavers' Row stood ajar.

Agnes stepped onto the familiar limestone step and knocked on the doorframe.

'Hello?' she called. 'Anybody home?'

The jangle of something metal falling from a height was followed by a bright, melodic voice.

'Com-ing! One minute!'

Footsteps sounded in the hallway and the door swung open.

'He-llo,' said the woman, her voice hitting two distinct notes.

Agnes took in the almost Amazonian stature of the figure facing her. The woman was dressed in paint-stained denim jeans and a man's undervest. A smear of grey dust marked her forehead, and she held a long, paint-smeared chisel in her right hand.

'What can I do for you?' she asked, and Agnes realised that she should have spoken sooner. She raised the green-ribboned patisserie box in her two hands, held it out as an offering.

'Sorry, yes. Hello.' Agnes stumbled, then let the rest of her words come out altogether, in a rush. 'I'm the previous owner of this house. You bought it from me, you see. I thought I should come and introduce myself. I'm Agnes.'

'Agnes!' said the woman, for all the world as if she'd only been waiting for the high delight of this moment. She slipped the chisel into her left hand, balanced the cake box on top of it, and thrust out her right hand to grasp Agnes by the elbow.

'Come in, come in. I'm Maeve. I'm so glad you've called.'

Agnes was pulled into the hallway. The old brown lino had been lifted, baring the concrete floor, and the wall on one side had a hole knocked through the middle of it.

'You're clearly busy,' said Agnes. 'I won't keep you from your work.'

'Oh no, please do!' said Maeve, continuing to move down the hall and into the old kitchen, giving Agnes no choice but to follow her. 'We were about to have our lunch. You'll join us.'

The kitchen also had been stripped to pink plaster walls and rough concrete underfoot. Below the back window, the old Belfast sink was propped up on a slightly skewed timber frame. A young girl was standing at a countertop jury-rigged from heavy planks. She was on her tippy toes, caught in the act of pressing the lid down on an over-filled sandwich toaster.

'Ah no—' said Agnes, but Maeve cut her off.

'Emer – this is Emer – get another cup out for Agnes, will you?'

The girl smiled shyly and wordlessly took the cake box from her mother's hand.

'I'm afraid we're still waiting for more furniture to be delivered.' Maeve reached for a flannel shirt that was hanging off a nail in the wall where a bleeding Sacred Heart, Agnes remembered, had hung before. Stretching her arms into the shirtsleeves, Maeve indicated that her guest might sit on either of two upended cavity blocks arranged near the front window.

'Thank you.' Agnes laid her basket on the floor and perched on the nearer block. An aroma of browning butter filled the room.

Maeve switched on the electric kettle that stood next to the sizzling sandwich maker. She took three plates from a box on the floor, held them under the running tap, then wiped them with a clean tea towel and laid them on the plank countertop before sitting opposite Agnes. She sat on the block as though there was nothing whatsoever askew with the arrangement, crossing one long leg over the other and wrapping her hands around her knee. Her whole body was so suffused with vitality, it was as if she had to hold herself still, to contain herself to the act of sitting down.

'Tea or coffee, Agnes?'

'Tea would be lovely, please.'

'Emer will make us a cup. Milk and sugar?'

'Neither, please. I take it black.'

'I hope it's not too shocking for you, seeing your old home in this state.'

Agnes opened her mouth to say that this had been, in fact, Cook's home, but she changed her mind.

'Not at all. I can't wait to see what you do with it.' She realised as she said it that this was true.

The girl, Emer, brought a toasted sandwich, cut into two rectangular pieces. Melted cheese and caramelised relish oozed onto the plate. She handed it to Agnes along with a pressed white linen napkin.

'C-Careful. It's hot,' she said quietly.

'Goodness. Thank you,' said Agnes.

'I have *lots* of ideas. The first step of my plan is to knock through that far wall.' Maeve pointed over her shoulder.

Balancing the plate on her lap, Agnes lifted the sandwich and took a bite.

'I wonder if you could recommend a local workman?'

At just that moment, Agnes' attention was focused on crispy buttered toast giving way to molten cheese.

Maeve grinned and leaned forwards.

'Good?'

Agnes swallowed.

'Delicious!' she declared, with such genuine pleasure that Maeve laughed out loud. It was a great hearty laugh, a prize laugh, and the thought occurred to Agnes that she would like to hear it again. To make Maeve Gaffney laugh was somehow its own reward.

'And now we must see what treat you brought,' said Maeve conspiratorially, 'in that very exciting box.'

17.

Blackberry Crumble

* * *

Agnes was concentrating on dispensing hot duck fat from the pan into an old, handleless cup when somebody knocked on the back door. She looked out through the kitchen window and spotted Bran's rear end poking out from amongst her hydrangeas.

'Come on in,' she said, projecting her voice as best she could.

The latch clicked on the door and Malachi Barry came in. Automatically, he lowered his head, having learned from sore experience.

'Ah now, Agnes,' he said. 'What are you at? Give me that.'

He took two steps to reach her and then wrapped his hand around the handle of the cast iron pan. She let him take the weight of it and stepped back, rubbing the strain out of her wrist.

'Will you kindly keep that animal of yours out of my flowers?' she said.

'I *was* trying to keep him out of your bit of duck,' he said.

'Well, don't think that *you* are going to get any either. It's all gone.'

'As if I'd take a morsel from a stingy old Prod like you.'

She cracked a smile. 'I licked the plate.'

He laughed. 'I always knew you were only pretending to be posh.'

'Call in that dog, will you? He'll scare away my goldfinches.'

Malachi opened the back door and whistled. Bran loped in sniffing the air.

'Brute,' said Agnes, taking a plate of fried liver from the countertop and placing it on the floor.

'So, what's broken this time?'

'I'm very sorry, Malachi, but the toilet seems to be blocked again.'

'Oh. Right.' His face fell. 'I'll have to run home for some tools—' He paused when he saw her biting the corner of her lip to keep from laughing.

'Bitch,' he said.

'Hah,' she said, using the tea towel now to wipe a single mirthful tear from the corner of her eye. 'I always knew you were only pretending to be polite.'

'Touché.'

'How's Bella?'

'Who?'

'Ah, Mal.'

'She's grand. Piling on the pounds.'

'Good for her. Tea?'

'Coffee, please, if you have it.'

Agnes handed him an age-speckled moka pot.

'So, what was it you wanted to see me about?'

He unscrewed the top of the pot and handed the separated parts to her.

Agnes turned her back to Malachi as she spooned coffee into the pot.

'I called in to the house on Weavers' Row,' she said.

'You met her then?'

'I did.' She turned the top on the pot to tighten it and lit the gas ring.

'Well?'

'She's certainly interesting.'

'Didn't I tell you? She's off her rocker, that one.'

'Perhaps she's simply eccentric.'

Agnes placed two espresso cups on top of two saucers on the kitchen table alongside a jug of custard and a metal trivet.

'She must be mad, for Christ's sake, to have bought that shack of yours.'

'That shack of *yours* too, don't forget.'

'I know.'

Malachi rubbed his two hands through his hair. He wasn't much to look at. He was too big and his facial features too broad and rugged. But his eyes were as brown and as kind as Bran's. And he did have beautiful hair, in fairness. It could do with a trim, though, Agnes thought.

'I suppose you won't say no,' she said, opening the oven door and handing him a pair of oven gloves.

'I feel a bit guilty, if I'm honest, about taking her money.' He bent and lifted the dish of hot, syrupy apple and blackberry crumble onto the waiting trivet.

'I admit I'm not entirely comfortable about it myself. Had I known the bidder was a woman on her own with a young daughter, I might have reconsidered Paddy O'Driscoll's paltry offer.' She was rooting around in a drawer for a serving spoon.

'I don't even have that excuse. I met her, face to face, and she talked me into it. It was like I was bulldozed or something, Agnes. She just kept talking *at* me until I said yes.' He poured the coffee and, putting the pot down, looked to Agnes for some sign that she knew what he meant.

She felt sorry for him. He was as defenceless against this Maeve Gaffney as she was.

'She *is* very convincing.'

'That's one word for her. I'd be inclined to go with bull-headed, wilful, mulish—'

'I found it!' Triumphantly, Agnes held the spoon aloft.

'About time,' he said.

'Bull-headed *and* mulish might be going a bit far. Did you not think she's very attractive?' Agnes dished crumble onto two chipped soup plates.

'I can't say I noticed,' said Malachi. He looked at his bowl and raised an eyebrow at Agnes.

'No?' She pulled his plate back and dolloped a second spoonful of crumble beside the first.

He nodded appreciatively.

'There's a fine Catholic serving for you,' she said, flooding his bowl with custard from the jug.

'That's more like it now,' he said, lifting his spoon. 'She's too tall.'

'I dare say you're right,' said Agnes, remembering Maeve towering above her in the doorway.

They didn't talk while they ate their dessert.

'Leave the pattern on, will you,' said Agnes, as Malachi scraped the last dregs of custard from his bowl.

'It's not often I get the real thing, Miss Beecher.'

'Will you keep an eye on her, Mal?'

He looked her in the eye and nodded.

'I suppose I'll have to.'

She nodded too. They had an understanding now and they both knew it.

'That dog of yours is farting more than ever. Take him away, would you? I can't stand the smell.'

'Come on, Bran,' he said. 'We know where we're not wanted.'

She smiled.

He stood.

Before he left, he picked up the still warm moka pot, twisted it open, and placed the separated pieces beside the sink.

18.

In Full Swing

* * *

All through September, Maeve worked on the house. By day, she demolished what was rotten and cleared rubble. She patched floorboards, scraped paper off walls, scoured metal and sanded woodwork. In the evenings, she drew sketches, ordered swatches and samples, then worked into the night to meet her submission deadlines at the magazine. By the time the end of the month rolled around, her plan was in full swing.

'This is going to be the making of us,' she said, taking a step backwards to admire her handiwork. 'I just know it.'

She stepped forwards again to accept the steaming mug of tea that Emer passed through the saucer-sized hole Maeve had just opened in the adjoining wall between the two cottages.

'You have to be brave in this life, Chicken.'

Emer didn't answer and Maeve didn't mind. She was used to Emer's quiet. She sometimes wondered if Emer didn't talk because she talked too much or if she talked too much to fill Emer's silence. It was as if, at the point in life where Emer was supposed to join the conversation, she had missed her cue, and now she was getting stuck. It would come good, surely, when the grief passed, and things were settled.

Maeve carried on talking.

'You have to grab the chances you're given to get what you want.' She took a sip of tea. 'Just look at all this extra space. We'll have all this side as a living room, and all that side as a kitchen, and no need at all for an extension. I'm going to paint this side purple, Cadbury purple with accents of gold, and I've already found a velvet sofa that will be perfect. You. Will. *Love* it.' Maeve put her mug down on the adjacent windowsill and swapped it for her sledgehammer. 'You can have a big bedroom on that side. I'm going to turn the whole upstairs of this side into a master bedroom, *en suite*. A boudoir.'

Maeve cleared dust from her throat.

'Stand clear!'

She stepped back on her right leg and balanced her weight before swinging the sledgehammer in a stroke that stretched the diameter of the hole in the wall from saucer to dinner plate.

* * *

By lunchtime the hole was roughly the size and shape of a double doorway and Maeve conceded she'd need professional help to go further. Emer made cheese toasties and they ate them sitting side-by-side on the front step.

'You've got the toasties nailed,' she said to Emer as she finished her sandwich, but Emer was concentrating on offering her crust in tiny pieces to a robin who was standing on the footpath. Maeve leaned back against the doorframe and watched as she drew the bird closer, crumb by crumb, until he was perched at the toe of her shoe. Emer held out a piece between her fingers. The robin nabbed it and flew away with the bread in its beak.

'Right then,' said Maeve, getting to her feet. 'We can't put off that mouldy bathroom any longer.'

Emer looked up with a blank face.

'Come on, it'll be fun.'

She gave Emer the task of levering the damp-loosened tiles from the wall.

'Just fling them into the bath,' she said, grinning. She positioned a speaker on the crumbling windowsill and scrolled her phone for Emer's old favourite – the *Shrek* soundtrack – and turned the volume up high, then sat on the edge of the bath and googled *how to disconnect a toilet*.

'Where would we be without the internet?' she said, three minutes later, as she selected a spanner from a paint tin full of tools and ducked her head into the nether regions of the toilet bowl.

'Dublin,' said Emer, under her breath.

'I heard that.'

'Did you hear *that*?' Emer held on to the tile she'd been about to smash and cocked her head to listen.

'Is there someone at the door?'

Emer nodded and tossed the tile into the bath.

Maeve stood up, put a hand to her hair, and brushed dust from the knees of her jeans. She walked downstairs and swung open the front door with a flourish designed to compensate for her dishevelled appearance.

'He-llo,' she said cheerfully, then took a backwards step. 'Oh.'

'Can I come in?'

'Of course.' *At last*. The thought must have warmed her expression because his face broke open.

She motioned him inside, then closed the door and moved towards the fireplace, drawing him all the way in.

'You found me,' she said.

'I think it's more the case that you found me.' His voice had matured. It was rounder now, more countrified, and deeper, as if his wealth weighed it down.

'A happy coincidence.' Maeve was speaking fast, working hard to keep her nerves from cracking her voice. 'Everyone's moving out of Dublin these days, it just makes sense, and this is such a lovely town—'

'Is that so?'

'That it is a lovely town?'

'That it just makes sense.'

'I—' She changed tack. 'Aren't you glad to see me?'

'Oh Maeve—'

Tim stepped towards her with his arms held out. Maeve shook her head sharply to stop him and to direct his attention back over his shoulder to where Emer was perched on the turn of the stairs.

'Tim—' Maeve began, then stopped.

Emer shifted under the attention and pressed her joined hands together between her knees.

'Oh,' said Tim, smiling. 'Hello. Who's this?'

Maeve opened her mouth, then decided against speaking.

Emer moved to the bottom step of the stairs. She held out her hand and introduced herself, just as Maeve had taught her.

'Hello. I'm Emer G-aaffney.'

So close. Maeve waited.

'Pleased to meet you, Emer Gaffney.' Tim smiled broadly and shook her hand. 'And how old are you?'

'Nine.'

Maeve held her breath. She could almost hear the cogs of Tim's brain clicking. He was holding on to Emer's hand for far too long. *Any second now*, she thought, the lightbulb was going to appear over his head. He drew his hand away from Emer's, an uncomfortably conscious movement, and slid it into his trouser pocket, then turned to face Maeve.

'She's not—?'

Don't tell him, said Greta, from somewhere behind Maeve's right shoulder. *You don't need—*

'She is.' Maeve hated the tremble she heard in her voice, her own vocal cords betraying her.

Tim glanced again at Emer, then shook his head as if he'd seen a unicorn or a UFO, something he couldn't believe in.

'I should go.'

'Ah no. No. Don't, please.' Maeve tried to laugh off the excess of emotion.

'I need to—'

'Stay for a cup of tea.' She pulled a jumble of coins from the pocket of her jeans and poured them into Emer's palm. 'Here. Run up to the shop for three scones, love, and get a jar of jam.'

'I-I-I'm—' Emer held out the legs of her dirty dungarees.

'You're fine.' Maeve brushed tile dust off her daughter's sleeves and pushed her out the front door.

'I can't believe it,' Tim said, when Emer was gone. He walked across the floor, the heel of one hand held to his forehead. At the window, he spun and faced her. He was silhouetted against the light, making it hard to read his expression.

'Believe it, Tim.'

'But you said—'

'I know what I said. Even so, she's yours.'

He buried his hands deep in the pockets of his trousers, as if he could hide his feelings there.

'You lied to me.'

She took one step towards him.

'I didn't *want* to.'

'You were, what, twenty? Why on earth would you want to keep the pregnancy?'

She took another step and reached out to touch his arm. This wasn't the time to tell him how much he'd hurt her. She'd been waiting for this moment, hoping for it, praying for it. *Don't fuck this up*. Deliberately, she softened her voice.

'Nineteen. And how could I *not* want to keep her, when she was all I had left of you?'

His chest rose and fell, rose and fell again. His hands slipped from his pockets and reached for her hips.

'Jesus.' His voice was a whisper.

She smiled.

It always worked.

His eyes softened and the corners of his mouth lifted.

She took the final step to close the distance between them, pressed the full length of her body against his. She felt his arms wrap around her, his right hand spread wide between her shoulder blades, his left sliding lower. She raised her chin and touched her lips to the skin of his jaw.

'Oh, Christ. Maeve—'

Upstairs, the *Shrek* soundtrack swelled to its romantic crescendo. Maeve was overcome with a feeling of relief. More than anything else, she wanted to laugh out loud.

And then, he pulled away. 'I can't believe this.'

'So you said.' Forgivingly, she smiled.

'I thought I was doing the right thing,' he said.

I've heard it all now, said Greta.

'So did I,' said Maeve. 'We both made mistakes.'

'I need time.' He put his hands back in his pockets.

'I'll be here. Whenever you're ready.' Maeve fought to keep her voice relaxed, to make this easy for him. She saw the flicker in his eyes at the suggestion, the minute expansion of his pupils, the way he sucked air into his lungs and straightened his shoulders. It was only a matter of time.

19.

Back Then, in Dublin

* * *

His bedroom, the bigger one at the front of the house, hit a reassuring note on the scale between health hazard, which was obviously scary, and clinically clean, which was even more scary but for different reasons.

Shoes and runners were scattered on the floor. A mug with an inch of cold tea in it sat on the bedside table, along with *East of Eden*, *Portnoy's Complaint*, and a Snickers wrapper. A navy and green tartan-print duvet cover was thrown back over the end of the slatted wooden bedstead. Tell-tale creases in the sheets marked where he'd slept, right in the centre.

Tim lifted a pile of clothes from a swivel chair and dumped them into the laundry basket that stood empty in the corner.

'Here, sit,' he said.

'Can I sit on the bed?' she asked, already sitting on the edge of it. 'My legs are wrecked.'

'Only if you promise not to get crumbs everywhere.' For a second, she thought he was serious. Then he laughed and came towards the bed. He bent and unlaced her Docs, pulled her socks off. 'Go on, swing your legs up.'

He sat opposite her, with his back against the foot of the bed, and pulled her feet onto his lap.

'So, what are *your* dreams, Maeve?'

She admired the way he'd worked around asking whether waitressing was the limit of her aspirations.

'I'm doing law,' she said, smirking. 'First year. I might be a bit too swotty for you.'

He rubbed a thumb into the ball of each foot.

'I walked into that.'

She didn't answer. Her brain was getting fuzzy at the edges. His hands had moved to her ankles. Her head was heavy, but her body felt weightless.

'Tim?'

'Yeah?' He looked up from under his fringe and she saw what he was hoping she would say.

'I'm really sorry . . .'

His face fell. 'Ah.'

'No, look – I'm actually knackered. Do you think we could just sleep for a while?'

'Sleep?'

'Yeah, *sleep* – you know, drop off, conk out – do they teach you those big words in your Pulitzer class?'

'Ah, yeah. I see the law student emerging now. Lift your feet, woman.'

He slipped out from under her legs, took her mug from her hand and stacked it inside his on the bedside table. He turned off the lamp, and walked around the bed in the pale yellow light that came from the street.

'Is it alright with you if I take my pants off?' he said in the dark.

She laughed.

'You mean your trousers?'

'Tuh. Yes, my *trousers*. Underpants on. Do you want to check?'

'Thanks. I'll take your word for it.' She heard the shuffle of his clothes, and by the light from the window she watched as he unbuttoned his shirt and shrugged it off. Under the covers, she wriggled out of her jeans and dropped them to the floor. She turned on her side, facing him. When she tucked up her knees, they bumped his. She didn't move away, and neither did he.

'Is this too weird for you?' she said.

'It's nice,' he said. 'A bit frustrating, maybe, but nice.'

'Sorry.' Maeve yawned. 'I'm just so—'

'Shush. Me too. Sleep.'

They were both quiet. She shifted her hip, settled herself against the firmness of the mattress, tucked her hand beneath the pillow. It was a very comfortable bed.

'Maeve.'

'Hmmm?'

She felt him tuck up the duvet under her chin and rub his finger down the length of her jawbone.

'You're gorgeous.'

She smiled. It was the last thing she heard before she fell asleep.

20.

Watching for Clues

* * *

Emer tried her best to keep her mother in the happy zone. She tried to maintain the cheerful, chatty Mammy who sang along to 'All Star' at top volume, and ruffled Emer's hair, and remembered to buy bread for school lunches.

Reading her mother's moods was like predicting the endings of Robin Stevens' mysteries. You had to watch for the clues. Emer's mother talked a lot but didn't always say exactly what she meant. 'Have you all your homework done?' was code for *my head's too busy to listen to you right now*. And, oftentimes, at night, her mother might say, 'You look tired, love,' which was really code for *I've had enough of talking to you so go to bed, love*.

'Let's go for a drive' was a danger signal, a warning that her mother was feeling trapped, like an animal in a cage. It was as if she had to let herself out every now and then, just to be sure the cage door wasn't locked. Emer knew it was important to always say yes to going for a drive.

'I'm trying as hard as I can' or 'I need a break' were signs that her mother had left the happy zone.

'I can't take any more' meant it was time for Emer to retreat and wait out the storm.

Sending her to the shop for scones, Emer knew, meant *I need you to stay out of the way*, and adding a request for jam meant *and stay away longer*.

So, she dawdled along the path to the shop, took her time debating the merits of raspberry jam over blackcurrant, and browsed the range of cakes for as long as she reasonably could. She didn't think about the man, or why he had seemed so astonished by her existence in the world. She focused instead on the choice between fruit scones and scones with blueberries, and wondered why blueberries didn't count as fruit.

'Having trouble choosing?' said a well-dressed woman who was waiting to use the tongs.

'S-Sorry.'

'Do you need help, pet?'

'No, thank you.' Emer put three scones into a paper bag and walked quickly to the checkout. She then had to make up for being rushed by dawdling even more deliberately all the way home. It was always better, in Emer's experience, to heed the signs.

When she got back to the house the man, Tim, was gone. The table was set with two plates and steam was rising from two mugs of tea already poured. Her mother's cheeks were rosy, and she was singing along to 'I've Got You Under My Skin'.

'Good girl,' she said, taking the paper bag of scones. She executed a perfect twirl before brushing the top of Emer's hair and tucking it back behind her ears. 'God, I love this song. Lady Gaga and Tony Bennett together, so good—'

'He's gone,' said Emer. 'Did I-I-I—? Was I too long?'

'Don't you worry one bit,' said Maeve, placing a scone on a plate and cutting it in half. 'He'll be back.'

'But who was he, Mammy?'

'Nobody,' said Mammy, which was code for *I'm not telling you* and confirmed for Emer that he *was* somebody, somebody important.

21.

This Famous Novel

* * *

'The week from hell, I'm telling you,' said Alison Rafferty, knocking back a third of her drink in one go. 'What's up with you?'

'Tim is writing again.' Nóinín squeezed the wedge of lime hard between her forefinger and her thumb and watched the juice drip into her gin and soda.

'Is that not a good thing?' Alison pushed a plate of breadsticks across the polished concrete surface of her kitchen island. They were the fancy handmade breadsticks. She'd gone to the English Market at lunchtime especially to get them, and the limes. You couldn't be sure of getting a lime in Drohid, though you could be damn sure Nóinín Corcoran would pass a remark if you tried to pawn her off with a regular ole slice of lemon.

Nóinín shook her head from side to side, wincing slightly while holding the first icy mouthful of gin in her mouth, waiting for it to warm up before she swallowed it.

'I needed that,' she said. 'It's not good. He'll only get morose again.'

'What's it about anyway, this famous novel of his?'

'Hah!' Nóinín laughed as if Alison had cracked a joke. 'The loss of innocence, apparently.'

'I love it. It's set at the back of the rugby club, so, circa 2007?'

Nóinín clinked the edge of her glass against Alison's.

'You betcha,' she said, and took another slug. 'Fun times.'

'You never know, maybe he'll surprise you this time and finish the thing.'

Alison nudged the breadsticks closer to Nóinín, who ignored them. She wasn't too bothered about Tim's writing, Alison calculated, if she was still resisting the carbs.

'Not a chance. He'll go at it hammer and tongs for a month, during which time he will lock himself in the attic and pretend that it's a Parisian garret or what have you. He'll refuse to shave, or wear anything other than jogging bottoms and his special moth-eaten woolly jumper. He'll live on coffee and biscuits, and we'll live on Dunnes' Simply Better lasagne, and there won't be a bed made or a child washed until he finally realises, *yet again*, that he's not Sebastian Barry and never will be. Then, he'll have a rant about artificial intelligence spelling the *Death of Art*, and dive headfirst into the slough of despond. Honest to God, I think the only reason he perseveres is to avoid taking a real job at the hotel with Daddy.'

'I thought he had a real job.'

'The *Drohid Echo*, is it? It's only a rag, Alison. They can't *give* the thing away. Tim's exposé on the state of the urinals at the GAA club was the highlight of the year. It's hardly Pulitzer material, now, is it?'

'Ah now.' Alison shrugged. 'He may as well have a go. Sure, it's harmless enough.' She was surprised at the bitter edge to Nóinín's voice. She'd always been envious of the Corcorans' relationship. If each of them on their own seemed to have a bit of a glow, together they glittered.

'He'll get over it,' said Nóinín. She picked up a breadstick and broke it in half, pointing one end at Alison. 'What's up with you anyway? It all sounded very urgent on the phone.'

Alison was sheepish. She didn't have anything as glamorous as a tortured artist husband to complain about, and the subject of Frank's long stints in Dubai was well and truly exhausted.

'Ah, it's only the fecking parent-teacher meetings. They want to throw Saoirse out of honours maths. She's delighted. I'm having none of it.'

'I thought you said Saoirse loved maths.'

'Did I? Well, it turns out Saoirse only loved Mr. MacNamara.'

'The fella with the cute arse?'

Alison couldn't help giggling. She appreciated the way Nóinín kept track of her infatuations. Her neighbour was good company, and company was the one thing Alison lacked.

'Yeah, him. *Ronan*.' She grinned. 'Shocking ginger hair, mind you. Anyway, he's gone off on paternity leave.'

'Very progressive,' said Nóinín.

'Yeah. They had twins, apparently.'

'Christ on a bike.' Nóinín shuddered.

'I know, yeah. Can you imagine?'

They both took a long swig of gin, to perish the thought.

'I quite like Dunnes' Simply Better lasagne,' Alison said.

Nóinín rolled her eyes.

'Hey!' She pulled her iPad from her handbag. 'Do you want a sneak preview of my new line of luxury leisurewear?'

Gratefully, Alison perched on the barstool next to Nóinín's and leaned in for a bit of retail therapy.

'I saw Pamela's little friend, the new girl, in the shop earlier. Didn't you say she was dressed to the nines when they came into your place?'

Nóinín flipped through the catalogue on-screen.

'Hmmm, yes. Totally Chic Parisian Schoolgirl.'

'The waif I saw was more Filthy Dickensian Urchin.'

'Really? Good bones, though, don't you think?' Nóinín paused in her scrolling and reached for a second breadstick.

22.

Lantern Slides

* * *

On the first Saturday in October, Malachi Barry turned up with a toolbox in hand and his dog in tow.

''Tis getting nippy,' he said, standing a couple of feet back from the doorstep and rubbing his hands together. Maeve noticed the half-moons of dirt beneath his nails.

'It's getting cold alright.' She stepped back to allow him inside.

'I'd like to help you get the old place sorted,' he said. 'I'm handy enough with a wrench.'

Watch yourself now, warned Greta.

'Can't hurt,' said Maeve.

'I hope not,' said Malachi Barry, looking puzzled.

Maeve showed him the leaking pipe under the bathroom sink.

'Plumbing is my forté,' he said, as if it was a joke.

When the work was done, she offered him a mug of tea.

'Thanks,' he said, and sat down opposite Emer without passing any remark on the fact that the erstwhile kitchen door was now serving as a kitchen table.

Emer didn't look up. She was in the middle of a game of solitaire.

Maeve spilled a sleeve of Jaffa Cakes onto a plate.

'Emer,' she said. 'Don't be rude. Put away the cards.'

'Yerra, what harm,' said Malachi, and he pointed out the four of spades she'd neglected to move. Emer's face lit up.

'You shouldn't encourage her,' said Maeve, putting his tea down in front of him.

'What other games do you know?' he asked Emer as she gathered the cards into a pile.

'Mousse,' she said.

'Mousse? I don't know that one.'

'She made it up,' said Maeve. She took a biscuit and bit into it.

'Is this a game of skill, Emer, or is it the luck of the draw?'

'It's all luck,' said Maeve.

'It is not.' Emer, for once, was vehement. 'If you p-play it smart, you always have a chance.'

Malachi nodded. 'Smart trumps lucky?'

'Almost every time.'

'Will you teach me?'

Emer looked up at him shyly, but Maeve could see she wanted to.

'Go on, Emer,' she said. 'I'll play too.'

Emer dealt the cards, seven each. 'So, eh, the first to get rid of all their cards wins,' she began. She spoke quietly, looking up at Malachi from under those fair eyelashes of hers.

'Got it,' he said. 'Go on.'

Malachi grasped Emer's rules easily. He threw his head back and laughed loudly when he won the second game.

'Beginner's luck,' said Maeve.

Don't encourage him, said Greta.

I'm not.

He was easy company, she thought, and she liked the way he talked to Emer. Emer liked it too, she could see that.

'Give them a good shuffle, Chicken,' she said, 'before you deal again.'

* * *

The very next day, on the dot of three o'clock, Maeve answered a discreet knock and found Agnes Beecher standing outside.

'Am I keeping you from your work again? You must tell me if I'm being a pest.' Agnes retreated, prepared to walk away.

Maeve saw the way the woman's eyes scanned her faded denims and grey vest.

'I'm afraid I don't observe a day of rest, Agnes,' she said, and held an arm wide in a gesture of welcome.

'Are you sure?' Agnes raised her right foot to cross the threshold.

'Certain. And believe me, if I wasn't happy to see you, I would tell you out straight.'

'Oh. Right. Well, that's good to know, I suppose.'

'Good. Come on in.'

Agnes walked around the newly expanded living room while Maeve arranged her best pottery cups, sugar bowl, and matching milk jug on the door-table. She wouldn't have it said that she didn't at least know how things *should* be done.

'Sorry,' she said, positioning a cushion on top of a concrete block for Agnes to sit on. 'Still no chairs.'

'Oh goodness, this doesn't bother me,' said Agnes, settling her bottom on the cushion. 'It reminds me of the picnics we used to have at point-to-point meetings.'

Maeve filled the teapot and sat down.

'Point-to-point meetings—?'

'Hmmm,' said Agnes, leaning down to pull a bundle of house magazines from her wicker basket. 'I bought these when I was redecorating *Ard na Mara*. They are quite out of date, I suppose, but you might find them useful.'

'Ah, do you know what?' said Maeve, splaying the magazines out across the table. 'You've found my weakness. I can't get enough of these.'

'They might not be to your taste,' said Agnes. She gave a coy glance around the room. 'It's hard to tell what your taste is, just yet, but I suspect it is rather good.'

It was a strange sort of compliment, but Maeve appreciated the vote of confidence.

'That's very nice of you to say, all things considered.' She laughed, and Agnes' face shone in response.

'I have a fairly recent copy of *Miller's Antiques* at home,' said Agnes. 'You're welcome to it, if you have any interest—'

'I'd love it. Thank you.' Maeve lifted the lid off the pot to check that the tea was drawn and began to pour. 'I take it you up-sized, Agnes, when you moved out of here?'

Agnes busied herself adding both milk and sugar to her tea.

Maeve recalled that Agnes had taken her tea black the last time, but she passed no remark.

'No. No, that's not the case at all,' Agnes went on, stirring vigorously. 'I could recommend a good workman, if you like—'

* * *

Eamon O'Neill, according to Agnes, was amenable and fairly honest.

'I got fed up of the big building sites,' he said, the following afternoon. 'Them big lads would only be working you like a machine.' He was a stocky, florid-faced man who spoke with a strong West Cork lilt and seemed fond of the sound of his own voice. 'I'm happy out now,' he continued. 'I can pick and choose, and take the jobs I like, like.'

'And does this look like one you'd like, Mr. O'Neill?' Maeve kept her voice flat, sensing that any hint of flirtation would be counter-productive.

'Well, girl, I wouldn't be up to any heavy lifting at all now.' He paused and let his eyes roll around the room, indicating the great scale of the work at hand. 'Would it suit you if I brought my young fella with me, the odd time, like, only when I'd need him?'

Maeve agreed that would suit her fine and invited Eamon to sit down and take a closer look at her sketchbook.

* * *

By the third Saturday in October, Malachi's visits were becoming a habit.

''Tis shocking out,' he said, standing two feet back from the doorstep with a cake box in his hands.

'So it is,' Maeve said, assuming he meant the weather. 'Come on in.'

She opened the box and transferred the cakes to a plate. There was an apple slice, a custard slice, a coffee slice, and a chocolate eclair. Maeve looked at him questioningly.

'That's the deal they do in the shop,' he said. 'Four cream cakes for a fiver.'

'Ah, I see,' she said, containing a laugh. It wasn't the fact that he opted for the deal that amused her, so much as his scrupulous honesty in telling her about it.

'Well, such an abundance of cakes deserves a proper pot of tea.'

She scalded her Nicholas Mosse forget-me-not teapot with water from the kettle.

He nodded. 'That's very nice.'

'Present from an old boyfriend,' she said, and watched as the corners of his mouth slackened.

'Funny sort of a present,' he said, taking a knife to the chocolate eclair and slicing it into three pieces.

Maeve raised her eyebrows at him. She wasn't sure what he meant to say. He didn't flirt with her, not in any direct sort of way. She found that disconcerting; it wasn't what she was used to.

'Funny sort of a boyfriend,' she said, leaning over and taking a piece of the cake from under the knife. His eyes followed her hand from the plate to her mouth.

'Tell me what I can do for you,' he said.

* * *

Jack O'Neill turned out to be a strapping boy of seventeen, six inches taller than his father and half as wide, but strong and eager.

'Will I take that for you?' he said to Maeve, on his first morning, when he met her on the stairs with a bucket of cement in her arms.

'Thanks, Jack.' She let him take it, knowing it would please him to help her in such a straightforward, chivalrous manner. 'You're very good.'

Jack nodded, then mistook the second last step of the stairs, and only barely managed to save the cement from spilling.

'I'm fine!' he said, blushing violently.

'You're grand, Jack,' she said.

Poor Jack, said Greta, though even she was laughing.

Maeve asked Eamonn and Jack if they'd like to join her for lunch, but they preferred to go home for an hour.

'Herself will have our dinner on the table,' said Eamon, giving Jack a paternal shove out the door.

So, Maeve ate her lunch alone, sitting on an upturned concrete block, staring at the bare walls, though in her mind's eye she was designing a set of bookshelves.

* * *

On the last Saturday in October, Maeve had Emer lie flat on the floor beneath the eaves so that she could draw an outline of her body in blue chalk.

'I-I-I've been murdered!'

'Ah, stop,' said Maeve, but Emer, giggling, had already splayed herself dramatically with one hand over her head and one leg bent. Maeve played along and drew the shape.

'Up you get, you goose. It's done.'

They both stood looking at the floor.

'Agnes Beecher says she knows where to get a cast iron bath. It's going to look fabulous right there.'

Emer nodded, but Maeve was distracted by the sound of a car pulling up. Malachi.

She had decided, lying in bed that morning, that she would discourage him from calling. It was a shame to do without his help, but there was something about him that made her uncomfortable. Malachi Barry wasn't straightforward. Or maybe he *was* straightforward and that didn't suit her.

She had stacked six black sacks full of rubbish outside the front door.

'Would you mind?' she asked, now, as he stood on the doorstep. 'I'd really appreciate it.'

'Right, I can do that alright,' he said, stepping away from her.

He didn't say another word as he loaded the rubbish into the back of his Land Rover. He was hurt, of course he was.

'Will you come back afterwards?' She was mixing her messages now, she knew that, but she couldn't bear the stoic stiffness of him. 'Emer would enjoy a game of cards.'

'Yerra, no.' He strode around the car and slipped into the driver's seat. 'I'll slip away home. There's a match I want to watch.'

Maeve pressed the door closed.

* * *

Contrary to Maeve's expectations, Tim had not returned. For over a month now, she had put on a full face of makeup every morning in combination with her work clothes. At every knock on the door, her heart had leapt. She'd been certain of him, convinced, again, by the lock of his arms around her body, but it seemed her power over Tim Corcoran lasted only as long as they were in the same room.

You're better off, said Greta.

'He's afraid,' she said, gripping the electric sander as she ran it up and down a doorframe.

Malachi would have done that for you.

'Oh, give over.' Tim would come around. She knew he would. She would roll out the red carpet and wait for him to land on it. In a way, it suited her. She needed time to fully set the stage.

23.

Back Then, in Dublin

* * *

She didn't open her eyes. It must have been a change in his breathing, she thought, that woke her. She moved her leg so that her foot lay against his, rubbed along the soft side of it with her big toe. She heard him swallow and take a deep breath. His hand cupped her knee, pressed forward, along her thigh to the summit of her hip bone. He raised his torso and shifted closer, aligning the length of his body – chest firm and belly tight – with hers. She wrapped her leg around his thigh, and her arm around his back, felt the flex of muscles beneath hot skin, threaded her fingers into the mess of his hair. He pressed his lips against her forehead. She lifted her chin so that her mouth found his. She felt his tongue curl around hers, questioning. She leaned away from him, wriggled out of her t-shirt. He groaned, a short, involuntary sound that came from somewhere deep and told the truth. He pulled her back, kissed her again, harder. He tasted of stout and custard creams. He smelled of tobacco and musk and a warm bed. He felt firm and strong and keen. She was overwhelmed by an avalanche of sensation: a lick in one place with a touch in another; a nip with a rub; a kiss with a push; her pulse and his, as if they were melting, melding together. He felt like something she'd never found before; he felt like the other half of herself.

* * *

In the morning, Tim insisted on calling a cab to take her home. He handed a folded note through the passenger-side window to the driver.

'I'll call you,' he said, with a double tap of his palm to the roof of the car as it slid away from the kerb. She risked a glance through the rear window and saw him, halfway up the path, head bent to the screen of his phone. She settled against the plastic-coated seat and closed her eyes. She tried to get back to it, to fix it in her mind before it was lost, the spinning, black hole feeling of it when, just for two or three or four seconds, the whole world fell away.

When they'd woken, he'd gone downstairs in his boxers and come back with two mugs of coffee. He'd stood alongside the bed, holding hers with the handle pointing towards her while she fixed a pillow behind her head.

'Thanks,' she'd said.

He'd grinned and slid into the bed beside her. She wondered how they'd reached this easy comfort so readily. Sure, they were both acting casual, but it wasn't hard. She felt relaxed, as if she had been unwound. He stretched his leg so that it lay against hers. His skin was cool and hers still bed-warm. With a miniscule movement of her thigh, she returned the pressure against his leg. She watched a smile curl the corners of his mouth.

'I'll have to get home,' she'd said, when he'd lifted his body off hers a half hour later. 'My mam's going to have my guts for garters.'

'Rather yours than mine,' he'd said, kissing her knee.

* * *

The taxi was stopped in traffic along the canal when her phone strummed.

I will call you. x

The driver met her smile in the rear-view mirror and winked.

24.

A Stroke of Genius

* * *

November was harsh. A north-east wind whipped down from the hills, skimmed the river, and slapped the exposed gable of the house at the end of Weavers' Row.

Eamon O'Neill began to regret his choice of projects. Oblivious to the weather, Maeve had had a *stroke of genius*, and was sure that a *tiny* extension would be the *transformation* of the place.

''Tisn't the right way, like, to be going about it,' Eamon had said to Jack, after she showed him her pencil sketch. Another builder might have told Maeve that 'twas pure madness to knock out an external wall of your home in mid-November, but Eamon wasn't one to be telling anything to a feisty woman like Maeve Gaffney. Besides, he knew full well, Maeve Gaffney would not have paid him a tack of notice, even if he was.

So, he'd brought Jack in to lend a hand and now the Belfast sink stood on its supporting frame, and the stone wall it had leaned against since Victorian times was gone for rubble. Only a sheet of heavy plastic hung across the gap, pinned to the ground by a row of red bricks and snapping every time the wind threatened to pull it loose.

''Tisn't the right way,' Eamon whispered to Emer when she handed him a cup of tea on Friday afternoon, but Emer only nodded. She, it seemed to Eamon, was well used to her mother having ideas.

Eamon had never worked harder in his life. He'd worked hell for leather all week, and now he was going to be late home for his dinner.

''Tisn't right,' he muttered to himself as he added an extra layer of plastic sheeting to insulate the gap, his lips clenched tightly around three half-inch tacks.

The boss was a looker alright, he thought, but that wasn't going to help him when Assumpta was drumming her fingers on the kitchen table, waiting for him to wash himself ahead of the table quiz at the GAA club. 'Twasn't like him to be late, she'd say. He'd had his head turned, that's what she'd say.

She'd be right, like, he thought.

'Twasn't the way she looked, though, this woman. The thing about Maeve Gaffney was the way she made him feel. She was sound out. She mucked in. She'd be working before he arrived every morning, and still working when he left. She asked his opinion on things, proportions and angles and the quality of timber. She cracked jokes and made fun of him, but in a way that made him feel half a foot taller.

'That shelf is crooked,' she'd announce, five minutes after she'd spotted him double-checking it with a spirit level, and then she'd laugh when he went to check it again.

She never demanded anything, but every Monday morning he'd find that she'd pulled something out, or torn something asunder, or knocked a hole in something, made some mad start on something that, sure as rain was wet and the sun sets westerly, must absolutely be done by the weekend if she and the child weren't to be left in the lurch – without a set of stairs, or front windows, or running water. Whatever the job, it had to be done. Somehow, the more she asked him to do, the more he felt bound to her. 'Twas as if she was allowing him to help her, just so that he could feel good about himself.

Well, this week Maeve Gaffney had bitten off more than Eamon O'Neill could chew. 'Twas her own bloody fault now if she was frozen solid for the whole weekend. Maybe 'twas just as well, he thought, spitting the last tack into his hand and hammering it home. It might keep her out of trouble. He folded up his ladder and carried it outside.

'Will ye be alright like that?' Eamon heard Jack asking Maeve when the van was loaded and they were ready to leave.

'Don't worry about us, Jack. We're two hardy women.' She gave his son a reassuring slap on the back.

'Come on out of that, Jack,' he said, banging the back doors of the van shut. 'Home time.'

25.

The Shakey Bridge

* * *

The wind got on her nerves. It took against her that weekend, like a maligned spirit, rapping at the plastic sheeting so that it ballooned and whooped, shrank and cracked, boomed and cackled, all day and all night. By the time Maeve gave up on sleep and opened her eyes on Sunday morning, had there not been Emer to think of, she would have taken down the damned plastic and let the wind have a free run of the house. But that would be another crazy thing to add to the list of crazy things she did. Sometimes protecting her own sanity and protecting Emer's belief in that sanity were diametrically opposed. The best thing, always, was to stay busy, to keep her mind focused on a task. The ceiling in the bathroom hadn't been painted yet, that was a good place to start, and Emer was keen to paste *Beano* comics on the inside of her wardrobe doors – that would keep her occupied, and out of the wind.

Maeve reached for her phone and swiped the screen. Her heart thumped. Below the time, 7.16am, but above the news headlines and an orange warning weather alert for high winds in the south-west, was one unread message. It was from Tim Corcoran. Pulling a pillow behind her neck, she slid it open.

Could they meet for a chat? Tuesday morning at Fitzgerald's Park.

That was in the city, she noted, well away from the prying eyes of Drohid.

The message had been sent at 3.54am, which meant that she must have slept, and that while she slept the wind had woken him.

She tapped the screen with the tips of her thumbs.

Of course.

She put the phone down on the bedcovers.
This was it.

* * *

The ten o'clock news was playing on the car radio when Maeve reversed into a space parallel to the park railings. She wrapped a scarf around her neck and lifted the roots of her hair with her fingertips before swinging her legs out of the car. As she locked the door, she glanced through the wrought iron railings, and saw him.

Tim.

Just there, on the far side of the lawn.

He was pacing the path in front of the museum, head down, hands thrust deep in his pockets. At the corner of the building, he turned and saw her. He stopped his pacing and stood, perfectly still. Maeve raised her hand to wave, but, taking in Tim's posture, thought better of it.

He didn't make a move towards her, just stood, watching. She steadied her pace, glad that she'd dressed for the weather in a denim skirt and warm boots and an Aran jumper under her leather jacket. It would have been silly to have arrived shivering, she thought, even if all he really got to see of her was her knees.

'Well, he-llo.' She let a question mark flirt around the end of her greeting.

'Fancy meeting you here.' A smirk flickered and his cheek dimpled.

'It's good to see you, Tim,' she said, because it was. All the time, months, *years* even, that she'd spent thinking about him had drained her. And now, having him right there, in the flesh, was like being plugged into a charger. She reached out a hand and touched his elbow, imagining she could hear the internal *bing* of a connection found.

He opened his mouth to respond, then appeared to double think himself. He still hadn't taken his hands from deep inside his pockets.

'Will we walk a bit?' He tilted his head towards the pond.

'Sure.' She moved in step beside him and, mirroring him, put her own hands in her pockets. 'I was beginning to think you didn't want to see me.'

'No. I just . . .'

'It's alright. You're married. I get it.'

'You're not?'

'I'm not, no.' He pointed out the landmarks as they walked, the sculpture of Adam and Eve, and the chubby Apple Woman sheltering in perpetuity beneath the spreading arms of an ancient purple beech.

'Look,' she said, pointing out a pair of mallard ducks huddled together in a nest made on the second tier of the dried-up fountain. 'They're shacking up for the season.'

'Don't they mate for life?'

She could tell by the way his voice dipped halfway through that he was regretting the question.

'That's swans,' she said.

'Right. Of course.'

He led her over the bridge that split the pond in two, to the path that ran through the rose garden. The rose bushes, mostly leafless and skeletal now, still supported a bloom or two, here and there, frosted cups held up to the sky.

'It must be lovely in summer,' she said.

He looked her in the eye. 'Gorgeous.'

She smiled.

'Come on,' he said, at last taking his hands from his pockets but lengthening his stride so she had to walk quickly to keep up. They came to a gate in the park railings, which he pulled open and led her through, down a slope to the bank of the Lee and then up a rising path to a suspended iron footbridge that spanned the river.

'Have you heard of the Shakey Bridge?' he asked, walking ahead of her along the narrow wood planks.

'Are you serious?' Even standing on firm ground, with one hand on the rail of the bridge, she could feel the vibrations of every step he took travelling through her wrist and up her arm.

'We're very literal people here in Cork,' he said. He stood at the centre of the bridge and beckoned to her to join him. 'Come on. It's fun.'

She felt it, the bounce of it, from the very first step. It made jelly of her legs, whomped up to her chest and dropped down again, only to meet the next wave on the way up. She laughed.

'I told you.' He laughed at her laughing, then jumped, to make more of it.

She looked into his eyes and saw the change in them, and she felt the change in herself, too. Somehow, all of their tension was absorbed by the motion of the suspension bridge, literally bounced out of them. He stepped, gently, along the wooden boards, until she could feel the heat of his body through his clothes. He slipped his hands behind her leather jacket, under her jumper, around her waist and up her back.

'There's a saying, you know,' Tim said, with an eyebrow cocked.

There it was, the fatal charm.

'Is there?'

'If you've never been kissed on the Shakey Bridge . . .'

God, she'd missed this, flirting – with intent.

'Go on.'

'Well, you're missing out. Bigtime.'

'My God, the poetry of it,' she mocked.

'Can I kiss you?' he asked.

'Did you ever have to ask?'

'Things have changed.'

'*I* haven't.' She lifted her chin and pressed against him, slipped her fingers into the gap at the back of his waistband, closed her eyes, felt a flutter rise from her belly.

Something hit off her foot.

'Sorry there. Sorry. Can I get by?' A woman in jogging gear had just wheeled a buggy over Maeve's big toe and showed no sign of stopping there.

'Oh sorry.' Tim leapt back, pressed himself against the bridge's handrail. Maeve followed suit.

'Sorry,' she said, not meaning it.

They watched the woman push her buggy off the bridge, then disappear up into Sunday's Well.

'Sorry,' said Tim, with a rueful expression.

She laughed.

'No, I mean it,' he said. 'Really. I'm sorry.'

'What for?'

'Ah, you know. It's not easy, this.'

'No. No, it's not.'

He led the way off the bridge, back towards the park.

'Want to go look around the museum? There's an exhibition about the War of Independence.'

'Oh, really?' Was it for this that he had arranged to meet? To see a museum exhibition? She couldn't make him out.

'My grandfather is in it.'

'Great,' she said. 'Yeah, sure. Let's go, then.'

* * *

Tim was leaning over a case that contained a pistol with the initials M.C. engraved into its wooden handle.

'Fascinating,' he said, meaning it.

He'd read every information sheet on every exhibit. They were in a small room at the top of the museum. There was no one to see or hear them.

'Do you not *want* to ask about your daughter, Tim?'

He straightened himself and looked at her, all hurt and confused, as if she'd torn a strip of skin off his back.

'Ah, Maeve—'

'Is that not why you arranged to meet?'

'Yeah. Well, of course, like.' She noticed the way his yacht-club accent fractured when he was upset.

'I sense a *but*.'

'Well, you know—' He'd got a grip on himself and succeeded in holding back the *like*.

'I know *what*, exactly?'

'It's been a very big shock, Maeve, discovering I have a child I knew nothing about.'

Ah sure, God love him. He's had a shock, said Greta, at peak sarcastic. Maeve shook her off.

'That's understandable,' she said. She put her hand on Tim's arm.

He turned on her. 'Why did you come to Cork?'

'What do you mean?'

'I mean, well, it feels a bit as if you came to hunt me down.'

As if he'd lifted the gun at her, Maeve fell backwards. He put a hand out to steady her, but the cabinet with Tom Barry's IRA uniform in it was rattled. A military medal fell off its stand and lay flat against the glass shelf.

'I'm not the enemy,' she said.

'Of course, not. Don't exaggerate.'

'I'm not stalking you, if that's what you think.'

'I know, I know. That's not what I meant. But seriously, of all the towns—'

She scoffed. 'I had to walk into yours.'

'*Well?*'

'I wanted a change. I got an incredible bargain on a great house in a beautiful location . . .'

'And just a coincidence that it's *literally* overlooking my back garden?'

'It seemed like fate.'

'Fate?'

'Yeah. Fate. Look, you're a free man. Make your own decisions.'

'But I'm not, am I? I'm not free.' He turned away and bent his head again to the case of Collins' memorabilia.

'*You* called me, Tim,' she said to his back. He didn't turn. 'I'm gonna go, alright. I'll see you when I see you.'

'Yep.'

She fixed her bag on her shoulder and walked away. She was two steps down the stairs when he called her.

'Maeve—'

She stopped and looked back. He'd run after her but stalled on the landing, as if he was afraid to get too close to her, and stood, gripping the handrail. She waited.

'I *will* call you.' Apologetically, he grinned.

She nodded once, then walked away.

26.

Back Then, in Dublin

* * *

Greta, it turned out, hadn't uttered a single cross word when Maeve finally got home from Tim's at nearly lunchtime. She was sitting at the kitchen table with a typed letter in her hand, and a sheet of paper laid out in front of her that looked like the results of blood tests.

'The prodigal daughter returns,' Greta said. She folded the pages in three and slipped them back inside an envelope.

'Ha, ha. You're very funny.'

'The ball was an all-nighter, was it? I hope you're getting paid overtime.'

Greta's smile was a thin, wobbly line across her face.

'Everything alright?' Maeve asked.

'Ah, yeah. Just the GP.' Greta pushed back her chair and stood. She folded the envelope and tucked it into the back pocket of her jeans, then crossed to the counter and held the kettle under the tap to fill it. 'My iron levels are low, she says. I'm to treat myself to a steak.'

'Yum. I'll join you. I hear dark chocolate is full of iron.'

Her mother took one mug out of the press and pointed to a second.

'Coffee, Maeve?'

Maeve said no, she needed a shower, and she was going to have to get her skates on if she wasn't going to be late for her tutorial at two o'clock.

* * *

She was late, in the end, but only because she stood outside the room replying to texts from Tim Corcoran.

Hey, you

                                          Hey you back

Was she free? She was. Did she fancy going to the cinema? Sure. Would they grab pizza before? Great, yeah.

* * *

Greta had a great deal more to say when Maeve slunk into the house at lunchtime for a second day in a row.

'What time of the day do you call this to be arriving home, young lady?'

Young lady. Jaysus. She hadn't heard that one since the time Greta discovered her belly-button piercing.

'Don't make a fuss, Mam. Please.' Maeve walked past her mother and dropped her coat over the rail as she ran upstairs.

'What in the name of God are you playing at?'

As if she didn't know, for Christ's sake. Maeve closed the bathroom door behind her, but Greta's voice carried easily through the entire house.

'Do you not have exams in a couple of weeks?'

Maeve didn't answer. She was brushing her teeth.

'You can have all the fun you want when you have a degree in your back pocket.'

Maeve pulled her makeup bag out from the press under the sink. She slid the pink, rectangular blister pack out of the side pocket where it usually lived between eyeliners and brow-fillers. The top row of blisters was squashed flat, with tiny, ragged shreds of foil decorating the flat side. Each little pill had been punched out on its allotted day of the week, each taken with a quick swig of water from the cold tap.

'I'm not working my fingers to the bone just so that you can be out gallivanting day and night like some trollop.'

Well, that was just lovely.

The side and bottom row blisters, beginning on a Friday, were intact. She stood with her head tilted, just looking at the packet. In her head, she recreated a picture of herself popping the pill onto her hand and passing it from palm to lips. She must have. Surely, she did?

'Are you alright in there?'

She definitely took it. Of course, she did. She wasn't that stupid.

'Maeve?'

Only today was Saturday.

27.

Chocolate Digestives

* * *

Malachi flipped the rashers in the pan, three for him and one for Bran. He cracked an egg on the edge and let it slip into the space between the rashers and the heap of fried onions. He put a plate on the counter, took ketchup and mustard out of the fridge, then shook the last of the bread out of the packet. There was only a heel left, not even enough for a sandwich. He'd have to go into town later on.

He arranged his plate of food and mug of tea on a side table beside his armchair and flicked on the telly. He'd missed the kick-off, but that was fine. Malachi had no patience for listening to overpaid pundits spouting shite about strategy.

Bran gobbled his allotted share and settled into his bed in front of the stove. He knew the routine. Neither of them would stir now until half-time, when Malachi would make another cup of tea and serve himself a squat tower of chocolate digestives.

The lack of a decent slice of bread left Malachi feeling deprived. He opened a mental list of things he needed to buy when he went to town. There was a bulb blown in the backyard light. He should get a new one. And socks. He needed new socks.

Twenty-five minutes ticked down on the match clock without either team scoring. It was a rubbish match. Malachi tipped his head sideways to look at the pile of old books and newspapers on the shelf beside the telly. At the very bottom was an old chess set. He hadn't played in years.

Bran stood up in his bed, turned around and sat down again. The fidgeting was contagious.

Malachi stood. He opened the door of the stove and threw in a log, the last in the basket.

'I'd better fill that,' he said and flicked off the telly.

Bran played around, chasing crows off the roof of the barn and checking on his hidden bones, while Malachi split logs to the size that fit through the stove door and tossed them into the basket. 'That'll do,' he said, when it was full, and Bran followed him inside.

Malachi put the basket down beside the stove and washed his hands under the hot tap. Then he lifted his waxed jacket from its hook and pulled it on. He looked into the old mirror that hung inside the back door and ran his thick fingers through his curls. *Need a haircut*, he thought. He lifted his chin, evaluating his reflected face, then shook his head and looked away.

He bent low to the bottom shelf beside the telly, pulled out the old chess set, and tucked it under his arm.

'Come on,' he said, giving Bran the nod. 'Let's go.'

* * *

'Would you not consider quarry tiles?' said Malachi, twenty minutes later, as he ran a hand down the long pine boards that Jack O'Neill had stacked, ready to be laid the following week.

'Too cold,' said Maeve, opening the packet of chocolate digestives Malachi had just handed her.

'They'd be far easier to keep clean,' he said.

'This isn't a farm, Malachi,' Maeve said, scoffing at him. 'A wooden floor is cosy.'

Malachi opened his mouth but reconsidered. There was only so much he could say.

He turned to Emer instead.

'So, what about it, Emer?' he said. 'Want to learn how to play chess?'

Emer looked to her mother and Maeve gave a small smile of encouragement.

Emer nodded, and Malachi found he was pleased.

He couldn't understand it himself. Maeve Gaffney was attractive. There was no denying it, regardless of what he'd said to

Miss Beecher, but he wasn't too smitten to see that she was too single-minded, too stubborn, *too much*.

The thing was, he couldn't resist trying to figure her out. There was something in the way she interacted with her daughter that contradicted her brazen manner. He'd thought about it when he was walking the fields, and when he was chopping logs, and when he was driving to town. She could only have been twenty or so having the baby. He had to wonder, why had she done it? Why had she committed herself to motherhood at such a young age, and why was such a good-looking woman still on her own? Was she protecting her daughter? Or was it that she was hung up on someone?

And what the hell was she doing in this wreck of a house? Half of him thought that Maeve Gaffney would make more of Weavers' Row than any of the small minds of Drohid had ever imagined possible. The other half of him believed she was on a fast train heading for Disaster, and that he had stoked the engine.

28.

Stir-Fry

* * *

By December, Mammy's tiny extension – the *scullery*, she called it – was all done. Eamon had built simple cupboards with long shelves above, and they were all, he insisted on telling Emer, *perfectly* level.

By lunchtime on Saturday, a brand-new cooker had been fitted and a brand-new fridge was making gurgly settling-in noises. All the rattly plastic sheeting had been folded away, and Emer and her mammy were sitting on fancy antique chairs arranged around a matching fancy antique table.

'Did she really have a s-spare t-table and chairs?' Emer liked the way she could rest her feet on the bar under the table. She reached for the ketchup bottle, squirted a wiggly line across a slice of white bread and squished that down on the top of her fried egg sandwich.

'She didn't say spare; she said *lying dormant*,' said Maeve. 'She's a very generous woman.'

Emer, having just bitten into her sandwich, decided not to ask what dormant meant. She watched as her mother ran her hand down the table's leg, again.

'I *love* the barley twist here—'

A loud *rat-at-at* sounded at the door.

'Mal,' Emer said, with her mouth full.

Mammy lifted a quizzical eyebrow and went to answer it.

There was no one outside.

'Must have been a ghost,' she said.

Emer went and craned her neck out the doorway. Mal was there alright. She could see the bottom half of him sticking out of the passenger door of the Land Rover.

'Mal!' Emer looked down at her socks.

He straightened himself too quickly and caught the back of his head on the doorframe.

'Feck it.' He rubbed his sore head. 'I've got a surprise for you, Miss Gaffney. Wait till you see this now.'

'I'll stick the kettle on.' Mammy slipped inside.

Bran hopped down from the passenger seat. Shoeless, Emer stepped into the street and stroked his neck. He licked egg yolk from her hand, making her laugh. She loved the way Bran always seemed to find a particular reason for liking her. Mal reached back inside the front of the car and pulled out a metal vice-like contraption.

'Right, you take that,' he said, and handed it to Emer.

'What is it?'

'It's a tree stand.'

The cold metal in her hand sent a shiver through Emer's arms. She hopped up and down on the spot.

'For a Christmas tree, Mal?' It was only a whisper, but he heard her. He was already pulling open the back doors of the Land Rover.

'That's right,' he said, hauling a bushy spruce to a standing position and then hoisting it onto his left shoulder.

'Lead the way, Miss,' he said, in the tone of exaggerated chivalry that made her feel like they were in an old black and white Christmas movie.

Emer held the front door open as wide as it would go while Mal carried in the tree. Maeve, hand aloft in the process of pouring water from the kettle into the blue flowery teapot, looked at Mal with a deliberately blank expression that Emer knew and hated. It was the face she used to hold a person at a distance.

''Tis cold out,' said Mal.

'Yes,' said Mammy, eyeing up the tree.

''Tis only a small one,' said Mal, though as he lowered the tree to stand it on the new floorboards, the top branch was bent flat against Maeve's freshly painted ceiling. 'I sell a few from my own land at the farmers' market, and I thought ye might like one.'

He stood still, one hand wrapped around the tree's trunk. Emer stood beside Bran, her fingers brushing the hair of his back. The three of them waited.

Mammy took her time putting the lid back on the teapot.

'That's very kind of you, Malachi,' she said, but stiffly. Her eyes met Emer's, and she smiled, but it was a sad little smile, like she was saying sorry about something.

'I can take it away. It was only that Emer said ye'd never had a real one,' said Mal, matching her tone, but Mammy talked over him.

'No, no. It's lovely,' she said. 'I'll grab a handsaw for you. You'll have to trim a bit off it.'

Decisions had to be made, then, about where the tree would look best, and how much needed to be cut off the bottom of it, and how much off the top, and which side should face out, and somehow the tension in the room dissolved in all the busyness of it. A box of lights and ornaments was located. Mammy scrolled her phone until she found Christmas FM. There seemed no question but that the three of them would decorate the tree together. Mal took all the high-up jobs, until they came to the final task of positioning a homemade angel made of toilet rolls and crepe paper.

'Emer made her at pre-school,' Mammy explained.

'I figured,' said Mal.

He hunched down so Emer could climb onto his shoulders. Then he stood up tall so she could reach the highest branch. She felt his hands wrapped tightly around her shins and knew he wouldn't let her fall.

'So—' said Mammy, when Emer was back on the ground.

'I'll be heading off, then,' said Mal, at the same moment.

Emer watched as her mother took a breath, and then spoke quickly, as if she'd decided something.

'Stay for dinner,' she said.

'Yerra, no,' said Malachi.

'It'll only be a stir-fry. You're more than welcome,' Mammy said it kindly, as if she meant it.

'Stir-fry?' Mal winked at Emer. 'Sure, who doesn't love stir-fry?'

'Great,' said Mammy. 'I'll get cooking, so. Will you light the fire for me?'

* * *

Emer watched Mal as he chewed and swallowed.
'What did you say this was?' he said.
'Stir-fry,' said Mammy, loading her fork.
'But this is pasta,' he said.
'So?'
'What did you say was on it?'
'I didn't.'
'It's Uncle Ben's k-korma sauce,' Emer explained. People tended to ask a lot of questions about her mother's cooking.
Mal burst out laughing.
'What?' asked Mammy. 'Do you not like it?'
'I love it,' he said.
Emer breathed out. She felt very happy just then.
After they'd eaten, Mammy made a pot of tea and the three of them sat around the table playing Mousse. They played for Ferrero Rocher sweets from the box that had appeared by magic from the lining of Mal's giant coat. Mal won the first game, but then Emer had a lucky streak and won three games in a row. She stacked her winnings into a little gold pyramid and laughed. Mal threw down his cards and leaned back in his chair. He spread his arms wide and let the front legs of the chair lift from the floor, thoroughly at ease in himself. Mammy poured more tea and stirred sugar into her own cup.

Quickly and without warning, she reached across and touched the hot spoon to the back of Mal's hand. He leapt from the sting of it, only barely managing to reclaim his balance and return the four feet of the chair, and his own two feet, to the ground.

'What the—?!' His voice sounded genuinely shocked.
'Sorry,' said Mammy, sucking the end of the spoon. 'I couldn't help myself.'
Mal straightened his chair and cleared his throat, rubbed a hand through his hair as if to compose himself. Emer glanced

towards her mother, but Mammy was relaxed, her attention engaged in thoroughly shuffling the deck.

'How about poker?' Mal asked.

Mammy laughed. 'And that is the point at which I send my nine-year-old daughter to her bed.'

Emer gathered her sweets.

'Goodnight,' she whispered.

'Goodnight,' her mother and Mal said together.

At the turn of the stairs, she slowed, listening.

'She's a good kid,' said Mal. Emer went up one more step.

'She is,' said her mother. There was undeniable doubt in her voice. Emer waited.

'Most kids would have asked for one more game,' Mal said.

'That's just it.' Mammy lowered her voice, but Emer could still hear. 'Sometimes I wish she would. I wish she'd fight back a bit.'

There was a small silence before Mal answered. Emer held her breath, listening hard.

'You enjoy a fight, don't you?'

Mammy laughed and said something in a low voice that Emer couldn't catch. She crept up the last two steps of the stairs and into her room.

Leaving the door half open, she stepped out of her jeans, got into her pyjamas, and climbed into bed. She stretched her legs under the tucked sheet without pulling it out from under the mattress. She liked the tightness of it, pinning her in place. She lay quietly, her head filled with words she'd have liked to have shouted at her mother, but knew she never would.

Mammy and Malachi seemed to have moved on to a new game. Mammy was humming a Dolly Parton song. Then it was Mal who was singing, in a low, low voice so that Emer couldn't make out the words. What would Granny have said? Mammy had often gone out on dates, even though Granny had always acted annoyed about it. But there had never been a man in the house after Emer went to bed. She'd never, not once that she could remember, heard a man's voice downstairs like that, a man singing. This must be what it was like to have a dad. She let one foot stray outward between the cold sheets, then pulled it in again to the warm spot in the centre. In her head, she played the day over again. It was all so normal, like something in a book or a film.

Her mother wasn't singing anymore. It was just Mal. Then, Mal stopped too. Then, a crash, and a scuffle, a chair or something falling over, maybe Bran thrashing his tail, then Mammy shouting.

'For Christ's sake, Malachi! Are you out of your mind?'

And then Mal, his warm voice still hushed, but audible.

'I'm sorry. Forget it ever happened.'

'Go home, will you.'

'I'm very sorry.'

'Just go. GO.'

One sharp bark.

'I am. I'm going.'

Chairs scraping. Heavy footsteps. The latch on the front door clicking.

'Goodnight, Maeve.'

'Would you go, please. Now.'

'I'm sorry, Maeve. It won't happen again.'

The door banging closed.

'You're right about that much.'

The Chubb key turning in its lock. The security chain sliding home. Her mother's voice.

'Fuck's sake.'

Emer rolled over to face the wall and pulled the duvet up to her ears. When Mammy's footsteps rounded the turn of the stairs, Emer held her breath. Her mother, she knew, was standing in the doorway. The loose board outside the door creaked once. Emer held her entire body still. She heard the slight rattle of the doorknob, and the door clicking shut.

29.

An Invitation

* * *

Maeve was deep in concentration, using a fine brush and some eye-wateringly expensive gold paint to add a Bohemian filigree pattern to her newly upcycled bedstead, when Emer arrived home from school with the news that she'd been invited on a playdate to a friend's house. This was good news. Emer had made mention of the girl once or twice. There had been a bit of *Pamela says this* and *Pamela says the other.*

'And where does Pamela live, exactly?' asked Maeve, still dabbing paint.

'Something P-Place? She said it's on the C-Cork road.'

Maeve lifted her brush. There had to be more than one Something Place in this town. Although then again, probably not. She lifted her brush.

'Cavendish Place?'

'Eh . . . maybe,' said Emer, with frustrating vagueness. 'P-Pamela says her dad can c-collect me.'

Maeve restarted her dabbing, even more cautiously than before.

'Not her mother?'

'Her mother is working. P-Pamela says it will be a really busy day for her.'

Maeve nodded.

'The eighth of December. Of course.'

'Why?'

'Oh, it's a traditional shopping day for culchies.'

Maeve was stalling for time. *What were the chances?*

'What did you say your friend's name was?'

'P-Pamela.'

Maeve took a deep breath.

'Her surname, Emer?'

'C-C-Corcoran.'

Maeve tapped the gold paint from her brush and wiped her hands.

'Has Pamela checked it's alright with her mam and dad?'

'She said she'll ask tonight. She said it's fine.'

Jesus Christ. Over all those years, in all that time, whenever she'd thought about Tim, she hadn't let herself think about his family. She knew there was a wife and children, but she'd blurred them into the background of her mental picture until they were nothing more than indistinct shadows.

Fecking hell. She'd never even thought about it, the possibility that the baby, his other baby, would intrude into *her* world. Life was stacking the game against her. Again.

'I was actually thinking you and I could go shopping on Friday, to the city—' Maeve watched Emer's face fall, her lips pressed thinly together. Her daughter wouldn't fight her. She knew that. If she said no, Emer would accept it. Better to put a damper on this whole situation. That would be the sensible course of action. It would be a very dicey play to encourage a friendship between the two girls – only asking for trouble.

Then again, she *could* just throw the ball back into Tim's court. He was free to say no to his daughter, to *both* of his daughters, if he wanted to. Maybe this was the chance to let him make a choice without her breathing down his neck. *Maybe,* he'd step up. She dipped her brush into the tin of gold paint.

'—But if you'd prefer to go to your friend's house, that's fine.'

30.

Thin Ice

* * *

'Daddy?' The Corcorans were, as usual, gathered around their sturdy dinner table. Tim was pouring wine for his wife and thinking how he should drive into the city to get a crate or two ahead of Christmas when Tadgh broke into his musings.
'What?'
'Don't say what, Tim,' said Nóinín. Tim threw her a look.
'Is there ketchup?' Tadgh persisted.
'No.' Tim sighed and sat down. 'You can't put ketchup on lasagne. It's sacrilege.'
Tadgh made a hoity-toity face and Nóinín laughed.
'That's a bit harsh, love.'
'He'll live.'
'Daddy?' Pamela this time.
'*Yes?*'
Nóinín smiled approval at his self-improvement.
'Can I have a friend over for a playdate on Friday?'
'Can I, too?' asked Tadgh, before Tim even had time to sip his wine. He raised a hand to stall their pleadings while he took a long slug.
'Yeah, sure. Just one each, mind.'
'Great,' said Tadgh. 'Shane wants to try out my Switch before he writes his Santa letter.'
Tim met his wife's eye and smirked. *Kids these days, eh?*
'Who are you inviting over, Pammie?' Nóinín asked, as she slid her portion of garlic bread onto Tadgh's plate.
'Emer.'

'Who?'

'The new girl. Emer Gaffney.' Pamela turned to Tim. 'I said you'd be able to collect her and drop her home. Is that okay?'

Tim coughed. *Sweet Jesus*. He reached for his glass, took a swig of wine, but coughed again.

'Are you alright?' asked his wife.

'Sorry,' he spluttered and held up his hand to excuse himself from the table. He took a cup from the draining board and filled it from the sink.

'That's very kind of you, Pamela, to ask the new girl over,' said Nóinín. 'I'm proud of you.'

Tim, listening with his back to the table, could sense Pamela's pleasure at receiving this sliver of praise from her mother. He had to put an end to this crazy situation now, before it got out of hand, *even more out of hand*.

'She seemed nice enough, Tim, and her mother could be a *very* good customer.'

Business, business. She can't help herself.

'Sorry. Bit of baguette went down the wrong way,' he said, sitting down. 'Ehh, I was thinking, though, they've got that ice-skating rink going again in the city. How about we do that instead on Friday?'

'*Class*,' said Tadgh. 'Shane'll love that.'

'Yeah, Dad. Me and Emer will love it too.'

'Emer and I,' said Nóinín.

'*Nobody* says that,' said Pamela.

'I meant—' said Tim, but it was useless.

'That's a brilliant idea, Tim. Well done,' said his wife, raising her glass to him from the opposite end of the table.

31.

My Husband the Novelist

* * *

Having made one dangerous play, Maeve couldn't resist making a second. The following morning, she walked up Main Street to Corcoran's Drapery and pushed the shop door open with a force that sent the service bell clanging. The woman sitting behind the counter closed her laptop and readjusted the green silk scarf knotted at her throat.

'Good morning,' she said, and rubbed her palms together cheerily. Her blonde hair was coloured, Maeve noticed, so subtly done that it might *nearly* have been highlighted by the sun. Her makeup, mind you, was anything but natural. Someone should tell her to lay off the bronzer. And those pristine fake nails told Maeve the only screwdriver she'd handled came with vodka and a swizzle stick. She was the sort of woman, Maeve thought, bitchily, who'd reached peak prettiness at twenty-one, then spent the rest of her life fighting to maintain her looks with ever increasing effort.

''Morning.' She held a tight rein on her voice, keeping it low and steady.

'Maeve, isn't it?' said Nóinín. 'You were in with us for the school uniform.'

Give the woman her due, she was an outstanding businesswoman. Either that or Tim had told her who Maeve was, in which case she had a remarkably cool head on her slender shoulders.

'That's right,' said Maeve. 'I actually came in because I'm afraid my daughter might have invited herself on a playdate to your house. I wanted to make sure it was okay with you.'

What Maeve really wanted, of course, was to find out how much Tim's wife knew. At the back of her head a concern niggled that she was letting her child wander innocently into the den of another lioness.

The woman laughed. Casually, she tucked her laptop away beneath the counter.

'Ah, don't worry – that's my husband's department. He has everything arranged. I know Pammie's looking forward to it.'

She was all easy charm, formidably polite, and Maeve began to regret coming. Nóinín Corcoran was giving nothing away.

'Okay. Well, that's grand, so. I was only checking—'

'Friday, isn't it? Tim would get nothing done anyway with the kids off school. He works from home. He's a writer, you know.'

Hah. That sounded like a boast you'd make to a stranger, not to a woman you thought of as competition.

'How wonderful.'

'Yes. He's a novelist.'

'Would I know any—?'

Nóinín cut her off.

'I'll tell you what,' she said, and Maeve spotted the hint of a twitch at the outer edge of her toothy smile. 'I'll give you his phone number, just in case you need to contact him in the meantime.'

Now Maeve wondered whether *she* was playing fair. This seemed too easy.

'Great,' she said, and pulled out her phone. 'Shoot.'

Nóinín called out a number.

'*Pamela's dad,*' Maeve said, making a show of pretending to add a new contact. 'Thanks.'

Nóinín allowed a pause to open up in the conversation. With a minute tilt of her head, she directed Maeve's attention to the rails of clothes on the shop floor.

'I might as well have a look around,' said Maeve, picking up on the cue. 'As I'm here.'

'Do,' said Nóinín, back on her track. 'I've got some lovely party clothes, just in time for Christmas.'

32.

The Eighth of December

* * *

The breakfast dishes were washed and put away, the pine floor swept and mopped, and the oak table polished with lavender-scented beeswax. New velvet cushions in gold and violet were plumped and positioned on the two deckchairs that stood in for a sofa, and a pile of high-end house magazines was stacked neatly on the make-shift concrete block coffee table.

Maeve was wearing her going-out jeans and her favourite boots, the tight ones that went all the way over her knees, and she'd done her hair in loose bouncy curls. She had walked to the shop for a lemon drizzle cake and come back with her arms full of orange chrysanthemums. She divided them between a dozen old jam jars and sauce bottles, then placed them on every available surface – the mantelpiece, the windowsills, and even the stopgap coffee table.

Emer was downstairs, dressed in the new outfit that Nóinín had effortlessly talked Maeve into buying, her hair done up in a Dutch braid. She was squeezed between the Christmas tree and the window frame now, watching for any sign of a car coming down Weavers' Row. Maeve couldn't bear to be in the same room as her. They were like loose wires, ready to spark off each other. Even the click-click of her own heels treading over and back between her wardrobe and her bathroom mirror was putting her nerves on edge.

At ten past ten, politely tardy, a bottle-green BMW coupé slid down the lane. Maeve stood on the landing, listening to the sound of car doors banging and Christmas baubles rattling on the tree, until the knock came.

'They're here,' Emer called in the sing-song voice that seemed to eliminate her stuttering.

'Com-ing!' Echoing the melody, Maeve tripped down the stairs. She dodged past Emer and pulled the door wide open.

'Good morning! Come in, come on in,' she said.

Beaming, Pamela stepped inside.

'Tim! What a lovely surprise.' Maeve cringed at the false note in her voice. 'Come in, please.'

'Hiya,' he said, with the wry grin of one bluffer to another.

'Come on in,' she said.

They were already in. She was repeating herself. Emer, she saw, was buttoning up her coat, signalling as loudly as Emer would dare that she was eager to leave. Pamela, on the other hand, was taking in the room with wide eyes. She was undeniably pretty, shorter and plumper than Emer, and had the same bright blonde hair as her mother.

'Will you have a cup of tea?' asked Maeve. 'I've got cake.'

'Are you sure you're okay with this?' asked Tim, talking over her. Maeve was still waving vaguely towards the tableau of flowers and baked goods.

'What? No, of course. I'm fine, absolutely fine.' She made a show of securing Emer's hat over her ears. 'As long as you are.'

'Right. We're all fine so,' said with a bright smile, so casually, just a regular Dad making sure everyone had their coat.

'You'll be good, won't you?' Maeve turned to Emer, who nodded and sidled closer to the door.

'Sure you won't stay for a quick cup?' Maeve tried once more, but Tim and Pamela were following Emer to the door.

'No thanks, Maeve.'

'Maybe later, then. What time will I expect you back?'

'What time suits you?'

'Oh, I'm easy.' She attempted a cheery laugh, but it misfired. She watched as Pamela waved Emer into the back seat of the big green car and slid in beside her. 'I might run in as far as the city, do a bit of shopping.'

'Three o'clock?' Tim stood with one leg in the well of the car.

She couldn't read him. He was being ridiculously laid back about taking his illegitimate offspring out for the day.

'You'll mind her, Tim?' she whispered to him, over the roof of the car.

He relented then and, for a second, broke out of the role he was playing.

'Of course I will,' he said, so gently that she felt her throat close up and tears sting the back of her eyes. She ducked to wave through the car window at the girls.

'Bye, Chicken, see you later,' she said, and they both waved back.

Tim Corcoran got into the driver's seat and pulled on his seat-belt, and then they were gone.

Maeve walked into the house and closed the door behind her. She needed to register the fact that Emer was gone, gone out for the day *with her father*. She couldn't have planned this if she'd tried. She sat at the table and cut herself a slice of lemon cake. He couldn't back away now. He wouldn't, not after meeting Emer and spending the whole day with her. She pulled the head of a chrysanthemum from its stem. All that was needed was to go gently with him, to make it easy.

She picked the petals, one by one, and let them rain onto her plate.

33.

Just a Regular Dad

* * *

It had been a strange day. Tim had set up his laptop at the coffee stall next to the ice rink, though he didn't pretend to himself that he would work. It was just a prop. He watched the boys flinging themselves recklessly onto the ice. Tadgh, he thought with unadulterated pride, had the perfect combination of his own athleticism and Nóinín's determination.

The girls took tentative steps around the edge of the rink, Pamela leading, always, and Emer staying within reach of the barrier. Pamela did most of the talking, but Emer seemed relaxed. They bent their heads together, whispering conspiratorially, and they laughed out loud when Shane landed flat on his backside.

'This is delicious, Mr. C-Corcoran,' Emer had said to him, when he took them for lunch afterwards. It was the only time she spoke directly to him – one stammered sentence, and it felt like a steak knife to his lungs.

The two girls, as far as he could tell, got on like a house on fire. *The two girls*, that was how he referred to them in his head, not his two daughters. Every time the thought occurred to him Tim pushed it back. No good could come from thinking about it. He hadn't gone looking for trouble. Trouble had come looking for him.

* * *

'Come in for a few minutes.' Maeve was all smiles. He'd reversed the car down Weavers' Row, intending a quick getaway.

'I really can't,' he said, through the car window. 'I have to get some work done.'

Emer, by this time, had climbed out and was standing on the front doorstep. Pamela had thrown her head against the back seat to demonstrate her boredom, but Maeve was holding her ground, standing close enough to the car that Tim's hand was brushing against the fabric of her jeans.

'Oh right, your work, of course,' said Maeve, 'I heard you're writing a novel.'

Christ. What else had Nóinín told her?

'It's nothing, really.'

'I'd love to hear more about it.' She smiled at him, the old smile, with all its confidentiality.

He resisted a mad urge to hook his finger inside her jeans pocket.

'Would you?' he said.

'Call over sometime.'

'I could do that alright, I suppose.' He was smiling now too.

'Well, sure you have my number now anyway.' Maeve threw a quick glance toward Emer. 'After the playdate.'

He pulled his arm back inside the car and put his two hands firmly on the steering wheel, but now felt reluctant to leave.

'She's very quiet,' he said.

'We complement each other, I suppose,' said Maeve.

'I was a bit worried. She really doesn't talk much.'

'No, she doesn't. She sings sometimes. She has a good voice, when she lets it out.'

Tim nodded. He didn't want her to think he was being critical.

'She's a credit to you, Maeve,' he said. He was happy with that. That was a good thing to say.

'Breeding beats feeding,' Maeve said, making air quotes with her fingers, 'as my mother would say.'

'Hah!' said Tim. 'How is the old bat?'

Inappropriately, Maeve laughed.

'Gone.' Her voice caught. 'She died. In the summer.'

'Oh God. Sorry.' *Damn it.* He should have left well enough alone. 'Sorry for your loss.'

Maeve nodded, in recognition of his contrition and his condolence both.

'Thanks,' she said.

He caressed the steering wheel, processing this new information.

'You're all on your own in the world, so?'

Maeve stepped back from the car onto the footpath. By small degrees, her smile widened, and her eyes shone with mischief. It was as if she was testing him, to see if he would move with her, like a child might try to pull a toy train with a magnet.

'Only during school hours,' she said. 'You know yourself.'

'I do,' said Tim, trying and failing to contain a grin.

34.

Inquisition

* * *

It was nearing the darkest day of the year and already the light was fading. Agnes leaned forward and checked the time on the display behind the steering wheel. It was only three o'clock. She would be inside, and locked up, before night fell.

Cautiously, she manoeuvred her car between the stone pillars that led to her cottage. The narrowness of the gateway had been one of the reasons she'd opted for a Fiat 500, the smallest car she could find. Other reasons included frugality and an unrelenting terror that she would kill a child. Agnes didn't like driving. She'd have avoided it altogether, but the two miles from *Ard na Mara* to town was too far to walk on days like this, when the rain was coming in sideways from the Atlantic.

Rounding the last bend in the lane she saw Malachi Barry's decrepit Land Rover parked at the side of the house. She pulled up alongside and gathered her shopping and the big bunch of burnt orange chrysanthemums lying on the passenger seat.

'I went a bit overboard yesterday,' Maeve had said, handing them through the car window as she was leaving. 'You'd be doing me a favour.' It was just like the woman: profligate and generous, both to a fault.

Agnes pulled up her hood and made a dash around the corner of the house. There was Malachi, as she expected, stacking split logs next to the back door. Bran barked once, and Malachi looked up.

'Out gallivanting again, I see,' he said.

'One of us has to have a life,' she said, and immediately regretted it. She could see by the set of his face that he wasn't in the mood.

Malachi upped the pace of his stacking.

'Don't leave without coming in to me, will you?' she said, by way of apology.

He grunted, and Agnes went inside.

She put the kettle on, put her groceries away, deposited the latest Graham Norton on the armchair by the range, ready for later.

'I put a hold on it for you, Miss Beecher,' Cáit at the library had said, producing the book from a closed cupboard behind her desk. 'I know how much you love him.'

They notice everything, Agnes thought, listening to the thud, thud, thud of logs landing one on top of another. She retrieved a tall crystal vase from a table by the window and arranged the long-stemmed chrysanthemums in it. She would cut some greenery from the garden whenever the rain let up. She leaned over the sink to tap a knuckle against the glass of the window, timing her knock to fall between his thuds.

Malachi raised his head.

'Tea's up,' she said, exaggerating the shape of the words so that her lips stretched thin. She turned and spooned tea leaves into a china pot.

He stood on the mat at the back door, shucking his coat from his shoulders while simultaneously toe-heeling his boots off.

Agnes pulled a towel from the oven door and tossed it to him. He caught it and rubbed his hair with it.

'I meant that for the dog,' she said.

'He'll shake himself—' He caught her eye-rolling glance around her tidy kitchen.

'He will not,' she said, giving the teapot a gentle swirl.

'Right. Sorry.' He knelt to rub down Bran's sopping coat.

Agnes watched him, the way he spread his hands wide along Bran's ribcage, then firmly down his legs, finally taking care to wipe any mud from his paws.

'Come on. Sit.' She filled his cup.

'That's lovely, Miss Beecher. Thanks,' he said, lifting it.
'What's up with you?' she said.
'What do you mean?'
'You're not yourself.'
'I'm grand.'
'You are not.'
'I am so. What *is* this, the Spanish Inquisition?'
'Hardly,' she said. 'That was your lot.'
He cracked a smile, but she knew it was only for her sake.
'You didn't even ask for a biscuit,' she said.
'Tuh,' he clucked his tongue. 'I wouldn't dare.'
'Just as well. I don't have any.'
'I have a box of Ferrero Rocher in the car,' he said. 'If you're desperate.'
She looked at him, puzzled. He'd brought her a box of Ferrero Rocher only the previous week.
'What? Were they on special offer or something?'
Unwillingly, he laughed.
'Yeah. Buy-two-get-one-free in Centra.'
'Hmmm. I see it all now.'
He topped up his own tea, over-filling it, so that there was no room left for milk. He stared at it and sighed.
'Why don't you bring her a load of logs, Mal? I'm sure she'd appreciate it.'
He raised his eyebrows at her, but they both knew there was no point in him pretending he didn't know who she was talking about.
'I can't,' he said.
'Of course you can. I have enough to keep me going. Give her whatever you would have given me for Christmas.'
Agnes felt a rush of blood to her cheeks and inwardly cursed it. They didn't usually make direct reference to the favours Malachi did for her. Theirs was an unspoken friendship. They both preferred it that way.
'It's not like I'm short of logs,' he said, putting down the tea-cup, having drained it a second time. 'It's not that.'
Just for a split second, a look of anguish crossed his features but he shook his head and settled his face into its usual solemn

expression. Agnes said nothing, waiting him out. She felt Bran's tail sweep against her leg. He was lying under the table, probably on top of his master's warm stockinged feet. Malachi was fiddling with the handle of the empty tea-cup, twirling it on its saucer. She closed her lips and held her breath so as to avoid wincing.

'She kicked me out,' he said, quietly, without looking up.

'Malachi Barry, *what* did you say to her?'

He put his head down in his hands and spoke to the table.

'T'wasn't what I *said* that bothered her.'

'Ah.'

''Twas only a kiss,' he said, clarifying the matter.

'No go?' she asked, though the answer was pitifully obvious.

'I feel like a fucking – sorry, Miss Beecher.'

'That's alright, I understand.'

'I feel like an idiot. I was sure she was giving me the, you know, I thought she was flirting with me.'

Agnes nodded.

'She does rather give that impression.'

He raised his eyes to hers, questioningly.

'I think she can't help it,' she said. 'It's just her way. She gave me a key to her house, you know, which seemed a bit, well, *familiar*.'

'She likes *you*,' he said huffily.

'She likes you too.'

He lowered his head, and she saw he was holding back tears. She pushed her chair back from the table and walked to the cupboard. From behind a twin pack of ground coffee, she extracted a packet of fruit shortcake biscuits. She got down a china plate, fanned half the biscuits across it, and placed it on the table in front of Malachi.

He sighed rather pathetically then reached out a hand.

'I knew you were hiding the biscuits,' he said.

'Don't push your luck.' She made a stage feint at pulling the plate away. 'Bring her a load of logs anyway. She could do with them.'

He looked up at her with much the same look on his face as Bran when he smelled toast.

'Do you think I should?' His voice had the ache of doubt in it. 'She wouldn't take it the wrong way?'

'*Is* there a wrong way, Mal?'

He shrugged and poured a third cup of tea from the china pot.

'You have fierce small cups,' he said, which was hardly what you'd call an answer.

35.

Filling the Void

* * *

Maeve invited her mother's cousin, Ailbhe, to come to Cork for Christmas.

'Bring the whole family,' she said. 'We'd love to have you.'

Ailbhe was kind, saying how much she'd love that were it not for a commitment already made and a party planned.

'Of course,' said Maeve. 'Sure, we might see you in the spring.'

* * *

'Would you and Jack like to join us for Christmas dinner?' said Maeve to Eamon O'Neill a week before Christmas. 'And Mrs. O'Neill too, of course.'

Eamon, who was in the process of packing up his tools, looked up at her as if she was telling a joke, a bad one.

'Ah now, go away out of that,' he said.

Maeve tipped her head to one side and smiled encouragingly.

'We'll be all on our own otherwise,' she said. 'We'd love to have you.'

Eamon, for once, stuck to a hard no, wouldn't even consider the possibility of it.

'We have our own crowd coming. 'Twouldn't be right,' he said, with uncharacteristic finality.

Maeve had figured it was a long shot anyway, and probably just as well. Neither of the O'Neill men were what you'd call sparkling conversationalists, though she held out considerable hope for the infamous Assumpta. All she wanted, really, was a gathering of people around the Christmas table, a buffer against the absence of her mother.

* * *

'I think I'll invite Agnes to dinner on Christmas Day,' she said to Emer that evening, while she was washing up their plates and Emer was drying.

'That would be weird,' said Emer.

'It would be a nice thing to do,' said Maeve. 'She'll be all on her own otherwise.'

No time like the present, Maeve thought, and she scrolled her phone to Agnes's number.

'Emer and I would love it if you would join us for Christmas dinner,' she said, when the preliminaries were out of the way.

There was a long pause on the other end.

'Only if it suits you,' said Maeve, unable to bear the silence. 'It's only that we'd be all on our own, you know, otherwise.'

'I'd like that very much,' said Agnes.

'Oh great—'

Agnes cut across her.

'But I'm afraid I have a previous commitment.'

'Oh, I see. Well—'

'It's Malachi Barry, you see. He usually comes over—'

Huh, thought Maeve, you never could tell. She knew they were neighbours, of course, but neither Agnes nor Malachi had given her any clue that they were on such friendly terms – the opposite, if anything. *Well, that's a shame*, she thought.

'Well, that's lovely—' she said, pausing while she considered what to say next.

'Unless—' said Agnes.

An invitation to Agnes's house on Christmas Day would be a blessing. *Ard na Mara* was so pretty, a dream of a house, and she'd have no cooking to worry about, no turkey threatening salmonellosis, but she *would* have to drive – she wouldn't be able to have a drink, and Emer would hate the idea, and they wouldn't be at home if Tim—

'Why don't you both come here to me?' Maeve said.

She thought she heard the sound of a tea-cup landing on a saucer, but otherwise nothing.

'Only if you'd like to,' she said, second-thinking the idea already.

'That would be a real treat,' said Agnes. 'But I'd have to check with Malachi.'

'I'll call him,' said Maeve. It was time she took control of the situation.

* * *

'Hello?' said Malachi, sixty seconds later. He was one of those people, Maeve noticed, who answered the phone with a question rather than a greeting, and since her name would have been displayed on his screen, the question was not *who* was phoning but *why* she was phoning.

'Was it you?' she asked, responding in kind.

'Was *what* me?'

Maeve sighed. This man had an uncanny knack for getting on her nerves.

'The firewood?' Without really thinking it through, she had been entertaining a vague hope that the sacks of split logs outside her door might have been from Tim. Malachi Barry hadn't even entered her head, but she saw now that he was a likelier candidate for a wordless gesture.

''Twas Agnes's idea,' he said defensively, *nervously*, as if she was likely to throw a hissy fit at him.

'Well, thank you,' she said, tempering her tone, and ploughing onwards before things got any more complicated. 'Let me make you dinner on Christmas Day, by way of thanks.'

'I can't—'

'Agnes said she'd love to come, but only if you will.'

'*Did* she now?'

'She did.'

'Yerra, I don't know.'

'I have you on speaker.' She didn't. Emer was upstairs.

"'Tis just, you know—'

'Emer would really like you to be here,' she said, inclining her head towards the empty chair where Emer *had* been sitting just a few minutes earlier.

'Well—'

'Oh, come on.'

'Can Bran come too?'

Maeve smiled. She liked to win.

36.

At First Light on Christmas Eve

* * *

Nóinín sat up and adjusted the pillows at her back.

'I'd better get cracking.' Tim was standing at the marital bedside holding an over-full mug of coffee. 'I have it all ordered, so it's just a case of nipping around and collecting everything.'

Nóinín took the mug and blinked the sleep out of her eyes. She winced as a waft of Tim's lemon verbena aftershave tainted her first sip.

'Don't forget the smoked salmon.' *Like last year*, she didn't add, because she didn't need to.

'I won't.'

'I need to get into the shop by half nine at the latest.'

'Don't worry.' He kissed her cheek. 'I'll be back in plenty of time to let you go.'

She listened to the sound of Tim's car accelerating out of Cavendish Place before putting her mug down on a coaster on the bedside table. She reached for the silver silk robe that lay draped over the end of the mahogany sleigh bed and slipped her arms through the sleeves. Taking her coffee, she stepped quietly along the landing, gliding over the ivory carpet, past the rooms where her children lay sleeping. Nóinín tried to remember the last time she'd even gone up the lop-sided flight of stairs that led to the attic rooms. From the day they'd moved in, Tim had laid claim to the top floor, refusing to let Nóinín measure it for carpet, saying they needed it for storage. She twitched in irritation now at the clamminess of the painted floorboards under her bare feet.

On the small landing at the top of the stairs Nóinín faced two closed doors. She opened the door of the front room, her intended guest bedroom, and looked inside. Suitcases and storage boxes were stacked around the walls. A golf bag and the sails from Tim's dinghy leaned against each other under the dormer window. A crate of wine and several tins of biscuits stood in a tower behind the door, preventing it from opening fully.

A blanket was spread over a suspiciously shaped bundle in the darkest corner. With one hand, Nóinín lifted it and witnessed Tim's pathetic attempt at hiding the kids' Santa presents.

'Hopeless,' she muttered, replacing the blanket just as she'd found it and pulling the door closed behind her.

The back bedroom door was stiff and more difficult to open, the reluctance resulting, she discovered, from a rug that had been laid over the entire floor. It was the thick-piled, handwoven monstrosity that Tim had bought in an online auction. He'd claimed it looked red on his computer screen. The reality was a lurid cerise. They had laughed about it. *Not to worry*, he'd said, he would return it. So much for that.

He had bought a desk too, evidently, and a captain's chair upholstered in oxblood leather. How civilised. The desktop, like the room, was devoid of clutter. There was only a chipped Jedward mug filled with pencils, and a closed laptop.

Nóinín sat in the chair and swivelled around to face the desk, then put down her coffee and lifted the lid of the computer. It pinged into life and requested a password.

Easy-peasy. Quickly, she typed CorcoransAbú!

The computer encouraged her to have another go. Unhesitating, she entered their house password again, without capitals. It didn't work.

Nóinín leaned back in the captain's chair and looked up through the skylight. It must be nice for Tim, she thought, sitting here surveying the clouds while she teetered in heels all day at the shop. She chose a little gold pencil from his collection and twirled it between her fingers, waiting for inspiration to strike.

Heyday. It was the title of a song that Tim, inexplicably, included on all his playlists. When the laptop insisted that she try again, she tapped the keys with matching insistence.

HeyDay, she typed, with the pencil gripped between her teeth. Only that morning, she'd heard him singing it in the shower.

HEYDAY.
heyday.
Heyday!

Lo and behold, she laughed to herself as the computer loaded files and opened itself up to her. It was nearly too easy.

He'd know, she thought. If she opened all his Word documents, he'd surely notice the same last-opened date on every file.

The cursor hovered over a document entitled *Heyday Baby*. It was the biggest file, by far, and it had already been opened that day. It was worth the risk, she thought, clicking on it.

And there it was, Tim's precious novel, all eighty-six thousand, seven hundred and six words of it. She skimmed through the pages, her eye catching on a word, a line, a phrase here and there. Something about a waitress with melting brown eyes, something about unbearable loss, something about an empty park bench. She scrolled back to the start and read the first line:

She looked like a Greek goddess.

Nóinín read on until she felt a blackness closing in from the back of her head to the front of her consciousness. She must have forgotten to breathe. Thinking she might faint, she put her head in her hands and sucked air into her lungs. What would he say, she wondered, if he found her here like this? Would he take this as his chance to walk away from her? Would he say it was just a story? *Was* it just a story?

She considered emailing the file to herself, then decided against it. She pulled the captain's chair closer to the desk, took a sip of lukewarm coffee, and began to read again, applying the full critical power of her mind to it.

37.

The Christmas Bird

* * *

At half past eight, Maeve joined the queue at the butcher's shop. The atmosphere, in determined contrast to the sky, was bright and cheerful. Maeve enjoyed the happy banter as wrapped and labelled parcels were handed over the counter, the cheerful exchange of season's greetings and best wishes. It wasn't until her turn came that she grasped the fact that, somewhere along the line, she'd missed a trick.

'What's the name?' said the spotty kid with the stupid sprig of plastic holly pinned to his striped apron. What was it with butchers and plastic greenery?

'Maeve Gaffney,' she said, giving him her broadest, most open smile.

He turned his back and wandered into the walk-in fridge at the back of the shop. An older man, probably the owner, nodded to the next woman in the queue and headed into the back room without a word.

'Nice to be known,' said Maeve, thinking out loud.

'Sometimes,' said the woman, smiling thinly. Everything about her was thin, Maeve thought. Her cheekbones were sharp and her neck was slim and sinewy.

'What was the name again?' Spotty MacHolly was back.

'Maeve Gaffney.'

'Are you sure?'

'Fairly sure,' she said, swallowing a laugh.

'I can't find anything,' he said.

Maeve looked at him blankly.

'Did you not order ahead?' said the thin woman.

'Oh.'

It was a thing. She knew it was a thing, ordering hams and turkeys for Christmas. Her mother had talked about it. Had Maeve thought about it at all, had she gone that far down the turkey thought process, she'd have thought it was a Dublin thing, a city issue. She'd have *thought* they'd have loads of turkeys in the country, *gangs* of them, running wild all over the place.

Still, there was no need to panic. It wasn't as if she needed to impress these people. She only needed to feed them.

'What have you got?' she asked Spotty.

He twitched an insolent eyebrow and raised his palms upwards in the universal signal of not giving a shit.

'I have a brace of quail,' said the older man, leaning over the counter and whispering in a shady way.

'How many is a brace again?' said Maeve, whispering back.

'Two,' he said.

Shite, she thought.

'Great,' she said, fixing an expression of festive delight on her face. 'I'll take them.'

38.

The Novelist Returns

* * *

With a six-kilo turkey under one arm, Tim turned the key in the lock and pushed the front door open. Nóinín was coming down the stairs, still in her dressing gown.

'Oh, hi,' he said, careful to keep the surprise out of his voice. It wasn't like his wife to be running late. She walked ahead of him into the kitchen and put her mug into the dishwasher. 'Are they still asleep?'

'Hmmm,' she said, closing the door of the dishwasher with particular care.

'I got the salmon,' he said, as he deposited the turkey on the marble countertop. 'It's in the car.' Tim enjoyed the hunter-gatherer satisfaction gained from the mammoth undertaking that was the Christmas grocery shop. Nóinín, it was becoming increasingly obvious, wasn't in the mood to be impressed.

'I must get dressed,' she said, sliding past him and making for the stairs. What exactly, he wondered, had she come downstairs to do? Certainly not to talk to him. That much was clear.

'Will you get home for lunch? I might make pancakes for the kids.'

Nóinín paused on the first step of the stairs.

'Not a chance, Tim.'

'I'll meet you at Alison's, so, will I?'

'You do that,' she said.

Something was up. What could possibly have happened in the hour and a quarter he was out of the house? There was no earthly way she could know, he thought. There was nothing *to* know, not really.

He had done nothing wrong. That was the thing that seemed so unfair to Tim Corcoran. At every step, he had only done what was right, yet over and over he was made to feel he was in the wrong. It was enough to make him wonder whether it wasn't time to try on a different, less honourable, idea of himself.

39.

Liebar Gustav 14

* * *

With a brace of quail and a miniature ham in a bag hanging from the crook of her elbow, Maeve locked her car and turned to the newly painted front door. She was happy with the colour. It was a heartening pinkish purple that reminded her of wild foxgloves and contrasted beautifully with the gilded wreath she'd fashioned from baubles and gold beads.

Whether by accident or design, the gold foil gift bag sitting on the doorstep could not have been better chosen to complete a perfect Christmas picture, so much so that Maeve was almost tempted to leave it in situ. *Almost.* She turned the key in the lock and dipped to pick up the bag, then shut the door with her bum and emptied her arms onto the dining table. I'll wait, she thought, eyeing the gold bag from the corner of her eye as she put the meat in the fridge and switched on the kettle. The sleeve of Weetabix sitting open on the countertop told her that Emer had been down.

She stood at the bottom of the stairs, listening. She could tell from the light on the staircase that Emer's door was standing open. She heard the bed creak and the turning of a page.

'Hello up there.'

'You were ages!'

'How about hot chocolate in bed?' She rubbed her hand along the bannister.

'Yes, puleease!' Emer sang it out.

Maeve laid a tray for her daughter, placing a mince pie on a china plate, even dusting it with icing sugar, and laying a dessert fork on the side. She loaded marshmallows on top of the hot chocolate and carried everything upstairs.

'I love you, Mammy.' Emer's face split wide with a toothy grin.

'Ah, don't worry. I'm only feeding you up before I put you to work in the kitchen. Do you want to peel a whole sack of potatoes or make a sherry trifle?'

'Eh . . . make a t-trifle?'

'I thought you'd say that,' Maeve laughed. 'Do you know how to make it?'

'I watched G-Granny.' Maeve saw her swallow a rogue lump in her throat.

She put her hand on Emer's forearm. Sometimes, it was better not to say the words.

'It's only fancy jelly, right? How hard can it be?'

'Piece of cake,' whispered Emer.

'That's my girl,' she said and wandered down the stairs.

Fairy lights shimmered off the surface of the gold bag, giving it life. She pulled it open and extracted the smaller of two parcels, each in the neat sort of wrapping, black paper and coiled gold ribbon, that was done with quick fingers by efficient shop girls. It had a tag attached. Maeve turned it over and read the words *For Emer*.

How are you going to explain that? asked Greta.

'Not now, Mam. Don't start.' said Maeve.

She tucked the parcel into her jacket pocket, putting it and her mother firmly out of her mind, and turned her attention to the other one. She slid a thumbnail under the single piece of tape and let the paper fall away revealing a bottle of perfume, Liebar Gustav 14 by Krigler. She gasped. She'd only ever mentioned it once, she was sure.

'It's legendary,' she'd gushed about the scent she would buy when she was rich and famous. 'Just imagine, you could close your eyes and know what it was like to stand close to Marlene Dietrich or Scott Fitzgerald.'

He found it, she thought, with the tips of her fingers pressed to her lips. *He remembered.*

She shook the gold bag upside down and a gift card fell out. '*You still look like a Greek goddess,*' it read. Nothing else.

She pulled the lid off the unassuming brown bottle and sprayed once onto the soft skin of her inner arm. She was overtaken by the scent of a garden in late summer, on a day when a thunderstorm had cleared the air and washed the foliage. Full-on lavender and geranium, but not sweet, it smelled of wealth, of leather and something sharper – it smelled of her mother's tea canister.

Maeve's eyes flooded with tears. She bit her lip and slipped the bottle back inside its gold and black box.

40.

Alison's Party

* * *

'There he is now.' Alison was relieved to see Tim coming through the kitchen door. Nóinín had arrived early, dressed in a showstopper sequinned gold mini-dress, and already glassy-eyed. She'd spent the last hour perched on a high stool at the kitchen counter, showing more leg than she should, sipping gin, and spitting venom. Her black mood was beginning to put a serious dent in the Raffertys' supply of Christmas spirit.

Alison beckoned to Tim. He responded with an automatic smile and proceeded to make his way through the assembled neighbours, shaking hands and clapping shoulders all the way. At last, he wrapped his arm around his wife.

'Come here,' said Nóinín, pinching the sleeve of his green cashmere jumper and pulling him closer. 'You've got to hear this.'

She held up a carrot stick and used it to point at Alison.

'What's this?' Tim raised a brighter smile and both eyebrows.

'Tell him what you told me,' said Nóinín, redirecting the carrot pointer from Alison to Tim.

'Ah, it's nothing much.' Alison looked around for a change of subject.

'*Tell* him,' Nóinín insisted, and again Alison regretted her generous measures.

'I was only saying how important it is, at Christmas, you know, to order everything in ad—'

Impatiently, Nóinín cut her off.

'That Gaffney woman made a holy show of herself in the butcher's.'

'She was calmer than I would have been, in fairness,' said Alison, keeping her voice light and thinking she wouldn't like to get on the wrong side of Nóinín.

'She'd have got nothing at all but for Alison's charity.'

'Ah now—' This was getting embarrassing. Alison would never have told the story had she known that Nóinín would make this big a deal out of it.

Tim threw her a quick glance that looked a lot like sympathy.

'Can you imagine *anyone* being that *stupid*?' Nóinín hissed the question at Tim and then waited, obstinately, for a response. Her face was pinched, two fine vertical lines drawn downwards from the corners of her mouth, making her look wooden.

Tim seemed stumped for an answer.

'I'll just go make sure the kids are okay,' he said.

Nóinín's face remained clenched in the same bitter expression, as if she was physically unable to let it go.

'Not at all,' said Alison, bolting. 'I'll check on the kids. You stay right here and enjoy yourselves.'

41.

Christmas Morning

* * *

'Rocking Around the Christmas Tree' came on the radio, and Emer turned it up. She felt a surge of satisfaction as she swivelled Granny's Waterford Crystal trifle bowl admiring her creation from every angle. She liked cooking, and she was good at it.

'You get it from me,' Granny always said.

Emer missed having Granny around, but she didn't miss the way Granny and Mammy would snap at each other, like narky turtles, all the time, but especially at Christmas. They were too different from each other to be stuck living together. Granny was always threatening to throw them out, and Mammy was always threatening to leave, and often Emer thought they really meant it, but in the end, they had gone on together, the Gaffney girls, until Granny died. It was a pity, Emer thought, that Granny couldn't see how pretty their new house was. Mammy was better at house-decorating than Granny, but Granny was better at cooking, and *definitely* better at Christmas shopping.

Last night, when Emer asked what was for dinner, Mammy had opened the fridge door and they had stood, side by side, looking at a saucepan full of Jamie Oliver's foolproof make-ahead gravy and the bowl of half-set jelly.

'Have a banana,' Mammy had said.

They'd made salt and vinegar Tayto sandwiches and watched *Die Hard with a Vengeance*.

'Your granny had a fierce soft spot for Jeremy Irons,' Mammy had said.

'Who?' said Emer, which led to watching *The Man in the Iron Mask*, which led to watching *Titanic*, but Emer had fallen asleep before the end. She didn't remember how she'd gotten to bed, and this morning was the first Christmas ever that her mammy had woken up before she did.

'Wake up, Chicken,' she had said, having to shout a bit because of the rain hammering down on the roof. 'Or you won't have time to open all your presents.'

She got a new Barbie from Santa, and a purple hairdryer, and in her stocking a hairbrush, a game called Yahtzee, and a new pack of cards. When she had opened everything, she gave her mammy the wristwarmers she had crocheted for her.

'Ooh! These are gorgeous,' Mammy had said, slipping them on and showing Emer that they fitted perfectly. Well, one was perfect, and the other was nearly perfect.

'I know you like p-purple and orange.'

'These are my favourite wristwarmers EVER!'

'You can cut the bobbles off, if you want.'

'Never.'

'There's something else.'

Her mother unwrapped a small keyring with a gold letter M attached to it. It had used up all of Emer's pocket money to buy it.

'M for Maeve.' She whispered it.

Mammy held it up and Emer could see the fairy lights on the tree twinkling in the gold surface.

'M for Mammy,' Mammy said, and she kissed Emer's cheek.

42.

A Feast

* * *

Maeve balanced the wrapped presents on either arm – a predictable bottle of Jameson for Malachi and equally predictable bottle of Baileys for Agnes. Everyone liked a bottle of something at Christmas, didn't they? She stalled at the turn of the stairs to listen to her daughter singing 'Rockin' Around the Christmas Tree' without a trace of a stammer.

Emer's attention was fixed on the meticulous decoration of Ireland's Tiniest Ham. She looked up and offered Maeve a half slice of pineapple.

'Do you want some?'

'Would I *like* some? No, thanks, Chicken, put it all on the ham.'

'It won't fit.'

'Right.'

Shite.

The thin woman at the butcher's shop had insisted that Pat – she and the butcher were on first-name terms – cut a chunk off the end of *her* ham and donate it to Maeve.

'I've ordered way too much,' the woman said, putting her pale hand on the sleeve of Maeve's coat. 'I always do.'

Of course she did.

Pat had demonstrated his objection by slicing off a piece that was hardly more than a fat rasher.

'Well, that's the handsomest ham I ever did see,' she said, now, and Emer glowed.

'You smell nice,' Emer said, when Maeve leaned in to kiss her.

'It was a present.' Maeve held her wrist out so that Emer could have a better smell.

'From who?'

'From whom.'

'You're g-getting like Granny.'

Was she? 'Come on, loads to do.'

Maeve stoked the red embers in the hearth and added a couple of Malachi's apple logs. She plumped up the sapphire-and-emerald-coloured cushions on the new sofa, and lit candles on the windowsills, the mantelpiece, and the table.

'That should hold back the dark.'

Emer folded a paper serviette so that Rudolph stood upright and set him among his comrades who were already beaming from three completed place settings, along with heaps of crepe-paper crackers and chocolate coins in shiny foil.

'Well done! Totally *Glitzy Kitschy Christmas*,' Maeve said and Emer beamed.

She jammed a tray of roast potatoes and another of Dunnes' *Simply Better* potato gratin into the oven.

'We won't go hungry.'

'P-parsley?' Emer was curling strips of smoked salmon on top of buttered brown bread.

'*Oui, Chef!*' Maeve picked sprigs of parsley from a bunch and passed them one by one to Emer.

'What do you call two p-potatoes wearing the s-same thing?'

Emer was already giggling and it was infectious.

'I dunno. What *do* you call two potatoes wearing the same thing?'

'Mashing outfits!'

'Oh, dear Lord, they're getting worse.'

'T-too much?' Emer asked, meaning the parsley.

'More is more,' said Maeve, meaning it all.

* * *

'Goodness! What clever girls you are – I can hardly believe my eyes!' said Agnes, handing over her hat, her scarf, and her leather gloves in turn to Emer. 'Whoever would have believed this place could be so transformed. My hat is off to you, ladies. *Chapeau!*' She gestured to the hat in Emer's hand, making Emer chuckle.

'Oh, it's just a bit of dollying up,' said Maeve. How nice it was to be praised. 'I've always loved playing house.'

'I brought some cheese.' Agnes handed Emer a box with the logo of an upmarket cheesemonger in the city. 'I hope that's alright.'

Maeve didn't get to answer because of a loud *rat-at-at* at the door.

'Mal!' Emer shouted.

'Don't shout.'

She was right, though. It was Mal.

Bran came in first. Malachi paused to wipe his shoes.

Maeve took a step back so that she and Emer and Agnes weren't all standing in a line, like a reception committee.

'Come in, come in,' Agnes said, sounding a bit like Greta, Maeve thought. 'Don't let the heat out, Malachi.'

'Yerra, 'tis rotten out.' He stood awkwardly on the *Stop Here Santa* mat holding a large paper bag from the same upmarket cheese shop in the city.

'I brought you some cheese,' he said.

'Typical!' Agnes said.

'What?' He looked worried. 'Is that wrong? You love cheese, don't you?'

'We do, Malachi.' Maeve stepped forward and accepted the bag from his hands. 'We love cheese.'

'Hang on.' He reached inside the lining of his coat and produced a bottle of port.

'Oh, well done,' Agnes said, and Malachi's face relaxed.

43.

High Spirits

* * *

The grown-ups were all very merry. Mammy told the story about the ham and the teeny-weeny quail in a way that made everybody laugh, and they all ate *loads* of roast potatoes.

'It is very good gravy indeed,' said Agnes.

'Well, the man did say foolproof,' said Maeve.

'Delicious,' said Malachi, flooding his plate.

They drank wine; and they talked louder than they usually would; and they laughed at all the cracker jokes, even the ones that weren't a bit funny.

'What do you call a turkey on Stephen's Day?' said Mal.

Emer shrugged.

'Fortunate?' said Agnes. She wasn't very good at jokes.

'That's not even a name!' said Mal, thrown off his stride.

Mammy roared laughing.

'What DO you call a turkey on Stephen's Day?' she managed to say.

'Oh! *I* know!' said Emer.

'Lucky,' Mal said quickly.

'But that's what I said,' said Agnes.

Mammy leaned sideways, trying to catch her breath, and Emer thought she might fall off her chair, but she righted herself just in time. Mammy'd had a bit more wine than Mal and Agnes because they both put their hands over the tops of their glasses and said they were driving, so Mammy emptied the bottle into her glass.

The laughter was catching.

Agnes told them how a woman called Mrs. Murphy used to put the turkey in the Aga when she got home from midnight mass and leave it in all night long.

'To make certain it was sufficiently desiccated,' Agnes said. Emer laughed because Mammy and Mal laughed. She guessed that desiccated wasn't what you wanted in a turkey.

Then her mammy told them about that time, when Emer was seven, that Granny decided to soak the turkey in a bin full of water and spices, because she saw Nigella do it on telly, and when she went out to the yard to get the bird on Christmas morning, the two legs were gone off it.

'What got it?' said Agnes.

Mammy nodded to Emer then to finish the story because she knew the ending.

'A fox!' said Emer, and everyone was astonished.

Mal won when he told a story about a turkey who hopped a fence, *like flipping Steve McQueen*, he said, to avoid the chop. Mammy held on to her sides and said it hurt, and Agnes took a linen hanky from her cardigan sleeve to wipe big, bright tears from her papery cheeks.

'Who's Steve McQueen?' Emer asked, but they were all laughing too much to tell her.

When they had recovered, Mammy gave Emer her cue to bring in the dessert. With her back turned, Emer lit a match and held it to the three sparklers stuck into the trifle, then carried the heavy bowl to the table as fast as she could.

Her mother and Mal and Agnes all clapped their hands and cheered.

'You do the honours,' Mammy said, handing her a big spoon for serving up.

The jelly was a bit soft, and the custard was a bit runny, but the hundreds and thousands she'd sprinkled on top looked pretty, even if the colours were spreading out of them into the cream, and everyone looked very happy when she passed around the little glass bowls that Mammy had bought specially.

'An authentic *zuppa inglese*!' said Agnes.

'I'd lick it off a sore leg,' said Mal.

Mammy said then that some sort of break was in order before the extensive cheese board could be tackled. The rain was still clattering down, and a stream ran the length of Weavers' Row.

'How about a game of Mousse?' Mal said. He rubbed his hands together dramatically to show Emer that he thought he would win.

'I'm afraid I don't know that one,' said Agnes.

'Not to worry, Agnes. We have the inventor of the game at hand and she's an excellent teacher.'

Emer felt a thud of pride in her chest.

'We'll want chocolate for the winners.' She set about gathering stacks of chocolate coins.

'And for the losers,' said Mammy.

'The secret is to sit beside someone who's kind.' With a blatant wink, Mal pulled his chair closer to Agnes, making her laugh out loud. 'But watch out for Emer, or she'll take you to the cleaners.'

'We'll see about that.' Agnes's face was lit up with glee. 'I can hold my own, wait and see. I was quite the shark, believe it or not, in my day.'

An hour later, Mammy and Mal had won one game each, Emer and Agnes were holding at two games each, and a tin of Cadbury's Roses had just been poured out on the table to up the stakes when the dragonfly knocker sounded loudly against the front door. Emer, Mal, and Agnes all looked to Mammy.

'Beats me,' she said, pushing back her chair and laying her cards face down on the table.

44.

Rudolph's Smiling Face

* * *

'Oh, hello,' said Mammy, when she opened the door. Then she stepped outside, pulling it closed at her heel. Emer saw Agnes raise her eyebrows in a question at Mal, and Mal shrugging his shoulders in return.

The front door was thrown open again and Emer saw her mammy fall into the room, as if she had been blown by a gust of wind. She was followed by a man who caught hold of Mammy's arm and held her up. His face was obscured by a tall collar turned up around it. His fair hair was plastered down his face and his grey tweed coat was dripping water onto the floorboards.

'Mr. Corcoran!' said Agnes, and Emer saw that it was Pamela's dad.

'Has something happened?' said Mal, standing up from the table.

Maeve pushed the door closed behind the man's back and the whole room, Emer felt – the four people, the pushed back chairs, the laid down cards, the logs on the verge of crumbling in the fireplace – all waited to hear what Pamela's dad had come to say.

'It's really coming down,' he said, seeming surprised by the jolly party.

''Tis wet alright,' said Mal.

'You're soaked through,' said Agnes.

Mammy pulled a tea towel from the handle of the oven door and passed it to Mr. Corcoran.

'Here,' she said. 'It's warm.'

'I only came out for a breath of air, you know. I thought I'd have a stroll along the river walk, but then the rain came down, and I saw the light in your window.' It seemed as if he couldn't stop talking. 'I'm sorry to interrupt—'

Everybody was standing up now. Mammy made a waving gesture with her hand, and they all stepped sideways as a group, closer to the fire.

'Sit down, please,' she said, waving Mr. Corcoran towards the new velvet sofa. His trousers were clearly soaking wet, so he stayed standing.

'I should go,' he said. He was fidgeting with his hands. He tapped his pockets as if he was looking for keys but didn't find anything.

'No.' Mammy stretched out her hand and grabbed hold of his arm. She had the look on her face that she got when she was keeping a secret.

'Come upstairs,' she said. 'I'll get you a proper towel.' She pulled Mr. Corcoran's arm and he followed her up the stairs like a robot or something. Mal and Agnes stood looking at each other, waiting to see what would happen next.

'Why don't we go ahead and play another hand of Mousse,' said Agnes, 'while they get themselves sorted.'

'Yerra, I might head off,' said Mal, tugging the hem of his cabled jumper down over his brown corduroy trousers.

Mal and Agnes both looked at the ceiling as the tip-tap-tip of her mammy's heels tracked across the wooden floor upstairs.

'You had better wait to say goodbye,' said Agnes.

Mal shook his head, but he sat down and vigorously shuffled the deck of cards. He dealt, and they played a hand of Mousse, which Emer won easily, and then another that, again, Emer won. She offered Mal and Agnes a sweet from her winnings.

'T-take what you like but not the hay-hay-zelnut whirl,' she said. They each reached out and took a chocolate.

'Is that your mammy's favourite?' asked Mal, and Emer nodded.

'Thank you, pet,' said Agnes.

From upstairs came the sound of lowered voices, muffled laughter, and bedsprings.

'Tuh. Bloody ridiculous carry-on,' said Mal under his breath. He scrunched the wrapper from a golden barrel and threw it onto the table.

'I think it's brightening up,' said Agnes, walking to the window.

'What?' said Mal.

'It's brightening up. The rain has stopped,' she said, with almost convincing good cheer. 'I vote for a brisk postprandial walk. What say ye?'

'I say you're mad, woman,' said Mal, but Agnes tilted her head in a meaningful way towards Emer.

'Come on, Grumpyboots, we'll have a Christmas constitutional. It's traditional, you know.' She was already gathering coats and handing them around, as if there was a rush about it, as if there was a danger they might miss something or, worse, *not* miss something.

* * *

A dark shelf of cloud was sliding steadily north-east towards the city, and the sun, as orange as a slice of carrot, was falling slowly towards the horizon, turning the river to lava.

'What's your favourite subject?' Agnes walked alongside Emer and kept up a happy chatter.

'English,' said Emer. 'No, s-singing.'

'Singing! Really?' said Agnes, failing to hide her surprise. 'And who's your favourite singer?'

'Billie Eilish.'

'Aha,' said Agnes. 'And is he handsome?'

Emer laughed.

'Eh, yeah.'

Mal walked behind them, with his hands buried deep into his pockets. He spat out words every now and then, but Emer couldn't decide if he was muttering to himself or to Bran. It was hard to tell.

The late break in the rain had brought people out and the path along the riverbank was busy. Emer saw a small boy looking wobbly on a new bike, and a girl going fast on a shiny pink scooter, and a man who was probably their grandad jogging behind them. She saw aunties wrapped up in giant scarves and bobble hats, and uncles kicking balls back and forth between them as they walked. She saw a girl pushing a toy pram, and when they got close enough, she saw the shiny black nose and brown eyes of a tiny puppy.

By the time Agnes and Emer, Mal and Bran reached the weir, the sun was dipping below the horizon – it was only half a slice of carrot now – and what warmth there had been in the day was gone.

'We had better turn back,' said Agnes, but her voice sounded unsure.

'Bloody ridiculous,' said Mal, but Emer could tell he was still talking to himself. He grunted his agreement with Agnes and whistled to Bran. They all turned around.

The cold came down with the darkness, forcing them to walk faster. They got back in what felt like very little time. All four of them slowed their pace as they approached the glossy purple door on Weavers' Row.

'I'll head off now,' said Mal, digging his car keys out of his coat pocket. He sounded like he wouldn't change his mind this time.

'Yes,' said Agnes. 'I'll say you—' She paused and looked questioningly into his face.

'Say I went home,' he said.

She nodded.

Emer watched their faces. She thought she should say something but couldn't think what it should be.

'Happy Christmas, Emer,' said Mal. He put his warm, broad hand on the top of her head. 'That trifle will go down in history.'

'Like Napoleon?' she said.

He smiled, a tight-lipped, sad sort of smile.

'That's right,' he said. He turned away and Bran followed at his heel.

'Bye, Mal,' she said, but he didn't seem to hear. She stood watching until the Land Rover turned onto Main Street before she turned to the door.

'Wait one moment,' said Agnes. She led Emer to the back door of her car. 'I was so concerned earlier about that smelly cheese, I left my presents in here.' She reached inside and took out a gift bag with Santa on it. 'Nothing new, I'm afraid,' she went on, 'just some old things I thought deserved a better home. You'll tell your Mam, won't you, that I said thank you for our lovely day.'

'C-Come in?' Emer shivered.

'I'll just see you safely inside. I wouldn't want to outstay—'

Before she could finish, the purple door swung open. Mammy stood with her hands on her hips. Backlit by the glow from inside, her face was dark, and she seemed even taller than usual. Her lips were pressed together, and her eyes were wide.

'Where the *hell* have you been?' she said to Emer, pulling her through the door by her coat sleeve. Emer caught her breath and tried to think of words that wouldn't cast blame on either Agnes or Mal.

'I—' Agnes tried to step inside, but Mammy blocked her, leaving her awkwardly off balance on the doorstep. 'I'm afraid I needed a breath of air. Too much port. Emer was kind enough to—'

'That's outrageous.' Mammy spat the words like darts. 'How *dare* you take *my* child from *my* home, without so *much* as a by-your-leave?'

'I'm so sorry, Maeve.' Agnes was flustered. A bright red stain was rising up her neck and cheeks as if some invisible person was colouring her in. 'I only meant to—'

'*Help*? Is that it? Do you think *you* know better than *I* do how to raise my *own* daughter? Are you implying that I'm a *bad mother*? Is *that* it?'

'Of course not. I—'

'On Christmas *Day*, of *all* days! I expected more of *you*, Agnes. I *thought* you were on my *side*.'

Tears pooled in Agnes's eyes. She took a step backwards, stumbling onto the road.

'Goodbye, Maeve,' she said. 'Thank you for the delicious meal.'

Mammy didn't answer. She closed the door and pulled across the chain, then bent down and turned the Chubb lock.

While her mother's back was turned, Emer slid the Santa bag behind the back of the sofa. She looked around for any sign of Pamela's dad but saw none. She was stuffing her gloves inside her coat pocket when Mammy rounded on her.

'How could you *embarrass* me like that?'

'S-Sorry,' Emer apologised. She felt sick. She had done something horrible. She must have.

'I've never been so *mortified* in my whole life. I came downstairs with Tim, all ready for a nice Christmas afternoon, and there you all were . . . *Gone!*'

Emer thought that was a funny way of saying it, and the thought must have played out across her face.

'Are you *laughing*?' Mammy's tone rose a pitch, and she poked her long, strong forefinger into Emer's collar bone.

'How.' Poke. 'Dare.' Poke. 'You.' Poke. '*Smirk* at me?' Poke. The last poke came with a good push behind it that knocked Emer back a step.

'I-I-I'm *not*, Mammy.' The words hardly came out because of the lump that was blocking her throat. Tears came then, lots of tears, rolling down her face and underneath her chin. She raised the sleeve of her jumper to wipe her nose.

'Don't,' said her mammy, and she put out her hand to hold back Emer's arm. Something in the fibres of Emer's jumper seemed to quell her mother's fury. She released a long, tormented groan of frustration.

'Why can't you see, Emer? I'm doing my best.' She reached over to the table for a serviette and handed it to Emer to wipe her face.

Emer undid her earlier careful folding of Rudolph's smiling face and blew her nose.

'Tim wanted to wish you a Happy Christmas,' said her mammy. 'He bought you a lovely present.'

Serviettes are useless for snot, Emer thought. She wiped, and wiped again, feeling all the while the force of her mother's disappointed eyes bearing down on her.

'Are you even listening to me?'

'Yes.' It was an automatic response. When Mammy got like this, Emer's head filled up with noise and made it very hard to hear anything at all.

'Imagine how we felt when we saw that you had just walked out. How could you be so *rude*?'

Emer didn't know how to untangle the mess of shame and anger in her stomach. It wasn't her fault. It would have been rude to have refused to go for a walk. Wasn't it rude to go upstairs and leave Agnes and Mal without explaining why? She stared down at the floor, counted the knots in the pine boards, and said nothing. The air in the room felt very still. A burnt-out apple log exploded in a finale of tiny red sparks and collapsed into a pile of hot ash. Emer could feel her own heartbeat pounding against her ribcage, and a shadowy darkness creeping in at the edges of her vision.

'Emer?'

Emer looked up at her mother. How *dare* she? How *could* she? Words, angry words, curse words, were flying, spinning inside her head, but she couldn't seem to make a sentence. She didn't have the courage to let the truth out, and her mixed-up brain couldn't find the words to form a lie.

'Don't you want people to *like* you, Emer?'

Yes, or no? Emer couldn't figure out which was the correct answer. Yes, she doesn't, or no, she does? Her mother was winding down. As long as Emer didn't aggravate her, it would be over soon.

She made a non-committal movement of her head.

Her mother sat down on the sofa and picked up the TV remote. She opened a menu and selected Indiana Jones.

'Sit down, Emer,' she said, patting the seat beside her.

Emer sat down at the opposite end.

'Truce?'

Emer nodded.

'I want him to like you,' said Mammy, hitting *Play*.

Emer said nothing.

45.

The Raiders March

* * *

Nóinín Corcoran poured a fresh glass of Chablis for her husband, filling it to the brim. It would be impossible to lift without spilling.

'Happy Christmas,' she said. She took a single piece of popcorn from the bowl that sat between them on the kitchen island, placed it on her tongue, and closed her lips around it.

Laughing, Tim Corcoran lowered his head to the glass and slurped, then raised his face to his wife. From beyond the double doors of the den, the driving beat of a John Williams theme thundered optimistically.

'Happy Christmas, honey.'

'You were gone ages,' she said. 'I called you.'

'Was I?' He took another slug of wine. 'Sorry. I left my phone at home.'

'I know.' She tipped her head towards the quartz countertop, where his phone was plugged into a charger.

'Ah thanks, hon. Where did I leave it?'

'Downstairs loo.'

'Right.' He nodded, confirming his hopelessness.

'So, you're alright now. Are you?' She drained her glass, and refilled it, then topped his up again, carefully, right to the brim.

Tim lifted the glass this time and the wine spilled over onto his hand. Nóinín took his wet hand in hers, bent her head, and licked wine from his skin. Her teeth scraped his knuckle. He didn't flinch.

'Right as rain.' He used his other hand to pull her body tight against his own. 'You smell nice,' he said.

'It's that perfume you gave me. I actually like it.'

'Hmmm.' He buried his head in her neck. 'Me too.'

46.

The Solace of Mince Pies

* * *

Malachi hung up his damp coat on the hook at the back of the door. It could drip away there onto the hard tiles and be damned. He kicked off his shoes, listening with some satisfaction as each one thumped against the skirting board and landed awkwardly. He'd had enough fecking etiquette for one day. He lifted Bran's water bowl, rinsed it out under the tap, refilled it, and placed it back on the floor. Bran shook himself out and rubbed his body against the leg of the kitchen table, then went and lapped water from his bowl.

'The gravy was salty.' Malachi gave the dog's head a rub and straightened up. He looked around the room that defined the size of his life, like a corral. He stuck his finger under the edge of thin oak veneer that was peeling from the cupboard door. He could rip it off, but then he'd have to look at the lousy chipboard underneath. He pushed it down again with the side of his thumb. He'd get a bottle of wood glue when the shops opened and stick it back. It would do.

'Bloody ridiculous carry-on,' he muttered again. 'What a fucking fiasco.'

As he stopped speaking, a dead silence seemed almost to ring in his ears, and it occurred to Malachi that the house was even quieter than usual. He listened and realised that his grandmother's clock, hanging where he'd put it above the table, had stopped. In all his rush to look respectable, to iron his shirt and brush his hair, he'd forgotten to wind it.

He looked over to the single recliner that faced the television. It had been a luxury, that chair, with its lumbar supports and its flip-up footrest and its ergo-feckin-nomic design. There wasn't really room for an armchair in the kitchen. He'd had to fold down both sides of the table and shove it back against the wall. He was only being practical. It didn't make sense to heat two rooms for one person.

He flicked the switch at the back of the kettle, took a teabag from the box on the counter and put it in a mug. Bran lay on the tiles at his feet, paws akimbo, belly raised for a rub.

'One person *and* a dog,' Malachi said, obliging with his stockinged foot. He opened a cupboard and took a box of Mr. Kipling mince pies from the shelf. He pulled one out, removed it from its crinkled foil tray and ate it, unthinking, in two bites. The kettle bubbled and switched itself off.

Malachi crossed to the clock. He opened the glass front and moved the hands to the right time. He found the key and turned it until the mechanism was fully wound, then went back to making his tea.

He'd given it his best shot. At least he could say that much. And if she only had eyes for Tim Corcoran, there was damn all he could do about it. Leave them at it, he thought. Maybe now the heavy, frightened feeling would go away.

'Yerra, fuck it anyway,' he said, and extracted another mince pie from the box.

47.

Home Alone

* * *

Agnes put her hand to the side of the radiator, as if she didn't already know it would be cold. She bent down and turned the dial at the side through the numbers, three, four, five, all the way around to MAX. The gurgling noise as it heated up grated on her nerves. She switched on the radio, hoping it wouldn't be hymns.

Thinking back to the morning, her feverish excitement, she stepped out of her good shoes and walked in her tights to the mahogany sideboard.

It was hymns.

She poured two long glugs of port into a crystal glass and carried the drink to a table in the bay window where one thousand pieces of a jigsaw had all been turned the right way up. That was how Agnes had put down the seemingly interminable hours before it was time to drive to Weavers' Row for Christmas lunch. The picture on the box was a cartoonish image of a bookshop: lots of books, a cat, and a lady's sunhat nonchalantly tossed on a wicker chair. No blue sky or large expanses of water. Agnes had learned her lesson on that score.

She took a sip of port and began separating out edge pieces. From deep in the jumble, she lifted a corner piece. That made four. It was good to have some sort of system. She'd get the edge finished, she figured, and then make herself a hot port to drink in bed.

An image of Maeve Gaffney standing on her doorstep, her shoulder turned and her face shuttered in disdain, intruded on Agnes' thoughts. The memory made her queasy. She'd never in her entire life felt so severely criticised. *I was wrong*, she thought, *I must apologise*. Obviously, she'd misread the situation and made a dreadful error. It was too awful to think about.

She'd got that Mary Morrissy novel from the library, thank goodness. She might stay in bed all day tomorrow and read. Who would ever know? Or care? Except for Malachi. *Poor Malachi*, she thought. In all likelihood, he wouldn't want to talk, but she'd light the fire in the morning and maybe make a crumble, just in case.

48.

Back Then, in Dublin

* * *

'You can't be pregnant,' he said, letting go of her hand, and immediately regretting it.

It was only six weeks after the ball. They were sitting on a bench in Merrion Square, the place thronged with students who'd finished their exams. Despite the nuisance of his finals getting in the way, it was fair to say that Tim Corcoran had had more sex in the last forty-two days than in the whole rest of his life put together. Conception occurring probably shouldn't have been all that much of a surprise.

'You just can't,' he said. 'It's not possible.'

'You can keep on saying that, Tim, if it helps you, but it's not going to make it true.'

She bent her head and let her hair fall down around her face. He heard the click of her back teeth as she clenched her jaw and realised she was trying not to cry.

'Sorry,' he said.

'It must have happened that very first time.'

'You're kidding.'

'I'm really not. *Jesus*, Tim.'

'Sorry, sorry. It's just—'

'I know, yeah.'

'Shit, like.'

She cracked a wry smile.

'Yeah.'

A couple dressed as Molly Bloom and James Joyce came strolling up the path, she twirling a parasol, he clutching a clipboard.

They took turns accosting likely customers as they came upon them.

'Could we interest you in a very special Bloomsday walking tour of Dublin?' said Molly to Tim.

'You're alright, thanks.' His eye flickered toward Maeve, and Molly Bloom's gaze followed his.

'Fair enough.' Molly gave him a sympathetic half-smile.

He wondered what she saw, what she thought of a young man looking bewildered at the side of a young woman looking distraught. Theirs, he imagined, was such an age-old, time-worn plot twist that even the original Molly Bloom could have read their story from their faces. Maeve's role, the poor unfortunate woman, caught out by biology, was well defined. Only his was in question. Was he the likeable good guy, or was he the flaky bastard? They were both about to find out.

He shifted along the bench until his hip bumped against Maeve's. He wrapped his arm around her. She flinched at first, but then let her head fall onto his shoulder.

'I don't know what to do,' she said.

He kissed the top of her head. She smelled, like always, of coconut and a florist's shop. She smelled, he imagined, like an island in the South Pacific. She belonged in a painting by Gauguin, lying on a beach wearing garlands of flowers.

'What are you thinking?' she asked, without lifting her head.

He decided against telling her how good she smelled.

'I love you,' he said. Tim had a certain idea of himself – a romantic ideal – and he said the words that made him feel he was at his best. This was not the moment to let himself down.

She sat up and looked him in the eye. Her face showed no expression.

'I love you,' he said again, smiling, and tucked a strand of her hair back behind her ear. He felt good, heroic even.

She put her hand on his thigh.

'What do you mean?'

What *did* he mean?

'I mean what people usually mean. I can't get enough of you. I can't bear to let you out of my sight. I want to be with you, always.'

She bit her lip, and he saw that she wanted to know what he meant in the context of her current predicament.

'I'm here,' he said. 'Whatever you decide, I'm here for you. I'll mind you.'

It was true, he thought. This would be hard for her, a tough decision, but he would see her through it. He felt proud of himself, of his gallant response, of his magnanimity. He was rewarded when her face brightened. The pressure of her hand on his thigh increased. She curved her body so that her breast was pressed against his heart, and he wasn't sure whose pulse he felt. Never before had he felt so vividly alive. It was like coming out of a dream state that had lasted his whole life, and for the first time ever being wide awake. She was like a drug. She made everything feel like *more*.

'I love the bones of you, Maeve Gaffney. I'm all yours.'

And then she laughed, that bright rippling, irresistible laugh of hers. All he wanted was to hear that laugh, and to be the one who made it ring out.

She twisted until she was sitting on top of him, straddling his legs. He put his two hands on either side of her head, pulled her mouth to his, and kissed her.

Somewhere to his right, Molly Bloom was still trying to sell a very special Bloomsday walking tour of Dublin. Maeve Gaffney brushed her left cheek against his and whispered in his ear.

'All mine?'

He let his hands fall to her shoulders, down her back, around her hips, under her ass, and he pulled her closer to him, so that she could feel just how much he meant it.

'Yes,' he said, but his voice was hoarse and hardly audible, so he cleared his throat and spread his palms wide and said it again. 'Yes.'

49.

St. Stephen's Day

* * *

She didn't even open the downstairs curtains, didn't once glance at the detritus of the previous day. One clean-up at a time, she decided, hustling Emer into the car.

She was a good mother. There was no point in dwelling on her mistakes, not when she had worked so hard. If she just stuck with the plan, she would give Emer the father she deserved. There was no time to waste. She needed to reset their relationship, get them back in their groove, move on.

'*Shrek*,' she said, through a mouth full of toast, as she reversed out of Weavers' Row. Automatically, Emer reacted to their shorthand, found the right music, and hit *Play*.

Maeve drove fast, tapping the steering wheel in time with the beat. She began, at first involuntarily, then deliberately, to sing along. She was aware of the sharp edge to her voice. It was too keen. Every so often, at the end of a chorus or the start of a new song, she consciously readjusted her tone. Emer sat passively beside her, face turned away, pretending to be sleepy.

She parked on the strip of wet gravel at the top of the beach. It was the long strand with the notorious riptides where they had twice already been warned not to swim. Maeve pulled Emer's hat down over her ears and tightened the cords to keep her own hood up.

'Come on.'

She was rushing, she knew, as if there was some terrible hurry. Her heart thumped with the urgency of it, to find somewhere to go, some other place to be, the desperate need to move through space to a different reality. She stretched her legs into long determined strides, up the strand, against the wind.

Over her shoulder, she saw Emer pressing her hands deep into her coat pockets and trotting in her wake so that the orange bobble of her hat bounced up and down as if it had a life of its own. She didn't know what else to do but bring Emer with her. *Keep moving*, that was the only strategy Maeve had. She leaned into the wind, squinting against the low glow of the winter sun, feeling the cold ache in her lungs, and the slip and give of the ground beneath her feet.

The sky was watery blue, as if someone had wiped it with a wet cloth, and the Atlantic was loud. Strong, lofty waves stretched high against the sky and crashed hard against the damp sand, raking it out, over and over, and leaving behind a bubbling froth of beige scum. Maeve walked as close to the water as she could without soaking her shoes. She let the last wash of each wave drive her up the beach and then she drifted again, outwards, as the water fell away. Emer walked on her left, the landward side, only an arm's length away. There was no silence to fill, no need to talk. The thunder of the ocean, the salty mist and blasting wind, took up all the space between them.

Maeve sensed Emer's pace slowing as they approached the freshwater stream that split the beach in two. On previous walks they had always called it a day here and turned back. Now, though, the rain that had soaked down from the fields had swollen the stream, so it was wider than usual and running fast. The force of it felt like a challenge to Maeve and she began to run. Without a word, she sped forward and leapt the stream, only catching the heel of her shoe in the water. She turned and waited.

Emer walked a few metres up the beach to a point where the stream could be negotiated by stepping over two miniature stony islands. In three hops, she got across.

Maeve saw the look of satisfaction on Emer's face when she landed on dry sand.

Catch her being brave, said Greta.
I remember.
'Good girl,' she said, smiling. That was all.

They pressed on, all the way to the headland where, beneath the shadow of the cliffs, the wind was cowed into a looming quiet.

Emer stood with her back to the cliff face and stared out at the sea. Her face was pale, and the orange of her hat accentuated the purple shadows under her eyes. Maeve could hear her counting the waves under her breath as they came.

'Is it true, the thing about every seventh wave being the biggest?' she asked without turning her head.

Maeve moved to stand close beside her. The sleeves of their coats squashed against each other.

'Sometimes, I think.'

Emer didn't reply. She wouldn't like an answer so vague. In Emer's book, things couldn't be *sometimes* true.

'It depends on how far the waves have travelled. They get blown up by the wind, by a storm, and they start off completely random, but form patterns as they go.'

Emer still said nothing.

'Like people, I suppose.'

Emer took a deep breath.

'Mammy?' she said.

Here we go.

'Yes, Chicken?'

'Is it so that I can be friends with P-Pamela?'

'What?'

'Is that why you want Pamela's dad to like me?'

It was Maeve's turn to look out at the sea. She let her eyes travel to the point where cloud boulders sat on the horizon. Maybe it was time she stopped making life easy for Tim Corcoran. Maybe what he needed was to have his hand forced. Maybe it was time to level the playing field. She tucked hair that had escaped from her hood back behind her ears.

'No. Well, yes. I suppose it *is* so you can be friends with Pamela,' Her voice was rising again, getting higher and thinner, as if it was being stretched. 'But it's for your own sake too, and for mine.'

A thin wave crept over the sand and Emer spotted a hermit crab scuttling ahead of it. She bent and picked it up, but it disappeared inside its borrowed shell.

'C-Clever thing,' she said.

'Hmmm.' Maeve waited.

'Why is it for my sake too?'

Maeve put her two hands to her temples and looked down at the sand.

'Mammy?'

'Because he's—'

Emer took an involuntary step backwards and slammed her back against the cliff, as if she felt the words coming before she heard them.

Maeve matched Emer's step, reaching a hand out to her.

Emer slid away sideways, her eyes wide, her face a picture of fear.

Maeve could see that her daughter was sorry she'd asked. Emer's courage, which rose so rarely, receded now as rapidly as the hissing waves.

'Stop, Mammy. *Please* stop.'

Maeve stood still, aware of her heels sinking into the wet sand. On her right, the Atlantic persisted. Emer moved away again and stepped onto the jagged rocks, as if she might try to make her way around the headland. Maeve stepped up beside her.

'We'd come out at the lighthouse, I think, if we could keep going.'

'But we c-can't keep going, can we?'

Maeve looked up at the height of the cliff, the treacherous looseness of the stony soil that made up the face of it, the rocks ready to topple.

'No,' she said. 'Not today.'

Emer's face was rigid.

'We don't have to think about it today. Alright?'

She held out her hand and waited.

Emer's chest rose and fell, and Maeve knew she was filing away the moment, putting it into a box that would go on a high shelf, which she might or might not ever open again. She didn't answer Maeve, but she wiped tears from her face and nodded her head and reached out to Maeve's hand and took it.

'I love you, Chicken,' Maeve said. Through her gloves, she felt Emer's fingers squeeze her own.

They turned and walked back along the beach, the wind at their backs now, whipping them along. In gusts, it cut their knees out from under them so that they were forced into a jog. When they came to the stream, Maeve let go of Emer's hand. She nudged her to go first. Emer took a run at it and leapt, held in the air by the wind so that, for a fraction of a second, she might have been flying.

Maeve landed in the sand ahead of Emer, her long legs giving her an advantage. She didn't hold out her hand this time but stayed close enough that the side of her arm rubbed against Emer's jacket. Again, the boom of the ocean precluded conversation, and anyway, there was nothing more to say.

'Chips?' Maeve asked, over the roof of the car. It was the first word she had spoken since they'd left the cliff. Emer was kicking sand from her shoes in the reedy grass. She pulled off her orange bobble hat and looked up. Her cheeks were stung pink from the wind.

'Ok,' she said, nodding. 'Chips.'

50.

Daddy's Girl

* * *

Nóinín parked at the back of the hotel and took the short route through the kitchens to reach the narrow corridor where her father's office was hidden. She was dressed in wide-legged woollen pants in winter white with a coordinating sweater and four-inch pumps in patent red. It was still Christmas, after all. She'd left Tim and the kids sprawled out in the lounge watching *The Empire Strikes Back*. In all likelihood they wouldn't even realise she wasn't in the house.

She tapped lightly on the office door with one hand while pressing down on the brass door handle with the other. She didn't wait for an answer; she'd sent a text to say she was on her way.

Paddy O'Driscoll was reclining in his leather chair with his feet on his desk and his hands joined on his belly.

'There's my flower,' he said, opening his eyes and raising the fingers of one hand in greeting.

'Hi, Daddy.' Nóinín walked around the desk and bent at the knees to peck her father's waxen cheek.

'That was some spread you put on yesterday.' He patted his girth. 'I'm still digesting.'

Nóinín walked slowly around the big desk, trailing her varnished fingernail along the surface of the wood, and perched on the hard chair Paddy had purposefully chosen for its singular lack of comfort.

'I have a problem, Daddy,' she said plainly.

Her father dropped his feet to the floor, pulled his chair closer to the desk, and leaned towards her.

'Oh?'

'I, well, *we* have a bit of a situation—'

Her father pressed his palms together.

'Well now, that usually only means one thing.' His voice was cross, immediately accusative. 'Is it you, or is it him?'

'*Him.*' She couldn't help sounding defensive. 'It's him.'

'I see. Do you want to tell me exactly what he's done? Or, more to the point, *who* he's done?'

Nóinín didn't hesitate. This was what she'd come for.

'Maeve Gaffney. The woman who bought—'

'I *know* who she is.' Her father swung back on his chair with a smirk on his face of grudging admiration for her husband. 'You're joking me.'

'I'm not.'

He caught her tone and corrected his posture.

'How do you know for sure?'

'He wrote it in his book.'

'His book?'

'His *novel.*'

'Fuckin' eejit.' Her father rolled his eyes and shook his head. He was clearly more upset by his son-in-law's lack of common sense than his infidelity. He drummed the fingers of his left hand against the desk. 'The house is in my name, pet. You've no worries there.'

Nóinín nodded. She'd thought it all through already.

'I don't want him to leave, Daddy.'

'No?'

'I don't want my name dragged through the dirt of this town.'

He tilted his head, allowing that that was exactly what would happen.

'And I like being a Corcoran. What would I do about the shop? My brand would be destroyed.'

'Are you sure?'

'I am. I don't want Pammie and Tadgh coming from a broken home. And,' she added, *generously*, 'he's not a bad father.'

'You've weighed it all up?'

'I have, Daddy. I'm sure.'

'Alright.' Her father was business-like now. Despite his solemn expression, Nóinín knew that there was nothing he enjoyed more than a problem to be *dealt with*. 'Does he know you know?'

'No.'

'Good girl. Keep it that way.' The rhythm of his drumming fingers sped up to a military ta-ta-ta-tum, ta-ta-ta-tum, ta-ta-ta-tum-tum-tum.

Nóinín waited.

'Right, look.' Her father spread both palms wide on the polished surface of his desk. 'You, play nice, right? Butter him up. Use your, what-do-you-call-it, *womanly charms*, right?'

'Yep.' Nóinín bit her lip but nodded agreement. 'I can do that.'

'Is there anything else I should know?'

'Pammie's got friendly with the little Gaffney one. She says they're besties.'

Her father took a minute to think about that. Nóinín knew he was looking for an angle, anything he could use for leverage. That was how he operated.

'Put an end to that,' he said. 'The sooner the better.'

'I'm not sure how I can—'

'Tell Pammie the girl has vicious nits,' he said.

Nóinín couldn't help returning her father's smile. He was enjoying this, she could tell.

'Jesus, Dad.'

'You must put your own kids first, love. That's your job.' He paused to think. 'And have a chat with Mary Joseph. She'll know what to do.'

'Yeah, alright.' She felt a bit nauseated. She'd rather deal with nits. She wouldn't admit to her father that she was still terrified of her aunt, but the fear must have shown on her face. Her father gave her a sympathetic wink.

'Don't worry,' he said. 'I'll take care of this.'

She was surprised to feel her eyes filling with tears. She shook them off and smiled her gratitude.

'Thanks, Daddy,' she said.

Her father walked around his desk and she stood, understanding that the meeting was at a close. He put his two hands firmly on her shoulders and kissed her cheek, then gave a slap to her back to return them both to their usual roles.

'You must give your mother the recipe for that gravy we had yesterday. I never get anything like that at home.'

'It was Tim made that,' she said, perfectly normally.

'Was it indeed? Good man, Tim. Isn't he a great fella for the cooking?'

'He is.'

'He is. I can see that, alright. Go on away home now and make two nice Irish coffees. Make them good and strong. Your mother puts Baileys in hers—' he carried on this inanity while he herded her out the door '—but personally now, I think you can't go wrong with a drop of Jemmie. Do you have Jameson at home, pet?'

'I don't know.' Nóinín was fully aware that she was being handled now, managed, but she liked it. Her father was the only person in the world to whom she could safely relinquish control. She did, in fact, know that there was plenty of whiskey in the drinks cabinet at Cavendish House, but it worked for them both that he made this gesture. She asked, he gave. It was a dynamic that allowed them both to feel normal, loved and loving, like ordinary humans.

'Go on down to Robert in the bar and tell him I said he's to give you a bottle of Jameson 18 from the stockroom. Alright?' This was the closer. All she had to do was agree now and the whole subject need never be raised between them again.

'Alright,' she said. 'Thanks, Daddy.'

'Right you are,' he said, and shut the door behind her.

51.

New Year's Day

* * *

'Lift your legs,' Mammy said.

Emer was eating a bowl of Crunchy Nut cornflakes at the oak table. She raised her two feet off the floor so that her mother could run the head of the hoover underneath. The untidiness of the living room, she could tell, was getting on Mammy's nerves.

'Here, look at this.' Mammy lifted a large gift bag from behind the sofa. 'I found mystery presents!'

Emer felt the punch in her lungs. She hadn't forgotten about the Santa bag; she had chosen not to remember it. She hadn't wanted to reignite any talk of Tim, and she hadn't wanted to think about the fact that neither Agnes nor Malachi had come back. If she had been brave, she might have hidden the bag inside her wardrobe, but who knew what trouble that would lead to later on. It had been simpler to consign it to a dark corner of her consciousness and hope that it would stay there.

'They're from Agnes,' she said.

'*What?*' Mammy stressed the 't' at the end of the word. *Not* a good sign. 'Why didn't you—?' She cut herself off.

'The s-small one is for me,' Emer said it quickly and her mammy duly handed over the smaller parcel. Then, more slowly, she said, 'And the big, the big one is for you.'

Mammy lifted the awkwardly shaped parcel from the bag. The wrapping paper was crinkled, and held together with long strips of tape.

'It's heavy enough,' she said. A twitch of tension played at the corners of her mouth. She cut the tape away with the edge of a knife and tore the paper, revealing at first only an extra layer of bubble wrap, but then, a gleaming five-branched silver candelabrum.

'Oh.'

Mammy was quiet.

'She s-said it was just old things.'

'It's too much.' Mammy gave a nod to the smaller parcel in Emer's hand. 'Open yours.'

It was obviously a book. Emer could understand that the silver candle holder was an over-generous gift, one that Mammy would never be able to repay, and therefore unacceptable, but hers was just a book. She turned the parcel over and began to peel off the tape.

'Hurry up, for the love of God.'

She was right. It was a book, an old one that looked as if it might easily have sat on Agnes's bookshelf since she was a girl. The cover was grass green, with an image embossed in gold of a girl kneeling in a patch of grass. From a flowerpot in her hands, a rose grew and spread out above her head, towards the title: *The Secret Garden*. The pages inside were thick and butter-coloured and interrupted by pretty illustrations that were each protected by a layer of transparent tissue paper.

Emer ran her finger over a drawing of a girl in a blue dress sitting on the arm of a chair. She was pale, with long, messy hair.

'Mammy, look,' she said, without looking up, thinking Mammy would see how much the girl looked like her.

'Let me see.' Mammy took the book and flicked to the title page. Her eyes opened wide, but she said nothing. Gently, she closed the book and put it down on the table, then lifted the candelabrum and turned it upside down to examine the base.

'You see these, here?' She pointed to a line of tiny marks pressed into the silver. 'They tell you who made it, and when.'

Emer peered at the marks while her mam searched on her phone. The first was a square with the initials TJ, then a shield with the letter M and a dot underneath, then a harp with a crown on top, and finally a woman sitting on a throne holding a flower.

'Who is she?'

'Hibernia,' said Maeve. 'It means it's Irish silver.' Mammy was scrolling, referring back and forth between her phone screen and the marks.

'Late 1700s, I think,' she said eventually. 'This is crazy. What was she thinking?'

'Maybe she didn't know.' Emer put her hand on the book.

'We have to give them back, Emer.' Mammy slid the book from under Emer's hand. 'I'm sorry, love. I'll make it up to you.'

Emer turned away. She picked up her bowl of Crunchy Nut cornflakes and poured what remained of them down the kitchen sink.

* * *

Mammy said it was best to get it over with. She was always like that when she was doing what she had decided was the right thing. It was as if she knew she had to act quickly, before some weaker part of herself would be swayed by temptation. She put the bag on the back seat and started the car, hardly giving Emer time to get in. Mammy drove fast, and she didn't talk. She didn't put any music on, instead just left the boring talking on the radio. Emer didn't say anything either.

The road was all uphill. A broad view of the sea had opened out on Emer's side when Mammy pulled in at an open farm gate, made a U-turn, and parked in a gateway on the other side of the road.

'This is it,' she said, and stalled.

Emer waited.

'Right, so,' said Mammy. She placed the bag on Emer's lap. 'You run in there.'

'Ah—'

'Don't *ah* me. You know full well you should have told me about them sooner. Tell her your mammy said that we can't accept them. Say there's a note in the bag.'

Emer got out of the car. She banged the passenger door closed behind her and stood looking at the high granite gatepost with its cast iron sign in blue and white. *Ard na Mara*, it said. *Ard* meant high, she knew, and *Mara* was the sea. The height of the sea? Was that what it meant? Or high above the sea? Behind her back, Mammy tapped her knuckle against the windscreen and Emer jumped.

She walked up the gravel path to the front door and pressed her index finger against the round knob of the doorbell. Straight away, the door swung open, as if Agnes had been standing waiting.

'Hello, Emer,' she said.

'Eh, Hello. I—' Emer found that she was out of breath. She held the Santa bag out in front of her and was grateful when Agnes lifted the weight of it out of her hands.

'You don't have to say anything. I understand.'

'I-I-I'm—' She wanted to say something kind, but the right words wouldn't come into her head. It would take too long to explain.

'You're alright, sweetheart.' Agnes seemed to swallow a lump in her throat. 'Go on away now, your mammy is waiting for you.'

Emer nodded and turned back down the gravel path. She could see her mother, sitting in the driver's seat, staring straight ahead.

52.

Back to School

* * *

On the first morning of the new term, they woke up late. Emer had slept through her alarm. The water in the shower was cold because Mammy hadn't turned the heater on. She couldn't find her tie. There was no milk for her cereal and no bread for her sandwiches. Her lunchbox, when finally she found it still in her school bag, was rancid with the smell of a mouldy clementine.

Emer scavenged the last crackers from the box of cheese biscuits – the saltless, seedy wholegrain ones – and wrapped them in tinfoil with a wedge of Camembert.

'Here,' Mammy said, whirling around the kitchen in her bathrobe. 'Take some of these.' She poured a fistful of walnuts into a plastic tub.

'We're not, we're not allowed nuts!' Exasperated, Emer dumped the nuts on the countertop.

'There must be some sort of fruit in here, for God's sake.' Mammy stood holding the fridge door open and muttering, as if she could make food appear by magic. 'Hah! Crisis averted.' She grabbed a carrot from the salad drawer and set about cutting it into sticks, like her life depended on it.

'I'd drop you up,' Mammy said at the front door, 'but the roads are very icy.' She tugged at Emer's hat and fussed with her school scarf.

'It's fine,' Emer said. 'I'm fine walking.'

'Good girl. Watch out for black ice.'

'What's black ice?'

'It's very thin, invisible ice that'll land you flat on your backside before you know what's happening.'

There wasn't much point in watching out for it so, was there, if it was invisible. Emer would never understand her mother, but she could tell that Mammy was relieved to see her going back to school. There'd been this big, unspoken thing hanging over them. The *elephant in the room*, it was called. *Giganotosaurus in the room*, more like.

Neither of them mentioned it, the thing that wasn't said at the beach. For what was left of the holidays, they had slept in every morning, then worked for a few hours on painting the kitchen. Emer liked brushing undercoat onto the skirting boards. She liked the smell of paint. She liked catching the running drips and wiping them sideways. She liked the way things could be changed so easily, made cleaner and brighter. She liked having her mother a few feet away, running a roller over the walls with reassuringly steady strokes. She liked that they could be close without needing to speak. She liked that, every now and then, her mother would say, 'Well done, Chicken. That looks *great*.'

They had let Spotify choose their music. It seemed safer that way.

In the evenings they'd watched movies. They'd eaten cheese at every meal but never mentioned Malachi or Agnes. It felt like a return to a familiar rhythm, comforting, easy. Emer, had she thought about it, might have said it was the path of least resistance. The fact was, she didn't think about it. It was there all the time, the knowledge, right at the back of her head, but she kept it in a kind of darkness, like the shadow world at the back of a brightly lit stage. If it didn't intrude on the action of the here and now, she didn't need to think about it.

Emer was late getting to school, but she wasn't the last. Pamela Corcoran came in the door right behind her. Emer opened her mouth to say something – *hello* or *happy new year*, she hadn't decided – but Pamela turned her face away. Side by side, the girls peeled off their coats and matching scarves and hung them up.

'Did you have a nice holiday?' Emer managed to say.

'Very nice, thank you,' said Pamela. She walked away without meeting Emer's eye.

The desks had been rearranged, spaced out so that each desk, with its pair of girls, stood alone. Miss Murphy pointed Emer to the desk directly in front of her own. Veronica Waugh was already seated in the other chair, talking to Sinead Hurley at the desk behind. Emer sat and took out her maths book and her pencil case and waited.

When Miss Murphy rapped the whiteboard with the tip of her marker for attention, Veronica twisted her body around in her seat.

'Sweet Jesus, girl, did something die in your sack?' she said, scrunching up her nose and curling her upper lip. 'That smell is rank, like.'

53.

The High-Bouncing Lover

* * *

Maeve picked her phone up from the bedside table and sent the text:

All clear.

She'd shaken out the bedspread and tidied the pillows by the time the reply came:

5 mins

She scrolled her phone and chose a playlist, then dropped her towel and stood naked in front of the mirror as Nat King Cole sang the opening line of 'Beale Street Blues'. Her stomach was flat, but she wasn't the slim girl she had been, back then. She had a dark bruise on her knee and no idea how she got it. It was a point of pride, the not knowing. She was too pale, but the moisturiser she'd slathered all over had left her skin bright and dewy. Her hair was still damp. She tousled it with her fingers and looked again in the mirror. She looked good. She *felt* good. She lifted the bottle of perfume from the shelf and dabbed the scent on her wrists, behind her ears, in the hollow of her clavicle.

You're going to hell for this, Maeve.
Oh fuck off, Mam.

No one, living or dead, was going to ruin this day for her. Excitement crackled upwards from the soles of her feet, like an electrical current seeking an exit point.

She looked again at the jersey dress she had planned on wearing, but left it where it was, arranged over the wicker bedroom chair. She opened her top drawer, found her pink silk bra and knickers, and draped them on the chair next to the dress. She slipped her arms into her mauve kimono and was tying the belt in a loose bow when the dragonfly knocker clapped twice.

'Hiya.' She opened the door just enough to let him slip inside.

'Hi yourself,' said Tim, stepping sideways and grinning as he took in what she was wearing. He was dressed for the weather, in boots, a dark ski jacket, and a petrol-blue woollen hat that set off his eyes.

A conversational chasm opened up between them.

'Would you like tea?' Maeve said, to fill the gap. She raised a hand towards the kitchen.

Tim looked down at the draped silk of her kimono sleeve.

'*Tea?*' He said it as if this was the most ridiculous suggestion he'd ever heard. With the back of his fingers, he touched her shoulder. His hand was warm, but the cold air he'd brought in with him chilled her bare legs. A shiver ran through her. With the pad of his thumb, he pressed the soft spot above her sternum.

A gasp turned into a laugh.

'No tea, then?' She reached up, pulled off his hat, and threw it over her shoulder. His blond hair stuck up in boyish clumps.

'No,' he said, 'not this time.'

Walking backwards, she led him towards the staircase.

54.

After the Bath

* * *

Tim leaned over the bath and kissed the wet skin of Maeve's shoulder. She was sleepy, and her cheeks were rosy.

'Bye, gorgeous.'

'Hang on two minutes,' she said, with her hand clasped to the back of his neck. 'I'll see you out.'

'Stay where you are,' he said. 'I'll pull the door behind me.'

It was just as well he'd said that, and that she hadn't been standing behind him in her silk robe when he opened the front door, because Sean Leahy was standing across the lane, leaning against the stone wall with his arms crossed and a half-smoked cigarette dangling from his lips. He dipped his head sideways in a beckoning gesture that left no room for doubt. This wasn't a chance encounter.

Tim stood tall and resisted the urge to shake his clothes straight.

'Sean?' he said, working hard to make a light-hearted query of it, a *fancy meeting you here* sort of tone.

'You're some fuckin' flowerpot,' said Leahy, just as lightly, and with a curling smirk that showed how much he was enjoying this particular task. Officially, he was a bouncer, employed to discourage the less desirable elements from frequenting the nightclub at the Drohid Arms, but every dog in the street knew that Sean Leahy took care of whatever dirty work Paddy O'Driscoll threw his way.

'Oh?' Tim searched his brain for something he might have done to annoy Paddy, aside from cheating on his only daughter.

'Paddy wants a word with you.'
Fuck.
'Grand, yeah. Sure, I'll wander on up there now and say hello.'
'I'll keep you company,' said Leahy, kicking off from the wall.
'No need.'
'Boss's orders.' Leahy shrugged.

* * *

In his office at the back of the Drohid Arms, Paddy O'Driscoll stood with his head bowed over a filing cabinet and his back to the door.

'Sit down,' he said, without turning, when Tim walked in.

Tim sat, forcing himself to slump and cross his legs in an attitude of ease.

Paddy continued to flick through files, taking out one after another, then returning them carefully, searching for some document that was vital to the conversation.

'Ah now, here we are,' he said eventually. He sat down at his desk and tapped the file, two quick taps of his middle finger. 'Do you know what this is, Tim?'

'No.'

'These are the completed documents on the purchase of Cavendish House, Tim.'

'Oh?' Tim's gullet baulked against the excess of spit that suddenly filled his mouth. He swallowed hard. 'You're very organised.'

'That's right, Tim,' said Paddy. 'I am. I am an organised man. It helps, you see, to know precisely where you stand in life.'

'Of course.'

'I'm not a fan of what-do-you-call-it, *ambiguity*.'

Silence yawned between them. Tim held eye contact with Paddy for as long as he was able but couldn't outlast his father-in-law's glare. Tim blinked first.

'I don't know what you're talking about,' Tim said, clambering for higher ground. He wasn't about to let Paddy bully him into submission.

'Alright, so. I'll tell you what, Tim. I'll spell it out for you.' Tim held his body completely still, girded against the onslaught he knew was coming.

'You,' Paddy continued, 'are playing away from home.'

'No, I'm—'

Paddy raised his palm to Tim.

'Don't fucking insult me, you little toerag. What do you take me for? Aren't you sitting in front of me right now with the smell of her still on you?'

Jesus Christ. How did he know?

'I—'

'Don't speak. Don't make it worse. Now, you listen to me.' Paddy leaned forward and drilled his index finger into the top of his desk, poking out the rhythm of his words. 'I'll *never* know what my daughter saw in *you*. You're nothing but a *gormless* little *shit* with a *big* head and no *balls*.' He took a breath. 'But to my e*ter*nal fucking dis*may*, she loves you.'

'Does she know?' The words were out of his mouth before Tim fully realised that he'd provided an admission of guilt. Paddy shook his head, as if impressed that anyone could be quite so stupid.

'No, Tim. She doesn't, and for *her* sake, I think it's better if we keep it that way. Are we in agreement so far, Tim?'

Tim nodded.

'I won't—' he began.

'No, you fucking *won't*. You won't go *near* Weavers' Row. You won't even *cross* the fucking *river*, Tim, without clearing it with me. And if I *hear* that you were within sniffing distance of that woman, I'll kick you out of this town *so hard* and *so fast* you'll think you're fucking Chuck Yeager. Do you *know* who Chuck Yeager is, Tim?'

Tim nodded. He'd read *The Right Stuff* more than once.

'Fucking *Noddy*, that's what you are. Fucking *Noddy* Corcoran,' Paddy barked out a harsh laugh. 'It has a ring to it.'

'Ah now—'

'Either *you* behave yourself, or *I* take measures to encourage young Ms. Gaffney to pack up her bags and her *pretty* little daughter and get out of Dodge. Are we *completely* clear now, Tim?

Tim nodded.

'There's no *ambiguity* about the situation, is there?'

Tim shook his head.

Paddy snorted. 'Get out of here.'

55.

Back Then, in Dublin

* * *

'You can't be pregnant,' said Greta Gaffney. She stood with her back to the kitchen sink, wiping her hands furiously on the bottom half of her apron.

Maeve sighed.

'And yet, here I am – pregnant.'

'How many weeks?'

'Not many. Seven, nearly eight.'

Greta nodded her head repeatedly in a business-like manner.

'Good. That's good.'

She sat down at the table in the chair beside Maeve's and took her daughter's two hands in hers.

'We can sort this out, love.'

'Go to England, you mean?'

'Yes.'

'No.'

'It will only be a few tablets, and a bit of a bad period.'

'No.'

'After a few months, you'll get over it, you know. You'll be able to get on with your life.'

'I want the baby, Mam.'

'Ah, love, come on. You'll have another baby when the time is right—'

'I want *this* baby.'

Maeve pushed back her chair and stood up. She moved away from her mother, put the kitchen table between them, like a safeguard.

'Ah now, Maeve. Don't go getting dramatic,' said Greta. 'You know I only want the best for you.'

'Tim is happy about the baby.'

'Tim's the father, is he? I haven't heard mention of him before this.'

Maeve looked down and spoke to the table.

'I met him at the May Ball.'

'This year's May Ball?'

Maeve nodded.

'Ah, love. You can't throw your whole life away on someone you've hardly known a wet weekend.'

'Don't make fun of me, Mammy. I love him, and he loves me.'

Greta stood up now and leaned across the table.

'Hah! And what would you know about love?'

Maeve released her frustration in a hoarse shout.

'More than *you* would anyway.'

She watched the tears flooding over the red rims of her mother's eyes. It was a low blow, and she knew it.

'Your father didn't want to know anything about you, Maeve.'

'I know, Mammy, but you kept me anyway, didn't you?'

Her mother looked her straight in the eye.

'Girls didn't have a choice in those days.'

Maeve drew breath. If her blow was low, her mother cut lower.

'Great, thanks. Good to know I was wanted.'

'Ah no, honey—'

'It's fine, Mam.'

'I didn't mean—'

'Ah, but you did.'

'Maeve—'

'Tim loves me, Mammy. He says he'll take care of us. Mind us, that's what he said.'

'It's early days, Maeve. What if he has second thoughts? You'll be stranded. No man likes to be trapped. Mark my words. If you trap him, sooner or later, he'll hate you for it.'

Maeve gathered up her bag, stuffed her sunglasses and her phone into it.

'Well, I appreciate the support anyway. Thanks very much.'

'Wait—'

'See ya, Mam.'

56.

A Common Enemy

* * *

'Sean Leahy's an idiot,' said Tim. He indicated the single ring on the tiny gas hob. 'Will I leave it turned on for a bit?'

'Yeah.' Maeve was shivering. 'I was just thinking I might have to put my woolly hat back on.'

'I wouldn't mind, as long as that's all you put on.' He poured hot water into two mugs. 'I'm sorry it has to be this way. I'd far rather we were tucked up in your cosy bed.'

So would Maeve. She could have lived without the novelty value of sex in a two-berth caravan perched on the edge of a cliff. It was the best he could come up with, Tim said. He'd called in a favour from his cousin who rented this place on Airbnb during the summer.

'Hey, look,' she said, raising the edge of the curtain that was closed around the head of the bed. 'We've got a sea view. That's hard to beat.'

'I'll find somewhere better, I promise.'

Maeve took a mug of coffee and lifted the duvet so he could climb back in beside her. A shower of impressive hail was clattering against the shell of the caravan. It made Maeve feel isolated, cut off from the real world. They might as well have been on another planet.

She cradled the mug in two hands and took a cautious sip.

It was becoming a habit, a post-coital hot drink and discussion of the state of affairs. It wasn't romantic, exactly, but she liked it, the domesticity of it. They were a team now, with a common enemy, and it wasn't even his wife. It was the two of them against the malicious forces of the big bad world. Love versus evil.

A week previously, Maeve had found her car clamped in the lane. It was blocking pedestrian access to the river walk, apparently. She'd had to pay a fine and apply for a resident's permit. Two days later, she had received a notice from the County Council informing her that recent renovations of a Building of Historic Special Interest, Class 9, were in breach of Part IV, Section 57 of the Planning and Development Act. She was instructed to desist from all further works and cordially invited to appear, in three months' time, before a committee at County Hall, where an appropriate fine and proper course of action would be determined. Tim, after a quick search online, had taken the notice and shredded it. It was a fake, he'd said, scoffing. Class 9 buildings were haysheds, and Paddy hadn't even taken the trouble to copy and paste the County Council logo.

And then, last night, she'd heard a noise in the lane. She'd taken a carving knife in her hand and gone out in the dark only to find Sean Leahy with one foot up on her garden wall, looking very much as though he planned to hop over it. He'd scowled at her, then caught the glint of the knife in the moonlight and slunk away. Maeve had debated whether or not to tell Tim. She didn't want him doing something rash.

'He said he was tying his lace,' she said now, striving to make a joke of it.

'Marra yah,' said Tim, and Maeve burst out laughing.

'Excuse me?'

'Marra yaaah.' He hammed it up.

'I'll never understand Cork people.'

'You don't have to.' He gave her a lascivious grin. 'I understand you.'

'That thing you did with your thumb was *very* good.'

'Might you even say *excellent*?' he asked, and she laughed again.

'You're not a bit needy, do you know that?'

'I can't help it.' His face fell serious and he wrapped his hand around her upper arm. 'When you turned up, I couldn't believe it was for me.'

'Of course it was for you.'

'Really?'

'*Yes*, really.'

'Well, I still can't believe it. I can't believe you still want me.'

Maeve pulled herself out of his grip and sat up facing him, careful that they weren't touching.

'I told you. You *know* that. It was you who—'

'I know. But I think I never quite believed it, even then. I always thought you were *way* out of my league, *way* too gorgeous to really want me. I mean, for God's sake, look at you.' He lifted his shoulders, so that his stomach muscles tightened, and ran his finger from under her arm, to her waist, and over the curve of her hip.

'*Too* gorgeous . . . so *that's* my problem, and there was I, all these years, wondering what I'd done wrong.'

Tim pulled her closer.

'You shouldn't have lied,' he said. He said it so softly, so regretfully, it knocked the wind out of her. Was it all her fault, all this mess? Would it all have gone differently if she hadn't lied?

'I'm sorry,' she said. 'I was trying to play fair.'

'I know you were. We both were. It was nobody's fault.'

She released a long sigh.

'What are we going to do?'

In answer, he kissed her, long and hard.

'Seriously, though?' She leaned backwards and put her hands on his chest.

'I told you, Leahy's an idiot. Don't let him intimidate you.'

'He frightened the living daylights out of me, Tim.'

'He won't hurt you. All he'll do is report to Paddy.'

'And then what? What happens if he sees us together?'

'He won't.' He looked around the caravan as if he was searching for something. 'Anyway, I've more important things to be worrying about.'

'What are you looking for?'

'This hat of yours.'

'Hah. Seriously?'

'Oh God, yes. Come on, you promised.'

He found the hat, put it on her head and kissed her nose, then whipped the duvet off her body. Maeve roared laughing, half from the fun of it and half from the shock of the cold air on her skin.

'Jesus Christ, Maeve. You're so fucking gorgeous.'

'Can I finish my coffee?'

'In a minute.'

57.

The First of February

* * *

The evenings stretched, and Mammy seemed to get happier. She was never tired and never done. It was as if she had a vision in her head that no one else could see, that only she could achieve. She had a mission; she was like the saints Sr. Mary Joseph talked about at assembly.

Every day, when Emer got home from school, the fire was lit, the sofa cushions were plumped, the floors mopped, and Beyoncé or Harry Styles was playing from the little blue speaker on the kitchen windowsill. Mammy might be sitting behind her sewing machine at the oak table making curtains, or she might be standing at the kitchen counter spooning hot chocolate into mugs, or she was in the garden, where every dead tree stump she excavated and every clump of brambles she cleared only drove her to do more.

On this particular Monday, Mammy had cleared a patch right outside the back door and had a bed ready for planting. Flowers, still in their pots, stood in holes, waiting to have their positions in life determined.

'How was school?'

'Fine.'

'Come on out,' Mammy said, when Emer stood in the doorway watching. 'I want you to plant the first flowers for me.' She waved a packet of bulbs so that they rattled.

'They're anemones,' she said. 'For St. Brigid's Day. We'll plant them today, and this time next year this whole place will be covered in blue and pink flowers. Like magic.'

Emer knelt on the damp earth next to her mother. Mammy showed her how to tickle the roots of the pot-bound plants and how to tuck compost around them. They planted shrubs first, then primulas and violas.

'For instant colour,' Mammy said.

Finally, one by one, Mammy dropped the little knobbly anemone bulbs into Emer's palm, and she pushed them into the soil.

'Will they not grow at all until next year?' she asked, disappointed that her contribution was so underwhelming.

'We'll see green shoots before too long. They're reliable little things,' said Mammy. 'Like you.'

She was certain it was a compliment, but something about the way her mother's voice dropped away at the end made Emer feel that reliability was also a failing, of imagination maybe, or of courage. She couldn't think of an answer, so she said nothing.

'Tell you what,' said Mammy, still full of the joys of spring. 'One of these days, I'll dig a pond and we'll get you a fish.'

Emer gasped at the thought.

'I could dig it,' she said.

Mammy laughed at her excitement and then looked around at a clear space near the boundary wall.

'That's my girl,' she said, and passed Emer a spade.

58.

A Promise

* * *

Maeve drove too fast and arrived too early. She drove the length of the beach and up the hill to the cliffs and pulled in at the entrance to the field. A hefty padlock was secured to the handle of the gate. There was nothing for it but to wait for him. She pulled her woolly hat down over her ears. She'd worn it specially, to make him laugh.

The day was dry, the sun climbing into a cloudless blue sky.

I should be in the garden, she thought, and then laughed out loud. It wasn't as if she was going to forfeit *this* for a couple of hours pulling brambles.

It was working out. She could feel it in her gut. Tim was relaxed with her now. He was funny and cheerful. He didn't talk about his marriage, and she didn't ask, but she felt they had crossed some invisible marker. He was *with* Maeve now. He just needed to find a way to leave *her*. Maeve didn't like to say her name, not even in her head. It was only for the children's sake he was staying with her. He'd said as much, more or less. But Emer was his child too. He just didn't know her yet. They didn't have a connection. That was the problem.

She saw his car then, as it made the turn onto the beach road. She got out and braced herself against the blast of sea air. She could see that he was smiling already as he parked his car nose to nose with her own.

'Hiya,' he said, climbing out.

'Hiya yourself,' she said. 'The gate's locked.'

'I have the key here.' He jangled the bunch in his hand and bent to open the padlock on the gate. 'We'd better pull the cars in off the road.'

He didn't say whether the precaution was to avoid the cars being damaged or to avoid them being seen, and she didn't ask him to clarify, but the practicality of it – both of them having to get into their cars and start the engines and manoeuvre through the gateway and park again, discreetly, on the inner side of the hedgerow – made their meeting seem illicit, more tawdry liaison than romantic rendezvous. Tim sensed it too, she thought. He walked from his car to hers and, quickly, kissed her lips.

'Hiya,' he said again, starting afresh.

'Hi.'

He took her hand in his and led her through the field. The long, dewy grass caught the sunshine in glinting sparks that blinded her eyes. You could walk right off the end of the cliff, she thought, if you weren't careful.

While Tim turned the key in the caravan door, she looked down to let her pupils readjust and noticed that the toes of her favourite boots were soaking wet.

'Open sesame.' He stood back and held the door open for her, then followed her inside. Straight away, he grabbed her and pulled her against him, his hand finding the gap at the waistband of her jeans and travelling downwards.

'Tim—'

'Hmmm?' He was opening the zip of her coat.

'Tim.'

'What?'

She imagined it then, a voice saying *don't say what*, but it was only her own voice. It seemed that Greta didn't come out here to the caravan. She probably felt it was beneath her dignity, Maeve thought. She was probably right.

'I was just thinking about Emer,' she said. Tim extracted his hand from her jeans. He looked at her but didn't say anything, so Maeve went on. 'She seems a bit down in the dumps.'

'You're worried about her?'

'I am. I feel a bit guilty, I suppose. We're so happy—' she smiled up at him.

'Yeah?' he grinned.

'Yeah.'

She kissed him, a long kiss with their two bodies pressed together inside the warm cocoon of their coats. It was Tim who pulled away this time.

'I can't encourage the friendship with Pamela. You know that. It just isn't—'

'Right. I know.'

'I'm sorry.'

'No, no. You needn't be. But maybe we could do something for her birthday.'

Tim looked at her blankly.

'It's next week.'

'Of course,' he said, chastened.

'Couldn't we do something together? The three of us?' She bent over and unzipped one knee-high boot, then the other, and kicked them off.

'The three of us?' The concept was obviously alien to him. 'Like what?'

He took a half step back from her, but she moved with him. She untucked his shirt and slid her hands underneath. His heart was beating hard against his chest wall.

'I dunno,' she said, unbuckling his belt. 'An outing of some sort. A picnic?'

'A picnic? In February?' He mirrored her actions and undid the button of her jeans.

'You'll think of something,' she smiled and kissed him. For a second, she nipped his lower lip between her teeth. He inhaled sharply. In one movement, she pushed his jeans and boxers down to the floor and pushed him backwards onto the bed.

'I will,' he said. 'I promise.'

59.

The Birthday Outing

* * *

Mammy pulled into a car park at the edge of town and Pamela's dad jumped into the passenger seat for all the world as if they were making a getaway from the scene of a robbery.

Don't spare the horses, Emer wanted to shout, but didn't.

'Hi, Tim,' Mammy said, as if this was all normal.

'Hi, Emer,' Tim said, turning his head to smile through the gap between the front seats. 'All set for an adventure Out West?'

'Ehm. Yes?' Emer said.

'You take charge of the music,' Mammy said then, passing Emer her phone. 'Tim's taste is not to be trusted.'

'*Shrek?*'

'*Shrek?!*' Tim looked puzzled.

'Go for it,' said Mammy, talking over him.

'Head for Macroom,' he said, indicating a turn to the right.

Tim gave directions to Mammy. Every now and then, he pointed to heritage signposts and talked about gun battles and ambushes. Mammy drove with her usual confidence, turning the steering wheel so that the car hugged every bend in the road. Tim's directions took them through Béal na Bláth, the place where his famous ancestor kept Michael Collins company, he said, in his hour of need. They drove on to Inchigeelagh, then Ballingeary, and the land got rockier and wilder looking.

In the car park at Gougane Barra, Emer sat on the back bumper while Mammy helped her lace up her new boots.

'Pull your socks up over your pants,' Tim said, and Mammy got a fit of giggles.

They divided the picnic between their rucksacks. Tim handed Emer a bunch of bananas and three apples to carry and play-acted teasingly about what was in his own bag.

They walked along Slí na Laoi, the stony path that followed the infant river all the way back to its source. Mammy walked in front and said something polite to everyone they met.

'Hello,' she said, and, 'lovely day,' every single time, but there weren't many hikers. It was still early in the year and the forest park was quiet.

Tim walked behind Emer, not saying much, which she liked.

'Now we'll see what you're made of,' he said when they reached the signpost that pointed up Slí na Sléibhe.

'Hah, do you think you can tire us out?' Mammy was still bouncing.

'I can but try,' he said.

Mammy laughed out loud and ran on again ahead of him and Emer.

'Catch me if you can, slow coaches!' She sang it out, and her voice scared a pair of blue tits from the budding branches of a fuchsia hedge.

They met nobody else at all on the mountain path. Tim seemed to relax, and Emer began to feel less awkward around him. At the very top of the path, with the whole wild countryside, the trees, the flat lake, and the widening river all laid out below them, they stopped and stood in a row, the three of them. Mammy took a tartan rug from her bag and spread it out on the rocky ground. Tim knelt and began unloading food from his bag.

'Ah, sugary duck,' he said, and Mammy giggled again.

'Sugary what now?'

'The flask's after leaking.' He upturned it, demonstrating that, but for a dribble of tea that spilled now in brown drops onto the grass, the flask was empty.

'This is serious,' said Mammy, though Emer could tell from the way she was smiling that it wasn't serious at all.

'No, it really is.' Tim peered inside the bag again, his face grave.

'I know I'm an addict and all, but I won't die.'

'No, but everything is drowned in tea!'

'The sausage rolls?'

Tim lifted a brown paper parcel from the bag and displayed a half dozen soggy sausage rolls. Mammy reached out and lifted one up between two fingers. It drooped miserably and Mammy laughed so hard the top half broke off and dropped back into the bag. She had to suck in a long breath to speak again.

'The cake?' It came out as half laugh, half breathless gasp. Emer by now was laughing too, and even Tim cracked a sorry sort of smile. With both hands, he lifted a cake box. The white cardboard was stained and dripping tea. He held the box out on his wide-spread palm and opened the lid. Emer and Mammy bent over to examine the contents. Inside was a mess of chocolate sponge dissolved in brown liquid with black syrupy cherries floating on top.

'Sugary duck, indeed,' said Mammy.

'Anyone for Black Forest Soup?' asked Tim, and Mammy tipped sideways with laughter.

An hour and a half later, they rounded the lake and took the turn that would lead back to the car park. Mammy, with her arm tucked under Emer's right elbow, was recounting the story of the time Emer had a loose tooth knocked out by an over-enthusiastic boy at the swimming pool, and the coach had dived to the bottom of the pool and retrieved it for her. Tim, laughing, had moved to Emer's left, so that she was flanked on either side. They fell into step together, three abreast, their boots hitting the path in time, step, step, step.

60.

A Bubble of Happiness

* * *

'I'm starving after that.' Maeve secured her seatbelt and put the car into gear. 'There's supposed to be a great pizza place out here somewhere – the crowd that make their own cheese – what do you say?'

Emer, leaning forward between the front seats, nodded her enthusiasm.

'Sure,' Tim said, without a trace of reluctance, and Maeve felt a bubble of happiness rise in her chest. 'I know exactly where it is. I'll direct you.'

The pizzeria turned out to be a whitewashed old farm building attached to a working dairy. Tim, still brimming with cheer, offered to run in and grab a takeaway.

'Let's bring it home. I'll get a bottle of wine too, will I?' He looked at Maeve.

The bubble deflated.

Tim carried on talking in the same accommodating tone of voice.

'That way you'll be able to enjoy some vino with your pizza.'

Maeve looked straight out through the windscreen and tightened her fingers around the steering wheel. She was aware that Emer, in the back seat, had sensed her tension. In the rear-view mirror, she could see her daughter's face was white and her jaw clenched. Emer was holding her breath, Maeve could tell, waiting for what she would say next.

'I'll get a selection, will I?' Tim ploughed on, apparently completely oblivious to the whitening of her knuckles. 'Any objections to pineapple?'

'Tim—' Maeve spoke. She shifted in her seat and turned her shoulders so that she could look him straight in the eye. 'It's Emer's birthday.'

That was all she said.

'Yeah.' Tim nodded and straightened his shoulders, as if to harness his courage.

'Let's just go into that restaurant and have a nice meal.' Maeve lightened her tone. 'Alright?'

She watched as Tim took two deep breaths.

'Right,' he said. He threw a brave smile to Emer. 'Let's go.'

They sat outside at a stone table next to a little fenced-off herb garden where a pair of early bumblebees were dancing over a burst of crocuses. Maeve passed no comment on the fact that it was still nippy for eating al fresco, or the fact that they couldn't have sat any further away from the pizza oven on the patio. She encouraged Tim to order a bottle of Nero d'Avola, but said she'd just have a Coke. He looked like he needed a drink, she said.

It seemed she was right. By the time they'd shared a plate of antipasti, Tim was on his second glass and regaining his earlier good humour.

'I have a p-pizza joke?' Emer said.

'Go for it.' Maeve watched as Emer took a drink, paused to create the necessary suspense.

'Nah, never mind.' Emer started giggling. 'It's too cheesy.'

Tim laughed.

Maeve groaned.

A waitress delivered their pizzas and went back inside the restaurant.

'No black pepper—' said Maeve.

'I'll get it,' said Tim helpfully.

'No, it's fine.'

'No, no.' Tim was jovial and already standing. 'It's my pleasure. Another Coke, Emer, while I'm there?'

'Yes, please,' said Emer. Tim nodded, smiling, and sauntered inside.

'Good pizza?' Maeve asked.

'Hmmm.'

And then, there was Tim, smiles all melted away, coming towards them with rushing steps, close to a jog.

'We have to go,' he said.

'Excuse me?' Maeve was holding a slice of pizza in mid-air.

'I'm sorry. Look, I've paid the bill. Can we go? *Now*.'

'Are you sick?'

'I'll explain in the car.'

'Can we get takeaway boxes? It'll only take a minute.'

'Eh—' He looked over his shoulder towards the patio. 'No, no. It's better if we just go. It's not worth it.'

Tim walked towards the garden's side gate while Maeve gathered her sunglasses and her phone from the table and packed them into her bag. She wrapped her arm around Emer's shoulder and followed Tim to the car park.

'Are you sick?' she asked again, when she'd slid into the driver's seat.

'Just drive on a bit.'

'What the hell?' Her voice rose, but she started the car. She navigated the tight turn left that led to the main road, then asked again.

'What the hell, Tim?'

'Alison fucking Rafferty, that's what.' He said it low, under his breath, as if he was afraid the woman would hear him. His face was chalk white and his skin was sweaty.

'And who, exactly, is Alison Rafferty?'

'Next-door neighbour. Nóinín's best friend.'

'Oh.'

'Yes.'

The yellow Saab slipped on through the countryside. They passed the Béal na Bláth monument again. Tim passed no remark on it this time.

The thought flashed across Maeve's mind that, in their hurry, they'd left Emer standing in the car park. She looked back over her shoulder, and there she was. Of course she was there. The panic subsided and Maeve looked again. Emer was staring out the side window, having done that thing she did, that trick she had of removing herself from reality. She glanced at Tim and saw a not dissimilar expression on his face.

'Look, maybe it's not a bad thing.'

Tim didn't answer.

'Maybe it's time you, *we*, came clean.'

Tim still didn't answer.

'You know, bite the bullet, get it over and done with.' She put her left hand on his leg.

'It's not like that, Maeve. I can't just do that. It's more complicated than you know, and I have children to think about.'

Maeve lifted her hand from his thigh and put it back on the steering wheel.

'Yes. You do have children.' Against her will, her voice got higher and thinner.

Tim's head bent low towards his chest. She had to listen hard to hear what he said next.

'I'm sorry,' he said. 'I'm not ready to take that step.'

Maeve drove on without speaking. She drove fast, took the bends wide, turning the steering wheel with the heel of her hand. She accelerated to overtake a tractor on a blind corner, and Tim put his two hands, splayed wide, on the dashboard in front of him. She tossed her hair and tutted once, in scorn, before braking hard enough to justify his cautionary action, then accelerating again. He turned and looked at her but said nothing.

When they came to the sign that said *Welcome to Drohid, Gateway to West Cork*, Maeve pulled in and stopped the car in a layby that was supposed to be reserved for Gardaí.

'Off you go then,' she said, jutting her chin in the direction of the dusty hedgerow.

'Yeah. You're right. I'll get out here,' he said, acting like it was his own idea. 'I'll buzz you tomorrow. I'll make it up to you, I promise.'

'I don't believe you have it in you,' she said, tipping the accelerator pedal before the car door had closed behind him.

* * *

Maeve played the *Shrek* soundtrack at full volume while they waited for a Lidl frozen pizza to cook. Then she wrapped Emer in a blanket on the sofa and they watched a five-episode marathon of *Gilmore Girls*. She kept all the words – all the accusations and blame that she wanted to spit at Tim – inside her head.

Let it go, said Greta.

Maybe her mother was right. She needed to think about something else.

'I have a plan,' said Maeve.

'A p-plan?' said Emer. Maeve ignored the anxious tone.

'Let's have a girls' day out.'

She'd take Emer to the city to buy new clothes. They'd get their hair done and go somewhere nice for lunch.

She talked about using some scraps of leftover fabric to teach Emer how to make a patchwork cushion cover. She talked about how wonderful it would be to live by the sea.

'I hate small towns,' she said, in the break between episodes while they were opening packets of salt and vinegar Tayto. 'I don't know what I was thinking, coming here.'

You came for him, Greta said.

Jesus, what was this with her mother being right all of a sudden? She came for him. She knew it. But it had been for *all* of them. They would *all* be happier, she'd thought. It had seemed to make so much sense.

When, close to midnight, Emer climbed into bed, Maeve followed her into her room and lay down next to her.

She rubbed her finger from Emer's forehead, down her nose, over her lips to her chin.

'That's how I used to make you close your eyes when you were a baby,' she whispered in the dark.

'I remember,' Emer whispered back.

'No, you don't.' A breath of quiet laughter.

'I do,' she said.

'Alright. I believe you.'

They lay quietly. Even with the windows closed, Maeve could hear the shushing noise of flowing water against the riverbank.

'Mammy?'

'Hmmm?'

'What's the difference between a good p-pizza joke and a bad pizza joke?'

'Oh God. Go on, what?'

'The delivery.'

61.

Back Then, in Cork

* * *

Tim sat staring at the countryside whipping past the train's window – the parched flat of the Curragh, the playground in Monasterevin, Friesian cows grazing the green fields of Tipperary – but he took in none of it. He was too busy rehearsing his break-up speech.

Plenty of lads went off to college and met someone new. Nobody really expected you to spend your entire life with the girl you snogged at the Leaving Cert results night disco. That wasn't part of the speech, mind you. He would say something about coming to the end of his days in college, about moving on, growing up, saying goodbye to childish things, blah, blah . . .

He didn't need to tell her about Maeve. There was no need to be hurtful, and anyway, she'd hear it on the rumour mill soon enough.

Spot on time, the train slowed and entered the long tunnel that presaged its entrance to Kent station. He took a big breath and steeled himself for the ordeal ahead. Just get it over with, he thought, and get the first train back to Dublin in the morning. Maybe he'd convince Maeve to fly to the states with him. He needn't come back to Drohid for years.

* * *

Nóinín hooked her arm through his as soon as he came through the barrier.

'I could have got the bus,' he said.

'I couldn't wait to see you.' She rested her head on his shoulder.

Automatically, his arm wrapped around her waist. She wasn't going to make this easy.

'Where are you parked?'

'Christ, yeah. I'm in the wheelchair space. Come on.' She laughed and extended her stride.

Tim couldn't help admiring Nóinín's innate sense of entitlement. It gave her a fearlessness that showed in all aspects of her life, including her driving. Nothing would do but to be the fastest out of the car park, the first away from the lights. She applied herself to negotiating the traffic on the Lower Glanmire Road. It wasn't until they hit a red light on the quays that Nóinín returned her attention to Tim.

'Well, any *craic*?'

Tim looked out the window. There was nothing between them and the oily depths of the Port of Cork but a few squat bollards and a line of yellow paint.

'Not a bit. Sure, haven't I been up the walls with exams.'

'I *do* have news.' She said it teasingly, throwing him a saucy grin before tipping her indicator and slotting into the faster moving right-hand lane. Tim didn't bother pointing out that they'd be turning left at the lights. He knew Nóinín was going to scoot up the outside of the traffic and then coerce her way back into the correct lane. He knew she couldn't help herself and, look, she'd get there faster. She always did.

'Oh?'

She let the question hang. They were rounding the Elysian, the tallest building in Cork and marker of the start of the dual carriageway. Nóinín moved through the gears and put her foot to the floor so that she could accelerate past a convoy of Dunnes' delivery trucks. Not until she had consolidated her position ahead of the traffic did she ease off the accelerator and put her hand on Tim's knee.

'Nóinín—' he said, thinking that maybe it would be better to cut her off at the pass. He knew by the way she was dragging this out that Nóinín's bit of news was something big.

'Will I tell you?'

'It's just—'

She swung the car neatly around the outside lane of the final roundabout and took the exit for West Cork and Drohid.

'Daddy bought us a house.'

'What? What do you mean?'

They were driving into the lowering sun. She took her sunglasses from their position as a hairband and put them on properly.

'Isn't it brilliant? Daddy said he could hardly believe his own luck. He only went along to the Beecher estate sale out of curiosity. He thought he might splash out and buy the grand piano. He's always wanted one, for the foyer, you know, so he could have someone play show tunes and what have you for wedding receptions.'

The car whipped under the Chetwynd Viaduct and Tim recognised the feeling he always got of passing from one reality to another, as if that giant metal arch had the power to realign his atomic structure. He'd be the Drohid version of himself now, for better or worse.

'He says nobody can get a mortgage. When the auctioneer looked for bids on Cavendish House, they didn't get the reserve. Nobody even offered an opening bid. They were all too afraid they might be held to it. Can you imagine?'

She was spinning this out, he could feel it.

'So, your father bid on it?'

'God, no.'

Oh. Tim had to admit to a pang of disappointment. He'd let himself imagine it – just for a split second – what it would feel like to turn the key on a house like that. There was something *fitting* about it.

'Then that's *not* the house he bought?'

'No . . .' She turned an excited smile to him. She looked good with the sun lighting up her face. 'No, *it is*. He waited until the auction was over and then he went to Agnes Beecher and made her an offer. She's *totally* strapped, you know.'

'No way.'

'She is. Daddy said she nearly took the hand off him to get a bit of cash.'

'Are you serious? Your father just bought you a house in Cavendish Place?'

'Us, Tim! He bought *us* a house in Cavendish Place.' She leaned sideways, flipped open the coin pocket behind the handbrake, and extracted a set of keys on a silver keyring. Nóinín dangled them on the end of her ring finger.

'Want to go take a look?'

* * *

Tim stood looking out the window of the drawing room. The old glass in the sash windows had sunk in ripples to the bottom of each pane so that the light coming through fell in tempered waves across the hardwood floor. The garden beyond was unkempt. The roof of an old wishing well was collapsing, the flowerbeds were full of weeds, and the trees needed pruning to clear the view of the river. Mind you, at least in its current state nobody could see him standing there in all his glory.

'It's gorgeous,' he said, without turning around.

'Hmmm,' said Nóinín from the chaise longue. 'The view's not bad from here either.'

He turned and smiled. He could tell that she had readjusted her posture, thrown back her shoulders and turned her hip, so that her nudity worked for and not against her. It was a tiny display of vulnerability of just the sort that had made him love her. The world saw Nóinín O'Driscoll, the spoilt bitch, but he saw a girl who really and truly loved him, a girl who could have anyone but wanted him. Being that man, the one who had tamed the town shrew, was intoxicating in itself, and it wasn't as if she didn't come with benefits.

She made room for him to lie beside her.

'Is it not a bit cheeky,' he asked, 'on somebody's antique couch?'

'It's *our* antique couch,' she countered, shifting so that she lay on top of him. 'I'll get it reupholstered.'

'You're remarkably blasé about this.'

'Maybe I am. It just feels like destiny, though – you and me, here, now – you know?'

He did. He knew exactly what she meant. All at once, his Drohid self had a pretty good future laid out. Suddenly, his Dublin life felt precarious. His relationship with Maeve seemed juvenile, ill-judged. Everything in this high-ceilinged, well-proportioned room felt, well, it felt right.

'I know,' he said. 'I do.'

62.

A Proposal

* * *

For a week after the pizza fiasco, Maeve told herself she was better off without him, that Emer didn't need him, and neither did she. For a week after that, she told herself that he would come round, that he just needed time, that he was scared, that was all – it was only natural – and she kept her phone nearby, with the volume turned up high, so she wouldn't miss any messages. And for a week after that she blamed her mother.

It was March when the text finally came asking her to meet him in the usual place at the usual hour, cool as a breeze, as if no time at all had passed.

He opened the caravan door before she knocked. He reached out and pulled her into his arms.

'Tim—' she began.

'Shush,' he said and pulled her coat from her shoulders. He covered her mouth with his to stop her talking, and he didn't let her speak until they were done.

'I missed you,' he said then, his face heavy with regret.

'Tim—' She sat upright and pulled the duvet around her body.

'What?'

She sighed.

'*What?*'

'I think I need to leave Drohid.'

'Hah,' he said, but it wasn't a laugh. There was a bitter twist to his mouth. 'I thought you wanted to be near me.'

'I did.' She lowered her voice. 'I do, but my house is too close to—'

'To *my* house?' He finished her sentence.

'Exactly.' She rushed on. 'I saw a place in the *Examiner* last week, out in Schull. It's perfect, only an hour away. I was kind of hoping you might think about—'

He didn't help her.

'You could come with me,' she said. 'Come with us.'

'I'd love to, Maeve. You know that, but it's complicated. You know it is.'

'Is it? Do you think you're the only one who's had to face tough choices? Do you think choosing love is easy? It's not easy. It's not even meant to be easy. It's hard, and it's scary, because loving means risking something. But it's not complicated.' She pulled her body away from his and stood up, naked, at the side of the bed. 'Life is complicated, but *love* isn't. Love is simple.'

63.

Three Things

* * *

Emer sometimes wondered if she actually *had* disappeared. It wouldn't have surprised her in the least if someone had sat on top of her or walked through her in the corridor. She had to remind herself, sometimes, to behave as if she could be seen, to make sure she wasn't caught staring at the other girls, to laugh when they laughed and not when they didn't.

Ever since her birthday, Mammy worked all the time, as if she was up against a clock that was ticking inside her head. It was a relief to Emer, every day, when she came through the front door, to hear the clatter of the sewing machine pedal, or the hammering of picture hooks into walls, or the scratch of sandpaper against the old dresser Mammy had found, literally in a ditch, and had decided to gild with gold leaf. It was a relief because she didn't know what the alternative was. She didn't know what would happen once Mammy's list of things to do was all done. Always, those days, her mother heard her come in, as if she had been listening for her, and always she stopped whatever she was doing and called out.

'How was school?'

Always, Emer said that school was fine.

And always, those days, Mammy had forgotten to eat, forgotten to do any shopping. She had forgotten to put away the breakfast dishes, forgotten to turn on the washing machine, and forgotten even to brush her hair. Every pathway in her brain was focused on one sole purpose: finish the house.

* * *

Sometimes, she'd pull money from her purse and send Emer up to the shop to buy the breakfast rolls they sold all day long. A couple of times, Emer offered to cook. One day, she bought bread and made toast and spooned beans on top, but the next day she made scrambled eggs and they stuck to the bottom of the saucepan, and Mammy scraped and scraped it with the edge of a spoon, and bent her head over the sink and groaned, and the next day they got breakfast rolls.

Emer learned to set the washing machine to a mixed load, so that nothing would run, and she learned to shake out her school pinafore and hang it up so that it wouldn't dry wrinkly. Once, she put it on and it was damp and itchy, and she worried that she'd get chilblains, but she didn't really know what chilblains were, so she put that, at least, out of her head.

Always, those days, Mammy worked late into the night and didn't get up in the mornings, so Emer stood in front of the bathroom mirror and brushed her own hair into a ponytail. She arranged two Weetabix side by side in a bowl and poured in just enough milk that they didn't get soggy. She made a ham sandwich and packed it in her lunchbox, and she closed the front door behind her, pulling it until she heard the lock click.

Because it was bright those mornings, and sunny, and even though it was still against the rules, Emer would turn left on the doorstep, instead of right, and take the river walk up to the footbridge. She liked the quiet of it. She felt more solid when there was no one to see her, or not see her.

And always, those days, she saw a heron standing on the opposite bank, alert, watching, her beak poised to snatch any silver streaking fish that passed too close.

'You can see me,' Emer would say, in her head, but the heron didn't so much as blink.

* * *

And so they drifted on until a day, a Friday, when three things happened all at once.

The river was running high, Miss Murphy said, and warned the class to stay away from it. Obediently, Emer walked home from school the way she was supposed to, across the big bridge, down Bridge Street, and left onto Main Street. Approaching the turning for Weavers' Row, she saw Agnes Beecher uncharacteristically loitering on the corner.

That was the first thing.

'I was hoping to catch you,' she said. 'I wanted to make sure you got this.' She handed Emer the same green book that she had given her at Christmas. The name was there – *The Secret Garden* – in the same gold writing. Emer looked down at the book in Agnes' hand but hesitated to take it. Nothing annoyed her mother more than people doing things behind her back.

'I-I-I c-can't take it,' she said, and shook her head.

'Oh, sweetheart, please,' said Agnes. 'It's only a harmless book, I'm not trying to convert you to devil worship, you know.'

'I know, but Mammy—'

'This is a gift from me to you, Emer. I don't know anyone who deserves to own this book as much as you do. It belongs with you.'

'C-Come down to the house. If—'

'It's no use. I tried before. Your mammy can't stand the sight of me, I'm afraid. I don't want to cause more upset, but when I saw the sign—' Agnes nodded her head down the lane and Emer turned to look.

The afternoon sun lit up the house against a massive heap of black clouds that hung above the river. A large red and black sign protruded from the front of the house so that it would be visible from Main Street. The agent's name was spelled out across the top of the board above unmistakable red letters: FOR SALE.

That was the second thing.

'Go on. Stick that in your bag and say nothing,' said Agnes, letting go of her grip on the book so that it fell and Emer caught it without thinking.

'Thank you.' Emer hugged it to her chest.

'You're more than welcome.' Agnes put one hand briefly on Emer's shoulder. 'Go on. Don't get into trouble.'

Emer stuffed the book into her bag and walked down the lane. She turned her key in the front door and went inside. Mammy was standing at the kitchen counter polishing a coffee pot.

'How was school?' she asked.

'Fine,' said Emer.

They both looked at the coffee pot.

'My secret weapon,' said Maeve. 'The smell of coffee ups the asking price by five per cent, you know. It's a proven fact.'

At that moment a crack of lightning lit up the room, followed the next instant by a thunderous boom. The massive heap of black clouds split open, and it started to rain.

That was the third thing.

64.

The Rain Didn't Let Up

* * *

Two hours later, Maeve stood waiting for the kettle to boil. She didn't want more tea, but it felt like the thing to do. It would, at the very least, give them both something warm to hold on to. The rain was still coming down in sheets, plastering the kitchen window, completely blocking the view.

'Will Rihanna be okay?' Emer asked.

'I'd say she's fine. She's a fish.'

'But what if the p-pond overflows and she gets washed out?'

'Then she'll be in Kinsale for dinner.'

'C-Can I bring her inside?'

'You're being silly, Emer.'

'*Please?*'

Maeve relented. Emer put a raincoat over her head and ran outside to rescue the fish. She put Rihanna into the trifle bowl and placed it on a window sill.

'She'll be safer there, won't she?' she asked.

That's Waterford Crystal, you know, said Greta.

'You worry too much,' said Maeve.

* * *

It rained all through the night, pelting hard against the skylights. It took a long time to get to sleep, and when her alarm went off in the morning, it was still raining. It was still raining an hour after that when she and Emer were sitting at the oak table eating Ryvita crackers spread with Nutella. Emer's head was stuck in one of her birthday books. *Sword of the Sun* it was called. Maeve, with undeniable urgency now, was turning over the property pages of the *Examiner*.

'I need to go shopping,' she said, looking up for long enough to refill her tea-cup.

'I'll c-come.'

'What? No,' said Maeve. 'You'd only be bored. I'll arrange some viewings for next week when you're at school.'

Emer's face twisted in confusion.

Maeve smiled.

'Ah,' she said. 'You mean the cupboards are bare again, are they?'

'A bit.'

'You're right. We'll just give it an hour until this rain lets up, will we?'

She turned to the next page of the property supplement and resumed her study.

* * *

The rain didn't let up. Maeve made more tea. Emer scraped out the end of the Nutella jar with a spoon. They'd had to give up on trying to listen to music because the little blue speaker couldn't compete with the noise of water spilling from the top gutter onto the roof of the scullery. When the first *rat-at-at* sounded on the front door, they didn't react. It might have been a branch falling or the crescendo of another cloudburst, but it came again, louder and more urgent: *rat-at-at*.

'Mal!' Emer pushed back her chair and jumped up. Maeve put down her cup and pressed her lips together.

'Wait,' she said. 'I'll get it.'

It was Malachi, of course it was, standing outside the door in a dun brown raincoat. Despite the hood that was pulled up over his head, the rain was running in rivulets down his solemn, concerned face.

'You'd better step inside,' said Maeve, pulling the door wide open. 'What on earth are you doing here?'

He flinched defensively and Maeve tempered her tone.

'What brought you out, I mean, in this weather?'

He scanned the room, surveying it.

'I thought as much,' he said, half under his breath. 'You fool, woman.'

'*Excuse me*?' Maeve, having just closed the door, turned the latch to indicate that she might open it again and invite him to leave.

'You need sandbags, Maeve. The river's going to burst the bank at high tide.'

Maeve dropped her hand from the latch and wrapped both arms around her body.

'But we're miles from the sea.'

''Tis still tidal at Drohid, though you'd hardly notice most years. They forgot about that when they built that new housing estate at Heron Ridge. They destroyed the floodplain. I'm telling you—' He paused, then lowered his voice. 'Listen to me, the water *has* to go somewhere, and that bank there' – he pointed towards the gap where the Saab was parked – '*right there* is the weakest point.'

'I don't understand.'

'Yerra, look, we all knew. I did, and Agnes Beecher did too.' He looked down at the floor where a mucky puddle was spreading from his Wellington boots. When he lifted his head again his cheeks had two pink dots on them. 'That's how you got your bargain riverside property.'

The words seemed to penetrate slowly through Maeve's brain until the light of full comprehension dawned on her.

'You *fuckers*.'

'Yes.'

Maeve's body crumpled forward, as if she'd been dealt a physical blow to the gut. Malachi stepped towards her and put his hands under her elbows, holding her up.

'Jesus Christ, Malachi.'

'I know. I'm heartily sorry. I really am.'

Maeve sucked in air. Holding tightly to his forearms, she straightened up.

'What do I do? *Tell* me.'

'Sandbags. Right now.'

65.

Floodgates

* * *

On the far side of the swollen river, a hundred yards upstream, two men wearing professional rain gear slotted heavy steel floodgates into concrete posts all along the bank where the river rubbed up against the gardens of Cavendish Place.

Inside Number Five, Alison Rafferty was hosting an impromptu gathering.

'Bring booze,' she'd texted out to each of her neighbours at lunchtime, and within the hour they had rung her doorbell, bottles of artisanal gin clutched under their golf umbrellas.

Nóinín, back from securing her shop, had gathered a crowd around her perch at the kitchen island.

'*And then*,' she said, with an insinuating wink, as she closed her account of how helpful the city firemen had been, 'the Chief carried me in his arms *all* the way to my car.'

'Ah now, that's not fair. How come you get all the fun?' Alison laughed and added a slice of orange to Nóinín's gin and soda. 'Sorry, hon, I'm all out of lime.'

Nóinín took a healthy slug and leaned closer to Alison.

'I'd swap a whole brigade of firemen for a dose of the attention Malachi Barry was laying on down at Weavers' Row.'

'What do you mean?' Alison raised one eyebrow. It was a skill she'd acquired in her teens through long practice and intent study of Vivien Leigh. 'No woman has ever managed to hold that fella's attention, and God knows we all tried.'

'Oh, I'm not saying anything now, only that big Land Rover of his was parked at the top of the lane all afternoon, and himself running up and down delivering sandbags and sandwiches. Bernie in Centra said he was like a madman, took one of every single chocolate bar on the display, and cleaned her out of salt and vinegar Tayto.'

'Go 'way! Malachi Barry with your woman from Dublin? He's a dark horse, that one.'

'Well, it seems she got under that shell of his.'

'Who got under who?' Nóinín's husband wrapped his arm around her shoulder and leaned in to join the conversation.

'Whom,' said Nóinín.

'Nobody says whom,' said Tim. He took the Jameson on ice that Alison was holding out to him and clinked his glass against hers.

'That Maeve Gaffney, apparently,' said Alison, 'and Malachi Barry. Isn't that hilarious?'

Tim Corcoran turned up the corners of his mouth.

'Hilarious,' he said, and knocked back his whiskey.

66.

After Dark

* * *

Malachi Barry emptied his own bag of groceries onto the kitchen table. He'd bought a chicken in the shop, in the hope that he'd convince Maeve to bring Emer and wait out the flood at the farm, but nothing would convince her. She wouldn't come with him, and she wouldn't let him stay. *Stubborn out*, that's what she was.

'I begged her,' he said to Bran, who had risen on his hind paws for a look at the bird. 'Get down from there.'

Malachi took the chicken and put it away in the fridge, then walked over to the sink to look out the window. Rain curtained the glass, obscuring his view of the yard. He turned and walked back to the table, cut a corner off the cheese he'd bought and held it out on his palm. Bran wagged his tail.

'Here. Have that.'

Delicately, Bran took the piece of cheese.

Malachi cut a slice and ate it, cut one slice more and gave it to Bran.

'We could have toast,' he said, and slid two slices from the large loaf into the toaster.

Over the table, his grandmother's clock ticked a stubbornly steady rhythm in counterpoint to the random dashes and whips of the weather. He walked back to the sink and tried again to see out of the back window, but, if anything, the rain was even worse than before.

When they'd eaten, Malachi boiled another kettle of water and carried it upstairs to the bathroom. He used the hot water to shave. He lathered soap over his body and then stood under the cold pulse of water from the showerhead to rinse it off. With a towel wrapped around his hips, he walked into his bedroom. He drew back the curtain and checked that the window was shut tight. Usually, he'd have had a view of the town from here, but not now. There was no view, no visibility, nothing at all beyond the falling sky.

In the darkness, he felt Bran settling into the duvet at the end of his bed.

'You're taking advantage now,' he said, but Bran didn't budge.

They lay still, the two of them, listening.

67.

Burst

* * *

High above the town, the last two nuns in Drohid Convent sat in the so-called sunroom, facing the valley. Sheets of falling water had blocked their view of the river all day, and now that it was night, even the town lights seemed in danger of being washed out.

'Go on, say it,' said Sr. Mary Joseph. 'I know you're dying to.'

'What's that, Sister?' said Sr. Francis, though it was true that the words *I told you so* had been on the tip of her tongue all evening.

'You were right. Had I taken Paddy's offer of a bungalow in the new estate, we'd be down there now, bailing out.'

Sr. Francis limited herself to a rueful smile. What point was there in trying to explain that the river was old? It was old and stubborn and wise to man's ways. It would rise now and show what real power looked like.

'Your brother meant well,' was all she said.

'He did in his eyeball. He wants this land, and he'll have it too. You know he will.'

Over my dead body. Sr. Francis kept the thought to herself. She put her hands into the pocket of her habit and found her Rosary beads.

Sr. Mary Joseph followed her lead and did the same.

'Will it burst, do you think?' she asked.

'It's burst already, girl,' said Sr. Francis. 'It's out of all control now. Do you not hear the roar of it?'

68.

Flood

* * *

Emer woke in her mother's bed in the dark. The downpour was still pelting against the roof slates. It wasn't the sound of rain falling you heard, it was the sound of it landing.

The space beside her in the bed was empty and cold, but she could hear clunking and thumping noises coming from downstairs. She grabbed a grey hoodie belonging to her mother from the end of the bed and pulled it over her head.

She found Mammy pulling towels from the hot-press under the stairs.

'Is the water c-coming in?'

Her mother didn't immediately answer. She was standing on the bottom shelf and stretching to reach the towels at the top.'

'Mammy?'

'We can stop it.' With a stack of tea towels in her arms, Mammy ran to the front door.

'Help me, Emer, please.'

Emer brought two bath towels, and Mammy pressed them into the gaps between the sandbags where water had begun to leak through.

'I think the soil is soaking up the water in the back garden, but in the lane it has nowhere to go. It must be over the doorstep.'

Emer ran to look out the window, but all she could see was her own pale face reflected in the glass.

'Can you give me a hand?' Mammy hauled a dry sandbag from the heap against the back door. Emer ran to help her. They took a corner each and dragged it across the floorboards to pile it against the wet ones at the front door, then did the same again with the next bag.

'See if there's anything else upstairs we can use.'

Mammy knelt on the floor, ramming a crocheted blanket under the edges of the sandbag wall. Straight away, the yarn darkened as it filled with brown river water.

'Get the dustpan,' Mammy shouted.

Emer, halfway up the stairs, turned back and ran to the kitchen.

'And the basin from the sink.'

Emer grabbed the basin.

'And an oven tray.'

Not understanding why, Emer pulled a tray from inside the oven.

Mammy took the oven tray and used it to catch the water that had begun to pool on the floor. She scooped it up and spilled it into the basin.

'You use the dustpan. See?' She demonstrated how Emer could do the same.

'It's working!' said Emer, but when Mammy ran to empty the basin into the kitchen sink, Emer couldn't hold back the flow and had to hop backwards out of the rippling influx.

'It's coming in, Mammy!'

'It won't be much. Don't worry. The tide has to turn.' Mammy stood looking at the steadily spreading puddle. She closed her eyes and breathed in very slowly, praying, maybe, or gathering strength.

'Alright,' she said. 'I'll need your help.'

She handed Emer a plastic grocery bag. Then she lifted one corner of the oak table and instructed Emer to fit the plastic bag over the table leg. Emer did as she was told, and Mammy tied garden twine around the top to hold it up.

'Waterproof stockings,' she said, as they repeated the process on all four legs. 'Very fetching.' Mammy laughed, but Emer knew it was the forced, empty kind of laugh that came when her mother was getting close to giving up.

By the time they had lifted the legs of the velvet sofa onto four upturned saucepans, a slick layer of muddy water had covered half the room.

'Oh, Mammy.' Emer pointed to the floor inside the back door where a long, fat garden worm was wiggling energetically inwards to escape the rising water that followed him in, seeping out from the wall of sandbags and moving fast.

'Ah.' Mammy stood at the centre of her home, with her pyjamas tucked into her wellies, her face red and sweaty. She looked at the worm and raked her hands through her hair. She turned in a slow circle. She shook her head, then looked straight at Emer.

'Upstairs. Now.'

69.

I've Got You

* * *

Maeve stepped down into the floodwater in response to a knock on the front window. The water was freezing. It soaked up her legs, crawling, like a living thing.

A wobbly line on the walls, four feet above the skirting boards, marked the extremity of the flood. The river had filled the kitchen cupboards and the hot-press. It had swamped the fireplace. It had climbed above the plastic bags wrapped around the legs of the oak table and soaked through the cushions of the purple velvet sofa.

'Oh. Thank God,' said Tim, when she pulled the window open. He was dressed in waders and wet gear. His face, in the dawning light, was strained. The rain had stopped, though the sky was the colour of wet cement, low and heavy-looking.

'The curtains!' Closing her eyes to the rest of the catastrophe, Maeve lamented the curtains. 'I should have taken down the curtains.' It was the only thing she could see that she could have done differently.

'Jesus Christ, Maeve.'

Maeve stepped back to make space, water swirling around her, and Tim made an attempt to climb through the window. His shoulders caught on the frame and, frustrated, he retreated to the footpath. 'Why did you not reply to my messages?'

You were a bit busy, said Greta.

'I was a bit busy,' said Maeve. Telling herself that the edge to his voice was only down to concern, she relented. 'Sorry.'

'No, I'm sorry,' he said, with his head stuck through the window. His eyes widened as he looked around the room. 'I was just so worried, all night long. I didn't sleep a wink, and then there was no sign of your car, and I thought that maybe you'd left, you know, gone somewhere.'

'Where would I go?'

'Sorry, no, of course. I was just so worried about you, both of you.'

'My phone's dead,' she said, explaining herself. 'We've no power.'

He looked up at Emer. She was standing on the turn of the stairs, just above the water.

'Are you okay?' Tim asked, over Maeve's head.

Emer nodded.

'You're a great girl,' he said, nodding back. He put a hand under Maeve's chin and raised her face to his.

'Come on, love. Let's get you out of here. You can do nothing until the water goes down.'

'But surely—'

'No. There's no point. Go on, get some warm clothes. We'll find somewhere to sit it out.'

'Where?' The word sort of fell out of Maeve, with no energy behind it.

'I know a place,' said Tim.

A knot of tension between Maeve's shoulder blades, the place where she held herself up, gave way.

'Okay so.'

She threw a change of clothes for each of them into a plastic shopping bag and passed it out through the window to Tim. Next, she helped Emer clamber out. Tim lifted her and sat her on the windowsill to wait.

'Come on,' he said to Maeve with a challenging grin on his face and his arms held wide. He took a step towards her and she fell into his arms, suddenly crumpling, as if the water had just at that moment soaked all the way through to her bones. Tim pressed her head into his chest and rubbed her hair and made shushing noises.

'You're alright now. I've got you.'

She felt a sob of relief rising in her chest.

'Thank you,' she said, holding on to the warm, dry reassurance of his body. 'I was at the end of my—'

'I know,' he said. 'Don't worry now. It's all over. Let me take care of you.'

She hung in his arms, completely worn out. She'd lost. She could see that now. She didn't have the money or the energy to start over in a house that was only going to flood, again and again. They'd blame it on climate change, she supposed, that incorporeal beast, not on their own greed, and most galling of all was the fact that Paddy O'Driscoll would get exactly what he wanted. He'd be rid of the thorn in his side and he'd gain a few more tarmacadamed parking spaces into the bargain.

'He's won, hasn't he?'

'What?'

'The fucking weather did the job for him. I've nothing left to fight for.'

'Don't think about it now. You need to take a breath. Come on.'

She nodded weakly.

'We'll have to take your car,' he said. She registered the wary note in his voice. He was calculating the risks, she thought, working out his chances of getting out of town with her without being spotted.

'Yeah, grand,' she said, exhausted. She had to close her eyes to focus on remembering where Malachi had said he'd parked it. 'It's up the hill.'

Tim carried Emer on his shoulders as he and Maeve waded up the lane. At the corner, Maeve threw a questioning glance towards the windows of the Drohid Arms.

'Don't worry,' Tim said. 'He's up the town already doling out free coffee to the army lads.'

In Main Street, water was gurgling up from the drains and lapping at the edges of the footpath, but Emer could walk without wetting her feet. They located the car and Maeve changed into dry jeans behind the shelter of the open door.

'Alright if I sit in?' asked Tim, holding his palm upwards and catching a stray drop of rain.

'Of course.' Maeve sat in the driver's seat and tied her laces. 'Right, tell me where to go.'

He took out his phone and thumbed a text message, pressed *Send*.

'High ground,' he said, with an encouraging smile.

70.

Photo Op

* * *

After a couple of failed attempts, Nóinín succeeded in hitting the button on the radio alarm clock. Her head felt like someone had poured concrete in through her eye sockets. She rolled over and reached in the opposite direction to see whether Tim could be prodded into producing a cup of coffee with a side of Solpadeine.

Tim wasn't there. His pillow was undented, and the sheet was still tucked in. Tim had never come to bed. He was probably up at the top of the house, tapping away at his Greek goddess. *Jesus.*

Her phone vibrated on the bedside table, and she picked it up – a message from Tim.

> Gone to lend a hand.
> Back by lunchtime.

That was Tim all over, always doing the right fucking thing.

Her phone buzzed again. Her father this time. Christ Almighty, did they all know what time her alarm went off? Yeah, they probably did.

> shop dry as a bone
> had leahy on watch all nite
> u shld get down here asap
> lots of cameras
> Dad XX

Her father was right. This was too good a publicity opportunity to be wasted. If the flooding was bad enough there might even be a national news crew.

But what to wear? She needed to look stressed but not haggard. One of those nice sailing jackets she'd got in would be just the ticket. She'd wear one that was a few sizes too big. That would look more dramatic.

71.

Resolution

* * *

Agnes pressed ground coffee into the moka filter, screwed the pot together, positioned it on the gas ring, and lit the flame. The clock on the oven flipped over from 07.59 to 08.00. Agnes hit the button on the top of the radio to turn it on – she would catch the local news – and placed a coffee cup on the counter beside the cooker.

Drohid's Main Street was passable this morning, the newsreader said in an unreasonably jaunty tone. The majority of businesses had escaped flooding, thanks to the new floodgates provided by the town council, but all of Arthur's Quay, Donovan's Quay, Brewery Lane, the river walk, and Weavers' Row were under significant amounts of water. Army personnel were working to rescue a number of small animals from the vet's surgery on Arthur's Quay and to remove cars that had been abandoned. The public were advised to avoid the town centre. Further updates would be issued by the town council throughout the day. *Stay tuned to 94.5 FM,* your *local radio for* your *local news.*

Paddy O'Driscoll's mouthpiece, that's all they were. Agnes turned the dial to Lyric FM where some wit was playing Chopin's 'Raindrop'.

She was determined now, after a night of soul-searching: she would unburden herself of this horrible guilt. She must. She would tell Maeve the whole truth, all of it, how she was strapped for cash even though everyone thought she was stinking rich, and how her pride and her greed had got the better of her, how selling the old house on Weavers' Row, while it still *could* be sold, had seemed a sensible choice, financially at least, and how, in all honesty, she hadn't given a second thought to the morality of it, or to the person who would buy a doomed home. She would make her confession, she would plead forgiveness, and then she would offer restitution.

Coffee gurgled up through the filter and the delicious aroma raised her spirits. There was plenty of space here at *Ard na Mara*. She would convince Maeve to come out and stay with her, at least while the house at Weavers' Row was being cleaned. There was no way anyone could stay in a drowned house with a small child. Maeve would see sense. Where else *could* she go?

And then, later on, they'd figure something out. Maeve and Emer could stay with her for as long as they wanted.

She picked up her phone and checked the screen. There were no messages. With the tip of her index finger, she tapped the *Contacts* icon and scrolled through the names: Fiat, the garage; Ann Fleming, her hairdresser; Joe Flynn, the electrician; Forde, the dentist; Maeve Gaffney.

With a hesitant fingertip, she hit *Call* and waited.

'Hello. This is Maeve Gaffney . . .'

It was a recorded message.

Agnes hung up. She was glad she had tried. Somehow, she felt better already. She would try again in a minute, and she would keep trying until Maeve answered.

On the radio, Marty Whelan was telling a joke about a bear who went into a bar and couldn't decide what to order.

Why the big pause? asked the barman.

I dunno, answered the bear, *I was born this way.*

Agnes smiled. She must remember that one to tell Emer.

72.

Getting off Lightly

* * *

Alison Rafferty kicked off her wellies at the back door and listened hard. *Not a peep, thank God.* She didn't know what had possessed her to go inviting the Corcoran kids to sleep over.

The new floodgates had worked a treat anyway. That was something. The lower level of the garden was a marsh, and the upper terrace was boggy, but it was the opposite bank that had given way. Cavendish Place had gotten off lightly.

The fresh air had cleared her head. A cup of tea and she'd be right as rain, then she'd make breakfast for the kids. Poor Nóinín would be paying the price right about now, she thought. Jesus, she'd really been laying into the gin and sodas, and pretty light on the soda. She'd even eaten a slice of focaccia. It wasn't like her.

Alison gave herself a pat on the back for having cleared all the glasses into the dishwasher before she went to bed. She hit the switch at the back of the kettle and used the remote control on the counter to turn on the radio.

Stay tuned to 94.5 FM, your *local radio for* your *local news,* said Carmel O'Reilly. Alison knew Carmel well. They'd served together for years on the committee of the convent school's parents' association. Alison scrolled through her phone to Carmel's number and fired a quick text.

* * *

> Hi Carmel
> What's the story?
> Can I go to the shops or what?

The reply pinged back while she was pressing her teabag against the side of her *Best Mum Ever* mug.

> Great drama
> Burly men in uniform left right and centre
> What more could you want?

Alison smiled. Carmel was always the best of *craic*. Between sips of tea, she sent a series of texts to everyone in her contacts who'd be worrying about her, and last of all a message to Nóinín asking if she was doing alright.

The reply came instantly in the form of a photo: Nóinín, dressed in a capacious white coat, her face a picture of empathy as she cradled a shivering golden retriever puppy in her arms.

73.

High Ground

* * *

Following Tim's directions, Maeve drove out of town heading south and took a left turn onto a narrow road that wound steeply up a hill and then down into a valley.

'Are you sure about this?' said Maeve.

'Keep going,' he replied, and she did. The road was wet and muddy and littered with snapped branches.

'Here,' he said, when after fifteen minutes they came to a wide junction that was flanked on either side by a butcher's shop and a pub with no name. Neither business was open for visitors. It was, after all, only a quarter past eight in the morning. He pointed to a narrow gateway at the side of the pub that led to a paved courtyard. 'Pull in there.'

She parked alongside the only other car in the yard, a pre-millennium Corolla. As they got out, she saw Emer pull her coat around her body. Even though the heater in the car had been on full blast, she still hadn't stopped shivering.

'What's the plan, Tim?' Maeve directed Tim's attention towards his daughter.

He nodded sympathetically.

'Trust me,' he said.

At that moment, a narrow plank door at the back of the pub swung open.

'Tim!' said a dark-haired man whose bulk almost completely filled the doorway. He beckoned them in. Tim paused to shake the man's hand, then turned to introduce Maeve.

'This is my cousin, William Corcoran.'

'Billy,' he said.

'Maeve Gaffney.' She took a firm grip of Billy's hand.

'I'm sorry now, but ye know it's Sunday, don't ye? I'm not licensed to open for hours yet.'

Tim turned on his smile.

'This is the woman I was telling you about, who's been renovating Weavers' Row. She was flooded out last night, Bill. You wouldn't deny her a hot cup of tea?'

Billy gave Tim a calculating look.

'You're *that* Maeve Gaffney.' He spoke slowly. 'Ah sure, no. I wouldn't turn ye away at all. Come into the snug.'

The snug, it turned out, was a small room, separated from the rest of the bar by stained-glass partitions, with two green leather benches on either side of a ring-marked table. Tim waited until Emer and Maeve had slid into opposite seats and then he sat down next to Maeve. Billy told them to make themselves comfortable and went away. They heard a clatter of cupboard doors before he came back with a little electric fan heater.

'Ye look frozen to the bone,' he said in his thick drawl as he plugged it in. 'Will ye not have a bit of hot breakfast?'

'You're very kind but—' Maeve felt a kick on her shin from Emer. 'Yes, thank you. That would be great.'

'You're a legend, boy,' said Tim.

'What have you been telling people about me?' Maeve asked, when Billy had left.

Tim threw a cautionary glance across the table to where Emer sat cleaning mud from under her fingernails.

'Billy knows the whole story.'

'Good to know *somebody* does,' said Maeve.

74.

To the Rescue

* * *

Malachi woke up with a start. Bran was licking his ear.

'Yerra, stop, you daft dog.'

He closed his eyes again, and tried to regain the dream, even just for a second, but she was gone, and Bran was persistent in conveying the urgency of his need to get outside. Stretching to pick up his phone, Malachi felt the ache in his arms. Carrying all those sandbags hadn't been as effortless as he'd let on. He looked at the time: 8.30am.

'*Shite.*'

Bran, making solid eye contact, whined in concurrence.

Malachi sat at the side of the bed and scratched his head. He'd been awake all night. He'd been awake when the rain stopped at half five, and he'd thought to himself that he'd wait until six and then drive down to the town to check on them, Emer and Maeve, and then he must have conked out.

'Shite,' he said again.

Bran whined, reiterating his agreement.

'Shower or no shower?'

Bran dipped his head to one side.

'You're right. There's not much point when I'm going to be up to my oxters in muck.'

Malachi pulled on jeans, a sweatshirt, and socks. His boots, he knew, were on the floor inside the back door. In the kitchen he went to make tea then, remembering that the kettle was upstairs, decided not to bother. He smeared butter on a slice of bread and ate it while he was pulling on his boots. He passed the last crust to Bran, who gulped it down and sat at Mal's knee, waiting.

'You want to come with me this time?'

Bran licked his hand, and Malachi almost laughed.

'You're a pal, do you know that?'

* * *

The flood had receded, but thick silty mud coated the surface of the street. Bits of rubbish, plastic bottles and streaks of paper lay wherever they had run aground. Malachi drove slowly as far as the entrance to Weavers' Row, but didn't turn in. The river was still lapping at the doorsteps.

He parked on Main Street. Bran, sitting on the passenger seat, gave a low growl.

'Wait here,' Mal said. 'I'll come back for you.'

He went into the Centra and bought two lattes and one hot chocolate. With the three takeaway cups balanced in the slots of a grey pulp cardboard tray, he waded through the water all the way down to the sandbagged door of Number Three. The end of the lane was so deep underwater that the fence that usually divided it from the riverside walkway was still half submerged.

The *rat-at-at* of his knock on the door seemed to travel along the surface of the floodwater, reverberating around him. He imagined the sound of it, riding like a twig all the way to Kinsale and on out to sea.

He knocked again, and again.

Nobody answered.

The curtains were open at one of the two windows, and he noticed the window frame was slightly ajar. It had been closed over, but not secured on the inside. He curled his fingers around the frame, pulled the window open and leaned inside.

'Maeve!' He felt awkward about shouting her name.

'Emer! Are ye there?'

He could see water on the floor inside the house. It was above the first step of the stairs and looked as though it had been a fair bit higher than that.

'Maeve!' He leaned further in, but his shoulders caught on the window frame, and he knocked the tray of hot drinks into the house. The cardboard tray tipped sideways and frothy milk spilled out to mix with brown water.

'Hello! Emer!' Malachi shouted louder and tried twisting his body sideways, but it was no use. He couldn't fit through the window.

'*Where the hell—?*' Huffing like a bull, Malachi pressed the window flush against its frame, and splashed back up the lane.

75.

A Long Story

* * *

Billy Corcoran brought plates of sausages and black pudding and two fried eggs each. As he laid the plate in front of her, Maeve noticed that his baby finger was shorter than it should have been, that it had no nail on it. It came back to her, then, the story about the hurling cousin who stole some fella's girl and paid the price in flesh.

'I'm sorry I've no bacon,' he said. 'I had rasher sandwiches for my tea last night. Will ye be alright without?'

'This is savage altogether,' Tim said, and Maeve resisted the urge to comment on his Corkisms.

Billy went behind the bar then and came back with a steaming glass of hot whiskey, complete with a cinnamon stick and a clove-studded slice of lemon, which he placed in front of Maeve.

'That will fortify you,' he said.

Maeve thanked him and took a sip from the glass. The hot toddy tasted of honey and spice, and the kick of the whiskey seemed to clear the damp out of her head.

'God, that's good,' she said, and offered the glass to Tim's lips. 'Have some.'

He winced and held up his hand in refusal.

'Too early for me. I'll stick to coffee.'

Maeve gave him a grateful smile, that he was allowing her this indulgence. It felt like an expression of empathy from both men, a nod of admiration for what she'd gone through and how well she'd coped. She felt the heat of the drink sinking through her and let herself think, for the first time since Malachi Barry had turned up with his awful revelation, that maybe the worst was over, that maybe she had turned a corner, that things were going to be alright.

'Will you not sit down with us?' she said to Billy.

'I will so.' He took a low stool from outside the snug door and pulled it up at the end of the table.

'Are you married, Billy?' Maeve wanted to know what had become of the girl so badly wanted.

'I'll tell you now, Maeve. That's a long story.'

'My favourite kind.' She gave him her best smile. 'I could do with a bit of distraction. Tell me what happened.'

Billy threw an *I-see-what-you-mean* look to Tim.

'She won't let up, Bill. You may as well tell her.'

'Alright. Let me get a real drink, so.'

He stood and walked to the bar, leaned over, and grabbed a bottle of Jameson.

76.

The Spare Key

* * *

When he opened the car door Bran yelped and wagged his tail.

'Not yet.' Malachi sat into the car and pulled the door closed. He pulled out his phone, found Maeve's number, and hit *Call*.

'Hello. This is Maeve Gaffney.' Malachi drew a breath, but Maeve's voice didn't give him a chance to speak. 'I'm unable to take your call, but please do leave a message.' The recording ended and a beep sounded. Malachi couldn't think what to say. He pressed *End Call* and put the phone on the dashboard.

'What do I do now?'

Bran made a low growling noise in his throat.

'What's that supposed to mean?'

Malachi picked up the phone and redialled Maeve's number. Again, he listened to her voice and, just ahead of the beep, he spoke.

'Eh, it's Malachi Barry here. I'm just calling to check that you're both alright. Let me know if I can help.' He paused. 'Bye now.'

He ended the call and sat staring at his phone's screen. Mindlessly, he scrolled backwards through his list of contacts until he saw Agnes Beecher's name. Could they be with her? The phone rang just once before she picked up.

'Hello.' Her voice was taut.

'Hello, Agnes. It's me.'

'Is something wrong? Are they safe?'

Her words told him all he needed to know. He would have hung up straight away, only he felt sorry for her.

'Divil the bit wrong, Agnes, so far as I know.'

'Have you been down there? They said on the radio that it's flooded. I was going to drive down myself, but you know Maeve—'

Running out of patience, Malachi cut her off.

'That's the thing, Agnes. I'm at Weavers' Row now. I'm sure they're fine, but there's no answer at the door. I'd feel better if I could just check inside, but I can't get in—'

It was her turn to cut him off.

'I have a key. Stay where you are. I'll bring it to you.'

'Agnes—'

She had already hung up.

'Right so,' he said, and put the phone back in his pocket. Bran leaned over and licked the back of Mal's hand.

'Good idea.'

He walked to the Centra again and dispensed black coffee into a takeaway cup, then queued at the deli counter for two sausage rolls, and a bag of sliced chicken for Bran. By the time he left the shop, it was raining again, fat drops splattering circles into the mud. He ran, sheltering the bag of sausage rolls inside his coat, aware of the ground slipping under his feet.

'It's like the end of the world,' he said, banging the car door shut behind him.

Bran stood up hopefully on the passenger seat.

'It's apoca-feckin-lyptic boy.'

77.

You'll Be Grand

* * *

It was raining again when they left the bar and her mammy held Emer's hand in hers so she wouldn't slip on the muddy tarmac.

'You'll have to drive,' Mammy said, handing her keys to Tim as they ran with their heads bent against the deluge. 'I'm well over the limit.'

'You only had a couple of hot toddies.'

'They were stiff ones.'

'I've never driven an electric car,' Tim said. He held his hands up to show how he didn't want to drive.

'There's nothing to it,' Mammy told him, and she held the passenger seat forward so that Emer could climb into the back. 'You'll be grand.'

Emer thought Tim said something else to her mother over the roof of the car, but she didn't hear what it was.

'I've got more immediate concerns than that today,' Mammy said, pulling her seatbelt across her chest and plugging it in.

Tim started the car and pulled out.

'I'll go back by the coast road, so,' he said to Mammy, and then, smiling over his shoulder, he said to Emer, 'Hold on tight!'

He manoeuvred the car cautiously from the courtyard and around the T-junction, but then gathered confidence once he was on the road to Drohid.

'She's pretty nippy,' he said, with a laugh in his voice as the car gained momentum on a long downward slope.

Mammy didn't answer. She'd gone quiet. Tim turned his face to her and put his hand on her leg.

He doesn't know the signs, Emer thought.

'Why didn't you come sooner?' There was a croak in Mammy's voice. It got too loud and then too quiet.

'What do you mean?'

She said nothing.

'I came at the actual crack of dawn. Like, I was *actually* looking out the window waiting for the sun to rise.'

'Why didn't you come last night?'

He didn't answer immediately. He acted as if he was concentrating on a bend in the road, but Emer could tell he was only pretending.

'You know why,' he said eventually, very quietly.

'That's bullshit.'

'It is not bullshit. You know very well that I have a family.'

'Are we not your family? Is Emer not your family?'

The words made Emer feel hollow inside.

'What do you expect me to do, Maeve?' Tim turned sideways in his seat. His face was red, and he spat his words. 'Do you think I can just—?'

Between the tight, angry faces, Emer saw a small, dark brown cow standing in the middle of the road. It took her a second to know what to do and then, as loud as she was able, she shouted.

'LOOK OUT!'

Tim turned back to the road and braked hard, swivelling the steering wheel to the left, avoiding the cow, and ploughing instead along the side of the ditch, briar roses scrawling the windows.

'Oh fu—' Tim began, as a small blue car reversed out of a pillared gateway into their path. Mammy, twisted sideways in her seat, put one hand over her own face and raised the other over the gap between the seats to shield Emer.

There was a sickening crunching sound that went on and on as the Saab's long nose inserted itself into the flank of the blue Fiat, folding it in half around itself and pinning it against the granite gatepost.

'Oh Jesus Christ,' said Tim, with his two hands clenched on the steering wheel.

'Are you hurt?' Mammy leaned between the front seats to see Emer.

Emer shook her head. The seatbelt had cut into the side of her neck, and her heart was hammering like a wild animal trapped inside her chest.

'No,' she said, as much because it felt like the only appropriate word to say as because she thought it was the correct answer to the question.

'Stay right there.' Mammy unbuckled her own seatbelt. She tried the door handle, but it was jammed. She turned her back to Tim and used both her legs to kick the door open, then climbed out.

Emer's heart kept pounding. She made herself take three deep breaths. Tim had put his head down on the steering wheel, as if he had fainted. The Saab's bonnet had popped and folded upwards, blocking the view. Emer couldn't see the driver of the blue car and she was too scared to crane her head for a better look. She didn't want to see someone bloodied, or worse. She turned her head to the high wall on her left. The brick was bright red from all the water that had soaked into it. Through the open passenger door, she could read the blue and white cast iron sign on the gatepost, the name of the house: *Ard na Mara*.

This was where Agnes lived.

That was the blue car Agnes drove.

Behind the car, in the middle of the road, the small brown cow stood, making exactly the noise Emer felt was trapped inside her head.

Bawling.

Mammy reappeared at the open door. Her hair was wet and plastered down her face.

'Tim! Are you alright?'

Tim raised his head.

'Yeah, I hurt my knee, off the car key, I think, but I'm okay.'

'I need help. Please. *Come on!*' Mammy reached in and pulled on his sleeve, then turned to Emer and reissued her warning, even more vehemently than before. 'Stay where you are. Do not move. I'll be back.'

She disappeared again. Tim tried and failed to open the driver's side door, so he clambered over the gear stick and crawled out.

'I'll get the cow,' he said, walking around the back of the car. With his two hands held out wide from his body, Tim walked at the cow.

'Hup, hup,' he said loudly. 'Get off the road, you fucking hoor you. Fuck off now.'

The animal looked shocked but stopped her braying. She kicked out a hind leg and trotted away, through the farm gateway opposite and up the lane, returning, in all likelihood, by the same route she had used to escape.

Tim rattled the heavy wrought iron gate out of the ditch and pulled it closed. He turned back then to the mashed-up cars, but stopped a yard away, stood like a statue, holding his two hands to his head.

'Maeve,' he said. 'You'll have to say that you were driving.'

'What?'

Don't say what, Emer thought, and then thought how bad the situation must be. Her mother's voice seemed strained and distant.

'Phone an ambulance, will you? She's not moving. I can't see her breathing.'

Tim took out his phone and stabbed at it. He turned to the wall to shelter the screen from the rain.

'Oh God. I can't find her pulse. Oh *God*. Tell them to hurry.'

'Hello,' said Tim, walking around the back of the Saab as he spoke. 'Yes. Ambulance, please. There's been a car accident. About two miles out of Drohid, out the coast road. Two cars.' Tim's words were chopped up, like he was answering a series of questions. 'Tim. Ehm, Corcoran. Yes. I don't know. There's a woman hurt. She's not breathing. No. Okay. Yes. Thank you.'

He put his phone in his pocket and walked back to the gatepost.

'They're on their way. They won't be long.'

'Thank God.' Emer could only just make out what her mother was saying.

'I can't be involved in this, Maeve,' said Tim.

'What?'

That was twice now her mammy had said *what*.

'Nóinín. If she hears that I was driving your car, it'll be all over. There's no way I can explain it.'

'Are you serious? I'm trying to keep this woman's blood inside her body right now. Do you think we could discuss this later?'

'I'll say I was walking by, okay? I'll say it wasn't your fault. I'll tell them about the cow.'

'I'm over the limit, Tim. You know that.'

Tim put his two hands on his head again, as if he could squeeze a solution out of his brain.

'Look, at the very worst, you'll lose your licence. I'd lose my marriage, my kids, my home, everything. Come on, Maeve, surely you can be reasonable.'

Emer held her breath, the better to hear her mother's reply. For a long moment there was no sound from the other car. The silence was interrupted by the wail of an approaching siren.

'*Please?*'

Across the road, the small brown cow had walked back down the lane and was standing with her head over the gate, watching.

'Maeve?'

Mammy didn't answer.

78.

Back Then, in Dublin

* * *

'She can't be pregnant,' said Maeve. 'How can she be pregnant?'
'She is.'
'Then you were still—' She paused. 'You were with *her*, were you, during your weekends in Cork?'
'Of course I wasn't. It was before. She's more pregnant than you.'
Maeve released a contemptuous scoff.
'You can't be more pregnant than someone else, Tim. It's an absolute. One is or one is not pregnant.'
He looked repentant, or maybe embarrassed. She was finding it hard to tell. Her heart was rapping against her ribcage, and she felt light-headed. She was standing at the bedroom window, her view dominated by the external structure of the Aviva Stadium soaring above her head. She'd have had to lean out the window to see the top of it. Two cars were parked in the driveway, along with a couple of bikes, all belonging to the other lads from Cork who shared the house. Everyone was home. Everyone was listening. They should have waited until they were alone, but he'd pulled her upstairs the minute he got back from Cork and dropped this bombshell. His ex was pregnant.
She sat down on the corner of his bed, took a long, deep breath, and waited for him to speak.
'What I meant was that it was before, you know, before I met you. It must have happened when I was at home for the Easter holidays. It was just . . . I was planning to break up with her . . . I didn't even—'

'Stop.'

But he didn't. He couldn't seem to stop talking.

'I think she did it on purpose, Maeve. I really do, the more I think about it. She knew I was going to break up with her once the exams were over. She knew I wasn't planning on moving back to Cork. I think she—'

'Stop.'

He sat down beside her at the end of the bed. Their knees, she noted, were nearly brushing the wall. It was a stupid place to sit.

'I'm so fucking sorry, Maeve,' he said. 'I don't know what to do.'

'Do you think I did it on purpose too?' she asked, looking straight ahead at the wall. It was painted a luminous shade of yellow, to counteract the shade of the stadium, she supposed. There was a bit of Blu Tack stuck to it, right in front of her face. She imagined scraping it off with the tip of her fingernail but couldn't quite bring herself to reach out and do it. She felt frozen, paused, stuck in that moment.

'Of course not,' he said. She listened to every sound, trying to analyse his tone for any hint of doubt.

'Why not?'

'Because I love you,' he said, without any hint of hesitation.

'But that doesn't mean anything, Tim.'

'It means I trust you. I know you wouldn't try to trap me.'

There it was. Her mother had warned her. *No man wants to be trapped*. Sooner or later, he would hate her for it. Sooner or later. He would *hate* her.

She stood up, turned, and put her back against the wall. He had his head down in his hands. She looked at his lovely golden hair, the way it curled against the skin of his neck.

'Well, you're off the hook on that score anyway.'

'What do you mean?'

He looked up at her. His face was stony white, bloodless.

'It was a false alarm.'

'You mean you're not pregnant?' It was there, unmistakable, the lowered tone of relief.

'You don't have to be with me unless you want to.'

She held his eye for as long as she could, but he looked away. He put his head down again and groaned.

'Can't you just support her?' Maeve said, clinging to a scrap of hope. 'You know, financially?'

'Hah.' His voice was bitter. 'That's the one thing I can't do. And if I don't, you know, *do the right thing*, I'll never again be able to show my face in Drohid.'

'Does that matter?'

'My folks will be shunned. I don't have a choice.'

'You always have a choice.'

He leaned forward and banged his head against the yellow wall.

'Oh God.'

'God won't help you,' she said. Her voice was hoarse. Her throat hurt from the strain of controlling it. Her next words came out in a whisper.

'You have to choose, Tim.'

She waited. Her legs felt shaky, and her lungs wouldn't fill up enough. From somewhere out on Lansdowne Road came the sound of a siren, the fire brigade, she thought. Downstairs, someone turned the radio on full blast and the chorus of 'Heyday' spilled into the space between them. Someone banged a cupboard door. Someone cursed. Someone laughed. Life went on.

When Tim raised his face to hers, she saw the wash of tears on his cheeks. He wiped his eyes, like a child, like a small, disappointed boy, but the tears kept coming. He put his hand out and caught hold of her fingers.

'I'm sorry, Maeve. I'm so fucking sorry.'

She nodded.

She looked into his eyes. Hyacinths, she thought. Remember that. His eyes were the blue of hyacinths. She rubbed her thumb along the flesh at the base of his palm, pressing hard, as if she might leave some mark on him, then pulled her hand away.

'Maeve—'

'Shush,' she said. She bent and let her cheek lie against his, kissed the tender skin in front of his ear.

'I'm yours,' she said, swallowing hard. 'No matter what.'

She stood, took her handbag from where it lay on his bed and slung it over her shoulder. She resisted the urge, a newly formed habit, to let her hand rest below her belly button.

'Maeve—' he said, but he didn't stand up.

She walked out of his room and down the stairs, unlatched the front door and pulled it behind her. Her head felt heavy, and she thought she might faint. She leaned against the wall as the space behind her eyes began to darken. She sank to the doorstep and dropped her head between her knees. She concentrated on breathing in, then breathing out, only distantly aware of the sound of the garden gate squeaking as it opened.

'Are you alright there?' Maeve looked up; it was one of Tim's housemates, the one who lived in his Cork jersey. 'Do you want to come inside?'

Maeve shook her head and rubbed the stream of snot and tears off her face.

'Can I not get you a glass of water or something?'

'No.'

'Will I get a taxi for you?'

She avoided meeting his eye, the embarrassment of it. She pulled herself to her feet and tossed her hair behind her shoulders.

'No, thanks. I'm grand.'

'Sure?'

She would get on with things. She would wait until he hated the girl who trapped him. She would wait for Tim Corcoran. They were destined to be together; she was certain of it.

'Absolutely sure.' She smiled broadly. 'Thanks anyway.'

79.

It Could Have Been Worse

* * *

It could have been worse, said Greta.
I know, said Maeve. *I know.*
Emer was fine. That was the thing Maeve held in the front of her head. She had to keep checking. She kept looking at Emer and asking, *Are you hurt?* And every time, Emer said *no*, as if it was the first time she was asked, as if she wasn't entirely certain herself.

Emer was fine. She had nothing more than a bruise on her collarbone and a small cut on her neck, both caused by her seatbelt. She was sitting on a stool now, leaning against the wall of the cubicle, watching in silence as a doctor closed a laceration to the inside of Maeve's left forearm with sixteen sutures.

'That was a nasty one,' said the doctor, laying down her equipment and taking up instead a clipboard and pen. 'Can you tell me how it happened?'

'I've no idea,' Maeve said, and it was true. The whole thing was a blur. She'd felt the stickiness of blood on her hands, but it hadn't occurred to her that it might be her own, not when there was so much more blood, pumping out, more than she could ever have imagined. It was like trying to hold back the flood waters all over again, only thicker this time and sickeningly warm.

'The paramedic's report says you climbed through a broken windscreen,' said the doctor. 'That would do it.'

'I suppose it would,' said Maeve blankly.

'You might have a small scar on your face, but it could have been much worse. It was a clean cut. I think it will heal up well.'

'Thank you, Doctor.' Maeve wasn't sure what else she was supposed to say. The doctor and the two nurses had all been polite, but cool. They'd taken blood tests without any comment. What they saw was a woman who had been drunk driving on a Sunday morning with her child in the back of her car. Given how little they must think of her, Maeve felt only admiration for their professional restraint.

'Have you someone to come for you?'

'No,' said Maeve.

'I can't let you leave on your own,' said the doctor.

'There isn't anyone. I'm from Dublin.' Maeve's mind was a complete blank.

'Is there a neighbour, maybe?'

'No,' said Maeve. Her nearest neighbour was Paddy O'Driscoll. She felt her eyes swim with tears.

'Mal,' said Emer, from her corner.

'Who's Mal?' said the doctor, scribbling something extra at the end of her notes.

'He's—' *He's the man who sold me a house he knew would flood*, she thought. The shock had worn off and she desperately wanted to close her eyes and go to sleep.

'He's our friend,' said Emer.

The doctor raised both her eyebrows at Maeve. There was no other option.

'Malachi Barry,' she said.

'Right,' the doctor said, and, somehow, she found him.

80.

The Weight of Water

* * *

'It could have been worse,' Mal said to her mother, holding his hand to her elbow to give her a boost into the Land Rover. Mammy turned her face away from him and said nothing. 'The rain's stopped anyway,' he went on, as if he couldn't help himself. 'That's something.'

It was late afternoon, and the setting sun was blazing across the hospital car park, turning brown puddles gold.

'Right so, little nugget.' He turned to Emer. 'You'll have to ride in the back with Bran. It's none too clean, I'm afraid.' He opened the door at the back and Emer climbed in. She took the bench seat behind her mother's back and Bran jumped up beside her. He looked at her with his head tipped to one side, then leaned forward and licked her hand. She rubbed the back of his neck and he settled himself alongside her, his warm body pressed against hers.

'You'll come back to my place for a bite to eat,' said Mal, leaning slightly forward in his seat as he navigated the lanes of a big roundabout and took the exit for Drohid. Emer could tell he had tried to make a statement of his invitation, but the question mark hung stubbornly at the end of it. It seemed that her mother hadn't heard, and Mal opened his mouth to ask again, but Mammy stopped him.

'I only want to go home.'

'To your own place?'

She just nodded and leaned her head against the glass pane of the car window.

Emer rubbed her fingers through Bran's fur. He readjusted his position so that his chin rested on her knee. She could see Malachi's eyes in the rear-view mirror. He was looking straight ahead, concentrating fiercely on the road, but just once, he caught her looking and bowed his head to her, as if to say she was doing something right, though what it was she couldn't tell. Maybe he was saying she was right to get him to come collect them. Maybe he was just letting her know that he could see her.

They drove on without speaking, under the viaduct, over the bridge that crossed the river, along the rock face, and past the giant billboard that said they should have gone to Specsavers. Malachi paused at the top of Weavers' Row, but the flood had receded, so he drove through the mud and pulled up close to the front door.

'Are you sure now? It's going to be shocking wet and cold in there.' He threw a look over the car seats towards Emer.

'We'll be fine,' said Mammy. 'We always are.'

'Let me come in and clear it out a bit. I can light a fire for you.'

'Maybe tomorrow, Malachi. Alright? I only want to sleep now.'

Bran didn't budge his head from Emer's lap.

'It could have been worse, you know,' said Malachi.

'So people keep saying.' Mammy tried to open the door with her injured arm. 'Shit.' Emer saw her wince with pain.

'They said she was stable. They wouldn't say that if they weren't fairly confident.'

'She never moved, you know. She never made a sound, or gave me any sign of what she was thinking.' Mammy's voice broke, 'I don't know if she knew it was me—'

'We've all made mistakes,' he said. 'You're not the first or the last to get into a car after a few drinks. It's hardly a—'

'Hah.' She made a fake laughing noise. 'A criminal offence, you mean? I believe you'll find it is exactly that.'

'Sorry. I'd be better off not talking. Ever.'

'You're alright, Malachi.' She turned to him, and Emer could see that she was trying to smile. 'C'mere, could you let me out of this tank?'

He got out and walked around the car to help her, then lifted Emer to the ground. At the gap that led to the riverside walk, a fat grey rat paused to watch them.

'Get away,' Malachi shouted, and the rat turned on its heel and scarpered.

'Let me clear the door for you.' He didn't wait for her answer, just set about lifting the sandbags from her doorstep. She handed him the key and he pushed the door inward, but then she put her hand on his arm.

'Thanks for the help,' she said.

'It will sort itself out,' said Malachi. 'Things usually do.'

Mammy didn't answer.

* * *

Emer stood in the centre of the room and turned in a slow circle. A slick of mud covered the entire floor, swirling in wave patterns, like a horrible brown carpet. Rihanna's bowl was lying upside-down on the ground. She went to pick it up.

'Leave it,' said Mammy. She closed the front door behind her, crossed the room, straight to the staircase, and walked upstairs without looking backwards. Emer, seeing no alternative, followed her.

Mammy sat on her bed and pulled at the laces of her boots. Emer helped her to get them off.

'Thanks,' she said, then rolled onto her side, turning away from the door. 'Thanks, Chicken,' and no more.

Emer left her and went to her own room. It was almost exactly as it had been before all this started, except for a pile of photo albums stacked on the floor, and two purple velvet sofa cushions leaning against the wall.

She changed into clean pyjamas, brushed her teeth and her hair, and got into bed. From downstairs, she could hear the blip-plink-dlip-plink-dripping. It felt as if the whole house was drip-drying, pulled downwards by the weight of water. She could hear the river too, still full and rushing. Every now and again she thought she heard the gurgling sound the water had made when it came under the door, but she couldn't muster the courage to walk downstairs to check. Something splashed nearby. It was inside the house, she was certain. She sat up straight in the bed, her pulse thumping in her throat. She pulled her dressing gown from the end of her bed and tied it tightly around her waist, then walked out onto the landing. She stood still at the top of the stairs, listening. The blip-plink-dlip-plink-dripping went on and on but there was nothing else. She put her head around the door of the ruby boudoir. Mammy's bandaged left arm lay above the covers, the rest of her tucked into a ball underneath. Emer got into the bed, curled against her mother's back, and slept.

81.

As Good as Family

* * *

Malachi turned the Land Rover around, drove back in the road to Cork city, and parked in the same spot in the hospital car park that he'd left less than an hour earlier.

'I won't be long,' he said, and Bran settled himself down on the passenger seat.

When he had asked earlier, a nurse with a long face had told him that Agnes was in surgery. This time, a smiling Malaysian nurse waved towards the room opposite the nurse's station.

'You'll have to wait a few moments,' she said. 'There's a Garda with her now.'

Approaching the open door, Malachi heard the strained tone of a man speaking to someone who he wasn't sure could hear or understand him.

'Is that alright, so? I'll leave you now, but I'll call back again tomorrow and see if anything at all has come back to you.'

Agnes said something then, but too quietly for Malachi to make out the words.

'Don't worry. I won't forget. I'll be sure to write that name down,' said the guard. 'You take care of yourself now.'

Around the corner of the door frame, Mal watched the guard, a man as tall and bulky as himself, patting the end of the hospital bed, as if he could inject a dose of strength through its frame. At the door, he stopped and looked hard into Malachi's face.

'Are you visiting Miss Beecher?'

'I am.'

'Are you family?'

'As good as. I hope.'

'And your own name?'

'Malachi Barry.'

The guard wrote down his name before slipping his pen into the rings of the notebook.

'Go on, so.'

'Thanks, Guard.'

Agnes was flat in the bed, with a sheet tucked up to her armpits and her thin, bare arms lying limp at her sides. Her forehead was wrapped in a wide bandage, and, under the sheet, both of her legs were raised on some sort of support.

'Mr. Barry,' she said, with a feeble grin, when she saw him. She spoke quietly, as if it hurt to breathe, but she was alert, perfectly herself.

'Miss Beecher.' Malachi wondered whether they had deliberately woken her up to speak to the guards. Wasn't that a thing they did in films?

With a twitch of her hand, she indicated that he should sit in the hard chair next to the bed. The seat of it, Malachi found, was still warm from the arse of the guard who had just vacated it.

'No grapes?' Agnes whispered.

Inwardly, Malachi cursed his empty hands. Why hadn't he stopped at the hospital shop for flowers? Because his heart had been beating in his ears with fear, that was why.

'There's a great big nil-by-mouth sign above your head,' he said.

Her smile wobbled and fell away.

'I was lucky.'

He surveyed the bank of monitors, the drips, the catheter bag, and the wire contraption over her legs.

'Yerra. If this is what you call lucky, I hope I'm nowhere near you when misfortune strikes.'

They were quiet for a minute. From the corridor, Malachi could hear the clatter of cups on a tea trolley.

'What happened, Agnes?'

Agnes shook her head only slightly and winced in pain.

'It's alright,' Malachi said. He covered her frail hand with his own and felt her fingers curl around his palm.

'I don't know,' she said, and paused for breath. 'It was so fast.' Another breath. 'I heard her voice.'

'Maeve's? You heard Maeve's voice?'

Agnes nodded.

'Was it her name you gave to the guards?'

'No.'

Malachi's stomach lurched.

'Was someone else there? Who was it, Agnes?'

She squeezed his hand as if to apologise.

'It was Bella,' she said.

'What?'

'On the road.'

Oh Jesus. It was all his fault.

'Bella was on the road?' He repeated the words incredulously, but he could see the sense of them as he spoke. He'd *stupidly* let the cows out of the byre and into the top field first thing, before he drove into town. In his rush, he must not have secured the field gate properly, and the farm gate at the end of the lane hadn't been closed in years. Not one cow in twenty would have bothered to stray that far, but Bella – Bella had an agenda.

Agnes only looked him straight in the eye.

'I'll kill her.'

'You won't. It's . . .' Her voice fell away. '. . . no one's fault.'

'I'm very sorry.' Malachi leaned forward and wrapped Agnes' hand inside both of his.

'Aren't we all?' she replied.

'I'm very sorry,' said the chirpy nurse, proving Agnes right as she approached the bed with a tray of medical equipment in her hand. 'Agnes needs to rest now.'

'I'll come back in the morning, alright?' He stood and took a step backwards from the bed, but Agnes clung to his hand.

'Bring grapes,' she said.

'You'll have me peeling them for you next, I suppose.' He gave her hand a final squeeze before he left.

He was still laughing to himself when the big guard rose from a chair in the corridor.

'Mr. Barry?' he said.
'Yes?'
'Sergeant John Molloy. Can we have a quick word?'
'I've left the dog in the car . . .' said Malachi.
'He'll be grand,' said the guard. 'This will only take a minute.'

82.

You'd Have to Be Mad

* * *

Nóinín Corcoran collapsed into her usual chair at the head of the kitchen table. She slipped her feet out of her shoes and curled her toes. There was something reassuring about the ache she felt in her arches.

'Well, I've sold every pair of Wellington boots and every raincoat in the shop, so there's the silver lining.' At the opposite end of the table, Tim was cutting slices from a shop-bought baguette. He didn't appear to have registered that Nóinín had spoken. She raised her voice. 'Not a drop got in. Thank God Daddy insisted on those floodgates.'

Tim made a non-committal sound at the back of his throat. He cut another slice of bread, and another, with a fastidiousness that was grating on Nóinín's last nerve, but she persisted. 'He was dead right. Those low houses on Weavers' Row got a good wash out.' She lifted her tone to make it a question, so that he would have to respond or else make an issue out of it.

'So I heard,' he said.

She smiled.

'You'd have to be mad to live over there. Anyone with an ounce of sense sold up and got out of it.'

'You're not wrong there.' With both hands, he picked up the breadboard and held it out to her. She took a piece of bread.

'Butter?'

'Yes, please.'

Slowly, she spread the butter all the way to the edges.

'What about you? Any news?'

It was a test, and they both knew it.

'Actually, yes. It was terrible. I saw that car crash on the coast road this morning.' His voice was hoarse. 'Did you hear about it?'

'I did, of course. It was all anyone could talk about all day. What do you mean you *saw* it?' She held the slice of bread halfway to her mouth, waiting for an answer.

'I went out for a jog. To see the flood, you know.' He dipped his spoon into his bowl of soup but, mirroring his wife, held it poised halfway to his mouth.

'Did you see it happen?' She took a bite of her bread, chewed slowly.

'No, I didn't. I was the first on the scene, though.' He brought the spoon to his mouth, swallowed. 'I called the ambulance,' he said.

'Was there loads of blood?' said Tadgh.

'Tadgh!' said Nóinín.

'No,' said Tim, offering his son a slice of bread. 'None at all.'

Nóinín turned her attention to Pamela.

'You're very quiet.'

'I'm fine,' said Pamela.

'Why don't you invite your friend Eilís to come over tomorrow?' She waved her spoon at Tim. 'You wouldn't mind, would you, Tim?'

'Not at bit,' said Tim. 'That would be grand.'

'Let's open a bottle of wine, shall we?' She smiled at Tim. 'I think we've earned a treat.'

83.

Cleaning Up

* * *

It was Malachi's *rat-at-at* that woke her. He stood on the doorstep with Bran at his side and a cardboard box full of cleaning products under his arm. Maeve, still in the clothes she'd worn the day before, held the door wide open.

'Malachi,' she said, but nothing further.

'Maeve.' He walked in. 'I'd have been here earlier, but I was above at the hospital.'

'Oh?' She was afraid to ask.

'She's alright, I think. She was asleep this morning, but she was awake last night.'

'Did she talk to you?' *Did she see what happened? Did she see who was driving?* Those were the questions Maeve wanted to ask but couldn't.

'The heifer calf on the road was one of mine. I'm desperately sorry, Maeve.'

'Aren't we all?'

'Yes,' he said. 'That seems to be the way of it alright.'

* * *

Beyond that, Malachi hardly spoke a word either to her or Emer. Maybe he was operating a policy of least-said-soonest-mended, or maybe, like her, he had run out of words.

There wasn't much call for conversation anyway. The things that needed to be done were all too obvious. Everything wet needed to be carried outside into the lane. The walls, the presses, the shelves, and the countertops all needed cleaning, and the floors needed to be swept out with a yard brush. Malachi, pointing to the bandage on Maeve's arm, insisted that she couldn't lift anything heavy. She stood with her arms crossed, watching, as he hauled the fridge out the front door. The new armchair went the same way, and last of all, the purple velvet sofa. She didn't say a word.

After a couple of hours, Malachi suggested they walk up to a coffee shop for some hot food.

'I can't face it,' she said.

Malachi looked at her for a long time, assessing her. She didn't have the energy to put on a show for him.

'Not to worry,' was all he said in the end, but he climbed into the Land Rover and drove out of the lane.

'That's weird,' said Emer. They both looked at Bran, who watched the car until it disappeared and then lay down across the open front door.

All of a sudden, Maeve was overcome with exhaustion. Her head felt weighted and her back slumped. Even pulling air into her lungs seemed an effort.

'My hand hurts,' she said, by way of explanation, and went upstairs. She lay down on the bed and curled into a ball.

She could hear Emer talking to the dog.

'I'll mind you until Mal gets back,' she was half-singing. 'I'll mind you.'

Maeve closed her eyes.

Then, Malachi shouting.

'Maeve!'

Footsteps thudding on the stairs, the bedroom door thrown back with a bang against the wall.

'Maeve—'

'What is it?' *What is it now?* she wanted to say but ran out of breath. She opened her eyes. 'What's wrong?'

'Nothing.' She saw it – the panic abating from his face. What did he think she could have done? 'Nothing,' he said again. 'I got you some lunch.'

He walked heavily down the stairs and went back to his car for the food and a tray of hot drinks. They ate sitting on the doorstep, where it was sunny.

'Yum,' Emer said into a long silence.

'Bran can't believe his luck,' Malachi added, with forced cheerfulness, as Maeve dropped a slice of chicken to the dog.

'You're very kind, Malachi,' she said, though she wished he would just go away so that she could sleep.

He lifted three industrial machines from the back of his car,

'This one's a generator, and this one's a wet vacuum,' he said, explaining everything to Emer, 'and this one's a dehumidifier. We'll have this place sorted out in no time flat.' He walked inside and put the generator down on the wet floor.

They worked all day. Malachi and Emer took turns operating the vacuum. Malachi used a crowbar to lift soaked floorboards so that Emer could suck water out from underneath. Maeve boiled water and sprayed disinfectant and wiped surfaces.

She was cleaning down the legs of the oak table when Bran rose from his position on the doorstep. He blocked the doorway and barked, and again, louder.

Two tall Gardaí in uniform stood in the lane outside.

'Quiet,' Malachi said, taking hold of Bran's collar. 'It's alright.'

'Oh God,' said Maeve. She felt her knees give way, just for a second, but she straightened up to her full height and stepped forward, pulling off yellow rubber gloves. She stretched out her right hand.

'Maeve Gaffney,' she said, and shook hands, firmly, with each of them.

84.

On the Turn of the Stairs

* * *

'Be a good girl,' Mammy said. With a guard standing on either side of her, she bent and kissed Emer's forehead. Emer bit the inside of her cheek so as not to cry.

'Don't worry a bit,' Mal said, but he wasn't looking at Emer. He was watching as they escorted Mammy to the squad car that was waiting at the top of the lane. One of the guards put his hand on Mammy's head so she didn't bump it getting into the car.

Then Mal put his hand on Emer's shoulder and steered her back inside the house. Bran came too.

'Did you, by any chance, manage to salvage a pack of cards?' Mal asked.

Emer had to think, but yes, they'd carried all the games upstairs. She nodded.

'That's great,' he said. 'We can have a game of Mousse.'

* * *

'Is Mammy going to jail?' Emer whispered. She put down a black jack, and Mal, having nothing to counter it, picked up ten cards. They were sitting on two pillows at the turn of the stairs. Bran lay across a step, level with Emer's shoulder, and Mal had his legs stretched out down the lower half of the staircase. The day was starting to fade, but Mal had a storm light at his elbow, ready for when they needed it.

'Yerra, don't be daft. What on earth gave you that idea?'

Emer looked through the spindles to the space where the two guards had just been standing.

'They only want to get a statement,' said Mal. 'She won't be long.' He played a five of spades.

'What's a s-statement?' She played a three.

'It's, like, the official story of what happened, all the little details. The guards will ask your mammy to tell them every single thing she can remember, as best she can.' He played an ace and switched the suit to hearts. 'The most important thing is that she tells them the truth.'

Emer picked up a card. 'If Mammy tells the g-guards a lie, will they p-pu—' She lowered her voice. 'Will they put her in jail?'

Mal looked up from the cards in his hand.

'Why would your mammy tell a lie?'

'I-I-I dunno.'

He played a queen of diamonds.

She put down a three.

'Do you think your mammy is going to tell a lie, Emer?'

'—'

He held the card he was about to play in his hand, waiting.

'Maybe,' she said.

He put down the card, a jack of clubs.

'What lie?'

She didn't answer.

'Tell me.'

'She's going to s-say she was driving the c-car.'

Mal was very still. Bran, wary, raised his head.

'Was she not driving the car, Emer?'

Tears filled her eyes and spilled over. She shook her head.

'Who was driving the car, if it wasn't your mammy?'

Bran licked tears from her cheek and Emer wrapped her arm around his body.

Mal put his hand on her head. She felt the warmth of it, and the gentle strength of his fingers threaded through her hair.

He whispered.

'Who was it?'

Emer was stuck. She didn't want to tell. She knew Mammy didn't want her to tell, and she didn't want everyone, Mal and the guards and everyone, looking at her while she said something different to what her mammy said. Mammy would say Emer was lying, and then no one would believe her. She didn't want to get blamed for a lie that wasn't hers. But she didn't want her mammy to take the blame for something she didn't do, something bad.

She said it under her breath, so quietly she could hardly hear her own voice.

'Tim.'

Mal seemed to have stopped breathing. He tapped the cards in his hand against the wooden step of the stairs, once, twice, three times.

'Tim Corcoran was driving your mother's car? He crashed the car? Is that right?'

She looked him in the eye then.

He waited.

She nodded.

'Okay,' he said. 'Don't worry about it. Alright?'

She nodded again, even though they both knew she didn't mean it.

They carried on, dealing the cards and playing them out, hardly talking at all. Emer won two games, and then a third. She could tell that Mal wasn't even trying but she didn't say anything.

When finally she heard her mother's key turn in the door, she felt a sick mixture of relieved and scared.

Mammy looked up at them, sitting there on the turn of the stairs. Something about them seemed to knock the last bit of energy out of her. She dropped her black leather handbag and her keys on the bare floor.

Mal stood up.

'I have to talk to you.'

'Thanks, Malachi. You're very good,' she said, in the tone of dismissal Emer had heard her mother use with workmen. 'Would you like to call over tomorrow?'

'*Now*, Maeve. Right now. I'm going nowhere.' Emer had never heard him sound so cross. She looked from him to her mother. Mammy was staring him down, as if she could literally will him out the door. Mal stared right back.

'Go to bed, Emer,' Mammy said.

Emer looked up the dark stairs.

'Here, take this,' said Mal, handing her the glowing storm lamp. With his other hand, he gestured Bran to heel.

She carried the lamp to her room and closed the door and sat at the end of her bed. She heard Mal shouting at Mammy, and she heard Mammy shouting back. She had to wonder why they sent her upstairs. She could hear every word.

'You *have* to tell them the truth.'

'I don't *have* to do anything. This is *my* life. It's got *nothing* to do with you.'

'What about your daughter? Keep on lying for that bastard and there's a fifty-fifty chance that girl of yours will be deprived of her mother.'

'Well, if I tell the *truth* there's a *one hundred* per cent chance she'll be deprived of her father.'

There was a pause, and then Mal spoke more quietly.

'So, it's true then, all the talk.'

'Hah! You too, Malachi?'

He didn't answer.

'Oh yes,' she said. 'It's all true.'

'He'll never leave her. You know that, don't you?'

'I love him.'

'I believe you.'

'He'll see it now. He'll understand that I love him more than she ever will, than she ever *could*. She doesn't have that kind of love in her. He'll see that now.'

'You're taking a very big risk.'

'They're not going to send a single mother to prison. It would be different if Agnes had died, then it would be manslaughter, but this is just—'

'Reckless endangerment?'

'Something like that.'

They were both quiet. Then Mal spoke in a low, forceful tone.

'I won't let you do this. Tell the guards the truth.'

'No. I won't.'

'If you don't, I will.'

'If you do—' Mammy's voice lowered to a hoarse growl. 'Don't you fucking dare, or I'll go into that river myself—' She said something Emer couldn't catch.

'Don't say that,' said Malachi. 'That's a shocking thing to say. You wouldn't—'

'I will. Be damn sure that I will, and I'll take her with me. I'm not leaving her alone.'

Emer heard the sound of glass breaking, the shuffle of a struggle, two loud barks, and then her mother's voice shouting, 'Get OUT of my house. OUT!' And then the sound of the front door banging shut.

Emer listened as her mother banged cupboard doors and crashed around the kitchen. There was nothing there, of course, to eat or drink, and pretty soon she heard Mammy's footsteps on the stairs. She heard the creak of the floorboard outside her bedroom door, and she imagined Mammy's hand on the brass doorknob, but it didn't turn. A moment later, she heard her mother's bedroom door slam shut.

She turned on her side and pulled the duvet over her head. It was as if her mind was snagged, caught on a thorn, forced to contemplate the one thought she'd been pushing and pushing and pushing away ever since that day on the beach at Christmas. Her entire mind was gripped by one single word.

Father.

85.

So Much to Do

* * *

'Get up, quick as you can.'

Emer had to rub her eyelids with the backs of her hands before they would open. Twisting her neck, she saw her mother, dressed to go out, in smart black slacks and her hair pinned into a tidy bun. She pulled the bedroom curtains wide and fixed them with their matching tiebacks. The sky was cloudless, an Alice in Wonderland shade of blue. Emer swallowed a hard lump in her throat and waited to hear what her mother would say about her betrayal.

'Can you find some clean clothes to put on?' Mammy asked, in a voice that was almost normal, but with a sort of determined cheerfulness that clipped it.

Emer nodded.

'Good girl. We have *so* much to do. The electrician will be here soon. He's promised to have us reconnected by lunchtime. I've got a bid on a second-hand sofa on eBay. I need to keep an eye on that. It's not great, but we can dolly it up with some cushions. It will do for viewings. I better go check on that. Can you hurry? We have so much to *do*.'

'What about s-school?' asked Emer, sitting up.

'I'll phone them. I think you'll be better off at home for a few days.'

Emer swung her legs out of bed and Maeve moved to leave. In the doorway, she paused.

'People outside our family don't understand us, Emer.'

Emer heard her mother's back teeth snapping against each other. She looked hard at her mother's face, at the harsh lines at the corners of her mouth. She couldn't think of an answer.

'You must never speak to strangers about family business. Do you understand?'

Mal's not a stranger, she said, shouted, screamed, but only inside her head.

'Can I trust you, Emer?'

Slowly, she nodded.

Her mother nodded back.

'Good girl. Get dressed. I need you to run up to the shop for scones while I make calls.' Her voice faded as she walked down the stairs. 'The best thing would be to hire a professional sanding machine. I wonder how much that will cost. Maybe I could ask Jack O'Neill to lend a hand.' She must have stopped at the bottom of the stairs and turned, because her voice came again, clear and strong. 'And brush your hair.'

When Emer got back from the shop, Mammy was holding two mugs of tea. The oak table was laid with two plates, a butter dish, and a crystal glass bowl filled with jam.

'Perfect timing, love,' she said, taking her seat. 'I'm ravenous.'

Emer sat down and took a scone.

'Oh. I forgot knives,' said Maeve. She jumped up from her seat and strode to the kitchen. 'I got all the dishes and all the cutlery washed this morning, but I'm going to have to buy some new tea towels, and a teapot too. The old one is cracked. I have the towels soaking in the bath, but I don't know if they can be salvaged. We're going to have to make do for a few weeks, you know, rough it a bit, until we get the house sold.'

Emer looked up from buttering her scone.

Mammy's eyes met hers.

'Don't worry,' her mother said. She reached with her knife for the butter. 'I have a plan.'

86.

Maeve Is Fine

* * *

They had almost finished their breakfast, and Maeve had regained a sense of equanimity, when her phone rang. She walked to the kitchen counter and picked it up. It was an unknown caller.

'Hello.'

'Hello. Am I speaking with Maeve Gaffney?'

'Yes.'

The voice hesitated, so that Maeve was left with a silent pause to fill.

'This is she,' she said, awkwardly.

'Mrs. Gaffney, I'm afraid I—'

'Ms.'

'Sorry?'

'Ms., not Mrs.' *Why did she say that? For God's sake.* 'Maeve is fine.'

Another pause. Maeve didn't fill it this time.

'Maeve.'

'Yes?'

'You gave your name as a contact for a patient who was admitted here last Sunday – Agnes Beecher.'

'I did, yes.'

Again, a too-long pause, as if the woman's batteries had run down.

'I have sad news, I'm afraid. The patient took a turn for the worse last night. She was taken to theatre for emergency surgery early this morning. The team did everything they could, but, sadly, Miss Beecher has died.'

'Thank you.' Maeve moved the phone away from her ear.

'Ms. Gaffney? Hello? Maeve? Are you—?' Maeve ended the call, cutting off the horrible voice. She couldn't bear the softness of it. Slowly and carefully, she placed the phone face down on the counter. She leaned her back against the wall and wrapped her arms around the centre of her body. She had to hold it together now.

Emer pushed her chair back from the table.

'Mammy?'

Maeve heard the voice, but it came from far away, somewhere not really *relevant* to her anymore.

At first very slowly, and then all at once, Maeve sank to the ground. She pulled her knees up and tucked her chin to her chest. She squeezed her eyes tightly shut. She said nothing, made no sound at all, but a low, moaning noise rang in her head, like an alarm going off.

87.

She'd Kissed Him, Once

* * *

Malachi was unhitching the trailer from his tractor when the phone in the inside pocket of his waxed jacket vibrated at a level that resonated uncomfortably through his lungs. He unzipped his coat and pulled out the phone – it was an unknown number.

Ignore it, he thought. He moved to put the phone away.
Better not, he thought, *just in case*.
'Hello?' he said.
'Malachi?'
'Who's this?'
'I'm so sorry to call you this early in the morning but—'
'Who did you say you were?'
'I'm sorry. I didn't. Look, this is Alison Rafferty.'
'Who?'
'I used to live up the road from you, Malachi.'
'Alison O'Toole, is it?'
'That's right.' She sounded relieved that he remembered her. She took a short breath, and then another, as if she was having trouble filling her lungs.
'What can I do for you, Alison?' he asked, adhering to form, and thinking it would give her time to gather herself. Bran, perched on the trailer, pricked one ear and leaned into Malachi's hand on his head.
'Well, actually, I hope I can do something for you.'
'Oh, yes?'
'This is a bit awkward. I hope you won't think I'm interfering.'

'Yerra, sure, I probably will, but fire away anyway.' He wanted to tell her to drop the put-on posh accent that sounded nothing at all like the Alison O'Toole who he'd kissed, just the once, at a GAA club disco. She'd kissed him, really. She'd been years older than him, a fact that he'd revelled in afterwards, but she must have regretted.

'It's about Agnes Beecher.'

Malachi's grip on the phone tightened.

'What?'

'She died this morning, Malachi. I'm sorry.'

'Oh.' He could think of no words to say.

'I thought you'd want to know straight away. I hope I did the right thing.'

He leaned against the side of the trailer.

'You did. You did the right thing.'

'Malachi.' She paused for a second. He sensed that she was deciding on something.

'Go on,' he said.

'I really shouldn't say, but there's something else you should know.'

'What is it?'

'My husband works with Matthew Dawson, you know, the Beechers' solicitor . . .'

Malachi listened while she recounted every word of what Matthew Dawson had told her husband on the phone that morning.'

'We were still in bed. I couldn't help overhearing,' she said, by way of excusing her indiscretion.

'I appreciate your telling me.'

'Let me know if there's any—'

He cut her off. 'Thank you.'

'Come on.' He beckoned, and Bran jumped down from the trailer. Malachi scrolled to Maeve's number, and pressed *Call*. Listening to the dial tone, he walked to the cab of the tractor and took his keys from the ignition.

'Hello. This is Maeve Gaffney. I'm unable to take your call, but please do leave a message.'

He kicked the back wheel of the tractor.

'Maeve. It's me. It's Malachi.' He was walking fast towards his car as he spoke, working hard to keep his voice casual. There was every chance she wouldn't know yet. 'I'm on my way to you now.' He let Bran jump in ahead of him, then sat into the driver's seat, started the engine. 'I'll be with you in ten minutes.' Who was there to tell her? Unless . . . unless she gave her name as a contact at the hospital. He dropped the casual tone, instead invested every bit of authority he could muster into his voice. 'Don't do *anything*, Maeve. Wait for me.' He tossed the phone onto the dashboard, slammed the gear stick into first and put his right foot to the floor.

88.

Sacrifice

* * *

You're strong, Maeve, said Greta.

Maeve stood looking around the room. She was so tired, *so* tired.

No daughter of mine ever gave up without a fight.

She needed to assess her priorities, decide what she needed to do, and what she needed to do first. She needed someone to take care of Emer. She'd told Malachi that she'd take Emer with her, and maybe she would, if it came to that, the last resort. She'd take Emer to hell with her, or wherever it was they'd end up, but she couldn't take Emer to prison.

'Do you remember Granny's cousin, Ailbhe? We went to her house for Christmas one year when you were little?'

Emer shook her head.

Maeve kept talking. 'Ailbhe's lovely. We always got on. She'll take care of you. I'll phone her. I'm sure she'll come straight away.'

Maeve wiped her nose and started moving around the room, fixing things, folding a napkin, pushing chairs into place under the table. She picked up the butter dish and fitted its lid, carefully, so that she didn't get any butter on it. She pushed it to the back of the counter top.

Emer stood like a statue, bone-white, her jaw slack in panic. The best thing would be to give her a job, keep her busy.

'Run upstairs and start packing a bag. You'll want your jeans and a tracksuit and, let's see, five or six tops and—'

'Are you g-going to jail?'

Maeve walked back to the table and picked up the bowl of raspberry jam.

'I don't know,' she said. She shook her head as if to reject the possibility and turned to face Emer. 'Hope for the best and plan for the worst. Isn't that what Granny used to say?'

Maeve smiled, and automatically, Emer smiled back.

'Go on. Run.'

Emer took the stairs one step at a time.

'Don't forget knickers and socks, and your toothbrush—' Maeve kept talking, as if this was a perfectly normal sort of situation, until the sound of sirens wailing stole away her train of thought.

Emer stalled halfway up the stairs.

Maeve stood still, listening.

The sirens were getting louder, getting closer.

'Oh God.' The bowl slipped from her hands and fell to the floor. The glass cracked, along a neat seam, and lay in two halves on either side of the pool of jam.

'I'll g-get it.'

'Leave it.' She held up her hand; she needed to listen to the sirens. They were at the bridge, she guessed. She stood up straight, steeling herself. She would be calm, and she would be dignified.

Good girl, said Greta.

She walked to the cupboard under the stairs, took out her bouclé tweed jacket and pulled it on. She tugged the hem of it, so that it would sit well across her back, and rubbed away the streak of raspberry jam that had splashed across her slacks.

She put her two hands on Emer's shoulders.

'This will only be for a few hours. They'll ask if there's someone you can stay with. Is there a friend at school you could—?'

'Mal?'

'No. No, it can't be Malachi.'

Maeve didn't hear what Emer said next. She was listening to the sirens. They were moving away. They weren't coming for her at all. Maybe it was nothing to do with her. Maybe it was some other emergency altogether, a burglary maybe, or a fire—

Maeve let go of Emer's shoulders and sprang to the front door. She threw it back and tumbled outside. She had to struggle not to slip on the mud as she ran up the lane to the main road. It was clear the Garda squad car had turned from Main Street onto the bridge. She stood and put her two hands to the crown of her head, for all the world as if she was being arrested.

The sound seemed to bounce around the lane, and then came clearly again, but from the opposite end, from the river.

'Oh, dear God.' All of a sudden, she understood what that meant. They weren't coming for her. They were going for Tim.

Someone had told them.

Tim would think it was her. He would think she had told the guards that it was him at the wheel. Someone had taken it away from her – her sacrifice – that opportunity to prove to him for once and for all that nobody could love him as much as she did.

She flung her body into a forward motion and tore past Emer, past the house, past the barrier that separated Weavers' Row from the river path. She stopped there and stood looking upstream towards the bridge.

'Oh,' she said. 'Oh, no.'

The river was swollen, flowing fast and littered with debris, the path completely submerged. She stood up to her ankles in muddy water. A Garda car was crossing the bridge, flashing blue lights set off theatrically by the backdrop of thunderous cloud rolling in from the south-west. At the far end of the bridge, it turned right, then disappeared behind the houses on the far side of the river. She stood transfixed until the blue lights re-emerged, visible through the wide garden at the side of Cavendish House.

Then, Maeve started running again.

'Mammy. *WAIT.*'

Maeve heard Emer's voice, but she didn't have time now. She had to tell him. He had to hear it from her, or he'd never understand, that she hadn't told them, that she loved him too much to have ever betrayed him. She didn't stop, didn't slow, didn't look back.

89.

Stop

* * *

'STOP!' a deep voice, a man's voice, roared.

Emer turned. It was Mal, skidding on the muck as he negotiated the lane. Bran, the nimbler of the two, was running at full pelt to Emer.

'Help,' she said. '*Please*, help.'

Bran stopped at her side, but Mal sprinted past, throwing up a spray of water with every step.

Mammy was waist high in the river now, fighting to keep her footing as the water rushed around her, still waving her hands in the air.

'It wasn't me,' she screamed. 'TIM! It wasn't me. I didn't tell them. TIM!'

Mal was up to his knees, wading out in long strides to get to her.

'MAEVE!' Mal's voice boomed. 'COME BACK.'

'MAMMY! COME BACK!' Emer shouted, in imitation, but her voice cracked at the end.

Emer could tell that her mother had heard from the way she stopped for a second and then straightened her back, all without turning her head. All at once, she reached out her hands and plunged into the river.

She swam two strokes, three, four, but the river tumbled over her, tugging her under and pulling her with it.

Emer heard a wordless screech an instant before she realised it had come from her.

Bran barked and barked.

Mal spun and climbed back out of the water.

'HELP HER!' Emer's scream found words this time.

Mal was panting. He didn't have breath to speak. Like a mad man, he peeled off his jacket and ran down the path. Emer saw the way he watched the water. He was trying to run faster than the river.

Bran ran ahead. At the point where the path met Weavers' Row, he stopped and barked, and that was where Mal dived headlong into the river and swam for the middle of it.

Mammy's body dipped under the water and disappeared, then surfaced again, and Emer held her breath. Mal would make it. He would get to the middle of the river and catch hold of her mother. He would save her.

He did it. He reached her. He grabbed her arm, but the river tried to pull her away from him. He lost his grip and had to grab her hair. He caught her. Mal caught Mammy.

He swam back to the river's edge where Bran, hoarse from barking, helped Emer to haul her mother onto the bank.

Mal, exhausted, hung on to the reeds at the water's edge.

Mammy lay motionless in an inch of dirty water.

'Roll her over,' Mal managed to say, trying to climb out.

Emer pushed her mother onto her side.

Bran licked Mammy's face, over and over again. That was what did it, what saved her. She coughed and vomited brown water onto the grass.

'Tim,' she whispered into the muck.

'Thank God,' said Mal. He was almost out, but his wet clothes were heavy, and he slipped. In slow motion, like in a cartoon, he fell backwards, into the rushing flow. He made big circles with his arms, but he couldn't get control.

Before Emer could even get to her feet, in a streak, Bran jumped across Mammy's body and leapt straight into the river. In seconds, he was at Mal's side, catching Mal's jumper between his teeth. Mal managed to wrap an arm around Bran's body and, together, they swam for shore.

It was harder for Emer this time. Mal was big and heavy, and he had no strength left in him. Once the top half of his body was on the bank he collapsed, face downwards, and she struggled to get his legs out of the river.

'Mal,' she said. 'Mal. Are you alright? Mal?'

He coughed and wriggled his body an inch further inland.

'Good dog,' he said.

Emer looked around. He wasn't on the bank.

'Bran?'

'Where is he?' Mal clambered onto his hands and knees.

Emer stood up and looked down the river. It was full of snapped branches and twigs and leaves and plastic bags and bits of rubbish, but she couldn't see Bran.

'Bran!' She ran down the bank and shouted.

Mal tried to stand but his legs went from under him.

'Bran!'

90.

Bran Was Gone

* * *

'It's your fault,' said Maeve, and Malachi turned to face her. She had risen to her knees but her whole body was shaking, whether from cold or fury he couldn't tell.

'Are you alright?' On his hands and knees, he crawled closer to her.

'You shouldn't have told the guards.' She pushed him away from her, but he persevered and tried to wrap his arms around her.

Maeve leaned back to gather force and slapped his face. She'd been holding that in, he thought, since she'd heard the truth about the house. He tried to hold still, to take the full force of her rage, but she flailed her fists against his ribs until he gave in and moved away from her.

'I warned you. I told you what I would do.' She was gasping for breath, but still possessed by whatever fire it was that kept her upright and fighting. 'If you loved me at all, you wouldn't have told them.'

'Listen to me,' he shouted. He lunged to grab hold of her elbows, pressed them tight against her body. He held her like that, both of them still on their knees, facing each other.

She glared at him with pure anger.

'Listen to me,' he said again. 'The guards got dashcam footage from a truck that passed ye on the road just before the crash. Tim Corcoran is caught on it, clear as day, driving your car.'

Maeve blinked. Water was seeping from her wet hair, down her forehead and into her eyes. Malachi let go of her arms, and she wiped her face.

'It's the twenty-first century, Maeve. You don't get to be a martyr.'

She sniffed and wiped her nose, but she didn't say anything.

He leaned forward, and her body moved towards his, so that just their foreheads met.

'I didn't tell them,' he said quietly.

She exhaled.

'I love him,' she said, and took a deep breath of air into her lungs. She was shivering.

He sighed heavily and rubbed his broad hands up and down her arms, to warm her. With the side of his thumb, he caught a crystal-clear tear that was streaking through the dirt on her face.

'Yerra, sure,' he said. 'I know that.'

91.

Nothing Left to Lose

* * *

Malachi told the ambulance crew that he was fine. He handed them back their grey woolly blanket and told them he just wanted to go home. They didn't give Maeve a choice: they gave her a shot of something and told her she'd need to have the wound on her arm cleaned and dressed. They bundled her into the back of the ambulance, and they took Emer with her.

He waited until they had driven away, then turned and walked along the riverbank. The ground was sodden, and the path was flooded in places, but Malachi was wet through already. He had nothing left to lose.

He scanned the banks on both sides, stopping to look closely wherever branches had fallen and created natural dams, any place Bran might have found a way out of the rushing current.

It wasn't possible that Bran and Agnes would both be taken from him on the same day.

Was it?

A black and white bundle curled amongst the reeds set his heart racing.

I knew it, he thought.

He ran to reach him, tripping forwards in his hurry. He tried to call out, but couldn't catch his breath.

Bran.

He slid down the edge of the bank, clinging to the reeds, trying to make out the form of a dog, but he saw what it was before he touched it – a dirty old anorak rolled up in a ball.

He wept then. He knelt on the mud, in the weeds and the wet long grass, and he clenched his hands, and he bent his head, and he felt it, that first shocking wallop of grief, hitting full force.

It blocked his windpipe. He swallowed it down and felt it churn in his gut. His stomach turned and he vomited, right there on the bank.

Fuck, he thought. He wiped his mouth and got to his feet. 'Fuck,' he said out loud. He climbed back up the slippery bank. 'FUCK.' He shouted it and got to his feet on the path. 'Fuck. Fuck. Fuck. Fuck.' He repeated it on every step forward, all the way back along the river path, blocking every other thought from his head. 'Fuck. Fuck. Fuck. Fuck.' He took the turn for Weavers' Row and ploughed on, past the house that used to belong to the Beechers' cook and past the house that used to belong to his granny.

He opened the door of the Land Rover.

'Fuck.' He kept his eyes away from the empty space on the passenger seat, and he turned the heat up full, and he drove home on his own.

* * *

The water in the shower was only lukewarm. Even after he'd dried himself and pulled on clothes, his fingers were stiff and burning sore, and he could hardly get his socks on. He was tired in his bones, and he felt as if the cold had gone right through him. Maybe it had.

He lay down on the bed and pulled the duvet over himself. His core temperature had probably been lowered, he thought, like the calf he'd seen as a child, caught in a drift of snow. He must have slept, then, because when he opened his eyes, the room was dark, but it didn't feel as if time had passed. He was still thinking the same thought, about the shivering calf, and how his father had brought it inside and wrapped it in his own coat and fed it hot mush.

He walked down the stairs and opened the fridge and took out a carton of tomato soup. He had to cut the top off it with a knife because his fingers still weren't working well enough to pull the folds apart, but he got it into a bowl and the bowl into the microwave and he pushed the buttons and gave it three minutes.

He stood in his stockinged feet and watched the bowl rotating. He plunged his fists into the depths of his fleece jacket. Down at the bottom of the right-hand pocket, his fingers found a gritty nugget. He pulled it out and looked at it: a bone-shaped dog treat, slightly furred. He held it in the palm of his hand and wondered what the hell was in it that made Bran crave them so badly – so much that he'd abandon his dignity and roll over on his back and cycle his paws like a circus performer.

Stupid dog.

The microwave binged.

Fucking stupid dog.

Fucking saved his life.

Malachi walked across the kitchen and dropped the dog treat into the bin. The boots he'd worn earlier were lying where he'd dropped them inside the back door, and right beside them stood his wellies, looking dry, at least, by comparison. He slipped his feet into them, grabbed his keys, and drove back to Drohid.

92.

A Wreath of Withered Laurel

* * *

Maeve didn't sit down when she got home from the hospital. She showered and dressed and pulled her wet hair into a ponytail. Then, she made a cheese sandwich for Emer, cut it into two triangles, and laid it on a plate.

'Don't answer the door,' she said. 'Not to anyone, do you understand?'

Emer, pale and wide-eyed, only nodded.

'I won't be long, I promise.'

Maeve walked to the Garda station and asked to speak with Tim Corcoran. She stood at the hatch and waited while the young guard went to find out if that was possible.

'He's not here, Maeve.' It was John Molloy, the same big, burly sergeant who had interviewed her. 'We released him.'

'Was he charged?'

'You know I can't—'

'Please?'

He sighed. 'What about you? Are you alright?'

Frustrated, Maeve tapped her knuckle on the polished wood of the countertop. She wasn't going to get anything from him.

'I'm fine,' she said, and turned away.

On the street outside, she stood facing the 1916 commemoration monument. A wreath of withered laurel was propped against the limestone plinth. Maeve pulled out her phone. Should she text him? Ask him to meet her? She didn't have the patience for that. What if he said no? She needed to speak with him. She needed to know that he'd heard her. With the phone in her hand, she started walking back down Main Street. She came to the junction with Bridge Street. Home, and Emer, was straight on. Without stopping to think, Maeve let her body take the left turn and kept walking over the bridge.

She was halfway up the tiled pathway when the front door of Cavendish House opened, and a man stood in silhouette against a golden light inside. Tim. He must have seen her coming.

He held the door wide open and stood sideways to draw her into the entrance hall.

'Come in,' he said.

Maeve was surprised. She wasn't expecting that.

'The kids are with the neighbours,' he said, as if that explained something.

Maeve looked around at the house. It was extraordinarily white, she thought. The walls, the stairs, and even the framed paintings were all in shades of white. A huge gilded mirror leaning against the wall accentuated the light and whiteness of the place. Only the crimson Axminster rug that ran down the hall provided a dash of colour.

'I—'

He cut her off. 'Are you okay?'

At the words, her heart stirred, but then she absorbed the coolness of his tone and the hard set of his face.

'I just want you to know that it wasn't me,' she said. 'It wasn't me who told the guards you were driving the car.'

'I know that.' His voice, she thought, had softened. He put his hand to her elbow and led her down the corridor but paused with his hand on the brass handle of a closed door. 'I know you would never have told them, Maeve.'

She exhaled and smiled up at him.

'Tim—'

'It was Emer, wasn't it?'

'No.'

'She's loyal to you. It only makes sense.'

'No.' She was stricken. Had the guards not told him about the truck driver with the dashcam? Or had Tim decided what he wanted to believe?

'Look, it doesn't matter now.' Tim turned the handle and opened the door. That much, she thought, was true. Maeve felt his hand held lightly, politely, to the small of her back as he led her into the kitchen. 'Sit down for a minute.'

A woman with shiny blonde hair splayed over her shoulder blades turned around from the window. Nóinín Corcoran's face was fixed in a brittle facsimile of a smile. She poured whiskey into three cut-glass tumblers on the table.

'Please, sit down, Maeve,' she said, her voice dripping with sympathy. 'We need to talk.'

Maeve stood with her two hands on the back on a kitchen chair. If she let go, she thought, she would fall to the porcelain floor. She looked to Tim for support and saw him swallow hard.

'Nóinín knows everything,' he said.

'Everything?' *Everything?* Maeve wondered. Did she know about the caravan at the beach? Did she know about that thing he did with his thumb?

'Everything. All the way back to the cocktail sausages,' said Nóinín, with a venomous laugh. 'Such a beautiful past you two have shared.'

Never before had Maeve quite comprehended the words *taken aback*, but she understood them then; she felt the meaning of them in the way her body physically recoiled from the malicious force of Nóinín's voice, from the blow of Tim's betrayal. She felt the sting at the back of her eyes. She blinked. There was no way on earth she would cry here in this room, in this house, *in front of them*.

'I should go,' she said. 'I left Emer—'

'I want *you* to know something,' said Nóinín, with a glance towards the hallway that told Maeve that she had heard every word said there. 'We – *Tim and I* – have agreed that we will support Emer financially. That is, of course, the right thing to do. But *know this*, Maeve, Tim married *me*. He didn't have to. I didn't trap him. I wasn't pregnant when he asked me to marry him. That happened after—'

'Don't,' said Tim. 'There's no need.'

Maeve looked hard at him, but he kept his eyes fixed on his wife.

'He *chose* me,' said Nóinín. 'Then and now, Tim chose *me*.'

93.

Try Me

* * *

Malachi went into the Drohid Arms via the staff entrance. He garnered a few curious looks, but nobody tried to stop him as he strode through the kitchen, found his way to Paddy O'Driscoll's lair and, without pausing to knock, walked right in.

'I hope you're pleased with yourself,' he said, without preamble.

Casting a newspaper aside, Paddy swung his feet from his desktop to the floor. 'What are *you* doing here?'

'I thought you and I should have a little chat.' Malachi sat down.

'You didn't bring your what-do-you-call-it, *mongrel* with you this time?'

Malachi put his hands on his knees and leaned forward. He looked hard into O'Driscoll's one good eye until the man blinked, and then he spoke.

'I'll drop the plans for my barn—'

'What will—?'

'Shut up,' he said. 'Shut up now and listen.'

Paddy gave the smallest possible inclination of his head and pushed himself upright in his seat.

'Right,' said Malachi. 'Put an offer on Maeve Gaffney's place, a decent offer – enough to cover her debts and have something left to start over.'

Paddy raised an incredulous eyebrow. 'You're suggesting that I buy her out?'

'You're getting what you wanted in the first place.'

'But nobody will bid on that house now. I could have it for tuppence.'

'*I* would.'

'You would what?'

'I would bid against you, Paddy. I can buy her out myself, if it comes to it.'

Paddy sat back in his chair, feigning nonchalance, but his pupils might as well have had dollar signs spinning in them, Malachi thought, with the way you could see the calculations running in his unfocused eyes.

'Sure, that would be an act of madness,' he said eventually. 'You'd be throwing your money away.'

'Maybe so.' Malachi smirked. 'But I'd get a fair deal of pleasure out of pissing you off. Maybe I'd let it out to some truly undesirable tenants, see how your guests would like that. I heard the council was looking for a halfway house for newly released prisoners.'

'You wouldn't dare.'

'Try me.'

'And if I were to go along with your plan—'

'I'll withdraw my planning application. You get your car park, *and* your wife gets her uninterrupted sea view.'

'And you'll make sure Ms. Gaffney relocates well away from here.'

Malachi sucked in a shallow breath.

'No man makes Maeve Gaffney do anything. Have we not all learned that much, at least?'

The tip of Paddy's tongue emerged between his lips.

'You know well what I mean. Don't go thinking you can pull a fast one over on me and then move her into your place.'

Malachi's right hand had stretched out from the side of his body, his fingers splayed, unconsciously seeking the top of Bran's head. He winced and clenched his fist. 'I know what you mean.'

Paddy had kicked back, relaxed into his cracked leather chair.

'Beyond the county bounds, right?'

Malachi shook his head.

'Jesus, you're like some fuckin' gombeen or some, some fucking—'

'Cowboy? I think that's the word you're looking for.'

'You've been watching too many westerns.'

'Hah.' Delighted, Paddy guffawed. 'You got me there.'

Malachi shook his head at the ease of Paddy's change of tone. This was all just business to him, and the shocking thing was, he enjoyed it. Paddy O'Driscoll *lived* for the closing of a deal. Malachi watched, in something close to awe, as the man smiled and thrust his hand out across the desk. Malachi looked at it, at the freckles on the back of it and the wiry hairs on the fingers. He wasn't entirely certain anymore exactly what the deal was that he was about to shake hands on.

'Come on,' said Paddy, stretching just a tiny bit further. 'You came to me this time.'

Malachi stood up to his full height, towered over Paddy O'Driscoll, and shook the man's hand, hard.

'Why does it always seem as if you're winning, Paddy?' He heard the catch in his voice and saw from the keen look on O'Driscoll's face that he too had heard it.

Paddy smirked. And then, he winked. The man actually had the gall to wink at him.

'Yerra, fuck you.'

With a smug grin, Paddy sat back and shrugged his shoulders.

'I get that a lot.'

94.

My Amazing Maeve

* * *

'Is everything alright, Mammy?'

Maeve had expected that Emer would have gone to bed, but there she was, sitting at the table with a game of solitaire spread out in front of her.

'You should be in bed.'

'You, you didn't say—'

'Go on.' She made an effort to speak gently. 'Go on up now, Chicken. Don't forget to brush your teeth. I won't be long behind you.'

Maeve kept her patience while Emer gathered up her playing cards and fastidiously packed them away in the box. And then she thought, *Emer would know*. Little girls always know when their best friend's birthday is.

'Emer?'

'Yes?'

'When is Pamela Corcoran's birthday?'

'Fourteenth of July,' Emer said, without a moment's hesitation.

'Are you sure?'

'Bastille Day,' she said. 'She's g-going to France to see the fireworks. Why?'

'Oh, nothing.'

'Goodnight,' Emer whispered, and Maeve only nodded. She didn't trust herself to speak.

When Emer had rounded the turn of the stairs, she pulled the bottle of wine out of her handbag, found the corkscrew, realised the bottle was screw-topped, opened it, and upended it into a mug.

She stood with her back against the Belfast sink and drank halfway down the mug, then hoicked herself up onto the countertop and sat with her legs swinging. Emer's birthday was February twelfth. Pamela was five whole months younger than Emer. What a grand act Tim had put on that day in Dublin, and the whole thing a lie. He didn't get *two* women pregnant accidentally. How could she ever have believed that? No. He'd chosen the golden girl, and he locked himself into that choice, retroactively, with a baby. He'd chosen the life he wanted – big fish in a small pond – and justified it to himself as doing the right thing.

All at once, it came clear to her: his dishonesty, his weakness, his downright *unworthiness*. Her chest constricted in pain and made her think of something Emer had said about the sound of rain. It's not falling you feel; it's the landing.

She reached for the bottle of Rioja and filled the mug to the brim.

'She was telling the truth,' Maeve said, out loud, and waited for a response. From her perch, she had a view of the whole ground floor – the dwindling fire in the hearth, the water-marked dining table, the two bare windows, stripped of their ruined curtains. She felt, though, that her mother was lingering around the sink. Probably, she had just finished washing up some other-realm dishes and was currently holding a phantom tea towel in her hands – her lovely, hard-wrung hands – and maybe she was leaning forwards, just a little bit, to get a view through the dark glass of the kitchen window.

'I've lost,' Maeve said, and when no answer came, she said it again, 'I've lost him.'

Dodged a bullet, more like, said Greta. She was folding the tea towel now, Maeve could tell, folding it in three, lengthwise, the way she always did before looping it over the rail on the cooker. She never liked to meet Maeve's eye when she was talking to her, really talking. Maybe this ghost bit she had going on suited her down to the ground: no eye contact, no touching, and the liberty to leave the room whenever she felt like it.

Maeve took another long slug.

'Who's my father?' she asked, not expecting an answer. She'd never got one before, after all.

He's a Spanish duke. That's where you get that black hair from, and those eyes of yours. We met that summer I told you about, when I went picking grapes. I always thought you'd figure it out.

Maeve laughed, then coughed as the wine went down the wrong way.

'You're joking.'

You'll never know, will you?

'Because you're only in my head?'

Pretty much.

It was too late. It always had been too late. The moment of her own creation never had and never would belong to her. It belonged to Greta and—

'A Spanish duke you say?'

She could hear her mother's laugh.

Hah. Oh yes, he had a coat of arms and everything.

'You can't joke about this. It's not fair.'

Whoever said any of this was fair? Nobody, that's who. Why do you keep on expecting some sort of cosmic justice? There is no jury sitting waiting to give you a gold star for being good, for being loyal and honourable. Don't you know by now that it's the brazen children, the brats and the charmers, who get all the sweets? What did you think was going to happen, Maeve?

That was the question she'd been avoiding for months. *What exactly did she think was going to happen?* Had she really believed that Tim Corcoran was going to walk out of his mansion, walk out on his gorgeous wife and his perfect family and – what – move into her ruby boudoir? Did she *ever* believe that could happen? Did she believe she was *that* irresistible? Did she think she only had to prove how much she loved him, and he'd drop his silver spoons and come running? *Did she?*

'Yes.'

Yes?

'No. I don't know. I thought he deserved a chance, a chance at happiness.'

With you?

'Yes, with me. With me and Emer.'

Well, he's had it. You gave him every damn chance he deserved.

'He's still her family.'

No.

'He *is*.'

He's not, Maeve. He's not, because he doesn't want to be. Wanting it matters more than DNA or paperwork. Wanting to be family, with honest, whole-hearted love, is all that really counts.

'But I'm not enough.'

Not enough? Bullshit. You're her mother.

'I don't know what I'm supposed to do now.'

There is no supposed to.

'Am I not supposed to have learned something from all this? Am I not supposed to have changed, somehow? Gotten wiser?'

Oh, love, but you have. You have changed.

How?

You're listening to me, aren't you?

'Hah.' Maeve laughed. She raised her mug into the air in salute. 'But I don't know what's the right thing to do. I don't even know what's the right thing for me.'

Ask yourself what's the right thing for Emer. That's your job.

'I know.' She heard it herself; she sounded like a sullen child saying she *knew* she had to learn her tables.

I know you know. Don't be cheeky.

The phantom tea towel whipped through the air and skimmed the side of Maeve's leg.

'Mammy.'

Maeve.

'I miss you so much. Sometimes I think my heart is weeping inside of me.'

I know, love.

The last log collapsed into the ashes, sending a dainty spray of sparks onto the hearth. Emer's pack of cards lay at the centre of the otherwise empty table. Her mug and the plate she'd had her sandwich on were turned upside down on the draining board, washed and left to dry.

'Are you there?'
I'm here.
'Aren't you going to say that you miss me too?'
How can I?
'How *can* you?'
Oh, Maeve. My amazing Maeve – how can I miss you when I'm stuck inside your head?

'Right.' She laughed. 'Makes sense.' She drained her mug and screwed the cap back on the bottle of Rioja. 'I should go to bed.'
Do that.
'Will you stay with me?'
Try and stop me.

95.

The First of April

* * *

Agnes Beecher's funeral service was surprisingly well attended, Alison thought, sitting in the second to last pew of St. Peter's. She wasn't familiar with the Church of Ireland service and didn't want to make a fool of herself. Oddly enough, it turned out that she *did* know the hymns. All those BBC dramas, she supposed, finally paying dividends.

Thomas Forde, the dentist who had been on his last legs even when Alison was small, was in the pew opposite with his back and his head bent over into a perfect question mark. Eamon and Assumpta O'Neill were together, shoulder to shoulder. Just in front of them, Ann Fleming, the hairdresser, was going fully welly on 'Oh Thou Great Redeemer'. She'd be a fan of *Call the Midwife* alright. The bona fide Protestants were further up, closer to the front. That shy girl who worked in the library was balling tissues one after another, the poor thing.

When the congregation stood, Alison recognised the flat, square back of Malachi Barry's head. He was in the front row, between the coffin and the Lord Mayor of Cork. He stood head and shoulders above everyone around him, his stocky neck looking almost blue above the collar of an expensive-looking black wool coat. He'd got a haircut, obviously, which struck Alison as a pity. His hair was the only thing he had going for him, in the looks department.

Paddy O'Driscoll, Alison was aware, had slipped in late and was lurking somewhere behind her. There was no sign of Maeve Gaffney, or of the Corcorans.

Nóinín wasn't talking to her since she'd found out that it was Alison who'd phoned Malachi when Agnes died.

'You just can't resist interfering, can you?' Nóinín had spat at her, after Tim was taken away in handcuffs.

'She'd have drowned herself,' Alison had said quietly, 'trying to get to him.'

'And?'

Alison had been shocked, then, by the viciousness of her friend's instinct for self-protection.

'And you'd have had to take in her child,' Alison had spat right back. 'Tim's child.'

'Don't be ridiculous.' Nóinín had narrowed her eyes. 'Nobody knew.'

'Oh, for heaven's sake. Everybody knew.' Here, in the house of God, Alison had to admit that she'd enjoyed watching the perfect face blanch and stiffen. 'Every dog in the street knew,' she had said, knowing that she was only twisting the knife.

Nóinín had placed her gin and soda down on a coaster and walked out the door without another word.

Poor Tim was going to be paying for his shenanigans for quite some time. He wouldn't go to prison, of course. Nobody could ever have thought he would. He'd do a bit of community service, that's what she'd heard on the grapevine, probably teach a creative writing course to disadvantaged youths or some such rubbish. It was Nóinín who'd be doling out the brunt of his punishment. Alison smiled to herself at the thought of an architect-designed, Tim-sized doghouse being constructed in the back garden of Cavendish House. He'd be on a tight leash, alright, but give it a few months and the Corcorans would be back where they belonged, glittering from the pages of the *Drohid Echo*, together.

The vicar pronounced a final blessing over Agnes Beecher in her casket and the organ piped up with something profound. Malachi and Matthew Dawson rose from their pews and took their places as pallbearers. With their arms wrapped around each other's shoulders, they led the procession down the aisle. What was the story, Alison wondered, that made Matthew take on such a task, at his age. Fair play to him, she thought, though she could see from the determined set of Malachi's jaw that he was taking more than his share of the weight.

She waited, as did almost everyone, to see the coffin placed inside the famous Beecher Crypt, a mausoleum built from that beautiful, white-streaked Cork limestone that couldn't be got anymore for love nor money. It had marble plaques on all four sides with dates going back to the early 1700s, generations, one after another, of the closest thing Drohid ever had to a royal family.

'Well, that's the end of an era,' someone said, a little too loudly, as people milled about in that awkward moment between the end of a funeral and the restart of life.

Alison stood to one side of the path until Malachi reached her. She put out her hand and grabbed hold of his lovely coat.

'Alison,' he said. 'You were good to come.'

'I wouldn't have missed it,' she said, and realised instantly how crass she sounded.

'You're honest anyway.' Malachi smiled. 'Agnes would have appreciated it. She had no idea how much people liked her.'

'We were all a bit shy of her.'

'That's it. Yerra, sure, she knows now,' his voice cracked, 'I hope.'

Poor Malachi, Alison thought. He was in bits.

'That's a fine coat,' she said, to relieve the tension. She picked a small feather off his lapel and tucked it inside her own pocket. He watched her do it but didn't comment.

'I splashed out,' he said. 'I didn't want her over on the other side saying I hadn't made an effort. She was a fussy old bag, you know.'

Alison nodded and a small silence loomed between them.

'I'm sorry about—' she began.

Malachi's attention was taken by his phone, which must have vibrated in his trouser pocket. He looked at the screen and held up one finger to Alison in a *hold on one second* gesture.

'Hello?' he answered the call.

Alison could hear the voice of a young woman or girl, but she couldn't distinguish the words.

'Yes,' Malachi said, turning sideways away from Alison. 'Yes, that's right. What? Jesus Christ, I don't believe it. No.' He turned another quarter circle so that Alison was once again looking at the back of his bare neck. 'No, no, there's no need for that. I'm on my way.'

He hung up the phone and swung back to face her.

'Everything okay?' she asked.

'I have to go. Sorry. I have to go. Will you tell them—?' He gestured towards the vicar and the Lord Mayor.

'That you were called away?' Alison suggested.

'Thanks,' he said. He put his hand on her arm. 'Listen—'

'What?'

'Thanks, alright.' He looked directly into her eyes and just for one split second Alison had the full attention of Malachi Barry. 'I mean it. Thank you.'

'Go on,' she said, dismissing him. She watched him break into a run so that his lovely coat caught the wind and spread out behind him.

'Go on,' she said again, into the breeze. 'Go do your thing.'

96.

Back Then, in Dublin

* * *

He stood on the doorstep and watched her as she walked away. Once, she put her hand out to catch hold of a railing. She stopped and slumped, as if she was feeling faint, and he made a move to follow her, but she stood up to her full height again, visibly pushed back her shoulders and walked on.

They all knew, all the lads, they all knew that Tim had got himself into a fine heap of shit. What a feckin' eejit. He'd had it all handed to him on a plate his whole life, that was his problem, didn't know when he had it good. The whole of Drohid was talking about the way Paddy O'Driscoll had bought the Beecher house and gifted it to his daughter and her boyfriend. How jammy could you get? And still the feckin' eejit goes and cheats and gets another girl pregnant. *Unbelievable*, that's what it was.

'Unbe-feckin'-lievable,' he muttered under his breath as he wiggled the key in the lock and pushed the door open.

Tim Corcoran was sitting on the second to last step of the stairs with his head in his hands.

'Was she okay?' Tim said, looking up. His face was streaked, and his eyes were shot with hot red lines.

'She didn't look well. Would you not go after her? Get her home, at least.'

'There's no point in dragging it out. It would only make it harder.'

'For you, you mean?' Malachi heard his voice hardening.

'For everyone.'

'Do you not have a duty of care or something?'

'Don't fucking lecture me, Malachi. You're no angel yourself.'

He had a point. It hadn't been deliberate, that time when he'd taken the tip off Billy Corcoran's finger with the hurley, but he couldn't exactly say he was sorry he'd done it either, or that he wouldn't make the same tackle again if the clocks were turned back. He stretched out his hand, and he pulled Tim to his feet.

'Yeah. There's a pair of us in it, I suppose.'

Tim staggered and put a hand on the wall to steady himself.

'Okay?'

Tim didn't answer. His face was washed again in tears.

'You could still catch her,' Malachi said. 'If you run.'

Tim shook his head.

'Are you sure you won't regret it?'

Tim swallowed hard. 'I'm sure I will. And it's killing me.'

Malachi nodded. 'You're a feckin' eejit, Corcoran. You know that, don't you?'

'I know it,' said Tim.

Malachi stepped ahead of him into the wrecked kitchen and filled the kettle.

'There's no treatment for it, no?'

Tim laughed bitterly.

'For being a feckin' eejit?'

'Yeah.'

'No,' said Tim. 'It's incurable. I just have to live with it.'

'I thought as much.' Malachi dropped teabags into mugs, took a carton of milk from the fridge and sniffed the top of it.

'What time does the match start?' Tim asked.

Malachi didn't answer. He finished making the tea and put a mug on the table in front of Tim. *Jesus Christ*, he thought. He'd moved on already. Tim Corcoran was a feckin' terminal case.

He left his own steaming mug of tea on the counter. He walked down the hall and out the front door and swung it shut behind him. Standing on the doorstep, he could see at a glance that the girl was gone around the corner. She'd be out on the main road by now. He wouldn't speak to her, even if he did catch up with her, but he thought he'd just make sure that she made it onto the bus.

97.

Mal Needs Help

* * *

Emer held the dustpan while Maeve swept the dust into it.

'Why are you bothering?' Emer said. Mammy was cleaning again, cleaning stupid things like windows and door frames, and the undersides of cupboard shelves.

'Pride,' Mammy said, poking the floor brush deep into the space under the bed. 'I won't have it said that I didn't know how things should be done.'

The head of the brush emerged again with a heap gathered. Something metallic rattled into the dustpan.

'What's that?' Emer said, but Mammy bent quickly and picked it up. She shook the dust off a gold chain.

'So that's where it went,' she said, with a sad sort of look on her face. She handed it to Emer. 'This is yours. It's from Tim.'

Emer took it and turned it over in her palm. It was a fine bracelet with a little gold bar that had her name written on it in swirly old-fashioned writing. She felt as if something hard was tightening around her chest.

'Why does it have my, my name on it?' she asked.

'He wanted it to be personal, I suppose. It's called an identity bracelet.'

'So that I know who I am? Like if I g-get hit on the head or something?'

Mammy smiled at that.

'No,' she said. 'It's a thing people give you to show that *they* know who you are, and to remind you that they love you.'

'But he didn't even know my name, did he? Before?'

'No. No, he didn't.'

Emer handed back the bracelet. 'I don't want it.'

'Tell you what, I'll put it away somewhere safe for you, in case you change your mind.'

Don't bother, Emer wanted to say, but she didn't.

'Do you know what would really be p-personal?' she said, instead.

'Go on, tell me.'

'It's not a joke, Mammy.'

'Alright. Go on, tell me what would really be personal?'

'A bracelet that said *Chicken* on it.'

Her mammy laughed, and Emer felt a squeeze of gladness that she could do it, that she could make her mammy happy.

'That can be arranged,' Mammy said, and bent her attention again to brushing the floor.

'Did you hear that?' Emer said. She waited, and it came again, the *rat-at-at* of the dragonfly knocker. She turned and ran down the stairs and opened the door.

'Hi, Mal,' she said, because it was him. Of course, it was.

'Hello, Emer,' he said. 'Is your mammy about?'

But her mammy was already there, coming to the door behind her.

'Is everything alright?' Mammy said. 'Come in—'

'No. No, I can't come in.' Mal's face was flushed, and his eyes were all rimmed with red, as if he'd been crying for hours and hours. 'I need ye to come out to the farm with me now. Come out and have dinner with me?'

'I'm sorry, Malachi,' Mammy said. 'I have so much to do. I just can't.'

'Maeve,' Mal said, 'I buried my friend today. I'm asking you, please, to come away with me now. Don't think about it. Just pick up your coat and come with me. I need your help.'

Mammy stood looking at Mal as if she was trying to read the inside of his head. She was going to say no, Emer thought. She was in her one-track-mind mode, and that track was all about getting packed and getting away from everyone in this town.

This little shithole, she'd called it, and not even said sorry to Emer for saying *shithole*.

'Why do you need help?' Emer asked.

'Oh just—' Mal's face broke open in a shy grin. 'I have this patient I have to look after, you see. He's going to need constant attention, and I only have this one pair of hands.' He held his palms upwards and shook his head, pretending he was sad, but smiling like a lunatic all the time.

'*No way?*' said Mammy, stepping into the doorway.

'He's in the car.'

Emer ran, but she couldn't get a view in through the high windows of the Land Rover. Mal jogged up behind her and pulled open the back door. And there, in a cardboard box that was lined with a black woollen coat, lying awkwardly on his side, with a bandage around his middle, two legs stuck out stiffly in casts, and a plastic cone on his head, was Bran.

'Oh,' said Emer. 'Oh Bran, oh Bran, oh Bran.'

'That's exactly what I said,' said Mal.

Emer put her hand on his back and Bran lifted his head and whimpered.

'Good God,' said Mammy. 'I can't believe it.'

'Yeah,' said Mal. 'I said that too. I thought someone was playing a joke on me, for April Fool's Day.'

'Is he alright?'

'Fractures to both forelegs, three fractured ribs, and bruising all over.'

'Poor Bran,' said Emer.

Bran attempted to wag his tail but managed no more than a flutter.

'Yeah. And near starved, of course, but not too dehydrated. It was having enough to drink that saved him, the vet said.'

'The irony,' said Mammy.

'Yeah. And he nearly got home, would you believe. A woman walking her dog found him on the riverbank just below my land. Somehow, he got out of the river at the right place, but he couldn't walk.'

'Poor, poor Bran,' said Emer.

'The vet wanted to keep him tonight but—'

'You wanted to go home, didn't you?' Emer said and Bran twitched his ear.

'But he'll have to be hand fed and carried around. If ye could just give me a hand—'

'*Of course* we will!' said Emer. '*Won't we*, Mammy?'

Mammy took a long time to answer. She seemed to be lost in a sort of daze. She looked at Bran for a long time, and then at Mal, and then at Emer.

'Yes,' she said eventually. 'Let me just grab a few bits in a bag.'

Emer looked deep into Bran's glossy eyes. Bran looked just as deeply into hers, then lifted his tail and brushed it against her arm.

98.

Cnoc Lios Críona
The Hill of the Fort of the Heart

* * *

It was dark by the time they pulled up in the yard. Maeve couldn't help feeling a spark of curiosity. She'd never been inside a genuine farmhouse before. It was smaller than she'd been expecting, and not especially attractive.

'The long one, there in the middle.' Malachi handed her his keys and went to lift Bran out of the rear of the Land Rover. Maeve went ahead and opened the back door, then held it wide so that Malachi would have a clear path.

'Stick the kettle on,' he said, pointing with his chin towards the kitchen counter. He carried the dog across the room and laid him in a wicker basket in front of the stove. He pulled cushions off the armchair and positioned them next to the basket.

'Will you sit with him, Emer?' He patted the cushions with his hand.

'Will I hurt him if I rub him?' Emer asked, and Maeve's heart went out to her.

'Maybe don't rub him,' she said.

'Just be gentle,' Malachi said. 'He'll let you know if you're hurting him.'

Maeve saw Emer leaning over to whisper something in Malachi's ear but couldn't hear what she said. Malachi only nodded in response and rubbed the outside of her upper arm before standing up. Without a glance at Maeve, he went back out to the car and returned a few minutes later with bags of groceries.

'Right, let's get organised,' he said, in an authoritative tone that she'd never heard him use before. She wasn't sure if he was trying to maintain a distance between them, or if he was simply preoccupied with looking after the dog.

'I'll start the dinner,' he said. 'Can you light the fire?'

* * *

Malachi gave Emer her plate of roast chicken, potatoes, peas, and gravy to eat on her lap, and gave her a second plate of chicken to feed in small pieces to Bran.

'Tanora?' he asked, holding out a glass.

'Thanks,' Emer said.

The kitchen table was small and pushed into a corner. The roasting trays that Malachi put straight on the table left barely enough space for their two plates, two glasses, and a bottle of wine. Malachi took what was obviously his habitual place, and Maeve sat at a right angle to him. Aware that Malachi's legs were under the table, she tucked her own beneath her chair.

'Gravy?'

She nodded, and he spooned it straight from the roasting pan onto her plate.

'You should have told me you were such a good cook,' she said.

He took a sip of his wine and put the glass down on the table.

'Would it have made a difference?' He kept his eyes fixed on his plate.

Don't complicate things, she wanted to say. *Don't hurt him*, said another voice in her head.

'I—'

'Don't,' he said, cutting her off. 'Do you know what's killing me?'

'Tell me.'

'It's that he was so close. If I'd walked my land after the flood, like I should have, I'd have found him.'

How like him to blame himself, when none of it would have happened if it wasn't for her, and her stupid obsession with . . . Abruptly, she realised that the feeling was gone. She didn't want to think about him anymore.

'How was the funeral?'

'It was good. Do you know, she had no idea at all how highly people thought of her. There she was, keeping herself to herself, hiding away with her books, trying not to be seen, and all the time people were out there *liking* her, only wanting a tiny bit of encouragement to be friends with her.'

'We left flowers, earlier.'

'I saw.'

'I know they don't make up for—'

'Leave it. There's no point in beating yourself up over things that are beyond your control. Let it go.'

'Hah. That's what my mother says.'

'Says?'

'Said,' she corrected herself. '*Sang*, actually. Herself and Emer had a big thing about that movie.'

'What movie?'

'*Frozen*.'

He looked at her blankly.

'Doesn't matter.'

They ate, and drank their wine, and talked in small bursts about unimportant things. After a while, Malachi stood and cleared the plates and put them in the sink. He tipped his head and looked over to check the dog.

'She's asleep,' he said, and handed Maeve a bobbly old Foxford blanket from the back of the armchair. She knelt and tucked it in around Emer's shoulders and kissed her forehead.

'I'm a crappy mother, do you know that?' she said.

'Don't be ridiculous. Do you want coffee?' Malachi asked.

Don't be ridiculous. It was the offhand way he said it that let her believe that he meant it.

'I'm good with the wine,' she said, sitting back at the table and pushing his chair out a little with the toe of her boot. 'Thanks.'

He opened a press and took out a second bottle of wine. He didn't look at her as he positioned the corkscrew on the top of the bottle. She was acutely aware at that moment that, if he opened it, he couldn't drive her home, but she couldn't tell whether he'd had the same thought. He sat on his chair just as it was, at right angles to the table, and stretched his legs along the side of hers.

'Knock that back,' he said, meaning the wine that remained in her glass, and when she had, he poured generous measures from the fresh bottle into both their glasses.

'I'm very sorry, Malachi.' She went to put her hand on his arm but thought better of it and twirled her glass instead.

'You got caught up with a rotten lot.' His mouth turned down at the corners and she could tell that he was thinking something he didn't want to say.

'Go on,' she said. 'Spit it out.'

'I just don't know what you ever saw in that feckin' eejit.'

'Ah, Malachi.'

'No, I mean, you don't seem like one who'd fall for all that floppy hair and bullshit.'

'No? Well, there you go. Turns out that's exactly what I am. Or was. I don't think it would happen now. It was a childish thing, you know. It got carried on way beyond what it should have.'

'Is he spectacular in the sack, or something?'

She laughed. 'You don't seriously expect me to answer that?'

'He'd have to have something special . . .' He looked at her sideways.

'To have landed me, you mean?'

He took a drink before he answered.

'To have kept you.'

'He didn't keep me.'

'But he could have. I told you – he's a feckin' eejit.'

'Thanks,' she said. 'I think.'

He pushed his glass towards the centre of the table, out of the way, and he laid his hand over hers.

She waited, but he didn't say anything, just rubbed the soft underside of her wrist with his thumb.

'Malachi—'

He still didn't speak, but twisted his hand and held onto her wrist as if he was measuring the strength of her pulse.

'You only want funeral sex,' she said.

He exhaled a laugh. 'Funeral sex?'

'Yeah. You know. Everyone gets this desperate ache after a funeral. It's like an evolutionary force or something, an urge to keep the species going.'

'And everyone gets it?' His eyebrows lifted comically.

'Oh God, yes.'

'And have you got something against funeral sex in general, or just with me?'

She thought for a second before she answered.

'I've nothing against funeral sex. When my mother died, I was gagging for it. I think that's probably how I ended up in this whole mess. Had I just gone and shagged someone, well—'

Malachi pushed his chair away from the table and stood.

'I'm making tea,' he said, his voice gravelly. 'Will you have one?'

'Sure. Yeah.' *I've hurt him*, she thought. *Again.*

She sipped her wine and watched him padding over the hard tiles in his thick socks, watched as he dropped teabags into a teapot and filled it from the kettle.

'A proper pot and everything,' she said, as much to break the silence as anything.

'In honour of Agnes,' he said, as he put the pot and two mugs on the table and sat down.

She watched as he poured milk into his mug, then looked around for a spoon. Not finding one, he picked up a fork, flipped it upside down between his fingers, and used the handle of it to stir his tea. A series of images flipped through her mind. In all the times she'd replayed every scene of her time with Tim, she'd missed something in the background.

'Malachi—'

'This isn't a funeral sex thing, Maeve. You know that, don't you?'

'You were there, in the kitchen—'

'What?'

'And on the doorstep. In Dublin.' Her eyes filled with tears. In her head, she was back there, in the loneliest moment of her life.

She looked up and saw it in his eyes. He'd known all along. He'd known everything. 'You were there.'

The corners of his mouth lifted in a sorrowful half-smile, and he nodded once.

'Why didn't you say?'

'I thought ye, yourself and Emer, and even that feckin' eejit Corcoran, deserved the chance at making a go of it, as a family, if that was what you wanted, and – I *did* try, you know.'

'You did.'

Jesus, how had she been so blinded by the shine off Tim Corcoran for so bloody long? He had wounded her, and she might have put it down to experience, but the baby inside her, Emer, had flooded her heart with perfect, unreserved love and she had never thought to separate the two things, the love for her child and the infatuation with the child's father. And all along she'd assumed that a love so pure couldn't be anything but mutual, that she must occupy as big a part of his heart as he did hers.

'I'm sorry, Mal. I couldn't see past the fairytale. Turns out I'm a hopeless bloody romantic.'

'Yerra, sure that's why I love you.' He stopped dead, as if just hearing for himself the words he'd said.

Maeve waited until his eyes met hers.

'Are you serious?'

'You know I am, Maeve,' he said, in a half-strangled voice. He cleared his throat and said it again, low and sure. 'You *know* I am.'

She fiddled with her hair. He was so . . . so straightforward. There was no flirting with him, no playfulness, no messing around. His honesty was something she didn't know how to handle. It wrong-footed her.

'What did Emer say to you?'

'When?'

'Earlier. When she whispered in your ear.'

He paused, probably weighing up his loyalty to Emer, she thought.

'She said everything is packed up. She said that you're leaving tomorrow.'

'It is. We are.'

'And she said that you said you'll never come back here, ever.'

Maeve nodded.

'That's true.'

'You got an offer on the house, did you?'

'Yeah. I got an offer too good to refuse.'

He looked into his mug for a long moment, then drank deeply from it.

'Good.'

'You're glad?'

'I'm glad you're free of it.'

'Me too.'

'Take the money and run.' He held her eye, as if he was making sure the message was hammered home.

'I will,' she said, nodding. It was a promise.

He put his hand under the seat of her chair and pulled it towards his until she was trapped between his legs.

'Do you want to come upstairs?' He whispered it.

She had a feeling of tension leaving her body, the way when the sun comes out you realise all at once how cold you were before.

'I do,' she whispered back. She put her hands on his thighs. 'But—'

'Ah.' His face fell.

'No, listen. I do, but not tonight.'

She leaned forwards and pressed her lips against his, but he pulled back from her, as if he didn't understand.

'But you're going tomorrow.'

'I'm not leaving the country, Malachi. You'll find me.'

'Don't say that—' His eyes were full of uncertainty. 'Not just for the sake of it.'

'I *want* you to find me. I'm *asking* you to come find me.'

'Oh.' He smiled.

She looked over her shoulder at Emer, panned out on the cushions on the floor.

'Can I sleep here tonight?'

'You can sleep there.' He nodded towards his armchair. 'I'll get blankets.'

He left then and she listened to the sound of his footsteps on the stairs and the creak of the upstairs floorboards under his weight. He was back in a couple of minutes with a faded hand-pieced quilt and a duvet that could only have been pulled off his own bed. Without uttering a word, he put the quilt over Emer. He held the duvet up between his two outstretched hands and gestured with a tip of his head that Maeve should move to the armchair.

'That's the ugliest chair I've ever seen,' she said, and he laughed, and she knew that they were alright.

She slid into the seat.

He shook the duvet up high and let it fall in a whoosh over her body.

'It's comfortable,' she said.

'It reclines, you know.' He leaned over her and pulled the lever so that her head went back and her legs went up.

'So it does,' she said, and scooched sideways to make space.

SEPTEMBER

99.

Filleann an Feall ar an bhFeallaire
Treachery Follows the Treacherous

* * *

Paddy O'Driscoll rapped his desk with a finality that indicated the weekly meeting was at an end and that his senior staff should set about their allotted tasks with all due speed and efficiency.

'Thanks lads,' he said, and then, with his head bent, 'hang back a minute, Tim, will you?'

Tim, who had barely raised his posterior from the hard plastic chair, swallowed a sigh and sat down again. MacSweeney gave him a sympathetic shrug and left.

'Some fucken cauliflower,' muttered Leahy on his way out the door.

Tim cleared his throat.

Paddy looked up, brow furrowed. 'You alright there?'

'Of course.' Tim sat up straighter.

'Thanks for taking care of the paperwork on the Weavers' Row property, Tim.'

'No problem.' It was galling enough to be conscripted into the family business; he wasn't about to give Paddy the soot of acknowledging what they both knew – that the Weavers' Row assignment was his own special penalty, designed, not just to inflict pain, but to put him in his place. 'She did well out of it,' said Paddy.

He meant Maeve. *Asshole*, Tim thought, but said nothing.

'I heard she was at the mart in Castleisland last month, bought herself a nice little Kerry cow called Liskillea Paula.'

Still Tim said nothing. Let Paddy make his jabs.

'She'd have an eye for the rare breeds alright, I'd say.'

Tim wondered whether Paddy's informers had shared the news that his precious daughter was up in Cork every second Saturday night. Special meetings of the fire department, she'd explained to Tim, over a couple of large gin and sodas.

Paddy pushed back his chair so that he could open his desk drawer.

'They're finishing up the job over the way this morning,' he said, tipping his head in the direction of the river. He took a key from the drawer and held it out across the desk. 'I want you to supervise it.'

'Grand,' said Tim, rising, at last, from his seat. He held out his hand, palm upwards, and let Paddy drop the key into it, then turned and moved towards the door.

'One more thing, Tim.' Paddy tapped his forefinger on the desk.

'What's that?' Tim held on to the doorknob.

'Don't be writing any more love stories, sure you won't?'

Tim left without answering. It was as much defiance as he could muster, that and taking the outlawed shortcut through the hotel kitchen to the back door. The key, a ridiculous affair with a six-inch shaft and a scrolled bow, felt hot and sweaty in his hand. He slipped it into his jacket pocket.

He didn't need the key, in the end. The purple front door had been removed and loaded, along with four sash windows and a cast iron fireplace, onto a truck headed for a reclamation yard in the city. Tim saw Eamon O'Neill rummaging around in the truck bed as if he was looking for something he might salvage.

'Okay there?' Tim kept his voice light, aware that he was branded as Paddy's deputy.

''Tisn't right,' said Eamon, without raising his head. ''Tisn't the right way of doing things.'

'Listen, Eamon,' Tim said, friendly like, 'Mr. O'Driscoll's looking for someone to put up a few shelves out at the house for his golfing trophies. Apparently, that big shot architect from Dublin was all about clean lines, or what have you.'

'No.'

'He pays well.'

'No.' Eamon looked up. The man's eyes were red-rimmed, as if he might have been crying, but his face was set hard. 'Don't ask again.'

Tim left him and approached the house. Leahy and young Jack O'Neill were manoeuvring an antique bath through the doorway.

'Nice bath,' said Leahy, leering.

Wishing he had it in him to punch the man, Tim sidled past and went inside.

There was nothing left but a shell. Every stick of furniture was long gone, every picture off the walls, every photo off the sills, not a trace of her left but the colours that she'd painted. He crossed to the stairs and put his hand on the top of the newel post, felt the warm sanded-smooth curve of it beneath his palm. He'd loved her. He'd loved her, and he'd known it, right from the start. But he'd made his choice long ago, and it had taken only that one lie to make it irrevocable. There was never any chance of going back. He'd known that too. He took two steps up the stairs.

No. It hurt too much. He couldn't take any more. He was only crucifying himself.

He walked back outside to the lane. Leahy, just like before, was leaning against the far wall and dragging on a cigarette.

'Had enough?' he asked.

'Get on with it,' said Tim, assuming control.

They both looked towards the JCB that was pulled up at the end of the lane. The driver was sipping from a takeaway coffee cup and scrolling his phone.

Leahy dropped his fag to the ground and crushed it with his foot, then put his fingers into his mouth and whistled. When the man looked up, Leahy gave him a double thumbs-up signal.

The driver nodded and took a moment to stow his coffee cup and his phone, then he slid the JCB into gear, engaged the engine, and drove straight through the gable wall.

100.

Noctilucent

* * *

With a ruler and a green biro, Emer drew a line under the end of her essay on *My Summer Holidays*. She closed her copybook and switched off the lamp on her desk. The sky beyond her window was close to dark and the big chestnut tree in the field was only a smudge now against the long grass. Up above, she could see stars, but straight out to the west, a high, wispy strip of night-shining cloud shimmered silver against deep blue. That must look beautiful, she thought, down at the beach. She couldn't see the water from her window, but she knew it was there, just behind the shadowed hill.

A sea view was beyond even their joint resources, Mammy had calculated. It would break them, she said.

Yerra, divil the bit, Mal had said back, but it turned out that Mammy was right. It had taken a lot of looking to find somewhere that had enough land for Mal and enough house for Mam, but they had both liked this place from the day they first saw it. Even though, according to Mal, it was *only a shack with notions in the farthest reaches of the arse end of nowhere*, and Mam said it was *nothing BUT potential*, they'd agreed it was perfect.

Mammy hadn't wanted to keep anything from their old house, but Mal had insisted she bring Agnes' oak table and chairs. He had insisted on bringing his ugly brown recliner, too, and Mammy had said that was *absolutely fine*, but, if he was determined to have it in the kitchen, they were going to need an extension, and that was how come they were both downstairs now, with a set of drawings laid out between them, vociferously debating the merits of French windows over sliding doors.

Emer hadn't put any of that in her essay.

She'd written about her first time going on a plane and how nice the ice-cream was in Italy, and about the frescoes in Pompeii, and the way the mornings smelled lemony. She didn't mention how Mal had lifted her onto his shoulders for a better view of the fireworks on Ferragosto, or how Mammy had wept when she opened the box with the amethyst ring inside.

Emer pulled down the sash to close the window. There were no curtains, yet, and she thought she might tell Mammy she liked it that way.

She hopped over the dog's bed and climbed into her own. Bran was getting old, Mal said. He was tired out after all his adventures. When Emer had asked if he could sleep in her room, she'd seen the look on Mammy's face and thought she was going to say no, but then Mal had said *Maeve*, in that way that he had, and Mammy had only laughed and said, *yeah, go on*.

Emer scrunched up her pillows and lay flat, with her right arm outstretched to reach Bran. She rubbed his head and scratched behind his ears. She might write about this, she thought, the next time they were given an essay for homework. She might choose *My Family* from Mr. Moriarty's list of titles, and she might write about Bran, and Mammy and Mal, and her new theory about how life is like a game of Mousse. You do need luck, and it's true that you have to play it smart, but really, the best thing is to have somebody kind at your side. A person, or a dog.

Bran licked her hand, then stilled, which was the sign that he was ready to sleep.

"Night,' Emer said, and closed her eyes. Of course, a dog couldn't play cards, she thought, though you never could tell for sure. With a dog as smart as Bran, she theorised, anything was possible.

She kicked the sheets loose and listened to the sounds of the house settling after the heat of the day, voices rumbling low, the fixed ticking of Mal's granny's clock. In her mind's eye, she saw the strand, the silver light in the sky mirrored, the waves slipping in and away, the ocean churning, restless, as if it knew something.

On the hard-packed sand, a little hermit crab danced sideways, then hid again in its cosy home, safe as safe can be.

Acknowledgements

Through squalls and storms, with wisdom, grace, and a wicked sense of humour, Polly Nolan has kept this ship we call my career on an even keel. She is, in a word, irreplaceable.

At Eriu, Deirdre Nolan saw sufficient potential in a sketchy proposal to place her faith in me. I remain enormously grateful. Lisa Gilmour has been an invaluable support as liaison and coordinator of practicalities.

At Bonnier UK, Sam Humphreys gained my absolute trust from first meeting. Her thoughtfulness, insight and calm efficiency were exactly what I needed. Leonie Lock has been my rock – kind, genuinely helpful, and confidence-inspiring in every circumstance. Natasha Drewett made valuable editorial comments, particularly on the writing of Emer's stammer. In copy editing, Gilly Dean waded through my Hiberno-English, pin pointed my mistakes and made truly useful suggestions. Emma Dunne, proof-reader, cast a keen eye over the final edits. Ella Holden, production controller, pulled the whole thing together. The cover designed by Jenny Richards continues to make my heart skip a beat.

At Echo, Juliet Rogers and Diana Hill have been impressive and thoughtful at every turn. The enthusiasm shown by Emily Banyard, Kaarina Allen and Ch'aska Cuba de Reed has made them a joy to work with.

The team at Gill Hess have done sterling work in promoting both *Last Chance in Paris* and *The Bridge to Always*. Declan Heeney braved the train to Cork to attend my launch, and kindly shepherded me around Dublin in the drizzle. At Cork City Library, Patricia Looney claimed me as one of her own. With great generosity, Vanessa Fox O'Loughlin held my hand through my first author event. Mairéad Hearne has been a very handy photographer and the best of company.

Booksellers have been amazing. John Breen (Waterstones) added my name to the long list of Cork authors he so heroically champions. Susan Walsh (Dubray) went beyond the call of duty. Simon Prim (Prim's) gave me a shout-out whenever he could. Fiona Farrell (Leaf and Bower) has been a bottomless well of enthusiasm and support.

Emer's jokes were gleaned, one by one, from the magnificent, moustachioed Marty Whelan on Lyric FM while I was on the morning school run.

Marian Nikel took on the dubious pleasure of reading my first draft and responded with kindness and intelligent critique. Rory Curtin, once again, rode to the technical rescue. Kieran Holland advised on matters bovine. Gráinne Murphy, my trusted wingwoman, provided cakes, days out, a water bottle and wise counsel. Aveen Boyce provided sanity checks when the walls were closing in. Jane McCarthy read this novel more times than anybody should. At every stage, she bolstered my courage and emboldened me to write the book I wanted to write.

At home, Michael, Mark, Kate, Alice and Grace taught me how to play Mousse, with all its attendant life lessons. Charlie has been by my side while every single word of this story was written. His loyalty inspired and sustained me.

To each and every person, and the one dog, who helped bring *The Bridge to Always* to bookshelves, my whole-hearted thanks.